New terrors

Ramsey Campbell was born in 1946, and has lived in Liverpool ever since (now with his wife Jenny and daughter Tamsin). After dawdling along in the Inland Revenue for four years, and enjoying himself rather more in Liverpool Public Libraries for another seven, in 1973 he took the risk of writing full-time, with Jenny's invaluable support. Other people who have encouraged him include his mother, August Derleth, his English teacher Ray Thomas, Kirby McCauley, Bob Lowndes, Carol Smith . . . Influences: Lovecraft, M. R. James, Leiber, Bloch, Aickman, Nabokov, Graham Greene, Alain Resnais, Hitchcock, all sorts of horror films he sneaked into the Essoldo London Road to see at the age of fifteen, and above all The Princess and the Goblin. *His novels include* The Doll Who Ate His Mother *(of which Bernice Williams Foley wrote: 'Thank goodness, this distasteful manhunt is fiction'),* The Face That Must Die, To Wake The Dead, *and he is currently working on one probably to be called* The Nameless. *His short stories are collected in* The Inhabitant of the Lake, Demons by Daylight, *and* The Height of the Scream, *and he has edited* Superhorror *and* New Tales of the Cthulhu Mythos. *One of these days he means to write a history of horror fiction. He reviews films and horror fiction (at least, for those few publishers who send out review copies) for BBC Radio Merseyside, and is president of the British Fantasy Society. In 1978 he was given both the British Fantasy Award and World Fantasy Award for best short fiction, though not for the same story.*

D1339894

New terrors

edited by Ramsey Campbell

Pan Original

Pan Books   London and Sydney

First published 1980 by Pan Books Ltd,
Cavaye Place, London SW10 9PG
This collection © Ramsey Campbell 1980
ISBN 0 330 26126 6
Set, printed and bound in Great Britain by
Cox & Wyman Ltd, Reading

for Cherry and Henry
with memories of grassy Wales

Contents

Acknowledgements

Robert Aickman for *The Stains* © Robert Aickman 1980;
Steve Rasnic for *City Fishing* © Steve Rasnic 1980; Lisa
Tuttle for *Sun City* © Lisa Tuttle 1980; Manly Wade Wellman
for *Yare* © Manly Wade Wellman 1980; Tanith Lee for *A
Room with a Vie* © Tanith Lee 1980; Daphne Castell and her
agent Virginia Kidd for *Diminishing Landscape with Indistinct
Figures* © Daphne Castell 1980; Marc Laidlaw for *Tissue*
© Marc Laidlaw 1980; Peter Valentine Timlett and his agent
Carole Blake for *Without Rhyme or Reason* © Peter Valentine
Timlett 1980; Bob Shaw and his agent Leslie Flood for *Love
Me Tender* © Bob Shaw 1980; Gene Wolfe and his agent
Virginia Kidd for *Kevin Malone* © Gene Wolfe 1980; Joan
Aiken for *Time To Laugh* © Joan Aiken Enterprises Ltd 1980;
Kit Reed and her agent A. P. Watt Ltd for *Chicken Soup*
© Kit Reed 1980; James Wade for *The Pursuer* © James Wade
1980; Graham Masterton for *Bridal Suite* © Graham
Masterton 1980; Dennis Etchison and Mark Johnson for *The
Spot* © Dennis Etchison and Mark Johnson 1980; Cherry
Wilder and her agent Virginia Kidd for *The Gingerbread
House* © Cherry Wilder 1980; Russell Kirk and his agent Kirby
McCauley for *Watchers at the Strait Gate* © Russell Kirk 1980;
Karl Edward Wagner for ·*220 Swift* © Karl Edward Wagner
1980; Errol Undercliffe and Montgomery Comfort for *The Fit*
© Ramsey Campbell 1980

Introduction

Nick Webb, then the fiction editor of Pan Books, proposed this book to me at the end of the 1978 British Fantasy Convention. Birmingham at Sunday lunchtime is a desert of concrete and dead restaurants; where better to discuss a book of contemporary terrors? Back at the hotel the conventioneers were being instructed in Tolkein, but we were champing hamburgers and imagining a book that would display today's masters of terror, both famous and potentially famous. Here, not without a struggle (Karl Wagner and Russell Kirk almost succumbed to the British postal troubles of mid-1979), is the first of its two volumes.

Why do people still read tales of terror? This is probably the hardest question in the field. 'Still' usually means either that the psychologists have exorcized our terrors or that 'reality' (nuclear and post-nuclear warfare, terrorism, and so on) is so disturbing that it makes the tale of terror redundant. I believe this book is an answer in itself, but my own response would be: some of the stories (Aickman's visions, Kirk's moral allegories) deal with states of being which are necessarily inexplicable, while the more openly horrific stories deal with fears and obsessions (which have certainly not been cleared away by science – indeed, science has created some of them) in a form sufficiently metaphorical to make them bearable to confront. Of course they include our own fascination with horror. Writers in this field expose the dark side of the imagination and at the same time keep the imagination alive. I believe this has never been so important as now.

Between Aickman and Wagner, two writers as different as they could be, are as many terrors as there are writers. Try not to read too many at once. They are best when read alone.

Ramsey Campbell
Liverpool, England
July 1979

Robert Aickman
The stains

*Robert Aickman is the finest living writer of ghost stories, and
nobody has advanced the form so significantly since Le Fanu.
I believe there is no author in the field more worth rereading.
In his essay in Gahan Wilson's anthology* The First World
Fantasy Awards *(which also contains the tale that gained him
the award, 'Pages from a Young Girl's Journal') he writes: 'I
do not regard my work as* fantasy *at all, except, perhaps, for
commercial purposes. I try to depict the world as I see it;
sometimes artistically exaggerating no doubt (artistically is
here a descriptive not a qualitative term), and occasionally
exaggerating for purposes of parable, as in my story "Growing
Boys". I believe in what the Germans term* Ehrfurcht:
*reverence for things one cannot understand.' (The essay is well
worth reading entire.)*

His books include The Late Breakfasters *(now back in print),*
Dark Entries, Powers of Darkness, Sub Rosa, Cold Hand in
Mine, Tales of Love and Death, *and the 'best of Aickman'
volume* Painted Devils. *He edited the first eight volumes of the*
Fontana Book of Great Ghost Stories, *with splendid
introductions. There is a great deal more to him for which I
have no room here, but some of it can be found in the first
volume of his autobiography, which was published as* The
Attempted Rescue. *It is about time someone published the
second.*

*Robert Aickman's combination of the supernatural (for
want of a better term) and the erotic is unique, and a perfect
start for this book.*

After Elizabeth ultimately died, it was inevitable that many
people should come forward with counsel, and doubtless
equally inevitable that the counsel be so totally diverse.

There were two broad and opposed schools.

The first considered that Stephen should 'treasure the memory' (though it was not always put like that) for an indefinite period, which, it was implied, might conveniently last him out to the end of his own life. These people attached great importance to Stephen 'not rushing anything'. The second school urged that Stephen marry again as soon as he possibly could. They said that, above all, he must not just fall into apathy and let his life slide. They said he was a man made for marriage and all it meant.

Of course, both parties were absolutely right in every way. Stephen could see that perfectly well.

It made little difference. Planning, he considered, would be absurd in any case. Until further notice, the matter would have to be left to fate. The trouble was, of course, that fate's possible options were narrowing and dissolving almost weekly, as they had already been doing throughout Elizabeth's lengthy illness. For example (the obvious and most pressing example): how many women would want to marry Stephen now? A number, perhaps; but not a number that he would want to marry. Not after Elizabeth. That in particular.

They told him he should take a holiday, and he took one. They told him he should see his doctor, and he saw him. The man who had looked after Elizabeth had wanted to emigrate, had generously held back while Elizabeth had remained alive, and had then shot off at once. The new man was half-Sudanese, and Stephen found him difficult to communicate with, at least upon a first encounter, at least on immediate topics.

In the end, Stephen applied for and obtained a spell of compassionate leave, and went, as he usually did, to stay with his elder brother, Harewood, in the north. Harewood was in orders: the Reverend Harewood Hooper BD, MA. Their father and grandfather had been in orders too, and had been incumbents of that same small church in that same small parish for thirty-nine years and forty-two years respectively. So far, Harewood had served for only twenty-three years. The patron of the living, a private individual, conscientious and very long lived, was relieved to be able to rely upon a succession of such dedicated men. Unfortunately, Harewood's own son, his one child, had dropped out, and was now believed to have disappeared into Nepal. Harewood himself cared more for rock growths than for controversies about South Africa or for other such fashionable church preoccupations. He had published two important books on lichens. People often came to see him on the subject. He was modestly famous.

He fostered lichens on the flagstones leading up to the rectory front door; on the splendidly living stone walls, here grey stone, there yellow; even in the seldom used larders and pantries; assuredly on the roof, which, happily, was of stone slabs also.

As always when he visited his brother, Stephen found that he was spending much of his time out of doors; mainly, being the man he was, in long, solitary walks across the heathered uplands. This had nothing to do with Harewood's speciality. Harewood suffered badly from bronchitis and catarrh, and nowadays went out as little as possible. The domestic lichens, once introduced, required little attention – only observation.

Rather it was on account of Harewood's wife, Harriet, that Stephen roamed; a lady in whose company Stephen had never been at ease. She had always seemed to him a restless woman; jumpy and puzzling; the very reverse of all that had seemed best about Elizabeth. A doubtful asset, Stephen would have thought, in a diminishing rural parish; but Stephen himself, in a quiet and unobtruding way, had long been something of a sceptic. Be that as it might, he always found that Harriet seemed to be baiting and fussing him, not least when her husband was present; even, unforgivably, when Elizabeth, down in London, had been battling through her last dreadful years. On every visit, therefore, Stephen wandered about for long hours in the open, even when ice was in the air and snow on the tenuous tracks.

But Stephen did not see it as a particular hardship. Elizabeth, who might have done – though, for his sake, she could have been depended upon to conceal the fact – had seldom come on these visits at any time. She had never been a country girl, though fond of the sea. Stephen positively liked wandering unaccompanied on the moors, though he had little detailed knowledge of their flora and fauna, or even of their archaeology, largely industrial and fragmentary. By now he was familiar with most of the moorland routes from the rectory and the village; and, as commonly happens, there was one that he preferred to all the others, and nowadays found himself taking almost without having to make a decision. Sometimes even, asleep in his London flat that until just now had been *their* London flat, he found himself actually dreaming of that particular soaring trail, though he would have found it difficult to define what properties of beauty or poetry or convenience it had of which the other tracks had less. According to the map, it led to a spot named Burton's Clough.

There was a vague valley or extended hollow more or less in the place which the map indicated, but to Stephen it seemed every time too indefinite to be marked out for record. Every time he wondered whether this was indeed the place; whether there was not some more decisive declivity that he had never discovered. Or possibly the name derived from some event in local history. It was the upwards walk to the place that appealed to Stephen, and, to an only slightly lesser extent, the first part of the slow descent homewards, supposing that the rectory could in any sense be called home: never the easily attainable but inconclusive supposed goal, the Clough. Of course there was always R. L. Stevenson's travelling hopefully to be inwardly quoted; and on most occasions hitherto Stephen had inwardly quoted it.

Never had there been any human being at, near, or visible from the terrain around Burton's Clough, let alone in the presumptive clough itself. There was no apparent reason why there should be. Stephen seldom met anyone at all on the moors. Only organizations go any distance afoot nowadays, and this was not an approved didactic district. All the work of agriculture is for a period being done by machines. Most of the cottages are peopled by transients. Everyone is supposed to have a car.

But that morning, Stephen's first in the field since his bereavement six weeks before, there *was* someone, and down at the bottom of the shallow clough itself. The person was dressed so as to be almost lost in the hues of autumn, plainly neither tripper nor trifler. The person was engaged in some task.

Stephen was in no state for company, but that very condition, and a certain particular reluctance that morning to return to the rectory before he had to, led him to advance further, not descending into the clough but skirting along the ridge to the west of it, where, indeed, his track continued.

If he had been in the Alps, his shadow might have fallen in the early autumn sun across the figure below, but in the circumstances that idea would have been fanciful, because, at the moment, the sun was no more than a misty bag of gleams in a confused sky. None the less, as Stephen's figure passed, comparatively high above, the figure below glanced up at him.

Stephen could see that it was the figure of a girl. She was wearing a fawn shirt and pale green trousers, but the nature of her activity remained uncertain.

Stephen glanced away, then glanced back.

She seemed still to be looking up at him, and suddenly he waved to her, though it was not altogether the kind of thing he normally did. She waved back at him. Stephen even fancied she smiled at him. It seemed quite likely. She resumed her task.

He waited for an instant, but she looked up no more. He continued on his way more slowly, and feeling more alive, even if only for moments. For those moments, it had been as if he still belonged to the human race, to the mass of mankind.

Only once or twice previously had he continued beyond the top of Burton's Clough, and never for any great distance. On the map (it had been his father's map), the track wavered on across a vast area of nothing very much, merely contour lines and occasional habitations with odd, possibly evocative, names: habitations which, as Stephen knew from experience, regularly proved, when approached, to be littered ruins or not to be detectable at all. He would not necessarily have been averse from the twelve or fourteen miles solitary walk involved, at least while Elizabeth had been secure and alive, and at home in London; but conditions at the rectory had never permitted so long an absence. Harriet often made clear that she expected her guests to be present punctually at all meals and punctually at such other particular turning points of a particular day as the day itself might define.

On the present occasion, and at the slow pace into which he had subsided, Stephen knew that he should turn back within the next ten to fifteen minutes; but he half-understood that what he was really doing was calculating the best time for a second possible communication with the girl he had seen in the clough. If he reappeared too soon, he might be thought, at such a spot, to be pestering, even menacing; if too late, the girl might be gone. In any case, there was an obvious limit to the time he could give to such approach as might be possible.

As the whole matter crystallized within him, he turned on the instant. There was a stone beside the track at the point where he did it; perhaps aforetime a milepost, at the least a waymark. Its location seemed to justify his action. He noticed that it too was patched with lichen. When staying with Harewood, he always noticed; and more and more at other times too.

15

One might almost have thought that the girl had been waiting for him. She was standing at much the same spot, and looking upwards abstractedly. Stephen saw that beside her on the ground was a grey receptacle. He had not noticed it before, because its vague colour sank into the landscape, as did the girl herself, costumed as she was. The receptacle seemed to be half-filled with grey contents of some kind.

As soon as he came into her line of sight, and sometime before he stood immediately above her, the girl spoke.

'Are you lost? Are you looking for someone?'

She must have had a remarkably clear voice, because her words came floating up to Stephen like bubbles in water.

He continued along the ridge towards her while she watched him. Only when he was directly above her did he trust his own words to reach her.

'No. I'm really just filling in time. Thank you very much.'

'If you go on to the top, there's a spring.'

'I should think you have to have it pointed out to you. With all this heather.'

She looked down for a moment, then up again. 'Do you live here?'

'No. I'm staying with my brother. He's the rector. Perhaps you go to his church?'

She shook her head. 'No. We don't go to any church.'

That could not be followed up, Stephen felt, at his present distance and altitude. 'What are you doing?' he asked.

'Collecting stones for my father.'

'What does he do with them?'

'He wants the mosses and lichens.'

'Then,' cried Stephen, 'you *must* know my brother. Or your father must know him. My brother is one of the great authorities on lichens.' This unexpected link seemed to open a door; and, at least for a second, to open it surprisingly wide.

Stephen found himself bustling down the rough but not particularly steep slope towards her.

'My father's not an *authority*,' said the girl, gazing seriously at the descending figure. 'He's not an authority on anything.'

'Oh, you misunderstand,' said Stephen. 'My brother is only an amateur too. I didn't mean he was a professor or anything like that. Still, I think your father must have heard of him.'

'I don't think so,' said the girl. 'I'm almost sure not.'

Stephen had nearly reached the bottom of the shallow vale.

It was completely out of the wind down there, and surprisingly torrid.

'Let me see,' he said, looking into the girl's basket, before he looked at the girl.

She lifted the basket off the ground. Her hand and forearm were brown.

'Some of the specimens are very small,' he said, smiling. It was essential to keep the conversation going, and it was initially more difficult now that he was alone with her in the valley, and close to her.

'It's been a bad year,' she said. 'Some days I've found almost nothing. Nothing that could be taken home.'

'All the same, the basket must be heavy. Please put it down.' He saw that it was reinforced with stout metal strips, mostly rusty.

'Take a piece for yourself, if you like,' said the girl. She spoke as if they were portions of iced cake, or home-made coconut fudge.

Stephen gazed full at the girl. She had a sensitive face with grey-green eyes and short reddish hair – no, auburn. The *démodé* word came to Stephen on the instant. Both her shirt and her trousers were worn and faded: familiar, Stephen felt. She was wearing serious shoes, but little cared for. She was a part of nature.

'I'll take this piece,' Stephen said. 'It's conglomerate.'

'Is it?' said the girl. Stephen was surprised that after so much ingathering, she did not know a fact so elementary.

'I might take this piece too, and show the stuff on it to my brother.'

'Help yourself,' said the girl. 'But don't take them all.'

Feeling had been building up in Stephen while he had been walking solitarily on the ridge above. For so long he had been isolated, insulated, incarcerated. Elizabeth had been everything to him, and no one could ever be like her, but 'attractive' was not a word that he had used to himself about her, not for a long time; not attractive as this girl was attractive. Elizabeth had been a part of him, perhaps the greater part of him; but not mysterious, not fascinating.

'Well, I don't know,' said Stephen. 'How far do you have to carry that burden?'

'The basket isn't full yet. I must go on searching for a bit.'

'I am sorry to say I can't offer to help. I have to go back.'

All the same, Stephen had reached a decision.

The girl simply nodded. She had not yet picked up the basket again.

'Where do you live?'

'Quite near.'

That seemed to Stephen to be almost impossible, but it was not the main point.

Stephen felt like a schoolboy; though not like himself as a schoolboy. 'If I were to be here after lunch tomorrow, say at half past two, would you show me the spring? The spring you were talking about.'

'Of course,' she said. 'If you like.'

Stephen could not manage the response so obviously needed, gently confident; if possible, even gently witty. For a moment, in fact, he could say nothing. Then – 'Look,' he said. He brought an envelope out of his pocket and in pencil on the back of it he wrote: 'Tomorrow. Here. 2.30 p.m. To visit the spring.'

He said, 'It's too big,' and tore one end off the envelope, aware that the remaining section bore his name, and that the envelope had been addressed to him care of his brother. As a matter of fact, it had contained the final communication from the undertaking firm. He wished they had omitted his equivocal and rather ridiculous OBE.

He held the envelope out. She took it and inserted it, without a word, into a pocket of her shirt, buttoning down the flap. Stephen's heart beat at the gesture.

He was not exactly sure what to make of the situation or whether the appointment was to be depended upon. But at such moments in life, one is often sure of neither thing, nor of anything much else.

He looked at her. 'What's your name?' he asked, as casually as he could.

'Nell,' she answered.

He had not quite expected that, but then he had not particularly expected anything else either.

'I look forward to our walk, Nell,' he said. He could not help adding, 'I look forward to it very much.'

She nodded and smiled.

He fancied that they had really looked at one another for a moment.

'I must go on searching,' she said.

She picked up the heavy basket, seemingly without particular effort, and walked away from him, up the valley.

Insanely, he wondered about *her* lunch. Surely she must have some? She seemed so exceptionally healthy and strong.

His own meal was all scarlet runners, but he had lost his appetite in any case, something that had never previously happened since the funeral, as he had noticed with surprise on several occasions.

Luncheon was called lunch, but the evening meal was none the less called supper, perhaps from humility. At supper that evening, Harriet referred forcefully to Stephen's earlier abstemiousness.

'I trust you're not sickening, Stephen. It would be a bad moment. Dr Gopalachari's on holiday. Perhaps I ought to warn you.'

'Dr Who?'

'No, not Dr Who. Dr Gopalachari. He's a West Bengali. We are lucky to have him.'

Stephen's brother, Harewood, coughed forlornly.

For luncheon the next day, Stephen had even less appetite, even though it was mashed turnip, cooked, or at least served, with mixed peppers. Harriet loved all things oriental.

On an almost empty stomach, he hastened up the long but not steep ascent. He had not known he could still walk so fast uphill, but for some reason the knowledge did not make him particularly happy, as doubtless it should have done.

The girl, dressed as on the day before, was seated upon a low rock at the spot from which he had first spoken to her. It was not yet twenty past. He had discerned her seated shape from afar, but she had proved to be sitting with her back to the ascending track and to him. On the whole, he was glad that she had not been watching his exertions, inevitably comical, albeit triumphant.

She did not even look up until he actually stood before her. Of course this time she had no basket.

'Oh, hullo,' she said.

He stood looking at her. 'We're both punctual.'

She nodded. He was panting quite strenuously, and glad to gain a little time.

He spoke. 'Did you find many more suitable stones?'

She shook her head, then rose to her feet.

He found it difficult not to stretch out his arms and draw her to him.

'Why is this called Burton's Clough, I wonder? It seems altogether too wide and shallow for a clough.'

'I didn't know it was,' said the girl.

'The map says it is. At least I think this is the place. Shall we go? Lead me to the magic spring.'

She smiled at him. 'Why do you call it *that*?'

'I'm sure it *is* magic. It must be.'

'It's just clear water,' said the girl, 'and very, very deep.'

Happily, the track was still wide enough for them to walk side by side, though Stephen realized that, further on, where he had not been, this might cease to be the case.

'How long are you staying here?' asked the girl.

'Perhaps for another fortnight. It depends.'

'Are you married?'

'I *was* married, Nell, but my wife unfortunately died.' It seemed unnecessary to put any date to it, and calculated only to cause stress.

'I'm sorry,' said the girl.

'She was a wonderful woman and a very good wife.'

To that the girl said nothing. What could she say?

'I am taking a period of leave from the civil service,' Stephen volunteered. 'Nothing very glamorous.'

'What's the civil service?' asked the girl.

'You ought to know *that*,' said Stephen in mock reproof: more or less mock. After all, she was not a child, or not exactly. All the same, he produced a childlike explanation. 'The civil service is what looks after the country. The country would hardly carry on without us. Not nowadays. Nothing would run properly.'

'Really not?'

'No. Not run *properly*.' With her it was practicable to be lightly profane.

'Father says that all politicians are evil. I don't know anything about it.'

'Civil servants are not politicians, Nell. But perhaps this is not the best moment to go into it all.' He said that partly because he suspected she had no wish to learn.

There was a pause.

'Do you like walking?' she asked.

'Very much. I could easily walk all day. Would you come with me?'

'I *do* walk all day, or most of it. Of course I have to sleep at night. I lie in front of the fire.'

'But it's too warm for a fire at this time of year.' He said it to keep the conversation going, but, in fact, he was far from certain. He himself was not particularly warm at that very moment. He had no doubt cooled off after speeding up the ascent, but the two of them were, none the less, walking reasonably fast, and still he felt chilly, perhaps perilously so.

'Father always likes a fire,' said the girl. 'He's a cold mortal.'

They had reached the decayed milestone or waymark at which Stephen had turned on the previous day. The girl had stopped and was fingering the lichens with which it was spattered. She knelt against the stone with her left arm round the back of it.

'Can you put a name to them?' asked Stephen.

'Yes, to some of them.'

'I am sure your father has one of my brother's books on his shelf.'

'I don't think so,' said the girl. 'We have no shelves. Father can't read.'

She straightened up and glanced at Stephen.

'Oh, but surely—'

For example, and among other things, the girl herself was perfectly well spoken. As a matter of fact, hers was a noticeably beautiful voice. Stephen had noticed it, and even thrilled to it, when first he had heard it, floating up from the bottom of the so-called clough. He had thrilled to it ever since, despite the curious things the girl sometimes said.

They resumed their way.

'Father has no eyes,' said the girl.

'That is terrible,' said Stephen. 'I hadn't realized.'

The girl said nothing.

Stephen felt his first real qualm, as distinct from mere habitual self-doubt. 'Am I taking you away from him? Should you go back to him?'

'I'm never with him by day,' said the girl. 'He finds his way about.'

'I know that does happen,' said Stephen guardedly. 'All the same—'

'Father doesn't need a civil service to run him,' said the girl. The way she spoke convinced Stephen that she had known all along what the civil service was and did. He had from the first supposed that to be so. Everyone knew.

'You said your dead wife was a wonderful woman,' said the girl.

'Yes, she was.'

'My father is a wonderful man.'

'Yes,' said Stephen. 'I am only sorry about his affliction.'

'It's not an affliction,' said the girl.

Stephen did not know what to say to that. The last thing to be desired was an argument of any kind whatever, other perhaps than a fun argument.

'Father doesn't need to get things out of books,' said the girl.

'There are certainly other ways of learning,' said Stephen. 'I expect that was one of the things you yourself learned at school.'

He suspected she would say she had never been to school. His had been a half-fishing remark.

But all she replied was, 'Yes'.

Stephen looked around him for a moment. Already, he had gone considerably further along the track than ever before. 'It really is beautiful up here.' It seemed a complete wilderness. The track had wound among the wide folds of the hill, so that nothing but wilderness was visible in any direction.

'I should like to live here,' said Stephen. 'I should like it *now*.' He knew that he partly meant 'now that Elizabeth was dead'.

'There are empty houses everywhere,' said the girl. 'You can just move into one. It's what Father and I did, and now it's our home.'

Stephen supposed that that at least explained something. It possibly elucidated one of the earliest of her odd remarks.

'I'll help you to find one, if you like,' said the girl. 'Father says that none of them have been lived in for hundreds of years. I know where all the best ones are.'

'I'll have to think about that,' said Stephen. 'I have my job, you must remember.' He wanted her to be rude about his job.

But she only said, 'We'll look now, if you like.'

'Tomorrow, perhaps. We're looking for the spring now.'

'Are you tired?' asked the girl, with apparently genuine concern, and presumably forgetting altogether what he had told her about his longing to walk all day.

'Not at all tired,' said Stephen, smiling at her.

'Then why were you looking at your watch?'

'A bad habit picked up in the civil service. We all do it.'

He had observed long before that she had no watch on her lovely brown forearm, no bracelet; only the marks of thorn scratches and the incisions of sharp stones. The light golden bloom on her arms filled him with delight and with desire.

In fact, he had omitted to time their progression, though he timed most things, so that the habit had wrecked his natural faculty. Perhaps another twenty or thirty minutes passed, while they continued to walk side by side, the track having as yet shown no particular sign of narrowing, so that one might think it still led somewhere, and that people still went there. As they advanced, they said little more of consequence for the moment; or so it seemed to Stephen. He surmised that there was now what is termed an understanding between them, even though in a sense he himself understood very little. It was more a phase for pleasant nothings, he deemed, always supposing that he could evolve a sufficient supply of them, than for meaningful questions and reasonable responses.

Suddenly, the track seemed not to narrow, but to stop, even to vanish. Hereunto it had been surprisingly well trodden. Now he could see nothing but knee-high heather.

'The spring's over there,' said the girl in a matter of fact way, and pointing. Such simple and natural gestures are often the most beautiful.

'How right I was in saying that I could never find it alone!' remarked Stephen.

He could not see why the main track should not lead to the spring – if there really was a spring. Why else should the track be beaten to this spot? The mystery was akin to the Burton's Clough mystery. The uplands had been settled under other conditions than ours. Stephen, on his perambulations, had always felt that, everywhere.

But the girl was standing among the heather a few yards away, and Stephen saw that there was a curious serpentine rabbit run that he had failed to notice – except that rabbits do not run like serpents. There were several fair-sized birds flying overhead in silence. Stephen fancied they were kites.

He wriggled his way down the rabbit path, with little dignity.

There was the most beautiful small pool imaginable: clear, deep, lustrous, gently heaving at its centre, or near its centre. It stood in a small clearing.

All the rivers in Britain might be taken as rising here, and thus flowing until the first moment of their pollution.

Stephen became aware that now the sun really *was* shining. He had not noticed before. The girl stood on the far side of the pool in her faded shirt and trousers, smiling seraphically. The pool pleased her, so that suddenly everything pleased her.

'Have you kept the note I gave you?' asked Stephen.

She put her hand lightly on her breast pocket, and therefore on her breast.

'I'm glad,' said Stephen.

If the pool had not been between them, he would have seized her, whatever the consequences.

'Just clear water,' said the girl.

The sun brought out new colours in her hair. The shape of her head was absolutely perfect.

'The track,' said Stephen, 'seems to be quite well used. Is this where the people come?'

'No,' said the girl. 'They come to and from the places where they live.'

'I thought you said all the houses were empty.'

'What I said was there are many empty houses.'

'That *is* what you said. I'm sorry. But the track seems to come to an end. What do the people do then?'

'They find their way,' said the girl. 'Stop worrying about them.'

The water was still between them. Stephen was no longer in doubt that there was indeed something else between them. Really there was. The pool was intermittently throwing up tiny golden waves in the pure breeze, then losing them again.

'We haven't seen anybody,' said Stephen. 'I never do see anyone.'

The girl looked puzzled.

Stephen realized that the way he had put it, the statement that he never saw anyone, might have been tactless. 'When I go for my long walks alone,' he added.

'Not only then,' said the girl.

Stephen's heart turned over slightly.

'Possibly,' he said. 'I daresay you are very right.'

The kites were still flapping like torn pieces of charred pasteboard in the high air, though in the lower part of it.

'You haven't even looked to the bottom of the pool yet,' said the girl.

'I suppose not.' Stephen fell on his knees, as the girl had done at the milestone or waymark, and gazed downwards through the pellucid near-nothingness beneath the shifting golden rods. There were a few polished stones round the sides, but little else that he could see, and nothing that seemed of significance. How should there be, of course? Unless the girl had put it there, as Stephen realized might have been possible.

Stephen looked up. 'It's a splendid pool,' he said.

But now his eye caught something else; something other than the girl and the pool. On the edge of the rising ground behind the girl stood a small stone house. It was something else that Stephen had not previously noticed. Indeed, he had been reasonably sure that there had been nothing and no one, not so much as a hint of mankind, not for a quite long way, a quite long time.

'Is that where one of the people lives?' he asked, and in his turn pointed. 'Or perhaps more than one?'

'It's empty,' said the girl.

'Should we go and look?'

'If you like,' said the girl. Stephen quite saw that his expressed response to the glorious little spring had been inadequate. He had lost the trick of feeling, years and years ago.

'It's a splendid pool,' he said again, a little self-consciously.

Despite what the girl had said, Stephen had thought that to reach the house above them, they would have to scramble through the high heather. But he realized at once that there was a path, which was one further thing he had not previously noticed.

The girl went before, weaving backwards and forwards up the hillside. Following her, with his thoughts more free to wander, as the exertion made talking difficult, Stephen suddenly apprehended that the need to return for Harriet's teatime had for a season passed completely from his mind.

Apprehending it now, he did not even look at his watch. Apart from anything else, the struggle upwards was too intense for even the smallest distraction or secondary effort. The best thing might be for his watch simply to stop.

They were at the summit, with a wider horizon, but still Stephen could see no other structure than the one before him, though this time he gazed around with a certain care. From here, the pool below them seemed to catch the full sun all over its surface. It gleamed among the heathered rocks like a vast luminous sea anemone among weeds.

Stephen could see at once that the house appeared basically habitable. He had expected jagged holes in the walls, broken panes in the windows, less than half a roof, ubiquitous litter.

The door simply stood open, but it was a door, not a mere gap; a door in faded green, like the girl's trousers. Inside, the floorboards were present and there was even a certain amount

25

of simple furniture, though, as an estate agent would at once have pointed out with apologies, no curtains and no carpets.

'Nell. Somebody lives here already,' Stephen said sharply, before they had even gone upstairs.

'Already?' queried the girl.

Stephen made the necessary correction. 'Someone lives here.'

'No,' said the girl. 'No one. Not for centuries.'

Of course that was particularly absurd and childish. Much of this furniture, Stephen thought, was of the kind offered by the furnishing department of a good Co-op. Stephen had sometimes come upon such articles on visits paid in the course of his work. He had to admit, however, that he had little idea when such houses as this actually were built at these odd spots on the moors. Possibly as long ago as in the seventeenth century? Possibly only sixty or eighty years ago? Possibly—?

They went upstairs. There were two very low rooms, hardly as much as half lighted from one small and dirty window in each. One room was totally unfurnished. The sole content of the other was a double bed which absorbed much of the cubic capacity available. It was a quite handsome country object, with a carved head and foot. It even offered a seemingly intact mattress, badly in need of a wash.

'Someone *must* be living here,' said Stephen. 'At least sometimes. Perhaps the owners come here for the weekend. Or perhaps they're just moving in.'

As soon as he spoke, it occurred to him that the evidence was equally consistent with their moving out, but he did not continue.

'Lots of the houses are like this,' said the girl. 'No one lives in them.'

Stephen wondered vaguely whether the clear air or some factor of that kind might preserve things as if they were still in use. It was a familiar enough notion, though, in his case, somewhat unspecific. It would be simpler to disbelieve the girl, who was young and without experience, though perfectly eager, at least when others were eager. They returned downstairs.

'Shall we see some more houses?' asked the girl.

'I don't think I have the time.'

'You said you had a fortnight. I know what a fortnight is.'

'Yes.' He simply could not tell her that he had to report for Harriet's astringent teatime; nor, even now, was that in the forefront of his mind. The truth was that whereas hitherto he had been trying to paddle in deep waters, he was now floundering in them.

The girl had a suggestion. 'Why not live *here* for a fortnight?'

'I am committed to staying with my brother. He's not very fit. I should worry about him if I broke my word.' He realized that he was speaking to her in a more adult way than before. It had really begun with her speaking similarly to him.

'Does your worrying about him do him any good?'

'Not much, I'm afraid.'

'Does your worrying about everything do *you* any good?'

'None whatever, Nell. None at all.'

He turned aside and looked out of the window; the parlour window might not be too grand a term, for all its need of cleaning.

He addressed her firmly. 'Would you give me a hand with all the things that need to be done? Even for a tenancy of a fortnight?'

'If you like.'

'We should have to do a lot of shopping.'

The girl, standing behind him, remained silent. It was an unusual non-response.

'I should have to cook on a primus stove,' said Stephen. 'I wonder if we can buy one? I used to be quite good with them.' Rapture was beginning.

The girl said nothing.

'We might need new locks on the doors.'

The girl spoke. 'There is only one door.'

'So there is,' said Stephen. 'In towns, houses have two, a front door and a back door. When trouble comes in at one, you can do a bolt through the other.'

'People don't need a lock,' said the girl. 'Why should they?'

He turned away from the filthy window and gazed straight at her. 'Suppose I was to fall in love with you?' he said.

'Then you would not have to go back after a fortnight.'

It could hardly have been a straighter reply.

He put one arm round her shoulders, one hand on her breast, so that the note he had written her lay between them. He remembered that the first letter written to a woman is always a love letter. 'Would you promise to visit me every day?'

'I might be unable to do that.'

'I don't want to seem unkind, but you did say that your father could manage.'

'If he discovers, he will keep me at home and send my sister out instead. He has powers. He's very frightening.'

Stephen relaxed his hold a little. He had been all along well aware how sadly impracticable was the entire idea.

For example: he could hardly even drive up to this place with supplies; even had his car not been in the course of an opportune overhaul in London, a very complete overhaul after all this anxious time. And that was only one thing; one among very many.

'Well, what's the answer?' Stephen said, smiling at her in the wrong way, longing for her in a very different way.

'I can't come and go the whole time,' said the girl.

'I see,' said Stephen.

He who had missed so many opportunities, always for excellent reasons, and for one excellent reason in particular, clearly saw that this might be his last opportunity, and almost certainly was.

'How should we live?' he asked. 'I mean how should we eat and manage?'

'As the birds do,' said the girl.

Stephen did not inquire of her how she came to know Shakespeare, as people put it. He might ask her that later. In the meantime, he could see that the flat, floating birds he had taken to be kites, were indeed drifting past the dirty window, and round and round the house, as it seemed. Of course his questions had been mere routine in any case. He could well have killed himself if she had made a merely routine response.

'Let's see,' he said. He gently took her hand. He kissed her softly on the lips. He returned with her upstairs.

It would perhaps have been more suitable if he had been leading the party, but that might be a trifle. Even the damp discolouration of the mattress might be a trifle. Harriet's teatime could not, in truth, be forced from the mind, but it was provisionally overruled. One learned the trick in the course of one's work, or one would break altogether.

There were of course only the bed and the mattress; no sheets or blankets; no Spanish or Kashmiri rugs; no entangling silkiness, no singing save that of the moor. Elizabeth had never wished to make love like that. She had liked to turn on the record player, almost always Brahms or Schumann (the Rhenish Symphony was her particular favourite), and to ascend slowly into a deep fully made bed. But the matter had not seriously arisen for years. Stephen had often wondered why not.

Nell was lying on her front. Seemingly expectant and resistant at the same time, she clung like a clam. Her body was as brown as a pale chestnut, but it was a strong and well-made body. Her short hair was wavy rather than curly. Stephen was ravished by the line of it on her strong neck. He was ravished by her relaxed shoulder blade. He was ravished by her perfect waist and thighs. He was ravished by her youth and youthful smell.

'Please turn over,' he said, after tugging at her intermittently, and not very effectively.

Fortunately, he was not too displeased by his own appearance. The hair on his body was bleaching and fading, but otherwise he could, quite sincerely, see little difference from when he had been twenty-four, and had married Elizabeth. He knew, however, that at these times sincerity is not enough; nor objectivity either. When are they?

'Please,' he said softly in Nell's ear. Her ears were a slightly unusual shape, and the most beautiful he had ever beheld, or beheld so intently.

He put his hand lightly on her neck. 'Please,' he said.

She wriggled over in a single swift movement, like a light stab from an invisible knife. He saw that her eyes were neither closed nor open, neither looking at him, nor looking at anything but him.

On the skin between her right shoulder and her right breast was a curious, brownish, greyish, bluish, irregular mark or patch, which had been hidden by her shirt, though Stephen could not quite see how. It was more demanding of attention than it might have been, partly because of its position, and partly, where Stephen was concerned, because of something vaguely else. In any case, it would mean that the poor girl could not reposefully wear a low-cut dress, should the need arise. Though it was by no means a birthmark in the usual sense, Nell had probably been lying on her front through chagrin about it. Upon Stephen, however, the effect was to make him love her more deeply; perhaps love her for the first time. He did not want her or her body to be quite perfect. In a real person, it would be almost vulgar. At this point, Harriet and Harriet's teatime came more prominently into view for a few seconds.

Nell might say something about the mark sooner or later. He would never take an initiative.

At the moment, she said nothing at all. He simply could not make out whether she was watching him or not. Her mouth was long and generous; but had not her whole proceeding been generous in a marvellous degree? He could not even make out whether she was taut or relaxed. No small mystery was Nell after years and years of a perfect, but always slow-moving, relationship with Elizabeth!

He kissed her intimately. When she made no particular response, not even a grunt, he began to caress her, more or less as he had caressed his wife. He took care not to touch the peculiar blemish, or even to enter its area. There was no need to do so. It occurred to Stephen that the mark might be the consequence of an injury; and so might in due course disappear, or largely so. In the end that happened even to many of the strangest human markings. One day, as the nannies used to say.

Suddenly she made a wild plunge at him that took away his breath. The surprise was directly physical, but moral also. He had found it a little difficult to assess Nell's likely age, and inquiry was out of the question; but he had supposed it probable that she was a virgin, and had quite deliberately resolved to accept the implication. Or so he had believed of himself.

Now she was behaving as a maenad.

As an oread, rather; Stephen thought at a later hour. For surely these moors were mountains, often above the thousand-foot contour; boundless uplands peopled solely by unwedded nymphs and their monstrous progenitors? Stephen had received a proper education at a proper place: in Stephen's first days, one had not made the grade, Stephen's grade, otherwise. Stephen's parents had undertaken sacrifices so immense that no one had fully recovered from them.

The last vestige of initiative had passed from Stephen like a limb. And yet, he fancied, it was not because Nell was what Elizabeth would have called unfeminine, but merely because she was young, and perhaps because she lived without contamination, merging into the aspect and mutability of remote places. So, at least, he could only suppose.

Soon he ceased to suppose anything. He knew bliss unequalled, unprecedented, assuredly unimagined. Moreover, the wonder lasted for longer than he would have conceived of as possible. That particularly struck him.

Nell's flawed body was celestial. Nell herself was more wonderful than the dream of death. Nell could not possibly exist.

*

He was fondling her and feeling a trifle cold; much as Elizabeth would have felt. Not that it mattered in the very least. Nell was no maenad or oread. She was a half-frightened child, sweetly soft, responsive to his every thought, sometimes before he had fully given birth to it. She was a waif, a foundling. And it was he who had found her. And only yesterday.

'Tell me about your sister,' said Stephen. He realized that it was growing dark as well as chilly.

'She's not like *me*. You wouldn't like her.'

Stephen knew that ordinary, normal girls always responded much like that.

He smiled at Nell. 'But what *is* she like?'

'She's made quite differently. You wouldn't care for her.'

'Has she a name?'

'Of a sort.'

'What do you and your father call her?'

'We call her different things at different times. You're cold.'

So she was human, after all, Stephen thought.

She herself had very little to put on. Two fairly light garments, a pair of stout socks, her solid shoes.

They went downstairs.

'Would you care to borrow my sweater?' asked Stephen. 'Until tomorrow?'

She made no reply, but simply stared at him through the dusk in the downstairs room, the living place, the parlour, the *salon*.

'Take it,' said Stephen. It was a heavy garment. Elizabeth had spent nearly four months knitting it continuously, while slowly recovering from her very first disintegration. It was in thick complex stitches and meant to last for ever. When staying with Harewood, Stephen wore it constantly.

Nell took the sweater but did not put it on. She was still staring at him. At such a moment her grey-green eyes were almost luminous.

'We'll meet again tomorrow,' said Stephen firmly. 'We'll settle down here tomorrow. I must say something to my brother and sister-in-law, and I don't care what happens after that. Not now. At least I *do* care. I care very much. As you well know.'

'It's risky,' she said.

'Yes,' he replied, because it was necessary to evade all discussion. 'Yes, but it can't be helped. You come as early as you can, and I'll arrive with some provisions for us. We really need some blankets too, and some candles. I'll see if I can borrow a Land-Rover from one of the farms.' He trusted that his confidence and his firm, practical actions would override all doubts.

'I may be stopped,' she said. 'My father can't read books but he can read minds. He does it all the time.'

'You must run away from him,' said Stephen firmly. 'We'll stay here for a little, and then you can come back to London with me.'

She made no comment on that, but simply repeated, 'My father can read *my* mind. I only have to be in the same room with him. He's frightening.'

Her attitude to her father seemed to have changed considerably. It was the experience of love, Stephen supposed; first love.

'Obviously, you must try to be in a *different* room as much as possible. It's only for one more night. We've known each other now for two days.'

'There's only one room.'

Stephen had known that such would be her rejoinder.

He well knew also that his behaviour might seem unromantic and even cold-hearted. But the compulsion upon him could not be plainer: if he did not return to the rectory tonight, Harriet, weakly aided by Harewood, would have the police after him; dogs would be scurrying across the moors, as if after Hercules, and perhaps searchlights sweeping also. Nothing could more fatally upset any hope of a quiet and enduring compact with such a one as Nell. He was bound for a rough scene with Harriet and Harewood as it was. It being now long past teatime, he would be lucky if Harriet had not taken action before he could reappear. Speed was vital and, furthermore, little of the situation could be explained with any candour to Nell. First, she would simply not understand what he said (even though within her range she was shrewd enough, often shrewder than he). Second, in so far as she did understand, she would panic and vanish. And he had no means of tracking her down at all. She was as shy about her abode as about the mark on her body; though doubtless with as little reason, or so Stephen hoped. He recognized that parting from her at all might be as unwise as it would be painful, but it was the lesser peril. He could not take her to London tonight, or to anywhere, because there was no accessible transport. Not nowadays. He could not take her to the rectory, where Harriet might make Harewood

lay an anathema upon her. They could not stay in the moorland house without food or warmth.

'I'll walk with you to the top of the clough,' he said.

She shook her head. 'It's not there I live.'

'Where then?' he asked at once.

'Not that way at all.'

'Will you get there?'

She nodded: in exactly what spirit it was hard to say.

He refrained from inquiring how she would explain the
absence of specimens for her father. Two or three stones
dragged from the walls of the house they were in, might serve
the purpose in any case, he thought: outside and inside were
almost equally mossed, lichened, adorned, encumbered.

'Goodnight, Nell. We'll meet tomorrow morning. Here.' He
really had to go. Harriet was made anxious by the slightest
irregularity, and when she became anxious, she became fren-
zied. His present irregularity was by no means slight already;
assuredly not slight by Harriet's standards.

To his great relief, Nell nodded again. She had still not put
on his sweater.

'In a few days' time, we'll go to London. We'll be together
always.' He could hardly believe his own ears listening to his
own voice saying such things. After all this time! After Elizabeth! After so much inner peace and convinced adoration and
asking for nothing more! After the fearful illness!

They parted with kisses but with little drama. Nell sped off
into what the map depicted as virtual void.

'All the same,' Stephen reflected, 'I must look at the map
again. I'll try to borrow Harewood's dividers.'

He pushed back through the heather, rejoicing in his sense of
direction, among so many other things to rejoice about, and
began lumbering down the track homewards. The light was
now so poor that he walked faster and faster; faster even than
he had ascended. In the end, he was running uncontrollably.

Therefore, his heart was already pounding when he discovered
that the rectory was in confusion; though, at the rectory, even
confusion had a slightly wan quality.

During the afternoon, Harriet had had a seizure of some
kind, and during the evening had been taken off in a public
ambulance.

'What time did it happen?' asked Stephen. He knew from

33

all too much experience that it was the kind of thing that people did ask.

'I don't really know, Stephen,' replied Harewood. 'I was in my specimens room reading the *Journal*, and I fear that a considerable time may have passed before I came upon her. I was too distressed to look at my watch even then. Besides, between ourselves, my watch loses rather badly.'

Though Stephen tried to help in some way, the improvised evening meal was upsetting. Harriet had planned rissoles sautéd in ghee, but neither of the men really knew how to cook with ghee. The home-made Congress Pudding was nothing less than nauseous. Very probably, some decisive final touches had been omitted.

'You see how it is, young Stephen,' said Harewood, after they had munched miserably but briefly. 'The prognosis cannot be described as hopeful. I may have to give up the living.'

'You can't possibly do that, Harewood, whatever happens. There is Father's memory to think about. I'm sure I should think about him more often myself.' Stephen's thoughts were, in fact, upon quite specially different topics.

'I don't wish to go, I assure you, Stephen. I've been very happy here.'

The statement surprised Stephen, but was of course thoroughly welcome and appropriate.

'There is always prayer, Harewood.'

'Yes, Stephen, indeed. I may well have been remiss. That might explain much.'

They had been unable to discover where Harriet hid the coffee, so sat for moments in reverent and reflective silence, one on either side of the bleak table: a gift from the nearest branch of the Free India League.

Stephen embarked upon a tentative *démarche*. 'I need hardly say that I don't want to leave you in the lurch.'

'It speaks for itself that there can be no question of that.'

Stephen drew in a quantity of air. 'To put it absolutely plainly. I feel that for a spell you would be better off at this time without me around to clutter up the place and make endless demands.'

For a second time within hours, Stephen recognized quite clearly that his line of procedure could well be seen as cold-blooded; but, for a second time, he was acting under extreme compulsion – compulsion more extreme than he had expected ever again to encounter, at least on the hither side of the Styx.

'I should never deem you to be doing that, young Stephen. Blood is at all times, even the most embarrassing times, thicker than water. It was Cardinal Newman, by the way, who first said that; a prelate of a different soteriology.'

Stephen simply did not believe it, but he said nothing. Harewood often came forward with such assertions, but they were almost invariably erroneous. Stephen sometimes doubted whether Harewood could be completely relied upon even in the context of his private speciality, the lichens.

'I think I had better leave tomorrow morning and so reduce the load for a span. I am sure Doreen will appreciate it.' Doreen was the intermittent help; a little brash, where in former days no doubt she would have been a little simple. Stephen had always supposed that brashness might make it more possible to serve Harriet. Doreen had been deserted, childless, by her young husband; but there had been a proper divorce. Harewood was supposed to be taking a keen interest in Doreen, who was no longer in her absolutely first youth.

'You will be rather more dependent upon Doreen for a time,' added Stephen.

'I suppose that may well be,' said Harewood. Stephen fancied that his brother almost smiled. He quite saw that he might have thought so because of the ideas in his own mind, at which he himself was smiling continuously.

'You must do whatever you think best for all concerned, Stephen,' said Harewood. 'Including, of course, your sister-in-law, dear Harriet.'

'I think I should go now and perhaps come back a little later.'

'As you will, Stephen. I have always recognized that you have a mind trained both academically and by your work. I am a much less coordinated spirit. Oh yes, I know it well. I should rely very much upon your judgement in almost any serious matter.'

Circumstanced as at the moment he was, Stephen almost blushed.

But Harewood made things all right by adding, 'Except perhaps in certain matters of the spirit which, in the nature of things, lie quite particularly between my Maker and myself alone.'

'Oh, naturally,' said Stephen.

'Otherwise,' continued Harewood, 'and now that Harriet is unavailable – for a very short time only, we must hope – it is upon you, Stephen, that I propose to rely foremost, in many pressing concerns of this world.'

Beyond doubt, Harewood now was not all but smiling. He was smiling nearly at full strength. He explained this immediately.

'My catarrh seems very much better,' he said. 'I might consider setting forth in splendour one of these days. Seeking specimens, I mean.'

Stephen plunged upon impulse.

'It may seem a bit odd in the circumstances, but I should be glad to have the use of a Land-Rover. There's a building up on the moors I should like to look at again before I go, and it's too far to walk in the time. There's a perfectly good track to quite near it. Is there anyone you know of in the parish who would lend me such a thing? Just for an hour or two, of course.'

Harewood responded at once. 'You might try Tom Jarrold. I regret to say that he's usually too drunk to drive. Indeed, one could never guarantee that his vehicle will even leave the ground.'

Possibly it was not exactly the right reference, but what an excellent and informed parish priest Harewood was suddenly proving to be!

Harewood had reopened the latest number of the *Journal*, which he had been sitting on in the chair all the time. His perusal had of course been interrupted by the afternoon's events.

'Don't feel called upon to stop talking,' said Harewood. 'I can read and listen at the same time perfectly well.'

Stephen reflected that the attempt had not often been made when Harriet had been in the room.

'I don't think there's anything more to say at the moment. We seem to have settled everything that *can* be settled.'

'I shall be depending upon you in many different matters, remember,' said Harewood, but without looking up from the speckled diagrams.

As soon as Stephen turned on the hanging light in his bedroom, he noticed the new patch on the wallpaper; if only because it was immediately above his bed. The wallpaper had always been lowering anyway. He was the more certain that the particular patch was new because, naturally, he made his own bed each morning, which involved daily confrontation with that particular surface. Of course there had always been the other such patches among the marks on the walls.

Still, the new arrival was undoubtedly among the reasons why Stephen slept very little that night, even though, in his own estimation, he needed sleep so badly. There again, however, few do sleep in the first phase of what is felt to be a reciprocated relationship: equally fulfilling and perilous, always deceptive, and always somewhere known to be. The mixed ingredients of the last two days churned within Stephen, as in Harriet's battered cook-pot; one rising as another fell. He was treating Harewood as he himself would not wish to be treated; and who could tell what had really led to Harriet's collapse?

In the end, bliss drove out bewilderment, and seemed the one thing sure, as perhaps it was.

Later still, when daylight was all too visible through the frail curtains, Stephen half dreamed that he was lying inert on some surface he could not define and that Nell was administering water to him from a chalice. But the chalice, doubtless a consecrated object to begin with, and certainly of fairest silver from the Spanish mines, was blotched and blemished. Stephen wanted to turn away, to close his eyes properly, to expostulate, but could do none of these things. As Nell gently kissed his brow, he awoke fully with a compelling thirst. He had heard of people waking thirsty in the night, but to himself he could not remember it ever before happening. He had never lived like that.

There was no water in the room, because the house was just sufficiently advanced to make visitors go to the bathroom. Stephen walked quietly down the passage, then hesitated. He recollected that nowadays the bathroom door opened with an appalling wrench and scream.

It would be very wrong indeed to take the risk of waking poor Harewood, in his new isolation. Stephen crept on down the stairs towards the scullery, and there *was* Harewood, sleeping like the dead, not in the least sprawling, but, on the contrary, touchingly compressed and compact in the worn chair. For a moment, he looked like a schoolboy, though of course in that curtained light.

Harewood was murmuring contentedly. 'Turn over. No, right over. You can trust me'; then, almost ecstatically, almost like a juvenile, 'It's beautiful. Oh, it's beautiful.'

Stephen stole away to the back quarters, where both the luncheon and the supper washing-up, even the washing-up after tea, all awaited the touch of a vanished hand.

The cold tap jerked and jarred as it always did, but when Stephen went back, Harewood was slumbering still. His self-converse was now so ideal that it had fallen into incoherence. The cheap figure on the mantel of Shiva or somebody, which Stephen had always detested, sneered animatedly.

But there Nell really was; really, really was.

In his soul, Stephen was astonished. Things do not go like that in real life, least of all in the dreaded demesne of the heart.

However, they unloaded the Land-Rover together, as if everything were perfectly real; toiling up the heather paths with heavy loads, Nell always ahead, always as strong as he: which was really rather necessary.

'I must take the Rover back. Come with me.'

He had not for a moment supposed that she would, but she did, and with no demur.

'It's rough going,' he said. But she merely put her brown hand on his thigh, as she sat and bumped beside him.

They were a pair now.

'It won't take a moment while I settle with the man.'

He was determined that it should not. It must be undesirable that the two of them be seen together in the village. Probably it was undesirable that he himself, even alone, be seen there before a long time had passed. He might perhaps steal back one distant day like Enoch Arden, and take Harewood completely by surprise, both of them now bearded, shaggily or skimpily. What by then would have become of Nell?

They walked upwards hand in hand. Every now and then he said something amorous or amusing to her, but not very often because, as he had foreseen, the words did not come to him readily. He was bound to become more fluent as his heart re-opened. She was now speaking more often than he was: not merely more shrewd, but more explicit.

'I'm as close to you as that,' she said, pointing with her free hand to a patch of rocky ground with something growing on it – growing quite profusely, almost exuberantly. She had spoken in reply to one of his questions.

He returned the squeeze of the hand he was holding.

'We'll be like the holly and the ivy,' she volunteered later, 'and then we'll be like the pebble and the shard.'

He thought that both comparisons were, like Harewood's comparisons, somewhat inexact, but, in her case, all the more adorable by reason of it. He kissed her.

38

At first he could not see their house, though, as they neared it, his eyes seemed to wander round the entire horizon: limited in range, however, by the fact that they were mounting quite steeply. But Nell led the way through the rabbit and snake paths, first to the spring, then upwards once more; and there, needless to say, the house was. Earlier that afternoon, they had already toiled up and down several times with the baggage. The earlier occupants had been sturdy folk; men and women alike; aboriginals.

It was somewhere near the spring that Nell, this time, made her possibly crucial declaration.

'I've run away,' she said, as if previously she had been afraid to speak the words. 'Take care of me.'

They entered.

When they had been lugging in the food and the blankets and the cressets and the pans, he had of policy refrained from even glancing at the walls of the house; but what could it matter now? For the glorious and overwhelming moment at least? And, judging by recent experience, the moment might even prove a noticeably long moment. Time might again stand still. Time sometimes did if one had not expected it.

Therefore, from as soon as they entered, he stared round at intervals quite brazenly, though not when Nell was looking at him, as for so much of the time she was now doing.

The upshot was anti-climax: here was not the stark, familiar bedroom in the rectory, and Stephen realized that he had not yet acquired points, or areas, of reference and comparison. He was at liberty to deem that they might never be needed.

Nell was ordering things, arranging things, even beginning to prepare things: all as if she had been a *diplomée* of a domestic college; as if she had been blessed with a dedicated mamma or aunt. After all, thought Stephen, as he watched her and intercepted her, her appearance is largely that of an ordinary modern girl.

He loved her.

He turned his back upon her earlier curious intimations. She had run away from it all; and had even stated as much, unasked and unprompted. Henceforth, an ordinary modern girl was what for him she should firmly be; though loyaller, tenderer, stronger than any other.

When, in the end, languishingly they went upstairs, this time they wrapt themselves in lovely new blankets, but Stephen was in no doubt at all that still there was only the one mark on her.

Conceivably, even, it was a slightly smaller mark.

He would no longer detect, no longer speculate, no longer be anxious, no longer imagine. No more mortal marks and corruptions. For example, he would quite possibly never sleep in that room at the rectory again.

Thus, for a week, he counted the good things only, as does a sundial. They were many and the silken sequence of them seemed to extend over a lifetime. He recollected the Christian Science teaching that evil is a mere illusion. He clung to the thesis that time is no absolute.

Nell had the knack of supplementing the food he had purchased with fauna and flora that she brought back from the moor. While, at a vague hour of the morning, he lay long among the blankets, simultaneously awake and asleep, she went forth, and never did she return empty-handed, seldom, indeed, other than laden. He was at last learning not from talk but from experience, even though from someone else's experience, how long it really was possible to live without shops, without bureaucratically and commercially modified products, without even watered cash. All that was needed was to be alone in the right place with the right person.

He even saw it as possible that the two of them might remain in the house indefinitely: were it not that his 'disappearance' would inevitably be 'reported' by someone, doubtless first by Arthur Thread in the office, so that his early exposure was inevitable. That, after all, was a main purpose of science: to make things of all kinds happen sooner than they otherwise would.

Each morning, after Nell had returned from her sorties and had set things in the house to rights, she descended naked to the spring and sank beneath its waters. She liked Stephen to linger at the rim watching her, and to him it seemed that she disappeared in the pool altogether, vanished from sight, and clear though the water was, the clearest, Stephen surmised, that he had ever lighted upon. Beyond doubt, therefore, the little pool really was peculiarly deep, as Nell had always said: it would be difficult to distinguish between the natural movements of its ever-gleaming surface, and movements that might emanate from a submerged naiad. It gave Stephen special pleasure that they drank exclusively from the pool in which Nell splashed about, but, partly for that reason, he confined his own lustrations to dabblings from the edge, like a tripper.

Stephen learned by experience, a new experience, the difference between drinking natural water and drinking safeguarded water, as from a sanitized public convenience. When she emerged from the pool, Nell each day shook her short hair like one glad to be alive, and each day her hair seemed to be dry in no time.

One morning, she washed her shirt and trousers in the pool, having no replacements as far as Stephen could see. The garments took longer to dry than she did, and Nell remained unclothed for most of the day, even though there were clouds in the sky. Clouds made little difference anyway, nor quite steady rain, nor drifting mountain mist. The last named merely fortified the peace and happiness.

'Where did you get those clothes?' asked Stephen, even though as a rule he no longer asked anything.

'I found them. They're nice.'

He said nothing for a moment.

'*Aren't* they nice?' she inquired anxiously.

'Everything to do with you and in and about and around you is nice in every possible way. You are perfect. Everything concerned with you is perfect.'

She smiled gratefully and went back, still unclothed, to the house, where she was stewing up everything together in one of the new pots. The pot had already leaked, and it had been she who had mended the leak, with a preparation she had hammered and kneaded while Stephen had merely looked on in delighted receptivity, wanting her as she worked.

He had a number of books in his bag, reasonably well chosen, because he had supposed that on most evenings at the rectory he would be retiring early; but now he had no wish to read anything. He conjectured that he would care little if the capacity to read somehow faded from him. He even went so far as to think that, given only a quite short time, it might possibly do so.

At moments, they wandered together about the moor; he, as like as not, with his hand on her breast, on that breast pocket of hers which contained his original and only letter to her, and which she had carefully taken out and given to him when washing the garment, and later carefully replaced. Than these perambulations few excursions could be more uplifting, but Stephen was wary all the same, knowing that if they were to meet anyone, however blameless, the spell might break, and paradise end.

Deep happiness can but be slighted by third parties, whosoever, without exception, they be. No one is so pure as to constitute an exception.

And every night the moon shone through the small windows and fell across their bed and their bodies in wide streaks, oddly angled.

'You are like a long, sweet parsnip,' Stephen said. 'Succulent but really rather tough.'

'I know nothing at all,' she replied. 'I only know you.'

The mark below her shoulder stood out darkly, but, God be praised, in isolation. What did the rapidly deteriorating state of the walls and appurtenances matter by comparison with that?

But in due course, the moon, upon which the seeding and growth of plants and of the affections largely depend, had entered its dangerous third quarter.

Stephen had decided that the thing he had to do was take Nell back quickly and quietly to London, and return as soon as possible with his reinvigorated car, approaching as near as he could, in order to collect their possessions in the house. The machine would go there, after all, if he drove it with proper vigour; though it might be as well to do it at a carefully chosen hour, in order to evade Harewood, Doreen, and the general life of the village.

He saw no reason simply to abandon all his purchases and, besides, he felt obscurely certain that it was unlucky to do so, though he had been unable to recall the precise belief. Finally, it would seem likely that some of the varied accessories in the house might be useful in Stephen's new life with Nell. One still had to be practical at times, just as one had to be firm at times.

Nell listened to what he had to say, and then said she would do whatever he wanted. The weather was entirely fair for the moment.

When the purchased food had finally run out, and they were supposedly dependent altogether upon what Nell could bring in off the moor, they departed from the house, though not, truthfully, for that reason. They left everything behind them and walked down at dusk past Burton's Clough to the village. Stephen knew the time of the last bus which connected with a train to London. It was something he knew wherever he was. In a general way, he had of course always liked the train journey and disliked the bus journey.

It was hard to imagine what Nell would make of such experiences, and of those inevitably to come. Though she always said she knew nothing, she seemed surprised by nothing either. Always she brought back to Stephen the theories that there were two kinds of knowledge; sometimes of the same things.

All the others in the bus were old age pensioners. They had been visiting younger people and were now returning. They sat alone, each as far from each as space allowed. In the end, Stephen counted them. There seemed to be eight, though it was hard to be sure in the bad light, and with several pensioners already slumped forward.

There were at least two kinds of bad light also; the beautiful dim light of the house on the moor, and the depressing light in a nationalized bus. Stephen recalled Ellen Terry's detestation of all electric light. And of course there were ominous marks on the dirty ceiling of the bus and on such of the side panels as Stephen could see, including that on the far side of Nell, who sat beside him, with her head on his shoulder, more like an ordinary modern girl than ever. Where could she have learned that when one was travelling on a slow, ill-lighted bus with the man one loved, one put one's head on his shoulder?

But it was far more that she had somewhere, somehow learned. The slightest physical contact with her induced in Stephen a third dichotomy: the reasonable, rather cautious person his whole life and career surely proved him to be, was displaced by an all but criminal visionary. Everything turned upon such capacity as he might have left to change the nature of time.

The conductor crept down the dingy passage and sibilated in Stephen's ear. 'We've got to stop here. Driver must go home. Got a sick kid. There'll be a reserve bus in twenty minutes. All right?'

The conductor didn't bother to explain to the pensioners. They would hardly have understood. For them, the experience itself would be ample. A few minutes later, everyone was outside in the dark, though no one risked a roll call. The lights in the bus had been finally snuffed out, and the crew were making off, aclank with the accoutrements of their tenure, spanners, and irregular metal boxes, and enamelled mugs.

Even now, Nell seemed unsurprised and unindignant. She, at least, appeared to acknowledge that all things have an end, and to be acting on that intimation. As usual, Stephen persuaded her to don his heavy sweater.

*

It was very late indeed, before they were home; though Stephen could hardly use the word now that not only was Elizabeth gone, but also there was somewhere else, luminously better – or, at least, so decisively different – and, of course, a new person too.

Fortunately, the train had been very late, owing to signal trouble, so that they had caught it and been spared a whole dark night of it at the station, as in a story. Stephen and Nell had sat together in the buffet, until they had been ejected, and the striplighting quelled. Nell had never faltered. She had not commented even when the train, deprived of what railwaymen call its 'path', had fumbled its way to London, shunting backwards nearly as often as running forwards. In the long, almost empty, excursion-type coach had been what Stephen could by now almost complacently regard as the usual smears and blotches.

'Darling, aren't you cold?' He had other, earlier sweaters to lend.

She shook her head quite vigorously.

After that, it had been easy for Stephen to close his eyes almost all the way. The other passenger had appeared to be a fireman in uniform, though of course without helmet. It was hard to believe that he would suddenly rise and rob them, especially as he was so silently slumbering. Perhaps he was all the time a hospital porter or a special messenger or an archangel.

On the Benares table which filled the hall of the flat (a wedding present from Harewood and poor Harriet, who, having been engaged in their teens, had married long ahead of Stephen and Elizabeth), was a parcel, weighty but neat.

'Forgive me,' said Stephen. 'I never can live with unopened parcels or letters.'

He snapped the plastic string in a second and tore through the glyptal wrapping. It was a burly tome entitled *Lichen, Moss, and Wrack. Usage and Abusage in Peace and War. A Military and Medical Abstract.* Scientific works so often have more title than imaginative works.

Stephen flung the book back on the table. It fell with a heavy clang.

'Meant for my brother. It's always happening. People don't seem to know there's a difference between us.'

He gazed at her. He wanted to see nothing else.

She looked unbelievably strange in her faded trousers and

the sweater Elizabeth had made. Elizabeth would have seen a ghost and fainted. Elizabeth really did tend to faint in the sudden presence of the occult.

'We are not going to take it to him. It'll have to be posted. I'll get the Department to do it tomorrow.'

He paused. She smiled at him, late though it was.

Late or early? What difference did it make? It was not what mattered.

'I told you that I should have to go to the Department tomorrow. There's a lot to explain.'

She nodded. 'And then we'll go back?' She had been anxious about that ever since they had started. He had not known what to expect.

'Yes. After a few days.'

Whatever he intended in the first place, he had never made it clear to her where they would be living in the longer run. This was partly because he did not know himself. The flat, without Elizabeth, really was rather horrible. Stephen had not forgotten Elizabeth for a moment. How could he have done? Nor could Stephen wonder that Nell did not wish to live in the flat. The flat was disfigured and puny.

Nell still smiled with her usual seeming understanding. He had feared that by now she would demur at his reference to a few days, and had therefore proclaimed it purposefully.

He smiled back at her. 'I'll buy you a dress.'

She seemed a trifle alarmed.

'It's time you owned one.'

'I don't own anything.'

'Yes, you do. You own me. Let's go to bed, shall we?'

But she spoke. 'What's this?'

As so often happens, Nell had picked up and taken an interest in the thing he would least have wished.

It was a large, lumpy shopping bag from a craft room in Burnham-on-Sea, where Elizabeth and he had spent an unwise week in their early days. What the Orient was to Harriet, the seaside had been to Elizabeth. Sisters-in-law often show affinities. The shopping bag had continued in regular use ever since, and not only for shopping, until Elizabeth had been no longer mobile.

'It's a bag made of natural fibres,' said Stephen. 'It belonged to my late wife.'

'It smells. It reminds me.'

'Many things here remind *me*,' said Stephen. 'But a new

page has been turned.' He kept forgetting that Nell was un-accustomed to book metaphors.

She appeared to be holding the bag out to him. Though not altogether knowing why, he took it from her. He then regret-ted doing so.

It was not so much the smell of the bag. He was entirely accustomed to that. It was that, in his absence, the bag had become sodden with dark growths, outside and inside. It had changed character completely.

Certainly the bag had been perfectly strong and serviceable when last he had been in contact with it; though for the moment he could not recollect when that had been. He had made little use of the bag when not under Elizabeth's direc-tion.

He let the fetid mass fall on top of the book on the brass table.

'Let's forget everything,' he said. 'We still have a few hours.'

'Where do I go?' she asked, smiling prettily.

'Not in there,' he cried, as she put her hand on one of the doors. He very well knew that he must seem far too excitable. He took a pull on himself. 'Try *this* room.'

When Elizabeth had become ill, the double bed had been moved into the spare room. It had been years since Stephen had slept in that bed, though, once again, he could not in the least recall how many years. The first step towards mastering time is always to make time meaningless.

It was naturally wonderful to be at long last in a fully equip-ped deep double bed with Nell. She had shown no expectation of being invited to borrow one of Elizabeth's expensive night-dresses. Nell was a primitive still, and it was life or death to keep her so. He had never cared much for flowing, gracious bedwear in any case; nor had the wonder that was Elizabeth seemed to him to need such embellishments.

But he could not pretend, as he lay in Nell's strong arms and she in his, that the condition of the spare room was in the least reassuring. Before he had quickly turned off the small bedside light, the new marks on the walls had seemed like huge in-human faces; and the effect was all the more alarming in that these walls had been painted, inevitably long ago, by Elizabeth in person, and had even been her particular domestic display piece. The stained overall she had worn for the task, still hung in the cupboard next door, lest the need arise again.

It was always the trouble. So long as one was far from the

place once called home, one could successfully cast secondary matters from the mind, or at least from the hurting part of it; but from the moment of return, in fact from some little while before that, one simply had to recognize that, for most of one's life, secondary matters were just about all there were. Stephen had learned ages ago that secondary matters were always the menace.

Desperation, therefore, possibly made its contribution to the mutual passion that charged the few hours available to them.

Within a week, the walls might be darkened all over; and what could the development after *that* conceivably be?

Stephen strongly suspected that the mossiness, the malady, would become more conspicuously three-dimensional at any moment. Only as a first move, of course.

He managed to close his mind against all secondary considerations and to give love its fullest licence yet.

Thread was in the office before Stephen, even though Stephen had risen most mortifyingly early, and almost sleepless. It was a commonplace that the higher one ascended in the service, the earlier one had to rise, in order to ascend higher still. The lamas never slept at all.

'Feeling better?' Thread could ask such questions with unique irony.

'Much better, thank you.'

'You still look a bit peaky.' Thread was keeping his finger at the place he had reached in the particular file.

'I had a tiresome journey back. I've slept very little.'

'It's always the trouble. Morag and I make sure of a few days to settle in before we return to full schedule.'

'Elizabeth and I used to do that also. It's a bit different now.'

Thread looked Stephen straight in the eyes, or very nearly.

'Let me advise, for what my advice is worth. I recommend you to lose yourself in your work for the next two or three years at the least. Lose yourself completely. Forget everything else. In my opinion, it's always the best thing at these times. Probably the only thing.'

'Work doesn't mean to me what it did.'

'Take yourself in hand, and it soon will again. After all, very real responsibilities do rest in this room. We both understand that quite well. We've reached that sort of level, Stephen. What we do nowadays, *matters*. If you keep that in mind at all times, and I do mean at *all* times, the thought will see you through. I know what I'm talking about.'

Thread's eyes were now looking steadily at his finger, lest it had made some move on its own.

'Yes,' said Stephen, 'but you're talking about yourself, you know.'

Stephen was very well aware that the sudden death some years before of Arthur Thread's mother had not deflected Thread for a day from the tasks appointed. Even the funeral had taken place during the weekend; for which Thread had departed on the Friday evening with several major files in his briefcase, as usual. As for Thread's wife, Morag, she was a senior civil servant too, though of course in a very different department. The pair took very little leave in any case, and hardly any of it together. Their two girls were at an expensive boarding school on the far side of France, almost in Switzerland.

'I speak from my own experience,' corrected Thread.

'It appears to me,' said Stephen, 'that I have reached the male climacteric. It must be what's happening to me.'

'I advise you to think again,' said Thread. 'There's no such thing. Anyway you're too young for when it's supposed to be. It's not till you're sixty-three; within two years of retirement.'

Thread could keep his finger in position no longer, lest his arm fall off. 'If you'll forgive me, I'm rather in the middle of something. Put yourself absolutely at ease. I'll be very pleased to have another talk later.'

'What's that mark?' asked Stephen, pointing to the wall above Thread's rather narrow headpiece. So often the trouble seemed to begin above the head. 'Was it there before?'

'I'm sure I don't know. Never forget the whole place is going to be completely done over next year. Now do let me concentrate for a bit.'

As the time for luncheon drew near, another man, Mark Tremble, peeped in.

'Glad to see you back, Stephen. I really am.'

'Thank you, Mark. I wish I could more sincerely say I was glad to *be* back.'

'Who could be? Come and swim?'

Stephen had regularly done it with Mark Tremble and a shifting group of others; usually at lunchtime on several days a week. It had been one of twenty devices for lightening momentarily the weight of Elizabeth's desperation. The bath was in the basement of the building. Soon the bath was to be extended and standardized, and made available at times to additional grades.

'Very well.'

Stephen had at one time proposed to tear back; to be with Nell for a few moments; perhaps to buy that dress: but during the long morning he had decided against all of it.

His real task was to put down his foot with the establishment; to secure such modified pension as he was entitled to; to concentrate, as Thread always concentrated; to depart.

He had not so far said a word about it to anyone in the place.

The two seniors changed in the sketchy cubicles, and emerged almost at the same moment in swimming trunks. There seemed to be no one else in or around the pool that day, though the ebbing and flowing of table tennis were audible through the partition.

'I say, Stephen. What's that thing on your back?'

Stephen stopped dead on the wet tiled floor. 'What thing?'

'It's a bit peculiar. I'm sure it wasn't there before. Before you went away. I'm extremely sorry to mention it.'

'What's it look like?' asked Stephen. 'Can you describe it?'

'The best I can do is that it looks rather like the sort of thing you occasionally see on trees. I think it may simply be something stuck on to you. Would you like me to give it a tug?'

'I think not,' said Stephen. 'I am sorry it upsets you. I'll go back and dress. I think it would be better.'

'Yes,' said Mark Tremble. 'It does upset me. It's best to admit it. Either it's something that will just come off with a good rub, or you'd better see a doctor, Stephen.'

'I'll see what I can do,' said Stephen.

'I don't feel so much like a swim, after all,' said Mark Tremble. 'I'll dress too and then we'll both have a drink. I feel we could both do with one.'

'I'm very sorry about it,' said Stephen. 'I apologize.'

'What have *you* been doing all day?' asked Stephen, as soon as he was back and had changed out of the garments currently normal in the civil service, casual and characterless. 'I hope you've been happy.'

'I found this on the roof.' Nell was holding it in both her hands; which were still very brown. It was a huge lump: mineral, vegetable, who could tell? Or conceivably a proportion of each.

'Your father would be interested.'

Nell recoiled. 'Don't talk like that. It's unlucky.' Indeed, she had nearly dropped the dense mass.

It had been an idiotic response on Stephen's part; mainly the consequence of his not knowing what else to say. He was aware that it was perfectly possible to attain the roof of the building by way of the iron fire ladder, to which, by law, access had to be open to tenants at all hours.

'I could do with a drink,' said Stephen, though he had been drinking virtually the whole afternoon, without Thread even noticing, or without sparing time to acknowledge that he had noticed. Moira, the coloured girl from the typing area, had simply winked her big left eye at Stephen. 'I've had a difficult day.'

'Oh!' Nell's cry was so sincere and eloquent that it was as if he had been mangled in a traffic accident.

'*How* difficult?' she asked.

'It's just that it's been difficult for me to make the arrangements to get away, to leave the place.'

'But we *are* going?' He knew it was what she was thinking about.

'Yes, we are going. I promised.'

He provided Nell with a token drink also. At first she had seemed to be completely new to liquor. Stephen had always found life black without it, but his need for it had become more habitual during Elizabeth's illness. He trusted that Nell and he would, with use, wont, and time, evolve a mutual equilibrium.

At the moment, he recognized that he was all but tight, though he fancied that at such times he made little external manifestation. Certainly Nell would detect nothing; if only because presumably she lacked data. Until now, he had never really been in the sitting room of the flat since his return. Here, the new tendrils on the walls and ceiling struck him as resembling a Portuguese man of war's equipment; the coloured, insensate creature that can sting a swimmer to death at thirty feet distance, and had done so more than once when Elizabeth and he, being extravagant, had stayed at Cannes for a couple of weeks. It had been there that Elizabeth had told him finally she could never have a child. Really that was what they were doing there, though he had not realized it. The man of war business, the two victims, had seemed to have an absurd part in their little drama. No one in the hotel had talked of anything else.

'Let's go to bed *now*,' said Stephen to Nell. 'We can get up again later to eat.'

She put her right hand in his left hand.

Her acquiescence, quiet and beautiful, made him feel compunctious.

'Or are you hungry?' he asked. 'Shall we have something to eat first? I wasn't thinking.'

She shook her head. 'I've been foraging.'

She seemed to know so many quite literary words. He gave no time to wondering where exactly the forage could have taken place. It would be unprofitable. Whatever Nell had brought in would be wholesomer, inestimably better in every way, than food from any shop.

As soon as she was naked, he tried, in the electric light, to scrutinize her. There still seemed to be only the one mark on her body, truly a quite small mark by the standards of the moment, though he could not fully convince himself that it really was contracting.

However, the examination was difficult: he could not let Nell realize what exactly he was doing; the light was not very powerful, because latterly Elizabeth had disliked a strong light anywhere, and he had felt unable to argue; most of all, he had to prevent Nell seeing whatever Mark Tremble had seen on his own person, had himself all the time to lie facing Nell or flat on his back. In any case, he wondered always how much Nell saw that he saw; how much, whatever her utterances and evidences, she analysed of the things that he analysed.

The heavy curtains, chosen and hung by Elizabeth, had, it seemed, remained drawn all day; and by now the simplest thing was for Stephen to switch off what light there was.

Nell, he had thought during the last ten days or ten aeons, was at her very best when the darkness was total.

He knew that heavy drinking was said to increase desire and to diminish performance; and he also knew that it was high time in his life for him to begin worrying about such things. He had even so hinted to Arthur Thread; albeit mainly to startle Thread, and to foretoken his, Stephen's, new life course; even though any such intimation to Thread would be virtually useless. There can be very few to whom most of one's uttered remarks can count for very much.

None the less, Nell and Stephen omitted that evening to arise later; even though Stephen had fully and sincerely intended it.

The next morning, very early the next morning, Nell vouchsafed to Stephen an unusual but wonderful breakfast – if one could apply so blurred a noun to so far-fetched a repast.

Stephen piled into his civil service raiment, systematically non-committal. He was taking particular trouble not to see his own bare back in any looking glass. Fortunately, there was no such thing in the dim bathroom.

'Goodbye, my Nell. Before the weekend we shall be free.'

He supposed that she knew what a weekend was. By now, it could hardly be clearer that she knew almost everything that mattered in the least.

But, during that one night, the whole flat seemed to have become dark green, dark grey, plain black: patched everywhere, instead of only locally, as when they had arrived. Stephen felt that the walls, floors, and ceilings were beginning to advance towards one another. The knick-knacks were dematerializing most speedily. When life once begins to move, it can scarcely be prevented from setting its own pace. The very idea of intervention becomes ridiculous.

What was Nell making of these swift and strange occurrences? All Stephen was sure of was that it would be unwise to take too much for granted. He must hew his way out; if necessary, with a bloody axe, as the man in the play put it.

Stephen kissed Nell ecstatically. She was smiling as he shut the door. She might smile, off and on, all day, he thought; smile as she foraged.

By that evening, he had drawn a curtain, thick enough even for Elizabeth to have selected, between his homebound self and the events of the daylight.

There was no technical obstacle to his retirement, and never had been. It was mainly the size of his pension that was affected; and in his new life he seemed able to thrive on very little. A hundred costly substitutes for direct experience could be rejected. An intense reality, as new as it was old, was burning down on him like clear sunlight or heavenly fire or poetry.

It was only to be expected that his colleagues should shrink back a little. None the less, Stephen had been disconcerted by how far some of them had gone. They would have been very much less concerned, he fancied, had he been an acknowledged defector, about to stand trial. Such cases were now all in the day's work: there were routines to be complied with, though not too strictly. Stephen realized that his appearance was probably against him. He was not sure what he looked like from hour to hour, and he was taking no steps to find out.

Still, the only remark that was passed, came from Toby Strand, who regularly passed remarks.

'Good God, Stephen, you're looking like death warmed up. I should go home to the wife. You don't want to pass out in this place.'

Stephen looked at him.

'Oh God, I forgot. Accept my apology.'

'That's perfectly all right, Toby,' said Stephen. 'And as for the other business, you'll be interested to learn that I've decided to retire.'

'Roll on the day for one and all,' said Toby Strand, ever the *vox populi*.

Mercifully, Stephen's car had been restored to a measure of health, so that the discreet bodywork gleamed slightly in the evening lustre as he drove into the rented parking space.

'Nell, we can leave at cockcrow!'

'I forgot about buying you that dress.'

He was standing in his bath gown, looking at her in the wide bed. The whole flat was narrowing and blackening, and at that early hour the electric light was even weaker than usual.

'I shan't need a dress.'

'You must want a change sometime.'

'No. I want nothing to change.'

He gazed at her. As so often, he had no commensurate words.

'We'll stop somewhere on the way,' he said.

They packed the rehabilitated car with essentials for the simple life; with things to eat and drink on the journey and after arrival. Stephen, though proposing to buy Nell a dress, because one never knew what need might arise, was resolved against dragging her into a roadside foodplace. He took all he could, including, surreptitiously, some sad souvenirs of Elizabeth, but he recognized plainly enough that there was almost everything remaining to be done with the flat, and that he would have to return one day to do it, whether or not Nell came with him. In the meantime, it was difficult to surmount what was happening to the flat, or to him. Only Nell was sweet, calm, and changeless in her simple clothes. If only the nature of time were entirely different!

'You'll be terribly cold.'

She seemed never to say it first, never to think of it.

He covered her with sweaters and rugs. He thought of offering her a pair of his own warm trousers, but they would be so hopelessly too wide and long.

Islington was a misty marsh, as they flitted through; Holloway pink as a desert flamingo. The scholarly prison building was wrapped in fire. Finsbury Park was crystal as a steppe; Manor House deserted as old age.

When, swift as thoughts of love, they reached Grantham, they turned aside to buy Nell's dress. She chose a rough-textured white one, with the square neck outlined in black, and would accept nothing else, nothing else at all. She even refused to try on the dress and she refused to wear it out of the shop. Stephen concurred, not without a certain relief, and carried the dress to the car in a plastic bag. The car was so congested that a problem arose.

'I'll sit on it,' said Nell.

Thus the day went by as in a dream: though there are few such dreams in one lifetime. Stephen, for sure, had never known a journey so rapt, even though he could seldom desist from staring and squinting for uncovenanted blemishes upon and around the bright coachwork. Stephen recognized that, like everyone else, he had spent his life without living; even though he had had Elizabeth for much of the time to help him through, as she alone was able.

Northwards, they ran into a horse fair. The horses were everywhere, and, among them, burlesques of men bawling raucously, and a few excited girls.

'Oh!' cried Nell.

'Shall we stop?'

'No,' said Nell. 'Not stop.'

She was plainly upset.

'Few fairs like that one are left,' said Stephen, as he sat intimately, eternally beside her. 'The motors have been their knell.'

'Knell,' said Nell.

Always it was impossible to judge how much she knew.

'Nell,' said Stephen affectionately. But it was at about that moment he first saw a dark, juicy crack in the polished metalwork of the bonnet.

'Nell,' said Stephen again; and clasped her hand, always brown, always warm, always living and loving. The huge geometrical trucks were everywhere, and it was an uncircumspect move for Stephen to make. But it was once more too misty for the authorities to see very much, to take evidence that could be sworn to.

The mist was more like fog as they wound through Harewood's depopulated community. Harewood really should marry Doreen as soon as it becomes possible, thought Stephen, and make a completely new start in life, perhaps have a much better type of youngster, possibly and properly for the cloth.

Stephen was struck with horror to recollect that he had forgotten all about the costly book which had been almost certainly intended for Harewood, and which Harewood would be among the very few fully to appreciate and rejoice in. The book had not really been noticeable at first light in the eroding flat, but his lapse perturbed Stephen greatly.

'A fungus and an alga living in a mutually beneficial relationship,' he said under his breath.

'What's that?' asked Nell.

'It's the fundamental description of a lichen. You should know that.'

'Don't talk about it.'

He saw that she shuddered; she who never even quaked from the cold.

'It's unlucky,' she said.

'I'm sorry, Nell. I was thinking of the book we left behind, and the words slipped out.'

'We're better without the book.'

'It wasn't really our book.'

'We did right in leaving it.'

He realized that it had been the second time when, without thinking, he had seemed ungracious about the big step she had taken for him: the second time at least.

Therefore, he simply answered, 'I expect so.'

He remained uneasy. He had taken due care not to drive past the crumbling rectory, but nothing could prevent the non-delivery of Harewood's expensive book being an odious default, a matter of only a few hundred yards. To confirm the guilt, a middle-aged solitary woman at the end of the settlement suddenly pressed both hands to her eyes, as if to prevent herself from seeing the passing car, even in the poor light.

The ascending track was rougher and rockier than on any of Stephen's previous transits. It was only to be expected, Stephen realized. Moreover, to mist was now added dusk. At the putative Burton's Clough, he had to take care not to drive over the edge of the declivity; and thereafter he concentrated upon not colliding with the overgrown stony waymark. Shapeless creatures were beginning to emerge which may no longer appear by daylight even in so relatively remote a region. Caution was compelled upon every count.

Thus it was full night when somehow they reached the spot where the track seemed simply to end – with no good reason supplied, as Stephen had always thought. Elizabeth would have been seriously upset if somehow she had seen at such a spot the familiar car in which she had taken so many unforgettable outings, even when a virtual invalid. She might have concluded that at long last she had reached the final bourne.

The moon, still in its third quarter, managed to glimmer, like a fragrance, through the mist; but there could be no visible stars. Stephen switched on his flash, an item of official supply.

'We don't need it,' said Nell. 'Please not.'

Nell was uncaring of cold, of storm, of fog, of fatigue. Her inner strength was superb, and Stephen loved it. But her indifference to such darkness as this reminded Stephen of her father, that wonderful entity, whom it was so unlucky ever to mention, probably even to think of. None the less, Stephen turned back the switch. He had noticed before that he was doing everything she said.

As best he could, he helped her to unload the car, and followed her along the narrow paths through the damp heather. Naturally, he could not see a trace of the house, and he suddenly realized that, though they struggled in silence, he could not even hear the gently heaving spring. They were making a pile at the spot where the house must be; and Nell never put a foot wrong in finding the pile a second, third, and even fourth time. Much of the trip was steep, and Stephen was quite winded once more by his fourth climb in almost no moonlight at all, only the faint smell of moonlight; but when, that time, he followed Nell over the tangled brow, the mist fell away for a moment, as mist on mountains intermittently does, and at last Stephen could see the house quite clearly.

He looked at Nell standing there, pale and mysterious as the moonlight began to fade once more.

'Have you still got my letter?'

She put her hand on her breast pocket.

'Of course I have.'

They re-entered the house, for which no key was ever deemed necessary. It might be just as well, for none was available.

Stephen realized at once that what they were doing was moving into the house pretty finally; not, as he had so recently proposed, preparing to move out of it in a short time. It was clear that once Nell truly and finally entered one's life, one had simply to accept the consequences. Stephen could perceive well enough that Nell was at every point moved by forces in comparison with which he was moved by inauthentic fads. Acquiescence was the only possibility. The admixture in Nell of ignorance and wisdom, sometimes even surface sophistication, was continuously fascinating. In any case, she had left familiar surroundings and completely changed her way of life for him. He must do the same for her without end; and he wished it.

The moonlight was now insufficient to show the state of the walls or the curiously assorted furnishings or the few personal traps he had omitted to bear to London. Stephen had worn gloves to drive and had not removed them to lug. He wore them still.

None the less, when he said, 'Shall we have a light now?' he spoke with some reluctance.

"Now,' said Nell. 'We're at home now.'

He fired up some of the rough cressets he had managed to lay hands on when he had borrowed the sottish Jarrold's Land-Rover.

Nell threw herself against him. She kissed him again and again.

As she did so, Stephen resolved to look at nothing more. To look was not necessarily to see. He even thought he apprehended a new vein of truth in what Nell had said on that second day, still only a very short time ago, about her father.

Nell went upstairs and changed into the dress he had bought her. She had done it without a hint, and he took for granted that she had done it entirely to give pleasure. In aspect, she was no longer a part of nature, merging into it, an oread. Not surprisingly, the dress did not fit very well, but on Nell it looked like a peplos. She was a sybil. Stephen was scarcely surprised. There was no need for him to see anything other than Nell's white and black robe, intuitively selected, prophetically insisted upon; quite divine, as ordinary normal girls used to say.

When he dashed off his gloves in order to caress her, he regarded only her eyes and her raiment; but later there was eating to be done, and it is difficult, in very primitive lighting, to eat without at moments noticing one's hands. These particular hands seemed at such moments to be decorated with horrid subfusc smears, quite new. Under the circumstances, they might well have come from inside Stephen's driving gloves; warm perhaps, but, like most modern products, of no precise or very wholesome origin. If ineradicable, the marks were appalling; not to be examined for a single second.

When Nell took off her new dress, Stephen saw at once (how else but at once?) that her own small single mark had vanished. She was as totally honied as harvest home, and as luscious, and as rich.

Stephen resolved that in the morning, if there was one, he would throw away all the souvenirs of Elizabeth he had brought with him. They could be scattered on the moor as ashes in a memorial garden, but better far. The eyes that were watching from behind the marks on the walls and ceilings and utensils glinted back at him, one and all. The formless left hands were his to shake.

In the nature of things, love was nonpareil that night; and there was music too. Nell's inner being, when one knew her, when one really knew her, was as matchless as her unsullied body. Goodness is the most powerful aphrodisiac there is, though few have the opportunity of learning. Stephen had learned long before from the example of Elizabeth, and now he was learning again.

Time finally lost all power.

The music became endlessly more intimate.

'God!' cried Stephen suddenly. 'That's Schumann!' He had all but leapt in the air. Ridiculously.

'Where?' asked Nell. Stephen realized that he was virtually sitting on her. He dragged himself up and was standing on the floor.

'That music. It's Schumann.'

'I hear no music.'

'I don't suppose you do.'

Stephen spoke drily and unkindly, as he too often did, but he knew that everything was dissolving.

For example, he could see on the dark wall the large portrait of Elizabeth by a pupil of Philip de Laszlo which had hung in their conjugal bedroom. The simulacrum was faint and ghostly, like the music, but he could see it clearly enough for present purposes, dimly self-illuminated.

He had taken that picture down with his own hands, years and years ago; and the reason had been, as he now instantly recalled, that the light paintwork had speedily become blotched and suffused. They had naturally supposed it to be something wrong with the pigments, and had spoken between themselves of vegetable dyes and the superiorities of Giotto and Mantegna. Stephen had hidden the festering canvas in the communal basement storeroom, and had forgotten about it immediately. Now he could see it perfectly well, not over the bed, but in front of it, as always.

'Come back,' said Nell. 'Come back to me.'

The music, which once, beyond doubt, had been the music of love, was dying away. In its place, was a persistent snuffling sound, as if the house from outside, or the room from inside, was being cased by a wolf.

'What's that noise? That noise of an animal?'

'Come back to me,' said Nell. 'Come back, Stephen.' Perhaps she was quite consciously dramatizing a trifle.

He had gone to the window, but of course could see nothing save the misleading huge shapes of the flapping birds.

He went back to the bed and stretched out both his hands to Nell. He was very cold.

Though there was almost no light, Nell grasped his two hands and drew him down to her.

'You see and hear so many things, Stephen,' she said.

As she spoke, he had, for moments, a vision of a different kind.

Very lucidly, he saw Nell and himself living together, but, as it might be, in idealized form, vaguely, intensely. He knew that it was an ideal of which she was wonderfully capable, perhaps because she was still so young. All that was required of him was some kind of trust.

Held by her strong hands and arms, he leaned over her and faltered.

'But whatever animal is that?' he demanded.

She released his hands and curled up like a child in distress. She had begun to sob.

'Oh, Nell,' he cried. He fell on her and tried to reach her. Her muscles were as iron, and he made no impression at all.

In any case, he could not stop attending to the snuffling, if that was the proper word for it. He thought it was louder now. The noise seemed quite to fill the small, low, dark, remote room; to leave no space for renewed love, however desperate the need, however urgent the case.

Suddenly, Stephen knew. A moment of insight had come to him, an instinctual happening.

59

He divined that outside or inside the little house was Nell's father.

It was one reason why Nell was twisted in misery and terror. Her father had his own ways of getting to the truth of things. She had said so.

Stephen sat down on the bed and put his hand on her shoulder. Though he was shivering dreadfully, he had become almost calm. The process of illumination was suggesting to him the simple truth that, for Nell too, the past must be ever present. And for her it was, in common terms, the terms after which he himself was so continuously half-aspiring, a past most absurdly recent. How could he tell what experiences were hers, parallel to, but never meeting, his own?

It would be no good even making the obvious suggestion that they should dwell far away. She could never willingly leave the moor, even if it should prove the death of her; no more than he had been able all those years to leave the flat, the job, the life, all of which he had hated, and been kept alive in only by Elizabeth.

'What's the best thing to do, Nell?' Stephen inquired of her. 'Tell me and we'll do it exactly. Tell me. I think I'm going to dress while you do so. And then perhaps you'd better dress too.'

After all, he began to think, there was little that Nell had ever said about her father or her sister which many girls might not have said when having in mind to break away. He would not have wanted a girl who had no independent judgement of her own family.

The processes of insight and illumination were serving him well, and the phantom portrait seemed to have dissipated completely. The snuffling and snorting continued. It was menacing and unfamiliar, but conceivably it was caused merely by a common or uncommon but essentially manageable creature of the moors. Stephen wished he had brought his revolver (another official issue), even though he had no experience in discharging it. He could not think how he had omitted it. Then he recollected the horrible furred-up flat, and shuddered anew, within his warm clothes.

For the first time it occurred to him that poor Elizabeth might be trying, from wherever she was, to warn him. Who could tell that Harriet had not made a miraculous recovery (she was, after all, in touch with many different faiths); and was not now ready once more to accept him for a spell into the life at the rectory?

Nell was being very silent.

Stephen went back to the bed.

'Nell.'

He saw that she was not in the bed at all, but standing by the door.

'Nell.'

'Hush,' she said. 'We must hide.'

'Where do we do that?'

'I shall show you.' He could see that she was back in her shirt and trousers; a part of the natural scene once more. Her white dress glinted on the boards of the floor.

To Stephen her proposal seemed anomalous. If it really was her father outside, he could penetrate everywhere, and according to her own statement. If it was a lesser adversary, combat might be better than concealment.

Nell and Stephen went downstairs in the ever more noisy darkness, and Nell, seemingly without effort, lifted a stone slab in the kitchen floor. Stephen could not quite make out how she had done it. Even to find the right slab, under those conditions, was a feat.

'All the houses have a place like this,' Nell explained.

'Why?' inquired Stephen. Surely Nell's father was an exceptional phenomenon? Certainly the supposed motion of him was akin to no other motion Stephen had ever heard.

'To keep their treasure,' said Nell.

'You are my treasure,' said Stephen.

'You are mine,' responded Nell.

There were even a few hewn steps, or so they felt to him. Duly it was more a coffer than a room, Stephen apprehended; but in no time Nell had the stone roof down on them, almost with a flick of the elbow, weighty though the roof must have been.

Now the darkness was total; something distinctly different from the merely conventional darkness above. All the same, Stephen of all people could not be unaware that the stone sides and stone floor and stone ceiling of the apartment were lined with moss and lichen. No doubt he had developed sixth and seventh senses in that arena, but the odour could well have sufficed of itself.

'How do we breathe?'

'There is a sort of pipe. That's where the danger lies.'

'You mean it might have become blocked up?'

'No.'

He did not care next to suggest that it might now be blocked deliberately. He had already made too many tactless suggestions of that kind.

She saved him the trouble of suggesting anything. She spoke in the lowest possible voice.

'He might come through.'

It was the first time she had admitted, even by implication, who it was: outside or inside – or both. Stephen fully realized that. It was difficult for him not to give way to the shakes once more, but he clung to the vague possibilities he had tried to sort out upstairs.

'I should hardly think so,' he said. 'But how long do you suggest we wait?'

'It will be better when it's day. He has to eat so often.'

It would be utterly impossible for Stephen to inquire any further; not at the moment. He might succeed in finding his way to the bottom of it all later. He was already beginning to feel cramped, and the smell of the fungi and the algae were metaphorically choking him and the moss realistically tickling him; but he put his arm round Nell in the blackness, and could even feel his letter safe against her soft breast.

She snuggled back at him; as far as circumstances permitted. He had only a vague idea of how big or small their retreat really was.

Nell spoke again in that same lowest possible voice. She could communicate, even in the most pitchy of blackness, while hardly making a sound.

'He's directly above us. He's poised.'

Stephen mustered up from his school days a grotesque recollection of some opera: the final scene. The Carl Rosa had done it: that one scene only; after the film in a cinema near Marble Arch. Elizabeth had thought the basic operatic convention too far-fetched to be taken seriously; except perhaps for Mozart, who could always be taken seriously.

'I love you,' said Stephen. No doubt the chap in the opera had said something to the like effect, but had taken more time over it.

Time: that was always the decisive factor. But time had been mastered at last.

'I love *you*,' said Nell, snuggling ever closer; manifesting her feeling in every way she could.

*

Curiously enough, it was at the verge of the small, lustrous pool that Stephen's body was ultimately found.

A poor old man, apparently resistent to full employment and even to the full security that goes with it, found the corpse, though, after all those days or weeks, the creatures and forces of the air and of the moor had done their worst to it, or their best. There was no ordinary skin anywhere. Many people in these busy times would not even have reported the find.

There were still, however, folk who believed, or at least had been told that the pool was bottomless; and even at the inquest a theory was developed that Stephen had been wandering about on the moor and had died of sudden shock upon realizing at what brink he stood. The coroner, who was a doctor of medicine, soon disposed of that hypothesis.

None the less, the actual verdict had to be open; which satisfied nobody. In these times, people expect clear answers; whether right or wrong.

Harewood, almost his pristine self by then, inquired into the possibility of a memorial service in London, which he was perfectly prepared to come up and conduct. After all, Stephen was an OBE already, and could reasonably hope for more.

The view taken was that Stephen had been missing for so long, so entirely out of the official eye, that the proper moment for the idea was regrettably, but irreversibly, past.

The funeral took place, therefore, in Harewood's own church, where the father and the grandfather of both the deceased and the officiant had shepherded so long with their own quiet distinction. People saw that no other solution had ever really been thinkable.

Doreen had by now duly become indispensible to the rector; in the mysterious absence of Stephen, to whom the rector had specifically allotted that function. At the funeral, she was the only person in full black. Not even the solitary young man from the Ministry emulated her there. It had not been thought appropriate to place Stephen's OBE on the coffin, but during the service the rector noticed a scrap of lichen thereon which was different entirely, he thought, from any of the species on the walls, rafters, and floors of the church. Performing his office, Harewood could not at once put a name to the specimen. The stuff that already lined the open grave was even more peculiar; and Harewood was more than a little relieved when the whole affair was finally over, the last tributes paid, and he free to stumble back to Doreen's marmite toast, and lilac peignoir. The newest number of the *Journal* had come in only just before, but Harewood did not so much as open it that evening.

As Stephen's will had been rendered ineffective by Elizabeth's decease, Harewood, as next of kin, had to play a part, whether he felt competent or not, in winding everything up. Fortunately, Doreen had been taking typing lessons, and had bought a second-hand machine with her own money.

The flat was found to be in the most shocking state, almost indescribable. It was as if there had been no visitors for years; which, as Harewood at once pointed out, had almost certainly been more or less the case, since the onset of Elizabeth's malady, an epoch ago.

A single, very unusual book about Harewood's own speciality was found. It had been published in a limited edition: a minute one, and at a price so high that Harewood himself had not been among the subscribers.

'Poor fellow!' said Harewood. 'I never knew that he was really interested. One can make such mistakes.'

The valuable book had of course to be disposed of for the benefit of the estate.

Stephen's car was so far gone that it could be sold only for scrap; but, in the event, it never was sold at all, because no one could be bothered to drag it away. If one knows where to look, one can see the bits of it still.

Steve Rasnic
City fishing

*Steve Rasnic appeared in my mail one day with four stories,
two poems, and a letter telling me about* Umbral, *the quarterly
of speculative poetry which he edits. Aside from living in
Colorado and writing (poetry published in some sixty
magazines; short stories; general education articles, and so on)
he is as enigmatic as his story. Here it is.*

After weeks of talking about it, Jimmy's father finally decided
to take his son fishing. Jimmy's friend Bill, and Bill's father
who was Jimmy's dad's best friend, also were to go. Their
mothers didn't approve.

Jimmy wasn't sure he approved either, actually. He had
somewhat looked forward to the event, thought that he should
go, but as the actual moment of departure approached he knew
fishing was the last thing he wanted to do. It seemed to be
important to his father, however, so he would go just to please
him.

'Now look what we have here, Jimmy.' Jimmy's father was
tall and dark-haired, and the deep resonance in his voice made
his every word seem like a command. He gestured towards a
display of tools, utensils, and weaponry. 'Hunting knife, pistol,
wire, gunpowder, hooks and sinkers, poles, small animal trap,
steel trap, fish knife, stiletto, .22 rifle, shotgun, derringer. You
have to have all this if you're going to get along in the wild.
Remember that, son.'

Jimmy nodded his head with hesitation.

Bill had run up beside him. 'See what I got!'

Jimmy had noted out of the corner of his eye a dark shape
in Bill's left hand. As he turned to greet his friend he saw that
it was a large, dead crow, its neck spotted with red.

'Dad caught it, then I wrung its neck while we had the feet
tied together. I thought I'd bring it along.'

Jimmy nodded his head.

There were loud screams and shouting coming from the house. Jimmy could hear his mother weeping, his father cursing. He walked up to the front steps and watched through the screened door.

He could make out Bill's father, his father, his own mother, and a young red-headed woman back in the shadows who must have been Bill's mother.

'You can't take them!' he could hear his mother sob.

Then there was a struggle as his dad and Bill's dad started forcing the women into the bedroom. Bill's mother was especially squirmy, and Bill's father was slapping her hard across the face to make her stop. His own mother was a bit quieter, especially after Bill's mother got hurt, but she still cried.

His father locked the door. 'We'll let you out, maybe after we get back.' He chuckled and looked at Bill's father. 'Women!'

It all seemed very peculiar.

As Jimmy's father pulled the battered old station wagon out of the driveway he began singing. He looked back over his shoulder at Jimmy and winked. Jimmy figured that singing was all part of fishing since first Bill's father, then Bill, joined in. Jimmy couldn't follow the words.

'Make a real man out of him, I think,' his father said to Bill's father. Bill's father chuckled.

They didn't seem to be getting any further out of the city. In fact, they seemed to be driving into the downtown section, if anything. Jimmy had never been downtown.

'Are you sure this is the right way to the stream, dad?'

Jimmy's father turned and glared at him. Jimmy lowered his head. Bill was gazing out the window and humming.

They passed several old ladies driving cars with packages and shopping bags filling the back seats. His father snickered.

They passed young girls on bicycles, their dresses fluttering in the wind. They passed several strolling couples, and a man with a baby carriage.

Jimmy's father laughed out loud and punched Bill's father on the shoulder. Then they were both laughing, tears in their eyes. Jimmy just stared at them.

The shopping malls were getting smaller, the houses darker and shabby.

Jimmy's father turned to him and said forcefully, almost angrily, 'You're going to make me proud today, Jimmy.'

Bill was beginning to get fidgety as he looked out of the window. Every once in a while he would gaze at the back of his father's head, then at the buildings along the street, then back out the rear window. He began scratching his arms in agitation.

Jimmy gazed out of his own window. The pavement was gettting worse – dirtier, and full of potholes. The buildings were getting taller, and older, the further they drove. Jimmy had always thought that only new buildings were tall.

They passed a dark figure, clothed in rags, crumpled on the sidewalk.

Jimmy's father chuckled to himself.

They had left the house at noon. Jimmy had just eaten the lunch of soup and crackers his mother had prepared, so he knew it had been noon.

The sky was getting dark.

Jimmy put his left cheek against the car window and tilted his head back so that he could see above the car. Tall smoke stacks rising out of the dark roofs of the buildings across the street blew night-black clouds into the sky. The smoke stacks were taller than anything he'd ever seen.

Jimmy felt a lurch as the car started down the steep hill. He had been in San Francisco once, and there were lots of hills that steep. He couldn't remember anything like that in their city, but then, he had never been downtown.

Bill was jerking his head back and forth nervously, his eyes very white.

The buildings seemed to get taller and taller, older and older. Some had tall columns out front, or wide wrap-around porches. Many had great iron or wooden doors. There didn't seem to be any people on the streets.

It suddenly occurred to Jimmy that the buildings shouldn't be getting taller as they went downhill. The bottoms of these buildings were lower than the ones further up the hill, behind them, so their rooftops should be lower too. That was the way it had been in San Francisco. But looking out the back window Jimmy could see that the roofs got further away, taller still as they descended the hill. The buildings were reaching into the sky.

Dark figures scurried from the mouth of an alley as they passed. Jimmy couldn't tell what they looked like; it seemed to be almost night time out.

Jimmy's father and Bill's father were perched on the edge of their seats, apparently searching every building corner. His father was humming.

Bill began to cry softly, his feet shuffling over the rumpled carcass of the crow.

The street seemed to get steeper and steeper. Occasionally they would hit a flat place in the road, the car would make a loud banging noise, bounce, then seemingly leap several feet into the air. The car was going faster.

His father laughed out loud and honked the horn once.

It was completely black outside, so black Jimmy could hardly see. The two fathers were singing softly again. The car was picking up speed with every clank, bounce, and leap. Bill was crying and moaning. Jimmy couldn't even see the sky any more, the buildings were so tall. And so old! Bricks were falling into the street even as they passed. Stone fronts were sagging, the foundations obscured by piles of powdered rock. Beams were obviously split and cracked, some hanging down like broken bones. Windowpanes were shattered, curtains torn, casements grimed. Jimmy couldn't understand how the buildings held themselves up, especially when they were so tall. Miles high, it seemed.

If he hadn't been taught better, he would have thought they hung down from the sky on wires. How else could they stand?

He was bouncing wildly up and down in the seat, periodically bumping into Bill, who was crying more loudly than ever. The car was like a train, a plane, a rocket.

A loud clank, then something rattled off to his left. He turned and saw that a hubcap had fallen off and was lying in the street behind them. Shadows moved in a side doorway.

The car was groaning. Bill's wails were even more high-pitched.

'Daddy . . . daddy, Bill's afraid!'

His father stared at the windshield. The car dropped another hubcap.

'Daddy, the hubcaps!'

His father remained motionless, his hands tightly gripping the wheel. A brick fell and bounced off the car. A piece of timber cracked the windshield.

The car squealed, roared, dropped further and further into the heart of the city. It seemed as if they had been going downhill for miles.

It suddenly occurred to Jimmy they hadn't passed a cross street in some time.

'Daddy . . . please!'

The car hit a flat section of pavement. The car body clanked loudly, the engine died, and the car rolled a few feet before stopping. They faced an old building with wide doors.

Jimmy looked around. They were in a small court, faced on all sides by the ancient buildings which soared upwards, completely filling the sky. It was so dark he couldn't see their upper storeys.

He looked behind them. The steep road rose like a grey ribbon, dwindling into nothingness at the top. It was the only road into the court.

Everything was quiet. Bill stared silently at his father. The dead crow was at his feet, trampled almost flat by Bill's agitated feet. The floorboard was filled with feathers, pieces of skin, bone and blood.

There were shapes in the darkness between buildings.

Jimmy's father turned to his friend. 'Bottom. We made it.' He began rummaging in his knapsack.

He was handing Jimmy the rifle, smiling, laughing, saying, 'That's my boy!' and 'Today's the day!' when the dark and tattered figures began closing in on the car.

Lisa Tuttle

Sun city

*Lisa Tuttle was born in 1952. She received a BA in English
from Syracuse University in 1973, and the John W. Campbell
Award for the best new science fiction writer of the year (in
conjunction with Spider Robinson) in 1974. She is a television
columnist and critic for Austin's daily newspaper (Texas), and
her stories have appeared in just about all the major science
fiction magazines being published as I write. But it was her
horror fiction I encountered first, and I was impressed by its
ruthlessness. Even her optimism is disturbing.*

It was three a.m., the dead, silent middle of the night. Except
for the humming of the soft-drink machine in one corner, and
the irregular, rumbling cough of the ice machine hidden in an
alcove just beyond it, the lobby was quiet. There weren't likely
to be any more check-ins until after dawn – all the weary cross-
country drivers would be settled elsewhere by now, or grimly
determined to push on without a rest.

Clerking the 11 p.m. to 7 a.m. shift was a dull, lonely job,
but usually Nora Theale didn't mind it. She preferred working
at night, and the solitude didn't bother her. But tonight, for the
third night in a row, she was jumpy. It was an irrational nervousness, and it annoyed Nora that she couldn't pin it down.
There was always the possibility of robbery, of course, but the
Posada del Norte hadn't been hit in the year she had worked
there, and Nora didn't think the motel made a very enticing
target.

Seeking a cause for her unease, Nora often glanced around
the empty lobby and through the glass doors at the parking lot
and the highway beyond. She never saw anything out of place
– except a shadow which might have been cast by someone
moving swiftly through the bluish light of the parking lot. But

71

it was gone in an instant, and she couldn't be sure she had seen it.

Nora picked up the evening paper and tried to concentrate. She read about plans to build a huge fence along the border, to keep illegal aliens out. It was an idea she liked – the constant flow back and forth between Mexico and the United States was one of the things she hated most about El Paso – but she didn't imagine it would work. After a few more minutes of scanning state and national news, Nora tossed the paper into the garbage can. She didn't want to read about El Paso; El Paso bored and depressed and disturbed her. She couldn't wait to leave it.

Casting another uneasy glance around the unchanged lobby, Nora leaned over to the file cabinet and pulled open the drawer where she kept her books. She picked out a mystery by Josephine Tey and settled down to it, determined to win over her nerves.

She read, undisturbed except for a few twinges of unease, until six a.m. when she had to let the man with the newspapers in and make the first wake-up call. The day clerk arrived a few minutes after seven, and that meant it was time for Nora to leave. She gathered her things together into a shoulderbag. She had a lot with her because she had spent the past two days in one of the motel's free rooms rather than go home. But the rooms were all booked up for that night, so she had to clear out. Since her husband had moved out, Nora hadn't felt like spending much time in the apartment that was now hers alone. She meant to move, but since she didn't want to stay in El Paso, it seemed more sensible simply to let the lease run out rather than go to the expense and trouble of finding another temporary home. She meant to leave El Paso just as soon as she got a little money together and decided on a place to go.

She didn't like the apartment, but it was large and cheap. Larry had picked it out because it was close to his office, and he liked to ride his bicycle to work. It wasn't anywhere near the motel where Nora worked, but Nora didn't care. She had her car.

She parked it now in the space behind the small, one-storey apartment complex. It was a hideous place; Nora winced every time she came home to it. It was made of an ugly pink fake-adobe, and had a red-tiled roof. There were some diseased-looking cactuses planted along the concrete walkway, but no grass or trees: water was scarce.

The stench of something long-dead and richly rotting struck

Nora as she opened the door to her apartment. She stepped back immediately, gagging. Her heart raced; she felt, oddly, afraid. But she recovered in a moment – it was just a smell, after all, and in her apartment. She had to do something about it. Breathing through her mouth, she stepped forward again.

The kitchen was clean, the garbage pail empty, and the refrigerator nearly bare. She found nothing there, or in the bedroom or bathroom, that seemed to be the cause of the odour. In the bedroom, she cautiously breathed in through her nose to test the air. It was clean. She walked slowly back to the living room, but there was nothing there, either. The whiff of foulness had gone as if it had never been.

Nora shrugged, and locked the door. It might have been something outside. If she smelled it again, she'd talk to the landlord about it.

There was nothing in the kitchen she could bear the thought of eating, so, after she had showered and changed, Nora walked down to the Seven-Eleven, three blocks away, and bought a few essentials: milk, eggs, bread, Dr Pepper and a package of sugared doughnuts.

The sun was already blazing and the dry wind abraded her skin. It would be another hot, dry, windy day – a day like every other day in El Paso. Nora was glad she slept through most of them. She thought about North Carolina, where she had gone to college, reflecting wistfully that up there the leaves would be starting to turn now. As she walked back to her apartment with the bag of groceries in her arms, Nora thought about moving east to North Carolina.

The telephone was ringing as Nora walked in.

'I've been trying to get in touch with you for the past three days!'

It was her husband, Larry.

'I've been out a lot.' She began to peel the cellophane wrapping off the doughnuts.

'Do tell. Look, Nora, I've got some papers for you to sign.'

'Aw, and I thought maybe you'd called to say happy anniversary.'

He was silent. One side of Nora's mouth twitched upwards: she'd scored.

Then he sighed. 'What do you want, Nora? Am I supposed to think that today means something to you? That you still care? That you want me back?'

'God forbid.'

'Then cut the crap, all right? So we didn't make it to our third wedding anniversary – all right, so *legally* we're still married – but what's the big deal?'

'I was joking, Larry. You never could recognize a joke.'

'I didn't call to fight with you, Nora. Or to joke. I'd just like you to sign these papers so we can get this whole thing over with. You won't even have to show up in court.'

Nora bit into a doughnut and brushed off the spray of sugar that powdered her shirt.

'Nora? When should I bring the papers by?'

She set the half-eaten doughnut down on the counter and reflected. 'Um, come this evening, if you want. Not too early, or I'll still be asleep. Say . . . seven-thirty?'

'Seven-thirty.'

'That won't cut into your dinner plans with what's-her-name?'

'Seven-thirty will be fine, Nora. I'll see you then. Just be there.' And he hung up before she could get in another dig.

Nora grimaced, then shrugged as she hung up. She finished the doughnut, feeling depressed. Despite herself, she'd started thinking about Larry again, and their marriage which had seemed to go bad before it had properly started. She thought about their brief honeymoon. She remembered Mexico.

It had been Larry's idea to drive down to Mexico – Nora had always thought of Mexico as a poor and dirty place, filled with undesirables who were always sneaking into the United States. But Larry had wanted to go, and Nora had wanted to make Larry happy.

It was their *luna de miel*, moon of honey, Larry said, and the Spanish words sounded almost sweet to her, coming from his mouth. Even Mexico, in his company, had seemed freshly promising, especially after they escaped the dusty borderlands and reached the ocean.

One afternoon they had parked on an empty beach and made love. Larry had fallen asleep, and Nora had left him to walk up the beach and explore.

She walked along in a daze of happiness, her body tingling, climbing over rocks and searching for shells to bring back to her husband. She didn't realize how far she had travelled until she was shocked out of her pleasant haze by a sharp cry, whether human or animal she could not be certain. She heard some indistinct words, then, tossed to her by the wind.

Nora was frightened. She didn't want to know what the

sounds meant or where they came from. She wanted to get back to Larry and forget that she had heard anything. She turned around immediately, and began to weave her way back among the white boulders. But she must have mistaken her way, for as she clambered back over a rock she was certain she had just climbed, she saw them below her, posed like some sacrificial tableau.

At the centre was a girl, spread out on a low, flat rock. The victim. Crouching over her, doing something, was a young man. Another young man stared at them greedily. Nora gazed at the girl's face, which was contorted in pain. She heard her whimper. It was only then that she realized, with a cold flash of dread, what she was seeing. The girl was being raped.

Nora was frozen with fear and indecision, and then the girl opened her eyes, and gazed straight up at Nora. Her brown eyes were eloquent with agony. Was there a glimmer of hope there at the sight of Nora? Nora couldn't be sure. She stared into those eyes for what seemed like a very long time, trying desperately to think of what to do. She wanted to help this girl, to chase away the men. But there were *two* men, and she, Nora, had no particular strengths. They would probably be pleased to have two victims. And at any time one of them might look up and see her watching.

Trying to make no noise, Nora slipped backwards off the rock. The scene vanished from her sight; the pleading brown eyes could no longer accuse her. Nora began to run as best she could over the uneven ground. She hoped she was running in the right direction, and that she would soon come upon Larry. Larry would help her – she would tell him what she had seen, and he would know what to do. He might be able to frighten away the men, or, speaking Spanish, he could at least tell the police what she had seen. She would be safe with Larry.

The minutes passed and Nora still, blindly, ran. She couldn't see their car, and knew the horrifying possibility that she was running in the wrong direction – but she didn't dare go back. A cramp in her side and ragged pains when she drew breath forced her to walk: she felt the moment when she might have been of some help, when she could have reached Larry in time, drain inexorably away. She never knew how long she had walked and run before she finally caught sight of their car, but, even allowing for her panic, Nora judged it had been at the very least a half an hour. She felt as if she had been running desperately all day. And she was too late. Much too late. By now, they would have finished with the girl. They might have killed her, they might have let her go. In either case, Nora and Larry would be too late to help her.

'There you are! Where'd you go? I was worried,' Larry said, slipping off the hood of the car and coming to embrace her. He sounded not worried but lazily contented.

It was too late. She did not tell him, after all, what she had witnessed. She never told him.

Nora became deathly ill that night in a clean, American-style hotel near Acapulco. Two days later, still shaking and unable to keep anything in her stomach, Nora flew back to her mother and the family doctor in Dallas, leaving Larry to drive back by himself.

It was the stench that woke her. Nora lurched out of sleep, sitting up on the bed, gagging and clutching the sheet to her mouth, trying not to breath in the smell. It was the smell of something dead.

Groggy with sleep, she needed another moment to realize something much more frightening than the smell: there was someone else in the room.

A tall figure stood, motionless, not far from the foot of her bed. The immediate fear Nora felt at the sight was quickly pushed out of the way by a coldly rational, self-preserving consciousness. In the dim light Nora could not tell much about the intruder except that that he was oddly dressed in some sort of cloak, and that his features were masked by some sort of head mask. The most important thing she noticed was that he did not block her path to the door, and if she moved quickly . . .

Nora bolted, running through the apartment like a rabbit, and bursting out through the front door into the courtyard.

It was late afternoon, the sun low in the sky but not yet gone. One of her neighbours, a Mexican, was grilling hamburgers on a little *hibachi*. He stared at her sudden appearance, then grinned. Nora realized she was wearing only an old t-shirt of Larry's and a pair of brightly coloured bikini pants, and she scowled at the man.

'Somebody broke into my apartment,' she said sharply, cutting into his grin.

'Want to use our phone? Call the police?'

Nora thought of Larry and felt a sudden fierce hatred of him: he had left her to this, abandoned her to the mercy of burglars, potential rapists, and the leers of this Mexican.

'No, thanks,' she said, her tone still harsh. 'But I think he's still inside. Do you think you could . . .'

'You want me to see if he still there? Sure, sure, I'll check. You don't have to worry.' He sprang forward. Nora hated his eagerness to help, but she needed him right now.

There was no one in her apartment. The back door was still locked, and the screens on all the windows were undisturbed.

Nora didn't ask her neighbour to check behind every piece of furniture after he had looked into the closets: she was feeling the loathing she always felt for hysterical, over-emotional reactions. Only this time the loathing was directed at herself.

Although one part of her persisted in believing she had seen an intruder, reason told her she had been mistaken. She had been tricked by a nightmare into running for help like a terrified child.

She was rude to the man who had helped her, dismissing him as sharply as if he were an erring servant. She didn't want to see the smug, masculine concern on his face; didn't want him around knowing he must be chuckling inwardly at a typical hysterical female.

Nora intended to forget about it, as she had forgotten other embarrassing incidents, other disturbing dreams, but she was not allowed.

She had a hard time falling asleep the next day. Children were playing in the parking lot, and her doze was broken time and again by their shouts, meaningless fragments of talk, and the clamour of a bicycle bell.

When, at last, she did sleep in the afternoon, it was to dream that she and Larry were having one of their interminable, pointless, low-voiced arguments. She woke from the frustrating dream with the impression that someone had come into the room and, certain it was Larry and ready to resume the argument in real life, she opened her eyes.

Before she could speak his name, the stench struck her like a blow – that too familiar, dead smell – and she saw the tall, weirdly draped figure again.

Nora sat up quickly, trying not to breathe in, and the effort made her dizzy. The figure did not move. There was more light in the room this time, and she could see him clearly.

The strange cloak ended in blackened tatters that hung over his hands and feet, and the hood had ragged holes torn for eyes and mouth – with a rush of horror, Nora realized what she was seeing. The figure was dressed in a human skin. The gutted shell of some other human being flapped grotesquely against his own.

Nora's mouth dropped open, and she breathed in the smell of the rotting skin, and, for one horrible moment, she feared she was about to vomit, that she would be immobilized, sick and at the monster's mercy.

Fear tightened her throat and gut, and she managed to stumble out of the room and down the hall.

She didn't go outside. She remembered, as she reached the front door, that she had seen that figure before. That it was only a nightmarish hallucination. Only a dream. She could scarcely accept it, but she knew it was true. Only a dream. Her fingers clutched the cool metal doorknob, but she did not turn it. She leaned against the door, feeling her stomach muscles contract spasmodically, aware of the weakness in her legs and the bitter taste in her mouth.

She tried to think of something calming, but could not chase the visions from her mind: knives, blood, putrefaction. What someone who had been skinned must look like. And what was he, beneath that rotten skin? What could that ghastly disguise hide?

When at last she bullied and cajoled herself into returning to the bedroom, the thing, of course, was gone. Not even the cadaverine smell remained.

Nightmare or hallucination, whatever it was, it came again on the third day. She was ready for it – had lain rigidly awake for hours in the sunlit room knowing he would come – but the stench and the sight were scarcely any easier to endure the third time. No matter how much she told herself she was dreaming, no matter how hard she tried to believe that what she saw (and smelled?) was mere hallucination, Nora had not the cold-bloodedness to remain on her bed until it vanished.

Once again she ran from the room in fear, hating herself for such irrational behaviour. And, again, the thing had gone when she calmed herself and returned to look.

On the fourth day Nora stayed at the motel.

If someone else had suggested escaping a nightmare by sleeping somewhere else, Nora would have been scornful. But she justified her action to herself: this dream was different. There was the smell, for one thing. Perhaps there was some real source to the smell, and it was triggering the nightmare. In that case, a change of air should cure her.

The room she moved into when she got off work that morning was like all the other rooms in the Posada del Norte. It was clean and uninspired, the decor hovering between the merely bland and the aggressively ugly. The carpet was a stubby, mottled gold; the bedspread and chair cushions were dark orange. The walls were covered in white, textured vinyl with a mural painted above the bed. The murals differed from room to room – in this room, it was a picture of a stepped Aztec pyramid, rendered in shades of orange and brown.

Nora turned on the air conditioning, and a blast of air came out in a frozen rush. She took a few toilet articles into the bathroom, but left everything else packed in the overnight bag which she had dropped on to a chair. She had no desire to 'settle in' or to intrude herself on the bland anonymity of the room.

She turned on the television and lay back on the bed to observe the meaningless interactions of the guests on a morning talk show. She had nothing better to do. After the network show was a talk show of the local variety, with a plain, overly made-up hostess who smiled, blinked and nodded a lot. Her guests were a red-faced, middle-aged man who talked about the problems caused by illegal aliens; and a woman who discussed the ancient beauties of Mexico. Nora turned off the set halfway through her slide show featuring pyramids and other monuments in Mexico.

The television silent, she heard the sound of people moving in next door. There seemed to be a lot of them, and they were noisy. A radio clicked on, bringing in music and commercials from Mexico. There was a lot of laughter from the room, and Nora caught an occasional Spanish-sounding word.

Nora swore, not softly. Why couldn't they party on their own side of the border? And who ever carried on in such a way at ten o'clock in the morning? But she hesitated to pound on the wall: that would only draw attention to herself, and she didn't imagine it would deter them.

Instead, to shield herself, she turned on the television set again. It was game-show time, and the sounds of hysteria, clanging bells and idiotic laughter filled the room. Nora sighed, turned the volume down a bit, and pulled off her clothes. Then she climbed under the blankets and gazed blankly at the flickering images.

She was tired, but too keyed-up to sleep. Her mind kept circling until she deliberately thought about what was bothering her: the man in the skin. What did it mean? Why was it haunting her?

It seemed more a hallucination than an ordinary dream, and that made Nora doubly uneasy. It was too *real*. When she saw, and smelled, the nightmarish figure, she could never quite convince herself she was only dreaming.

And what did the hideous figure itself mean? It must have come crawling out of her subconscious for some reason, thought Nora. But she didn't really think she had just made it up herself – the idea of a man draped in another's skin stirred some deep memory. Somewhere, long before, she had read about, or seen a picture of, a figure who wore the stripped-off skin of another. Was it something from Mexico? Some ancient, pre-Columbian god?

Yet whenever she strained to recall it, the memory moved perversely away.

And why did the dream figure haunt her now? Because she was alone? But that was absurd. Nora shifted uncomfortably in bed. She had no regrets about the separation or the impending divorce; she was glad Larry was gone. They should have had the sense to call it quits years before. She didn't want him back under any circumstances.

And yet – Larry was gone, and old two-skins was haunting her.

Finally, worn out by the useless excavations of her memory, Nora turned off the television and went to sleep.

She woke feeling sick. She didn't need to turn her head or open her eyes to know, but she did. And, of course, he was in the room. He would come to her wherever she fled. The stench came from the rotting skin he wore, not from a neighbour's garbage or something dead between the walls. He didn't look like something hallucinated – he seemed perfectly substantial standing there beside the television set and in front of the draperies.

Staring at him, Nora willed herself to wake up. She willed him to melt and vanish. Nothing happened. She saw the dark gleam of his eyes through ragged eye holes, and she was suddenly more frightened than she had ever been in her life.

She closed her eyes. The blood pounding in her ears was the sound of fear. She would not be able to hear him if he moved closer. Unable to bear the thought of what he might be doing, unseen by her, Nora opened her eyes. He was still there. He did not seem to have moved.

She had to get out, Nora thought. She had to give him the chance to vanish – he always had, before. But she was naked – she couldn't go out as she was, and all her clothes were on the chair beside the window, much too close to him. In a moment, Nora knew, she might start screaming. Already she was shaking – she had to do *something*.

On fear-weakened legs, Nora climbed out of bed and stumbled towards the bathroom. She slammed the door shut behind her, hearing the comforting snick of the lock as she pressed the button in.

Then she stood with palms pressed on the Formica surface surrounding the basin, head hanging down, breathing shallowly in and out, waiting for the fear to leave her. When she had calmed herself, she raised her head and looked in the mirror.

There she was, the same old Nora. Lost her husband, driven out of her apartment by nerves, surrounded by the grey and white sterility of a hotel bathroom. There was no reason for her to be here – not in this building, not in El Paso, not in Texas, not in this *life*. But here she was, going on as if it all had some purpose. And for no better reason than that she didn't know what else to do – she had no notion of how to start over.

Nora caught a glimpse of motion in the mirror, and then the clear reflection of the one who had come for her: the lumpish head with the mask of another's face stretched crudely over his own. She looked calmly into the mirror, right into the reflections of his eyes. They were brown, she realized, very much like a pair of eyes she remembered from Mexico.

Feeling a kind of relief because there was no longer anywhere else to run, Nora turned away from the mirror to face him, to see this man in his dead skin for the first time in a fully lighted room. 'She sent you to me,' Nora said, and realized she was no longer afraid.

The skin was horrible – a streaky grey with ragged, black edges. But what of the man underneath? She had seen his eyes. Suddenly, as she gazed steadily at the figure, his name came into her mind, as clearly as if he had written it on the mirror for her: Xipe, the Flayed One. She had been right in thinking him some ancient Mexican god, Nora thought. But she knew nothing else about him, nor did she need to know. He was not a dream to be interpreted – he was here, now.

She saw that he carried a curved knife; watched without fear as he tore seams in the skin he wore, and it fell away, a discarded husk.

Revealed without the disfiguring, concealing outer skin, Xipe was a dark young man with a pure, handsome face. Not a Mexican, Nora thought, but an Indian, of noble and ancient blood. He smiled at her. Nora smiled back, realizing now that there had never been any reason to fear him.

He offered her the knife. So easy, his dark eyes promised her. No fear, no question in their brown depths. Shed the old skin, the old life, as I have done, and be reborn.

When she hesitated, he reached out with his empty hand and traced a line along her skin. The touch of his hand seared like ice. Her skin was too tight. Xipe, smooth, clean and new, watched her, offering the ritual blade.

At last she took the knife and made the first incision.

Manly Wade Wellman
Yare

*Manly Wade Wellman was born in Angola in 1903, but now is
thoroughly identified with North Carolina, where he lives with
his equally charming and hospitable wife Frances (who used to
contribute to* Weird Tales, *and who has now returned to
writing).*

*Manly is a large gentlemanly Southerner who drinks
tumblers of Jack Daniels and smokes horrid cigars. He has
written under many pseudonyms, listed (along with much more
essential information) in* Who's Who in Horror and Fantasy
Fiction. *His books include* Who Fears the Devil? *about the
occult fighter John (who now also figures in novels),* Lonely
Vigils, The Beyonders, The Old Gods Waken, After Dark,
Sherlock Holmes' War of the Worlds *(written in collaboration
with his son Wade, and unpublishable in Britain) and the huge
collection* Worse Things Waiting. *This last won the World
Fantasy Award, as well it might, and in 1978 he was given the
North Carolina Award for Literature. August Derleth called
his stories of John 'sui generis and at the same time authentic
American folklore'. This is true also of 'Yare'.*

They were four in the last grey of evening, by the windblown
coals of the fire with utensils propped ready. Trees tufted this
slope below Black Ham Mountain, with grassy stretches between. Young Hal Stryker felt privileged to be there. He let
the others study his flowing sandy hair and his patched jeans.

'This here is Hal Stryker, the feller I said I'd fetch,' Poke
Jendel introduced him when they arrived. 'Hal, shake hands
with Seth Worley and with this here beardy one. He's Reed
Lufbrugh, he makes a good distill of blockade and looks to me
he fetched on some in a jug. Seth and Reed, Hal's a lowlander
who wants to see how we do things up here in the mountains.'

'Such as this fox hunt,' amplified Stryker. 'I've heard about how you hunt foxes, but it's better to see a thing done than hear about it.'

'Truer word was nair spoke,' approved Seth Worley, lean as a hunting knife and as ready looking with his black hair and ploughshare jaw. Jendel was the smallest man there, but hard-knit, shrewd about his horsey face, with broad hands that were wise with guns, tools and especially with a banjo. Lufbrugh was the oldest, with thinning grey hair, a bush of beard, moustaches that curled like buffalo horns. They sat on square chunks of rock, rough-clad, good-humoured. All had brought guns but Stryker. These were laid carefully, within quick reach of hands.

Tied to nearby roots strained half a dozen dogs. All but one were brown-blotched hounds. The exception was of a Scandinavian breed, heavy furred, with ears that stood up expectantly.

'Them dogs is ready to go,' declared Worley, 'and I aim to hark at them a-running something down tonight.'

He arranged the joints of two chickens in a skillet above the coals. Poke Jendel stirred meal and water and salt into another skillet for pone. Lufbrugh unstoppered his jug. Each drank in turn, with the jug draped on a forearm. 'Good,' Stryker praised the sharp tang of the liquor.

'Better'n the government whisky,' said Lufbrugh. 'Pure as spring water. Naught touched it but the wood of the keg and the copper of the still and the clay of the jug.'

Stryker studied the rock on which he sat. 'It looks as if a house was built here once.'

'Long years back,' nodded Jendel above the pone. 'Feller they called Yare lived here. His house is gone and so's he. I don't recollect him, he was before my time.'

'What kind of name is Yare?' wondered Stryker.

'Just only a nickname, I reckon,' said Jendel. 'I don't know his true name. Folks just called him Yare.'

'I was a young chap when Yare was a-using round here-abouts,' contributed Lufbrugh, the jug in his lap. 'He come from somewheres outland, he allowed he loved the animals and hated the hunters.'

'How did that suit the people?' asked Stryker, who was no enthusiastic huntsman himself.

'They fussed with him and he fussed with them,' replied Lufbrugh. 'He had powers from somewhere, I heard say. Could fetch down a rain by a-singing a certain song, could kill a crop in the field if so happen he didn't like the feller who'd planted it.'

'My old daddy done told me about him,' elaborated Jendel above his cooking. 'If you killed a deer, he'd set his big old handprint in blood on to your door, and the blood wouldn't dry, would drip and drip for days.'

'I've heard that same thing,' said Worley, shaking dark powder into the chicken gravy. 'This ain't no poison spell, boys, just some instant coffee. It goes good thattaway.'

'Well, but you say this Yare is dead,' said Stryker.

'So folks say,' said Lufbrugh. 'Me, I ain't nair yet heard tell where his grave might could have been dug.'

Jendel took knife and fork and cautiously turned the cake of pone in his skillet. 'Near about time to set them dogs on,' he said.

'I'll do that,' volunteered Worley, rising and unsnapping the leashes from the collars. He walked a few steps with the dogs, until they bunched and sniffed the ground attentively. Then they sprang away, noses to earth. They ran towards where, about the distant hunch of Black Ham Mountain, rose a pale melon of a moon. The men watched them.

'We're near about ready to eat,' said Jendel at length. He cut wedges of pone and slid them on to paper plates. Worley forked on juicy pieces of chicken. Lufbrugh passed out iron knives and forks. Stryker bit into his chicken. It was as savoury as Worley had promised. Away in the dimness, a dog bayed tremulously, musically.

'That there's Tromp,' Jendel informed them. 'I'd know him amongst a thousand.'

'Don't you follow them?' Stryker suggested.

'Nair a step, son,' said Lufbrugh, spooning gravy on his pone. 'Not this here bunch of smart dogs. We sit and hark at them a-singing, and directly they fetch what they're after back to us here, close to where it wants to hole up.'

'I hear tell the lowlands hunters ride after a fox with red coats on,' said Jendel. 'A sight of trouble to do that.'

Another dog's voice pealed like a bell.

'That's my Giff,' Worley told them. 'When he talks up thataway, the trail's hot. They're a good piece off from here already.'

'And they'll fetch him back,' predicted Lufbrugh, gnawing at a drumstick.

Stryker ate pone and gravy. 'What you said about that man Yare is interesting,' he prompted.

'I know you, Hal,' grinned Jendel. 'You enjoy to hear about hants and witches and all like that.'

85

'You say he lived here. Right where we are now.'

'His house got burnt off these here very stones,' said Lufbrugh.

'Why?' asked Stryker.

'Folks didn't much like Yare.'

They watched Stryker, and he smiled. As Jendel had said, he liked this sort of story, here in this sort of place, at this time of the night, with the dogs baying at a distance.

'Why didn't they like him?' he asked, because they waited for him to ask it.

'Well, he fussed with folks about hunting,' said Lufbrugh between mouthfuls. 'He loved animals another sight better'n folks – wild animals, that is. Yare didn't value cows or chickens or hogs, said they was tame, deserved to die. Folks figured he stole such things at night and ate them up. But he hated deer killing, coon killing, even fish catching.'

'Did he have any family?' asked Stryker. 'A wife?'

'Nair girl would have looked at him,' said Lufbrugh. 'Hairy, the way he was.'

'How hairy was that?'

'All over,' replied Lufbrugh. 'Not just a beard like mine. His face was all hair, even the nose, the one-two times I seen him. And his arms, his hands, a-sticking out of his old clothes, they was hairy, too, like on a bear or a wildcat. Dark hair, no shine to it. Pure down ugly to look at.' Lufbrugh bit into the drumstick. 'Better off dead, if he is dead.'

'He'd have to be better'n a hundred by now,' said Jendel.

'My old granddaddy lived past a hundred,' Worley said. 'Walked a couple miles, a-gathering walnuts, the morning of the day he died.'

'And Yare was long and tall,' resumed Lufbrugh. 'Must have been near seven foot. With long arms, they like to drag on the ground.'

Stryker was silent, trying to visualize such a figure. Jendel ate chicken and pone.

'Like what I say, I wasn't round here when he was,' he said. 'But a heap of folks said Yare wasn't true human blood, he'd been born of some kind of devil blood.'

'He looked devilish enough,' endorsed Lufbrugh. 'And cut up devilish enough. Scared folks, maybe even killed a couple of fellers—'

'I've heard tell that a couple of hunter nair come home from time to time,' nodded Worley. 'Nobody found their bodies.'

'Nobody found Yare's body,' said Lufbrugh.

Remotely, the dogs lifted their voices together, like a choir.

'They're sure enough on to something,' said Jendel. 'They're a-trying now to catch up on it.'

They finished eating, to the remote music. Jendel threw scraps into the fire, which crackled hungrily. Lufbrugh passed the jug again. The moon soared well above Black Ham Mountain.

'Now, hark at them dogs,' said Worley.

The chorus lifted, far off to one side, as though the pack were following a trail along the slope. Joy was in the voices, and deadly intent.

'They reckon they're a-getting close,' decided Worley. 'Soon's they can see what they're after, they'll purely get a move on.'

The clarion voices rang together, then all died out but one.

'Tromp,' Jendel identified it. 'He must be a-leading the way just now.'

Those cries grew fainter.

'They're a-heading away after it, but they'll fetch it, sure enough, back here,' said Lufbrugh confidently. 'Somebody want another whet out of this here jug?'

It went the rounds.

'Now,' said Stryker, 'what about the question of whether this Yare is dead or not?'

'Oh, hell,' said Worley, wiping his mouth, 'you know how some folks are, a-talking. They'll tell you that their corn dies down with a blight, or their dogs go mad and have to be shot, and they figure Yare's got something to do with it. Or they see something at the window, and get pestered about that.'

'I've heard such stuff as that,' chimed in Jendel. 'How if he comes up and looks in at your window, somebody in your family dies.'

'Do you hold with that, Poke?' inquired Lufbrugh.

'Nair said I did, but I know folks that does.'

Worley drank again. 'All right,' he addressed Stryker. 'Weuns been a-telling you tales. It's your turn now. Tell us some of these here things Poke says you seen and done.'

'Do that thing, Hal,' encouraged Jendel.

Stryker did so, somewhat hesitantly. He told of how he had managed to destroy an evil spirit that haunted an ancient stage house on a half-forgotten road, and of how he had managed to get into a remote cabin literally besieged by evil, cunning trees, and then had managed to get out again. As he spoke, he watched his companions. They acted as though they were weighing every word he spoke.

'Shoo,' said Jendel at last. 'You done done more such things than air one of us has, Hal. And the doing of it must have sure enough done something for you.'

Remotely, the dogs bayed on their resolute quest.

'What do you mean by that?' Stryker demanded.

'You been up against hants and all like that. You whupped them. That means, you've found out how.'

'I don't see that I have,' said Stryker, mystified.

'Like when you're in a war,' offered Lufbrugh. 'They train you, they give you a gun, call you a soldier. Only you ain't no such thing, no soldier, till you been in where the shooting is and seen the monkey show, so to speak it.'

The dogs sang to them again, far away there somewhere. They sounded more excited, less light-hearted.

'Hark at them,' spoke up Worley. 'They might could have caught a glimp of what they want to catch up with.'

A series of half-screaming yelps.

'Old Tromp, a-telling the others he'll lead,' Jendel said approvingly.

'Son,' said Lufbrugh to Stryker, his voice weighty, 'what you tell us gives me the thought you're what we've been a-needing here in the Black Ham neighbourhood.'

'Me?' Stryker half cried out.

'You done been a-studying these things,' said Lufbrugh. 'You can figure what to do in some cases.'

The fire flickered there among them, lighting the faces that looked at Stryker. Jendel put wood on the blaze. It fought briefly with the fuel, then sent up tongues of flame, yellow as butter. The dogs sang to them again, they sounded nearer by now.

'What does all this have to do with fox hunting?' Stryker asked.

'Fox hunting?' said Lufbrugh after him.

'Who said aught about foxes?' inquired Worley.

'Why—' Stryker stammered. 'Why, I came out here with Poke because you were going to hunt a fox.'

'I nair said pea turkey to you about foxes,' said Poke solemnly. 'Back yonder at my place, I said we were a-bringing out our dogs here tonight, and did you relish to come along.'

'Are you having some kind of fun with me?' challenged Stryker, half angrily.

'No, Hal.' Jendel's voice was patient. 'I might could have fooled you up a tad, but we're dead serious about this. On account of them strange things you narrated to us. We'd had the word on you about them before now.'

'Them witches and hants and them,' added Worley. 'And you a-being able to do something about them if they come a-pestering you.'

Stryker stared at them, from one solemn face to another. 'Well,' he said slowly, 'I've had some unusual experiences. I didn't think you'd believe them.'

'We believe,' said Lufbrugh. 'We come out here to believe. Look, son,' and his beard jutted emphatically, 'that's why we had Poke to fetch you out with us tonight.'

'I don't get it,' groaned Stryker, fidgeting on his rock.

'Ain't it a natural fact that if a man's had them experiences you say you had,' said Jendel, 'been up against such things and made out to handle them some way – he's got a power, ain't he?'

'What Poke means,' said Worley from his own rock, 'he can do away with such things.'

'That's the old supposition,' admitted Stryker, feeling a chill in his stomach.

'Then look, Hal,' urged Jendel. 'Hark at me good. It ain't no fox that we come out here tonight to have the dogs run.'

'In God's name, what is it then?'

'Shoo,' said Jendel, 'we been a-talking about that. It's Yare we fetched them out after.'

The dogs bayed, and the sound of baying was stronger, it was nearer. Stryker jumped to his feet.

'If this is a joke—' he began.

'If it was a joke, it'd be a plumb foolish one,' said Jendel. 'It ain't nair joke, Hal. We mean the last mumbling word of it.'

They sat on those rocks that once had held up a house, sat like a panel of judges passing sentence on him. The moonlight picked out their faces.

'We come out here to track up on Yare, once for all,' said Jendel. 'To stop what he does hereabouts. And you're the one is a-going to stop it for us.'

'You're all out of your heads!' cried Stryker.

'If that's a fact,' said Lufbrugh, 'you'll have you the chance to find out directly. Because they're a-running Yare in here to us, like a fox to his hole.'

The voices of the pack rose louder, louder, building a crescendo.

'They can see him now,' said Worley expertly. 'They're a-running him fast.'

'And he wants to hole up right where we are,' said Jendel. 'Where he used to live. Hal, I said it's up to you.'

'Up to you, son,' said Lufbrugh, as though he pronounced a benediction.

The excited clamour of the chase grew louder. Across open ground towards them came something, swift as a shadow.

It was big and black, Stryker saw as he faced towards it. A bear, or a midnight bull, would be that size. The dogs thronged after it, leaping to close in.

The others had risen, their rifles in their hands. Stryker, weaponless, snatched a pole from the stack of firewood. It was perhaps four feet long, sharpened to a rough point. It might help in a fight. A fight – his blood stirred at the thought.

He stepped away from the fire. The ground seemed to quake under him. Whatever the something was, it had come near enough to see. It came swiftly at a crouch, huddled and huge. Its long forelimbs swept like shaggy wings, close to the ground. Suddenly it rose erect in front of him.

It loomed like a rearing horse. It plunged uncouthly against the night sky, those great shaggy arms outflung. Stars winked around it. He wondered why nobody fired, and it occurred to him that shots might not hurt it. It closed in.

Rakelike paws swooped at him. The moonlight touched what must be a face higher up, dark and tufted except for pale crumbs of eyes, so close set that they almost merged. Jagged picket rows of teeth.

Then the dogs were upon its bushy flanks. It screamed deaf-eningly and floundered back from Stryker, its paws slapping right and left. He caught a pale shimmer through the fur on one arm, a glint as of ivory. A dog yelped in agony as it flew through the air like a blown leaf. The grotesque hugeness shook itself free from the pack and clumped towards Stryker again.

A wave of foul stench smote his nostrils, so overwhelming that he tottered as at a blow. The shaggy shape rose against the sky. The coat of hair rippled. He had another glimpse of streaky pallor, like a row of naked ribs. Desperately he swung the pole with both hands. The blow rang where it struck, as though on a dulled gong. The creature did not even flinch under the impact. It clawed for him. His shirt ripped and he threw himself backwards and fell head over heels. As he rolled over and came up on one knee, it towered above him again. It hunched great shoulders, bannered with black hair. It stunk so strongly that Stryker's eyes swam. The talons scooped for him.

He whirled the pointed pole in his hands, sharp end forward. He jabbed frantically, and the murky bulk dodged away. The dogs snarled and yelped and danced all around.

'Yare!' he cried its name at it. And it knew its name, it heaved its shoulders and snarled back at him.

Who was Yare, what had Yare become? This floundering, looming entity, wing-armed, talon-fingered, was grown out of Yare who had loved the wild, had hated tame mankind. It wanted to fight, it must be fought, this dark blotch in the dancing glow of the moon.

Somehow he got the pole in position. Again he jabbed, trying without real hope to keep the murky bulk away. He saw the shaggy face open up, with teeth like a monstrous skull. It slammed itself at him.

His pointed pole struck into something, as into earth. Above his head rang a deafening scream of startled pain. The stench welled around him like a foul torrent.

The ramming force of his thrust had brought him to his feet again. He surged forward with the pole. The giant shadow almost enveloped him. Then, abruptly, it gave back. With all his summoned strength he drove the pole in and in.

It had floundered down, it sprawled and thrashed there. A paw raked upward at him. He felt the sting of talons on his cheek. Leaning all his weight on the pole, he felt it strike into something other than what he had transfixed. Into earth, pinning the shape there like a gigantic insect upon a card. His mind churned within him and he staggered away and slammed to the grass. He dreamed horribly of something.

His senses returned to him furtively, as though they were not quite sure that they should come back. Voices chattered. Then he felt hands upon him. He blinked his eyes, and he could see. Jendel was on one side of him, helping him to his feet. Worley came up on the other, an arm around him.

'He sure enough gouged you,' Jendel babbled. 'Looks like as if a knife come on your cheek. Let me have that there jug, Reed.'

Lufbrugh passed it to Jendel, who sloshed it at Stryker's

face. The liquor stung sharply, and helped clear his head. He touched his face timidly. It was wet with blood, with the whisky.

'None of you got into the fight,' Stryker said.

'None of us could have done aught,' Lufbrugh replied. 'It was up to you.'

'Got a clean handkerchief?' Worley asked, his hands at Stryker's pockets. 'Here you are, hold it there. It'll staunch up the blood.'

Stryker wadded the handkerchief against the wound. 'What happened?'

'What happened?' Lufbrugh echoed him. 'You done what we fetched you here to do. You finished Yare off.'

Stryker looked at Jendel for some sort of enlightenment.

'Yonder he lies.' Jendel pointed. 'When you got up against him with just a stick, we wondered ourselves if things hadn't gone against us. But you stuck right through where he was biggest. Spiked him to the ground. No, Hal, don't go over yonder.'

'He's dead,' said Worley.

'Dead all the way through,' amplified Lufbrugh. 'All the way back along them years. He stinks rotten.'

Stryker gazed. The great shadowy form lay motionless in the soft moonlight. Around it capered the dogs, weaving a pattern. They did not venture too near.

'He appears like to be just bones inside his skin,' said Lufbrugh. 'Not even them dogs want air part of him.'

'He done slapped my Giff clean out of this life,' mumbled Worley miserably. 'Crushed him like a duck egg.'

'That there's too bad, Seth,' Lufbrugh comforted him. 'I knowed you valued that there dog a right much. Thought the world of him. Too bad it happened.'

All of them walked away from the patterned rocks, the motionless fallen bulk of what had been something called Yare.

'You know, fellers,' said Lufbrugh, 'that there pole that Hal Stryker took into the fight with him? It was an ash pole.'

'Ash pole,' Stryker echoed him tonelessly.

'Sure thing. Ash. I've talked to old Injun fellers round here, they used to allow ash was something you could use to fight evil spirits with. It must have done its part just now.'

Stryker mopped his bloody, sweaty face. Wearily he walked along with the others. The dogs followed them, all but the one that lay limply apart from that larger dead mass.

'What shall we do with the body?' Stryker asked all three of them at once.

'Hell,' said Jendel, 'we won't do aught with it.'

'We'll just leave it where it is,' seconded Lufbrugh.

Already they were a considerable distance from where those things had happened. They quickened their feet. They headed towards where a tiny point of radiance made a token of a cabin in the night.

Tanith Lee

A room with a vie

*Tanith Lee is prolific and mysterious. She was born in north
London in 1947 and began writing at the age of nine. She has
been a library assistant, a clerk, a shop assistant, an art student
for a year. 'In 1976 I was able to jettison these interruptions
and become a full-time writer. I am interested in classical
music, painting, reading, cinema, all of which influence my
writing. In fact, I am influenced by everything which I see and
which happens to me.' So far she has firmly refused most
invitations to appear at conventions, though people tell andy
offutt that she is 'nice to look upon'. Perhaps she is too busy:
between 1975 and 1979 she wrote ten adult fantasy novels,
three more for children, five for young adults, three radio plays
and a large number of short stories. Her imagination seems
indefatigable.*

*Here is a tale in a setting far from the vivid fantasy worlds
of* The Birthgrave *and* The Storm Lord *and* Volkhavaar – *a
contemporary tale which follows through its implications with
nightmare logic.*

'This is it, then.'

'Oh, yes.'

'As you can see, it's in quite nice condition.'

'Yes it is.'

'Clothes there, on the bed. Cutlery in the box. Basin. Cooker.
The meter's the same as the one you had last year. And you
saw the bathroom across the corridor.'

'Yes. Thank you. It's all fine.'

'Well, as I said. I was sorry we couldn't let you have your
other room. But you didn't give us much notice. And right
now, August, and such good weather, we're booked right up.'

'I understand. It was kind of you to find me this room. I was
lucky, wasn't I? The very last one.'

'It's usually the last to go, this one.'

'How odd. It's got such a lovely view of the sea and the bay.'

'Well, I didn't mean there was anything wrong with the room.'

'Of course not.'

'Mr Tinker always used to have this room. Every year, four months, June to September.'

'Oh, yes.'

'It was quite a shock last year, when his daughter rang to cancel. He died, just the night before he meant to take the train to come down. Heart attack. What a shame.'

'Yes, it was.'

'Well, I'll leave you to get settled in. You know where we are if you want anything.'

'Thank you very much, Mrs Rice.'

Mr Tinker, she thought, leaning on the closed door. *Tinker.* Like a dog, with one black ear. Here, Tinker! Don't be silly, she thought. It's just nerves. Arrival nerves. By-the-sea nerves. By-yourself nerves.

Caroline crossed to the window. She stared out at the esplanade where the brightly coloured summer people were walking about in the late afternoon sun. Beyond, the bay opened its arms to the sea. The little boats in the harbour lay stranded by an outgoing tide. The water was cornflower blue.

If David had been here, she would have told him that his eyes were exactly as blue as that sea, which wasn't at all the case. How many lies there had been between them. Even lies about eye colour. But she wasn't going to think of David. She had come here alone, as she had come here last season, to sketch, to paint, to meditate.

It was a pity, about not being able to have the other room. It had been larger, and the bathroom had been 'contained' rather than shared and across the hall. But then she hadn't been going to take the holiday flat this year. She had been trying to patch things up with David. Until finally, all the patching had come undone, and she'd grasped at this remembered place in a panic – I must get *away.*

Caroline turned her back to the window. She glanced about. Yes. Of course it was quite all right. If anything, the view was better because the flat was higher up. As for the actual room, it was like all the rooms. Chintz curtains, cream walls, brown rugs and jolly cushions. And Mr Tinker had taken good care of it. There was only one cigarette burn in the table. And probably that wasn't Mr Tinker at all. Somehow, she couldn't imagine Mr Tinker doing a thing like that. It must be the result of the other tenants, those people who had accepted the room as their last choice.

Well now. Make up the bed, and then go out for a meal. No, she was too tired for that. She'd get sandwiches from the little café downstairs, perhaps some wine from the off-licence. It would be a chance to swallow some sea air. Those first breaths that always made her giddy and unsure, like too much oxygen.

She made the bed up carefully, as if for two. When she moved it away from the wall to negotiate the sheets, she saw something scratched in the cream plaster.

'Oh, Mr Tinker, you naughty dog,' she said aloud, and then felt foolish.

Anyway, Mr Tinker wouldn't do such a thing. Scratch with a penknife, or even some of Mrs Rice's loaned cutlery. Black ink had been smeared into the scratches. Caroline peered down into the gloom behind the bed. *A room with a view*, the scratching said. Well, almost. Whoever it was had forgotten to put in the ultimate double-'u': *A room with a vie*. Either illiterate or careless. Or smitten with guilt nine-tenths through.

She pushed the bed back again. She'd better tell the Rices sometime. God forbid they should suppose she was the vandal.

She was asleep, when she heard the room breathing. She woke gradually, as if to a familiar and reassuring sound. Then, as gradually, a confused fear stole upon her. Presently she located the breathing sound as the noise of her own blood rhythm in her ears. Then, with another shock of relief, as the sea. But, in the end, it was not the sea either. It was the room, breathing.

A kind of itching void of pure terror sent her plunging upwards from the bed. She scrabbled at the switch and the bedside light flared on. Blinded and gasping, she heard the sound seep away.

Out at sea, a ship mooed plaintively. She looked at the window and began to detect stars over the water, and the pink lamps glowing along the esplanade. The world was normal.

Too much wine after too much train travel. Nightmare.

She lay down. Though her eyes watered, she left the light on.

'I'm afraid so, Mrs Rice. Someone's scratched and inked it on the wall. A nostalgia freak: *A room with a view*.'

'Funny,' said Mrs Rice. She was a homely woman with jet black gipsy hair that didn't seem to fit. 'Of course, there's been two or three had that room. No one for very long. Disgusting. Still, the damage is done.'

Caroline walked along the bay. The beach that spread from the south side was packed with holidaymakers. Everyone was paired, as if they meant to be ready for the ark. Some had a great luggage of children as well. The gulls and the children screamed.

Caroline sat drawing and the children raced screaming by. People stopped to ask her questions about the drawing. Some stared a long while over her shoulder. Some gave advice on perspective and subject matter. The glare of sun on the blue water hurt her eyes.

She put the sketchbook away. After lunch she'd go further along, to Jaynes Bay, which she recollected had been very quiet last year. This year, it wasn't.

After about four o'clock, gangs of local youth began to gather on the esplanade and the beach. Their hair was greased and their legs were like storks' legs in tight trousers. They whistled. They spoke in an impenetrable mumble which often flowered into four-letter words uttered in contrastingly clear diction.

There had been no gangs last year. The sun sank.

Caroline was still tired. She went along the esplanade to her block, up the steps to her room.

When she unlocked the door and stood on the threshold, for a moment—

What?

It was as if the pre-twilight amber that came into the room was slowly pulsing, throbbing. As if the walls, the floor, the ceiling were—

She switched on the overhead lamp.

'Mr Tinker,' she said firmly, 'I'm not putting up with this.'

'Pardon?' said a voice behind her.

Caroline's heart expanded with a sharp thud like a grenade exploding in her side. She spun around, and there stood a girl in jeans and a smock. Her hand was on the door of the shared bathroom. It was the previously unseen neighbour from down the hall.

'I'm sorry,' said Caroline. 'I must have been talking to myself.'

The girl looked blank and unhelpful.

'I'm Mrs Lacey,' she said. She did not look lacy. Nor married. She looked about fourteen. 'You've got number eight, then. How is it?'

Bloody nerve, Caroline thought.

'It's fine.'

'They've had three in before you,' said fourteen-year-old Mrs Lacey.

'All together?'

'Pardon? No. I meant three separate tenants. Nobody would stay. All kinds of trouble with that Mrs Rice. Nobody would, though.'

'Why ever not?' Caroline snapped.

'Too noisy or something. Or a smell. I can't remember.'

Caroline stood in her doorway, her back to the room.

Fourteen-year-old Mrs Lacey opened the bathroom door.

'At least we haven't clashed in the mornings,' Caroline said.

'Oh, *we're* always up early on holiday,' said young Mrs Lacey pointedly. Somewhere down the hall, a child began to bang and quack like an insane automatic duck. A man's voice bawled: 'Hurry up that piss, Brenda, will you?'

Brenda Lacey darted into the bathroom and the bolt was shot.

Caroline entered her room. She slammed the door. She turned on the room, watching it.

There *was* a smell. It was very slight. A strange, faintly buttery smell. Not really unpleasant. Probably from the café below. She pushed up the window and breathed the sea.

As she leaned on the sill, breathing, she felt the room start breathing too.

She was six years old, and Auntie Sara was taking her to the park. Auntie Sara was very loving. Her fat warm arms were always reaching out to hold, to compress, to pinion against her fat warm bosom. Being hugged by Auntie Sara induced in six-year-old Caroline a sense of claustrophobia and primitive fright. Yet somehow she was aware that she had to be gentle with Auntie Sara and not wound her feelings. Auntie Sara couldn't have a little girl. So she had to share Caroline with Mummy.

And now they were in the park.

'There's Jenny,' said Caroline. But of course Auntie Sara wouldn't want to let Caroline go to play with Jennifer. So Caroline pretended that Auntie Sara *would* let her go, and she ran very fast over the green grass towards Jenny. Then her foot caught in something. When she began to fall, for a moment it was exhilarating, like flying. But she hit the ground, stunning, bruising. She knew better than to cry, for in another moment Auntie Sara had reached her. 'It doesn't hurt,' said Caroline. But Auntie Sara took no notice. She crushed Caroline to her. Caroline was smothered on her breast, and the great round arms bound her like hot, faintly dairy-scented bolsters.

Caroline started to struggle. She pummelled, kicked and shrieked.

It was dark, and she had not fallen in the grass after all. She was in bed in the room, and it was the room she was fighting. It was the room which was holding her close, squeezing her, hugging her. It was the room which that faint cholesterol smell of fresh milk and butter. It was the room which was stroking and whispering.

But of course it couldn't be the damn room.

Caroline lay back exhausted, and the toils of her dream receded. Another nightmare. Switch on the light. Yes, that was it. Switch on the light and have a drink from the small traveller's bottle of gin she'd put ready in case she couldn't sleep.

'Christ.' She shielded her eyes from the light.

Distantly, she heard a child crying – the offspring probably of young Mrs unlacy Lacey along the hall. 'God, I must have yelled,' Caroline said aloud. Yelled and been heard. The unlacy Laceys were no doubt discussing her this very minute. The mad lazy slut in number eight.

The gin burned sweetly, going down.

This was stupid. The light – no, she'd have to leave the light on again.

Caroline looked at the walls. She could see them, very, very softly lifting, softly sinking. Don't be a fool. The smell was just discernible. It made her queasy. Too rich – yet, a human smell, a certain sort of human smell. Bovine, she concluded, exactly like poor childless Sara.

It was hot, even with the window open.

She drank halfway down the bottle and didn't care any more.

'Mr Tinker? Why ever are you interested in him?'

Mrs Rice looked disapproving.

'I'm sorry. I'm not being ghoulish. It's just – well, it seemed such a shame, his dying like that. I suppose I've been brooding.'

'Don't want to do that. You need company. Is your husband coming down at all, this year?'

'David? No, he can't get away right now.'

'Pity.'

'Yes. But about Mr Tinker—'

'All right,' said Mrs Rice. 'I don't see why I shouldn't tell you. He was a retired man. Don't know what line of work he'd been in, but not very well paid, I imagine. His wife was dead. He lived with his married daughter, and really I don't think it suited him, but there was no alternative. Then, four months of the year, he'd come here and take number eight. Done it for years. Used to get his meals out. Must have been quite expensive. But I think the daughter and her husband paid for everything, you know, to get a bit of time on their own. But he loved this place, Mr Tinker did. He used to say to me: "Here I am home again, Mrs Rice." The room with his daughter, I had the impression he didn't think of that as home at all. But number eight. Well, he'd put his ornaments and books and pieces round. My George even put a couple of nails in for him to hang a picture or two. Why not? And number eight got quite cosy. It really *was* Mr Tinker's room in the end. My George said that's why other tenants'd fight shy. They could feel it waiting for Mr Tinker to come back. But that's a lot of nonsense, and I can see I shouldn't have said it.'

'No. I think your husband was absolutely right. Poor old room. It's going to be disappointed.'

'Well, my George, you know, he's a bit of an idiot. The night – the night we heard, he got properly upset, my George. He went up to number eight, and opened the door and told it. I said to him, you'll want me to hang black curtains in there next.'

Beyond the fence, the headland dropped away in dry grass and the feverish flowers of late summer to a blue sea ribbed with white. North spread the curved claw of Jaynes Bay and the grey vertical of the lighthouse. But the sketch pad and pencil case sat on the seat beside Caroline.

She had attempted nothing. Even the novel lay closed. The first page hadn't seemed to make sense. She kept reading the words 'home' and 'Tinker' between the lines.

She understood she was afraid to return to the room. She had walked along the headlands, telling herself that all the room had wrong with it was sadness, a bereavement. That it wasn't waiting. That it wasn't alive. And anyway, even sadness didn't happen to rooms. If it did, it would have to get over that. Get used to being just a holiday flat again, a space which people filled for a few weeks, observed indifferently, cared nothing about, and then went away from.

Which was all absurd because none of it was true.

Except, that she wasn't the only one to believe—

She wondered if David would have registered anything in the room. Should she ring him and confide in him? Ask advice? No. For God's sake, that was why she was imagining herself into this state, wasn't it? So she could create a contact with him again. No. David was out and out David would stay.

It was five o'clock. She packed her block and pencils into her bag and walked quickly along the grass verge above the fence.

She could walk into Kingscliff at this rate, and get a meal.

She wondered who the scared punster had been, the one who knew French. She'd got the joke by now. A room with a vie: a room with a *life*.

She reached Kingscliff and had a pleasantly unhealthy meal, with a pagoda of white ice cream and glacé cherries to follow. In the dusk the town was raucous and cheerful. Raspberry and yellow neons splashed and spat and the motorbike gangs seemed suitable, almost friendly *in situ*. Caroline strolled by the whelk stalls and across the car park, through an odour of frying doughnuts, chips and fierce fish. She went to a cinema and watched a very bad and very pointless film with a sense of superiority and tolerance. When the film was over, she sat alone in a pub and drank vodka. Nobody accosted her or tried to pick her up. She was glad at first, but after the fourth vodka, rather sorry. She had to run to catch the last bus back. It was not until she stood on the esplanade, the bus vanishing, the pink lamps droning solemnly and the black water far below, that a real and undeniable terror came and twisted her stomach.

The café was still open, and she might have gone in there, but some of the greasy stork-legs she had seen previously were clustered about the counter. She was tight, and visualized sweeping amongst them, ignoring their adolescent nastiness. But presently she turned aside and into the block of holiday flats.

She dragged up the steps sluggishly. By the time she reached her door, her hands were trembling. She dropped her key and stifled a squeal as the short-time automatic hall light went out.

Pressing the light button, she thought: Supposing it doesn't come on?

But the light did come on. She picked up her key, unlocked the door and went determinedly inside the room, shutting the door behind her.

She experienced it instantly. It was like a vast, indrawn, sucking gasp.

'No,' Caroline said to the room. Her hand fumbled the switch and the room was lit.

Her heart was beating so very fast. That was, of course, what made the room also seem to pulse, as if its heart were also swiftly and greedily beating.

'Listen,' Caroline said. 'Oh God, talking to a *room*. But I have to, don't I? Listen, you've got to stop this. Leave me alone!' she shouted at the room.

The room seemed to grow still.

She thought of the Laceys, and giggled.

She crossed to the window and opened it. The air was cool. Stars gleamed above the bay. She pulled the curtains to, and undressed. She washed, and brushed her teeth at the basin. She poured herself a gin.

She felt the room, all about her. Like an inheld breath, impossibly prolonged. She ignored that. She spoke to the room quietly.

'Naughty Mr Tinker, to tinker with you, like this. Have to call you Sara now, shan't I? Like a great big womb. That's what she really wanted, you see. To squeeze me right through herself, pop me into her womb. I'd offer you a gin, but where the hell would you put it?'

Caroline shivered.

'No. This is truly silly.'

She walked over to the cutlery box beside the baby cooker. She put in her hand and pulled out the vegetable knife. It had quite a vicious edge. George Rice had them frequently sharpened.

'See this,' Caroline said to the room. 'Just watch yourself.'

When she lay down, the darkness whirled, carouselling her asleep.

In the womb, it was warm and dark, a warm blood dark. Rhythms came and went, came and went, placid and unending as the tides of the sea. The heart organ pumped with a soft deep noise like a muffled drum.

How comfortable and safe it was. But when am I to be born? Caroline wondered. Never, the womb told her, lapping her, cushioning her.

Caroline kicked out. She floated. She tried to seize hold of something, but the blood-warm cocoon was not to be seized.

'Let me go,' said Caroline. 'Auntie Sara, I'm all right. Let me go. I want to – please—'

Her eyes were wide and she was sitting up in her holiday bed. She put out her hand spontaneously towards the light and touched the knife she had left beside it. The room breathed, regularly, deeply. Caroline moved her hand away from the light switch, and saw in the darkness.

'This is ridiculous,' she said aloud.

The room breathed. She glanced at the window – she had left the curtains drawn over, and so could not focus on the esplanade beyond, or the bay: the outer world. The walls throbbed. She could *see* them. She was being calm now, and analytical, letting her eyes adjust, concentrating. The mammalian milky smell was heavy. Not precisely offensive, but naturally rather horrible, under these circumstances.

Very carefully, Caroline, still in darkness, slipped her feet out of the covers and stood up.

'All right,' she said. 'All right then.'

She turned to the wall behind the bed. She reached across and laid her hand on it—

The *wall*. The wall was – *skin*. It was flesh. Live, pulsing, hot, moist—

It was—

The wall swelled under her touch. It adhered to her hand eagerly. The whole room writhed a little, surging towards her. It wanted – she knew it wanted – to clutch her to its breast.

Caroline ripped her hand from the flesh wall. Its rhythms were faster, and the cowlike smell much stronger. Caroline whimpered. She was flung backwards and her fingers closed on the vegetable knife and she raised it.

Even as the knife plunged forwards, she knew it would skid or rebound from the plaster, probably slicing her. She knew all that, but could not help it. And then the knife thumped in, up to the handle. It was like stabbing into – into meat.

She jerked the knife away and free, and scalding fluid ran down her arm. I've cut myself after all. That's blood. But she felt nothing. And the room—

The room was screaming. She couldn't hear it, but the

scream was all around her, hurting her ears. She had to stop the screaming. She thrust again with the knife. The blade was slippery. The impact was the same. Boneless meat. And the heated fluid, this time, splashed all over her. In the thick unlight, it looked black. She dabbed frantically at her arm, which had no wound. But in the wall—

She stabbed again. She ran to another wall and stabbed and hacked at it.

I'm dreaming, she thought. Christ, why can't I wake up?

The screaming was growing dim, losing power.

'Stop it!' she cried. The blade was so sticky now she had to use both hands to drive it home. There was something on the floor, spreading, that she slid on in her bare feet. She struck the wall with her fist, then with the knife. 'Oh, Christ, please die,' she said.

Like a butchered animal, the room shuddered, collapsed back upon itself, became silent and immobile.

Caroline sat in a chair. She was going to be sick, but then the sickness faded. I'm sitting here in a pool of blood.

She laughed and tears started to run from her eyes, which was the last thing she remembered.

When she woke it was very quiet. The tide must be far out, for even the sea did not sound. A crack of light came between the curtains.

What am I doing in this chair?

Caroline shifted, her mind blank and at peace.

Then she felt the utter emptiness that was in the room with her. The dreadful emptiness, occasioned only by the presence of the dead.

She froze. She stared at the crack of light. Then down.

'Oh no,' said Caroline. She raised her hands.

She wore black mittens. Her fingers were stuck together.

Now her gaze was racing over the room, not meaning to, trying to escape, but instead alighting on the black punctures, the streaks, the stripes along the wall, now on the black stains, the black splotches. Her own body was dappled, grotesquely mottled with black. She had one white toe left to her, on her right foot.

Woodenly, she managed to get up. She staggered to the curtains and hauled them open and turned back in the full flood of early sunlight, and saw everything over again. The gashes in the wall looked as if they had been accomplished with a drill or a pick. Flaked plaster was mingled with the – with the – blood. Except that it wasn't blood. Blood wasn't black.

Caroline turned away suddenly. She looked through the window, along the esplanade, pale and laved with morning. She looked at the bright sea, with the two or three fishing boats scattered on it, and the blueness beginning to flush sky and water. When she looked at these things, it was hard to believe in the room.

Perhaps most murderers were methodical in the aftermath. Perhaps they had to be.

She filled the basin again and again, washing herself, arms, body, feet. Even her hair had to be washed. The black had no particular texture. In the basin it diluted. It appeared like a superior kind of Parker fountain-pen ink.

She dressed herself in jeans and shirt, filled the largest saucepan with hot water and washing-up liquid. She began to scour the walls.

Soon her arms ached, and she was sweating the cold sweat of nervous debility. The black came off easily, but strange tangles of discoloration remained behind in the paint. Above, the holes did not ooze, they merely gaped. Inside each of them was chipped plaster and brick – not bone, muscle or tissue. There was no feel of flesh anywhere.

Caroline murmured to herself. 'When I've finished.' It was quite matter-of-fact to say that, as if she were engaged in a normality. 'When I've finished, I'll go and get some coffee downstairs. I won't tell Mrs Rice about the holes. No, not yet. How can I explain them? I couldn't have caused that sort of hole with a knife. There's the floor to do yet. And I'd better wash the rugs. I'll do them in the bath when the ghastly Laceys go out at nine o'clock. When I've finished, I'll get some coffee. And I think I'll ring David. I really think I'll have to. When I finish.'

She thought about ringing David. She couldn't guess what he'd say. What could *she* say, come to that? Her back ached now, and she felt sick, but she kept on with her work. Presently she heard energetic intimations of the Laceys visiting the bathroom, and the duck-child quacking happily.

She caught herself wondering why blood hadn't run when the nails were hammered in the walls for Mr Tinker's pictures. But that was before the room really came to life, maybe. Or maybe the room had taken it in the spirit of beautification, like having one's ears pierced for gold earrings. Certainly the knife scratches had bled.

Caroline put down the cloth and went over to the basin and was sick.

Perhaps I'm pregnant, she thought, and all this is a hallucination of my fecundity.

David, I am pregnant, and I stabbed a room to death.

David.

David?

It was a boiling hot day, one of the last-fling days of the summer. Everything was blanched by the heat, apart from the apex of the blue sky and the core of the green-blue sea. Caroline wore a white dress. A quarter before each hour, she told herself she would ring David on the hour: ten o'clock, eleven, twelve. Then she would 'forget'. At one o'clock she rang him, and he was at lunch as she had known he would be, really.

Caroline went on the pier. She put money into little machines which whizzed and clattered. She ate a sandwich in a café. She walked along the sands, holding her shoes by the straps.

At half past four she felt compelled to return.

She had to speak to Mrs Rice, about the holes in the walls.

And then again, perhaps she should go up to number eight first. It seemed possible that the dead room would somehow have righted itself. And then, too, there were the washed rugs drying over the bath that the unlaceys might come in and see. Caroline examined why she was so flippant and so cheerful. It was, of course, because she was afraid.

She went into the block, and abruptly she was trembling. As she climbed the steps, her legs melted horribly, and she wished she could crawl, pulling herself by her fingers.

As she came up to the landing, she beheld Mr Lacey in the corridor. At least, she assumed it was Mr Lacey. He was overweight and tanned a peachy gold by the sun. He stood. glowering at her, blocking the way to her door. He's going to complain about the noise, she thought. She tried to smile, but no smile would oblige.

'I'm Mr Lacey,' he announced. 'You met the wife the other day.'

He sounded nervous rather than belligerent. When Caroline didn't speak, he went on, 'My Brenda, you see. She noticed this funny smell from number eight. When you come along to the bathroom, you catch it. She was wondering if you'd left some meat out, forgotten it.'

'No,' said Caroline.

'Well, I reckoned you ought to be told,' said Mr Lacey.

'Yes, thank you.'

'I mean, don't take this the wrong way, but we've got a kid. You can't be too careful.'

'No. You can't.'

'Well, then.' He swung himself aside and moved a short way down the corridor towards the Lacey flat. Caroline went to her door. She knew he was watching her with his two shining Lacey piggy eyes. She turned and stared at him, her heart striking her side in huge bruising blows, until he grunted and went off.

Caroline stood before the door. She couldn't smell anything. No, there was nothing, nothing at all.

The stink came in a wave, out of nowhere. It smote her and she nearly reeled. It was foul, indescribably foul. And then it was gone.

Delicately, treading soft, Caroline stepped away from the door. She tiptoed to the head of the stairs. Then she ran.

But like someone drawn to the scene of an accident, she couldn't entirely vacate the area. She sat on the esplanade, watching.

The day went out over the town, and the dusk seeped from the sea. In the dusk, a police car came and drew up outside the block. Later, another.

It got dark. The lamps, the neons and the stars glittered, and Caroline shuddered in her thin frock.

The stork-legs had gathered at the café. They pointed and jeered at the police cars. At the garden pavilion, a band was playing. Far out on the ocean, a great tanker passed, garlanded with lights.

At nine o'clock, Caroline found she had risen and was walking across the esplanade to the holiday block. She walked right through the crowd of stork-legs. 'Got the time?' one of them yelled, but she paid no heed, didn't even flinch.

She went up the steps, and on the first flight she met two very young policemen.

'You can't come up here, miss.'

'But I'm staying here,' she said. Her mild voice, so reasonable, interested her. She missed what he asked next.

'I said, what number, miss.'

'Number eight.'

'Oh. Right. You'd better come up with me, then. You hang on here, Brian.'

They climbed together, like old friends.

'What's the matter?' she questioned him, perversely.

'I'm not quite sure, miss.'

They reached the landing.

All the way up from the landing below, the stench had been intensifying, solidifying. It was unique. Without ever having smelled such an odour before, instinctively and at once you knew it was the perfume of rottenness. Of decay and death.

Mrs Rice stood in the corridor, her black hair in curlers, and she was absentmindedly crying. Another woman with a handkerchief to her nose, patted Mrs Rice's shoulder. Behind a shut door, a child also cried, vehemently. Another noise came from the bathroom; someone vomiting.

Caroline's door was wide open. A further two policemen were on the threshold. They seemed to have no idea of how to proceed. One was wiping his hands with a cloth, over and over.

Caroline gazed past them, into the room.

Putrescent lumps were coming away from the walls. The ceiling dribbled and dripped. Yet one moment only was it like the flesh of a corpse. Next moment, it was plaster, paint and crumbling brick. And then again, like flesh. And then again—

'Christ,' one of the policemen said. He faced about at his audience. He too was young. He stared at Caroline randomly. 'What are we supposed to do?'

Caroline breathed in the noxious air. She managed to smile at last, kindly, inquiringly, trying to help.

'Bury it?'

Daphne Castell

Diminishing landscape with indistinct figures

*Daphne Castell didn't answer my letter which asked what she
had been up to since the last time I used one of her stories, and
it is quite possible that she was too busy to respond. When I
wrote about her in* Superhorror *I noted that she teaches ESN
children, evening classes on effective speaking and English for
the profoundly deaf, plays percussion in a band, sings contralto
in a choir, broadcasts on BBC, lives in Oxford with three
eccentric children and five evil cats, and is interested in all
manner of things. Her work has appeared in* Fantasy & Science
Fiction, New Worlds, Amazing, Science Fantasy, *various
anthologies and a host of journals. She dreams most of her
plots, and this may be the most dreamlike of her tales, and the
most subtly disturbing.*

At the top of the hill, I stopped for a moment, before coasting
down the last great sweep of road.

My friend's estate lay under the sunset, basking submissively
in its medieval colours. In this lonely bay, a niche in the curved
heights of hills, I looked down over little trailing plumes of
blue smoke from a dozen roofs, no more. They invited comment, and then companionship. Not entirely distinct from the
small clouds which skirted hillsides, or from the ground-cling-
ing mists which masked marshes or snared thickets, they were
still strong with the scent of humanness; and the mist and the
clouds were the persuasive voices of wild places.

The thin trembling sticks of saplings blemished the new
brown ploughland, as young as the baby crows that squawked
in nests, high in the elms but still a hundred feet below me.
There were very small blue and yellow flowers in a bracket of
earth mounted on the stone wall round my solitary bay, and
something lacewinged and skinny was hatching out from a

chrysalis at my elbow. Spring was at its beginnings, and so many things were young and small and new that they had more power to spread and overtake than you would have thought possible. You looked at an elm tree and saw its significant rough power, not the brown heart-rot that ate away its strength in age and disease. The ploughed earth ran at your feet, a simple and elementary statement of all foundations, but everywhere runnelled and channelled with fine feathery green, the new-planted stuff that disdained and conquered its sources.

The coming of evening quietened even the light wind that had done no more than move the old tufts of last year's seed pods, and I felt frost coming quietly with the night, and shivered, and got into my car.

The visit was so ill-arranged, really almost inexplicable. I had known him, but not seen him, for many years, I had read with interest of his work, I was on holiday in these regions, and a little bored.

We talked on the phone, and he had referred vaguely to what he was doing now, and said that he was taking a break. I might come and stay with him for a few days perhaps? I would be very welcome. But don't decide in too much of a hurry. There was really nothing to do there. 'It's all being done, anyway,' he said, laughing faintly over the telephone. 'It takes care of itself, my research.'

The idea of research that you started, and that then proceeded happily and perhaps inevitably of its own accord, pleased and attracted me. He was always such a gentle, apologetic person. He seemed to approach the processes that he set in motion with polite caution, as if he hoped not to offend them by influencing them at all. This was understandable – after all, for much of his life he was in close contact with the mentally disturbed, and with their investigators and protectors and interpreters. It was sometimes difficult to know which of these people was the most easily roused. Certainly I have seen a specialist near to frothing at the mouth, at a suggestion that some of his patients were not nearly fit to be loosed upon society; and I have seen a nurse actually strike heavily a new trainee who had been impatient with some old man, lugging him about like a sack.

My friend hovered about these distinctive little worlds, never really resting in any of them, observing and using, and sensibly not involving himself too far or too deeply, like so many men.

Like his name, he remained aloft and distant – I have forgotten to say that he was called Peregrine, Peregrine Ogden. He wasn't married, and his friends did not use his first name – I don't know why, except perhaps that in friendship, as in knowledge and observation, he did not settle closely, or cling, only touched in passing, and remained near but apart. It is not easy to call a man by his Christian name when his attention is partly elsewhere.

My own name is John Bates – my acquaintances, and my one or two friends call me 'Jack', and the laboratory assistants and technicians call me 'Batesy', behind my back. I am not in the least like my friend Ogden, but we used to get on very well indeed, in a quiet way, though I cannot truthfully say I have ever understood him. However, he tells me that he doesn't understand me, or at least cannot appreciate the way in which the mind functions in a man of my type, which comes to almost the same thing.

I drove slowly and peaceably as usual, conscious now that I was slightly nonplussed about how I was going to meet him, and what we were going to say to each other. I contemplated with dismay the idea that we might say everything we had to say in the first hour or two, and then not really be able to speak to each other for the rest of the few days I was to remain there. As the lancets of trees striped past my window in the late sun, I was wishing I had not decided to come; only commonsense told me that this had happened so often on other visits to other places, and that I would no doubt enjoy myself very much, when the initial embarrassments and insistence upon courtesies had been overcome. And there would be other people there, I assumed. It was a very large place; and the dead relative had left him a good deal of money with it.

I wondered what his research was exactly – he had plenty of room for it, as I could see. I drove through a barely noticeable metal gate and along a weedy stretch of gravel path. Then there was another entry – this time a pair of high old stone pillars with some sort of mythical bird on each, and no gate. The bird, I thought, was a phoenix open-mouthed with envy and ecstasy, poised and just about to arise in renewed life, balanced on one toe and a crude stone ball that might have represented a new world.

The pillars extended and dwindled rapidly down into an ancient wall on each side of the drive. The round tops of the walls were mossy, sage-green and orange with lichen, and under them stones had crumbled out like pieces of rotten cheese, leaving holes bordered by lips and teeth of more rotting stone. In the park beyond the fences that followed the disappearance of these walls, deer ambled in sparse, anxious herds, taking off with huge fretful leaps as my car came level with them.

I fancied that their hides looked pitted and motheaten, with lack of care, like the wall, but they did not stay still long enough for me to be sure. Perhaps Ogden's relative had not left him so much money that he could afford to keep the estate going smoothly.

But when I reached the house itself, it was apparent that a good deal had been spent on retaining its massive dignified charm. Smoothly reticent about its age, it contained a number of styles, none of them recent, all of them harmoniously blending. The colour of the walls was indescribable – dull cream with apricot shadows moving imperceptibly into grey stone shaded with moss and stencilled with small creepers, with here and there an unobtrusive patch of old mellow brick, lined with thick dark timber. Even a small modern shed, which obviously housed an electric generator, sheltered itself apologetically in shrubs, and appeared to have attempted to reduce its new wood as quickly as possible to a shade congenial to the more aristocratic tones that neighboured it.

Perhaps the only discordant note was struck by the statue of a man that stood some way off amongst the trees. It was extraordinarily modern – it wore clothes; and, in fact, I might have been able to mistake it for a more than ordinarily motionless human being, except for the pitted grey stone texture of the face, and the arms and legs, which were not covered. I thought that Ogden's relative must have been unusually eccentric, to cover his statues with simulacra of clothing; and then I wondered whether Ogden himself had changed, or extended his personality to encompass a new oddity.

The small patches of vivid orange lichen that had grown on the old wall along the driveway grew on the statue too, and on the roof of the house I was looking at, and above some of the windows. I have always liked the colours of lichens and mosses, and this particular orange was a charming flare of contrast.

There seemed to be absolutely no one around, but it was obvious that I was approaching the house by the back quarters, and therefore I presumably had quite a long way to go before I found living company, apart from the deer.

I could not imagine how guests had approached in their

coaches, in times gone by, invited to some wedding festivity or to celebrate Christmas with Ogden's ancestors. There must be a broader sweep of drive, perhaps with an entry on to some old coach road, now closed and gone, turned into farmland, perhaps.

I had stopped the car at first sight of the house, preserved and almost new-looking in its well-cared-for serenity, and now I drove on, through two more sets of stone entries and several arched gateways, presumably once leading to mews and kennels, since the drive gave way first to paved stone, and then to cobbles.

Once more I stopped the car, anxious not to miss any entry to the part of the house in which Ogden lived. From the passage in which I was now, several other large passages led off. They all appeared to be covered in, and some had walls all along them, but some were open to the weather in many places, and it seemed possible to run in and out of one side of a passage, into another, and so to another. I could almost have driven the car in and out of each aperture, like a horse in a bending race, at a gymkhana. I got out to explore one passage. There was absolutely nothing in it, except for a few large doors, locked and barred. At the end, in the open air, stood a large iron trolley. To this day I have no idea whether it was ever used, or for what purpose. There was so much about the house I never discovered.

At the end of another passage, I thought I could just see the figure of a woman, her head bent to one side as if she were listening. However, when I moved towards her, she disappeared round the corner of the passage, and although I stepped outside as quickly as I could, she was not visible outside the passage, along the wall. It was as if she had stepped sideways into some other dimension. I did not see her again, and I have no idea who she was, though I think, from what I learnt later, that she must have been a patient.

All the passages were empty, and all the doors in them were closed, and even when they looked as if they might easily be unbarred, they led only to the outside – perhaps at some former time there had been other outbuildings attached to them.

I thought it better to drive on, though I seemed to be taking a long time, by this route, to get to the house proper. My arrival, at last, was quite unexpected. I turned through one more pair of high gates, masking everything before me from sight, and found myself facing a lower, smaller portion of the house, more informal and cottage-like, apart from a high central part, rather like a flat-roofed water tower.

Round the circular gravel patch in which the drive ended were several cars, and a number of people were moving quickly in and out of the building. It was such an odd sensation to have been driving through and past apparently uninhabited buildings for so long, and now to find this busy corner of human beings, that for a moment I was almost uneasy. It was so stupid, for obviously the whole of the house was too big to be lived in, and Ogden and his friends, or staff, or whoever the cars belonged to, would not waste any time in wandering through the unusable part of it. They would come straight here. At the same time, looking back on the areas I had left, I could see that they were sometimes used by somebody for something. A group of heads had gathered in one of the more distant windows, obviously to watch the activities near the water tower buildings. I could see a hand waving from the window, and one of the people near me responded cheerfully, with a wave of his own.

I could see Ogden now, and he hadn't changed. He was apparently deep in conversation with a friend or employee, and he was wearing a white coat. From time to time he looked absently round him, as if he were expecting some event. And so he was, of course – he was awaiting my arrival, but he hadn't yet noticed the car. As I edged it gently forward, it shuddered a little, as it does occasionally when I drive it too slowly. As I brought it to a halt, I noticed a slow puff of some kind of vapour or smoke coming from an upper window of the tower. Even above the engine I heard a sharp thumping blast of sound, and then there was another puff, this time of a different colour, a sort of dim pink. It could have been flame-lit smoke, or a crowd of very tiny fragments of something.

Ogden saw the car and started forward, his face open with welcome. He looked really pleased to see me. Most of the people with him had hurried into the building. I got out of the car, and he exclaimed, and shook my hand, and patted me on the shoulder, and made all the proper remarks about how long the time had been, and how little the changes.

'An unsuccessful experiment?' I asked, gesturing at the smoking window. At once, the expression on his face changed peevishly.

'Oh, a great disappointment, really, my dear Bates, you remember how *wrong* things can go. And we were really rather looking forward to seeing the results of this. We didn't expect quite such a disaster, though I suppose one must be prepared for anything, and it was just on the cards that a similar sad thing might happen.'

I was rather struck by the tone of mourning in which he referred to a sad thing happening. Ogden had always been dedicated, of course, but experiments can always be set up again. Nothing is unrepeatable. I said something of the sort, as I was getting my bag out of the car, and Ogden sighed.

'This one would only be repeatable by sweet chance, I'm afraid, my friend. Some experiments, as you know, demand the cooperation of human beings, and the human element is always unpredictable. Tell me, what do you think of the place?' He said this with childlike eagerness.

'Marvellous!' I said. 'But so huge I was almost afraid to venture in. How on earth do you look after it all?'

He looked round him thoughtfully, and I heard from him a deep sigh as if of pleasure and refreshment. Certainly the trees and the sweep of grass and the old distant building were a fulfilment in themselves.

'I think, you know, I really think the place looks after itself. Or at least, the parts of it sometimes seem self-sufficient. There are plenty of – er – plenty of people scattered about in it. They all do their own work, where it's necessary, Bates, where it's necessary. And where it isn't—' he shaded his eyes with his hand, and looked beyond me and into long distances, apparently lost in the intricacies of his own musings.

'Where it isn't—?' I prompted him, remembering the uncared-for wall.

'Oh—' he waved a dismissive hand '—well, where it isn't, things are probably self-renewing, like trees or other living things, or perhaps they simply fade and crumble and decay, and that, too, in its own way is very picturesque and satisfactory.'

He called over a pleasant, round-faced man in a green jacket, who picked up my bag and beamed at me.

'Charley Tent,' introduced Ogden. 'Part nurse, part orderly, part guardian, entirely whole, kind, helpful human. Not a dissident notion in him, no maladjustment anywhere.' It seemed to me rather a dubiously detailed compliment, but Charley Tent obviously liked it.

'Not many we can say that of here, Mr Ogden,' he grinned,

but Ogden, for a moment, looked distinctly put out.

'That's not fair, Charley – they're all settling in their various ways – well, most of them.' His eyes strayed unhappily towards the window in the tower-like building.

'That's all right, Mr Ogden, only my little way, you know that,' said Charley, not at all disturbed. 'Very nice to meet you, sir. I do hope you'll find it both interesting and peaceful here. Our work, Mr Ogden's, that is to say, but we're all with him in it, absolutely heart and soul, our work, sir, couldn't possibly be more fascinating or more worthwhile. I hope you'll stay to see that for yourself.

'And the place, sir, well, you can see that already – we're very fortunate indeed, that Mr Ogden should have needed us to help him here, don't you think that already, sir?' He looked anxiously at me, almost as if he were wagging a non-existent tail, and I thought him a simple and warming personality – a bit gushing, true, but very much at one with his own way of life.

Ogden introduced me to half a dozen more of his staff, or friends, or colleagues – it's still difficult for me to know what to call them. There was Margaret, a still, kindly person, thick-set and reassuring in a tweed suit, a specialist of some kind, I didn't catch what.

There was a tall slender foreign girl, Magdalen Anima, of all unlikely things a most expert anaesthetist, so Ogden assured me, shy but smiling. I wondered if there were more than a trace of self-consciousness about him, as he introduced her. She was certainly very lovely and poised, as darkly beautiful and well-groomed as a model.

There was Henry, Bruggins, or Druggins, whose surname I never did learn properly – perhaps I wasn't paying sufficient attention after Magdalen. Henry was a doctor, and so were two or three more of them – a man called Sayers, with a perpetual tic, and sandy, greying hair, Stein, very silent, short, fat, dark – Macdonald, whom I remembered vaguely from a convention in London, a gawky young man with an irritating laugh. There were two or three nurses, too, and a scattering of the psychiatric arts.

Ogden produced two of them with great pride, from the crowd, like a magician with a rabbit from a hat, and I wondered again why they were all gathered on the ground in front of the building. But perhaps they had anticipated the technical trouble that led to the explosion or whatever it had been.

'Dr Aimy,' said Ogden almost formally, 'and his colleague, Dr Briars, both of them extremely interested in our work here, and really responsible in the main for our successes. If I hadn't persuaded them to leave their Geneva and their Toronto clinics respectively – well, the place wouldn't be here, it wouldn't be working, and now I'm wasting your time, because we're all going in to have food in a moment, and when Charley has taken your bag up, you'll be meeting all these quite splendid people properly and talking to them as you would wish.'

Aimy and Briars, plump, fair men, remarkably alike, smiled at me with sleepy sympathy, and continued a subdued conversation, after just the little break necessary to say something polite. One of them – Aimy, I fancy – patted Charley on the shoulder affectionately, as if he hadn't seen him for a while. Indeed, as I followed Charley through the gently dispersing nuclei of people, most of them seemed to have some greeting or smile for him, and one or two shouted anxious questions, to which he replied reassuringly.

We went in under the tower, turned right, and found ourselves in yet another of the long bare passages, punctuated with barred doors.

'Will the car be all right there?' I asked.

Charley turned, with a smile and a nod, and shifted my bag to his other hand. 'I'll move it for you – soon as I've seen them serving dinner, I'll go and see that it's put away in one of the garages.'

'That's kind of you,' I said, 'but don't miss your food for me. Oh, and let me know where the garage is, won't you? I'd hate to come to the day of my departure, bags packed and everything, and then find I'd mislaid my car.'

Charley answered quite seriously: 'Well, I'll tell you what, sir, you wouldn't be the first. Of course, if you consider what we've got here—' but then his voice died away and he seemed to be communing contentedly with himself, as he went before me, down the long bare windswept passage.

We trod through a couple of completely empty rooms, through a short, dark annexe of some kind, and up a flight of carpetless stairs.

'The Vera Locke wing, this is,' explained Charley. 'Come here with all her money, she did, not a friend or relative to leave it to, and she give it all to Mr Ogden. "Peregrine," she says – I can hear her hoarse old voice now, "People think I'm as mad as a hatter, and they're not far wrong" – but of course she had a lot of sane moments, sir, they all do – "but," she says to him "I'm giving you all my money now, because I've known you for years, and I know you'll either do me some good, or you'll do someone else some good. And if you can't do anything else man, and I'm pushing up the daisies, for heaven's sake use it to put some central heating into this benighted dump." That's what she said, sir, and we're going to have that done. Only we haven't got round to it. We've got a lift in, though, which was another thing she fancied. I'll show you, in case you want it – but it's a bit further over, round the other side of the building, away from most of the offices, but near the gardens, the herb gardens that is and the knot garden. Here's your room, sir. I brought you the quickest way, though you mightn't think it.'

The room was extraordinarily pleasant and comfortable, very low, with long, low, white-painted windows, and natural-coloured wooden walls and floor. There were large hand-made rugs on the floor, and a brilliant patchwork quilt on the enormous bed. There were several large cupboards, not with doors but with bright, woven hangings, and a number of mirrors, as if whoever had planned the room fancied that people might enjoy watching themselves from all angles. The windows were open, and I could smell the old-fashioned scent of clove-pinks.

'This is delightful,' I said. 'Mrs Locke – Miss Locke? – must be pleased, in her moments of clarity, with what her money has done?' I looked inquiringly at Charley, and he obliged me with an evasive reply. 'Well, she's still here, yes, but in a sense, she doesn't know much of what goes on about her. Poor lady! Yes, it's a nice room, isn't it? Mr Ogden, he always says that people, and where and how they fit in are the most important things he knows, never mind what they've done in the past, or how wrong the human race has been. Mr Ogden says we must concentrate on getting even a small part of it right, in the mind, you know, not so much the body, and if we get the mind comfortable and suited in itself, whatever that happens to be for it, then we shall be doing as we ought to.'

'And what do you think about the body, Charley?'

He looked sorrowfully at me. 'I wish I knew – when I looks about and sees what some of them can do to themselves, just for want of understanding, and sheer common care and affection and attention – I was thinking of things like drink and drugs, you understand, sir, but mostly of little things like not feeding themselves properly, because they was in a depression, or always knocking the same place, partly out of awkwardness, but partly because they've picked that spot out deliberately, to kind of pay themselves back for something – they couldn't tell you what, and I can't, though Mr Ogden might know. And then there's those that'll really tear themselves, not all the time, only perhaps when they see or hear one thing, or when there's something particular they've got on their plate, or perhaps on some days of the week – we get a lot of what they call the autistic ones, here. He has mostly those, and some with schizoid tendencies.'

Charley brought the words out smoothly enough, and with a lack of self-consciousness that told me how long he must have been helping Peregrine Ogden with his work.

Observation and treatment of mental diseases is not something I know much about, but I knew how well Peregrine had succeeded in many of the cases he undertook – though who can ever say how much of a cure is due to the work of the psychiatrist, and how much to the efforts of a patient? When the mind is not quite submerged enough for it to have lost all desire to return to dry land, it will sometimes, somehow, reach out from what seems a wild waste of uncontrollable waters, and cling to the most unlikely spar of rescue, and somehow bring itself ashore. It hadn't happened, evidently, to Vera Locke.

Charley laid my bags beside the bed, and quietly straightened rugs, pulled curtains across, for it was nearly dark now. He showed me how to find light switches, and politely guided me out of the room towards the lift.

'Nice and new, it is, all clean pink paint.' And it was, a smooth curving expanse of pillars and panelling and decoration, with a small moving box that slid up and down so silently you couldn't hear it from outside the panels. As I stepped into it, something nagged at my attention. I stopped and leaned back to look sideways – I had been right. Something about the pillars at the side, and the decorations above reminded me of a woman's limbs – curving, rounded cylinders, stretching up, as if she lifted her arms straight above her hair, from the bend of her waist, above her hips. The head must be turned sideways, because the flow of the decoration was so much like spread curls, running along the top of the lift. Charley's thick fist, laid negligently just above the waist, somehow enhanced the impression.

'This is really a most unexpected place, in many ways,' I said.

'Ah. Depends on what we expect, don't it, sir? Preconceived notions, what they say. I wish I knew what some of those poor folk expect, I really do.' It was spoken with affectionate, but disquieting passion. 'Still,' communed Charley to himself, 'Mr Ogden knows most of it, and we watches. We takes hints, and does a bit of guiding, whenever it seems, like, necessary. It'd surprise you how many find themselves here, what've been pretty well lost for good, it seems like, in other places.'

'I'm sure,' I said inadequately. Charley's passionate concern for the misplaced mind in a world of solidly domiciled minds shamed me deeply. It was not that I did not feel the same concern; it was more that I had never taken it upon myself to be its champion, its protagonist against the invisible hydra monster, mist-world of delusion. I suppose that basically, in my core of being, I like a world of construction. I have always supposed that you could never mix construction and delusion. How wrong I was!

We went downstairs in the lift, and round a number of turns in the everlasting long high passages. At one stage I was not in the least surprised to find myself under the cone of a medieval dovecote, or pigeon house. It was a little like the Colosseum, with its tiers of roosting perches, but no windows, of course.

'Hello, Marion.' Charley opened a door, and peeped in, smiling. It was most extraordinary – I tried to follow him in, but you could hardly enter the place for the crowded, happy noise of children bustling about the place, swinging on each other's hands and playing, falling over unsteady feet, half-singing as they went. You really could not find room, for the place was full, or seemed full, to capacity. Yet there was only a pretty, middle-aged, rather haggard woman, very skinny, crouched in a corner. She had the deepest, most welcoming smile. I have felt the same sensation once in a house where a very successful party had been held, just after the last of the guests had left.

'Going well, is it, dear? Mr Ogden's ever so pleased, I know,' said Charley tenderly. She nodded and smiled that beautiful, enveloping smile, full of secret and undirected happiness, but her eyes were turned upon other corners of the room, and I am quite certain she saw neither of us, though she obviously heard Charley.

I seemed to be fending off small humanity at large, as we

staggered out, but really I was most unclear about what had actually happened.

'Marion'll be going soon, I should think – as clear as ever I saw. You could feel it yourself, couldn't you? Now wasn't that lovely, don't you think?' Charley guided me skilfully by the elbow round another of the interminable bends.

I didn't know what to say. 'You mean you think she'll be fit to leave?' I asked. 'It seemed to me—'

Charley interrupted reproachfully. 'Oh, she wouldn't want to say leave – not *leave*, that is. Not that any of us'd want to – though there's a lot who've got good other places to go to. No, no, I meant her treatment was obviously coming along so successful – nearly there, she is. I wish I'd be able to find something as good.'

I wanted to pursue the topic of Marion's fitness or unfitness for real life – she had looked to me so totally remote from human communion, but this was a new and fascinating side track.

'Do you mean you had treatment of this sort, or something like it once?'

'Oh, yes, but with me it didn't really take – or perhaps you could say it wasn't needed. I was too near to normal you see. I came back before Mr Ogden could properly get to me.' It seemed an odd way of putting it. Charley threw back his head and laughed, a clear chuckle of enjoyment, full of kindness and indulgence. 'I was very near what they called a mass murderer, you see. I couldn't see my way to bringing up a family in this nuclear world we've got now. So I shot my wife and the kiddie, and I went out with the rifle. That's where I'm a bit unclear, but I must have been near enough insane then, because I wanted to go and shoot a whole lot of innocent people who might have had different ideas about living in the nuclear society. Just as well the police caught up with me then, and of course, when Mr Ogden asked to have me, partway through treatment – silly, isn't it, I still keep fancying what he might have made of me if only I'd been that bit further off. But I had to come back – oh, I'd had fancies, grant you, but then they were based on something very near and real.'

I don't deny that this revelation came as a shock to me; but there was something about the atmosphere of the whole place, which cushioned the shock, as it were. And, in fact, my attention had already been caught by clean white doors opening off to the right, through which I fancied I could see perhaps familiar instruments and equipment, and smell well-known odours. There would have to be laboratories in a place like this, of course. It has always seemed to me that a well-kept, well-equipped laboratory, preferably without other research workers, but with perhaps one unobtrusive assistant, must be the nearest thing to perfection that the limits of our unsatisfactory sciences can show. I had begun insensibly to edge towards the white doors, each with its little oval window, shining like a tender jewel.

Charley's arm drew me firmly onwards, as he observed: 'I expect Mr Ogden'll want to show you over them himself, personal. Then there's the computer, too. We had another patient left us another legacy to pay for that – mind, I don't want to give the idea a lot of them die. Most of them is a great success. It's rare we has one die, but some of 'em prefer to give us something before they go on to the next stage.'

At the very point of my muttering: 'Computer! Good gracious, his own computer,' Charley threw open a large, ornately panelled door with a flourish, and I was in the dining room. It was a pleasantly luxurious place, with good thick carpeting, small tables, none holding more than six people, concealed lighting, and, I was pleased to see, waitress service at the tables. The walls were elegantly dressed with pale-green Regency striped paper, and the carved wooden pairs of wall candlesticks that adorned them at intervals were beautifully designed. A view of the lawns and some of the trees was framed in the heavy brown velvet curtains.

Charley left me with a slight mutter, and went forward rather quickly to shut a pair of doors that lay just open beyond them.

I could catch only a glimpse of a much more disordered series of tables, and figures either motionless or moving very quickly. One pair appeared to be waltzing, and were leaning back from each other at an extreme angle that reminded me oddly of something I had seen.

'Patients' dining room,' said Charley apologetically, and then, with perhaps slight reproach, to Peregrine Ogden, who was waving at me from a window table: 'The new guest, Mr Ogden – the guest, I should say, anyway, and the doors were open again, sir.'

'Doesn't matter, doesn't matter,' Peregrine tapped a fork on the table, and one of the stout, kind-eyed women came over to bring me a menu. The two doctors, Aimy and Briars, Magdalen

Anima, and the taciturn but amiable Henry Bruggins or Druggins, shared the table. Charley disappeared towards a table in the darkest corner of the dining room. Apparently all staff here ate together. Even the waitresses, when they had ascertained (from Charley, of course) that no one else was to come, sat down together at a larger table along one side of the room, and had their own meal.

'I suppose not all your patients will eat,' I remarked, for want of something better to say. Ogden put down his fork and looked at me with an air of pleased surprise.

'There, now,' he nodded at Aimy. 'I knew it. I knew that keen analytical mind of yours would begin to enjoy itself as soon as you got here.' Aimy smiled back at me, and said, 'Yes, yes, indeed!', in what sounded like a rather complimentary tone of voice. I wondered what my research colleagues, and the rather objectionable technicians who call me 'Batesy' behind my back would have felt about the respect of those around me now. Surprised, I am almost certain.

'Now just what made you draw that conclusion, in particular, I am wondering?' asked Briars, lighting a cigarette. I do object to people who smoke between courses. But I suppose all of us need some dummy, some crutch, to support us against too much contact with rude reality.

'Oh, the patient Charley called Marion,' I explained. 'I could see that she was quite removed from the normal commerce of the everyday world – or at last, I hope I am allowed to say that. I'm speaking as someone with no knowledge whatsoever, of course.'

'But that's good, that's very good,' said Magdalen Anima, with a shake of her pretty hair, 'for one so new to the place to see and feel that. It's wonderful for Marion, isn't it?'

Fortunately, some soup was brought for me. I ate it, without knowing quite what reply to make.

In the meantime Ogden was continuing to congratulate himself on the inspiration that had led him to invite me. I was surprised to hear how much he remembered about me.

'You'll like it here, you in particular,' he was saying. 'The peace, the tolerance. We have to have tolerance, of course.'

'An essential,' smiled Aimy. 'But then tolerance should be an essential to all human creatures who do not consider that, being founded from the animal, they have a duty at times to make obeisance to it.'

'And the laboratories, you'll be welcome to go there, use

them, browse if you want to,' Ogden was saying to me, 'help if you want, don't if you don't want. Small staff, well-trained, decent people with nice manners and a genuine interest in research.' I had almost forgotten that such people existed. 'Some of our work comes fairly near your own field, you see,' continued Ogden. 'One can't always tell just what part chemistry will take in the troubles of our people.

'The child with galactosaemia, phenylketonuria, born into a scheme of nourishment foreign to its own body, but undoubtedly born of human parents. Of course, that could be true of so many more – how are we to know? In our own way, Dr Aimy and Dr Briars and I try to find out – but it is a small way, as I have said. Charley, perhaps, does even more, for he is in everyone's world at once, and feels empathy with whatever strange place it may seem to be.'

'And yet he once could not tolerate his own world,' I could not resist remarking. Ogden looked at me with troubled concentration. 'Ah, he told you. Yes, he would do. He's taken a great liking to you. We could all see that. I think he'd want you to stay.' He laughed a little, and so did Magdalen.

'You see,' said Briars, leaning forward, 'we all of us believe here that there is some way for these people out of the intolerable impasse in which they find themselves. The mind cannot discover an existing remedy – so it makes one. Or perhaps these minds are already born knowing of states of existence which are not yet here. So they look for them. To people existing in what they would call a normal state, these people are mad.'

'Charley wasn't mad, of course,' said Ogden. 'He would have taken a great deal more stress without actually going beyond the irrecoverable point.'

'And what a real treat it is for all of us now to know that we share these experiences with a man like Charley!' This enthusiasm came, quite uncharacteristically it seemed to me, from Henry Bruggins/Druggins? 'A fully rounded man, a persona *per se*, a fellow who has accepted and remembered and come to terms with all he has executed.'

It seemed to me that Charley had executed his family – I could not quite believe it possible to come to terms with that. But, of course, it was not my field. In the peace of one's laboratory, one deals with absolute quantities, named substances, infinite but determinable variables. There are as many possible results as one cares to take the trouble to find. But one must use only known facts, naturally, to explore the unknown.

'Which reminds me,' said Ogden, thoughtfully prodding at the holes in a clogged salt cellar with an unused fork, 'has anyone been to see Lawrence today?'

Aimy clapped his hands in almost childlike glee: 'But, my very dear colleague, you have missed a genuine experience – the most splendid thing! In fact, I would go almost as far as saying that he is one of this institution's greatest successes – better than dear Vera, and such a great comfort after that unfortunate affair with the Twist boy.'

The atmosphere round the table turned sad and stilted. Ogden looked stiffly at me, and said: 'But tell me about Lawrence. I noticed he hadn't had meals for some time.'

'It is virtually impossible to approach him, for some yards round,' said Aimy merrily, 'and then when he walks, you know, on his accustomed paths, his repetitive tread, there are turns at which you really cannot see him. And the colours – the colours he produces are quite beyond imagination. I wish I could compare them to anything. You must simply see for yourselves. I believe he has begun to assimilate red a little – you remember the red business – the screams at the buses, the pillar boxes. No, I am sure I could distinguish a little red today – he has somehow internalized that.' Everyone laughed at this, and I looked at Ogden, perplexed, I may as well confess.

'Highly autistic type of patient,' said Ogden, in an aside. Not that that explained anything.

I tried to look as if I was participating, but, as usually happens, it was not a successful attempt.

Magdalen, obviously a most intuitive person – almost a telepath, one would say, only I do not believe in that sort of thing – felt it her duty to assist me.

'There is much we can do – much our dear and talented Peregrine can do – to help such lost minds find a more congenial track. At last, perhaps, in fact, nowadays in most cases, they find and retrieve the route for which they originally looked. Then they take it, of course.'

'Take it?'

'Adjust themselves into their new settings,' explained Ogden. 'The things, or the directions, or the modes of behaviour, or the people they need are within their reach suddenly. It is as if they have been looking with their eyes closed, or in total darkness, as if something living underwater was looking for something living above water.'

'Or in a vacuum, sir,' Charley had come over, apparently having finished his meal, and was leaning rather familiarly behind Ogden, with his hands on the back of his chair. 'Just as well not too many of our customers want the almost impossible, wouldn't you say, Mr Ogden?'

In spite of his gay smile, Ogden looked at him reproachfully. Obviously Charley had touched upon a sore spot. 'That wasn't too good, Charley. Really not too good. Now would you say that was anyone's fault? Anyone's at all? And who could have got nearer to it than us? Eh? I suppose it counts for something that poor Mr Anstruther's last days were such utterly happy ones? He was quite convinced of it himself, and that usually helps so much.' But it seemed that no one could be annoyed with Charley for long, and Ogden's tones ended up in indulgence, though Charley looked perhaps a little crestfallen.

'Well, you know how it is with me, Mr Ogden – plain jealous, and I don't have to tell anyone that. They all know it here, and it's plain to see. Here I am cured, and never another chance, and I see all this going on around me – oh well, who am I to complain? There can't be many men have a happier life than meself. I think I was upset too, in a way, over Mr Anstruther – I mean, I knew within meself that it was impossible, but it didn't seem so, and everyone else seemed so sure.'

'Everyone has a failure,' said Briars heavily. 'Life would be too full of miracles to be good for us, otherwise. A proper balance of failures is essential to nature.'

'Are you talking about the – ah – the explosion?' It seemed unmannerly curiosity, but I felt I had to know. The pink confetti-like stuff – I would really rather not be sure, but it seemed necessary at least to ask. If they refused to give details, that would, in its way, be equally satisfactory.

'Dear, dear, yes. I suppose that was all it seemed,' said Ogden unhappily, and the others were silent.

We seemed to have ended our meal. Peregrine Ogden asked me to come and have coffee with him, in his study, but excused himself first for ten minutes. He had a patient to talk to.

Charley went off by himself, whistling, with a friendly nod back to me. I had the curious feeling that if I had shown any anxiety, he would have trotted back, and kept me company, even to standing guard outside my room, while I slept. But, on the contrary, I had begun to feel as if this were a place I had been looking for for a great while, without ever being able to formulate to myself any very exact image of what I hoped to find.

I looked out through the full warm curtains at the dimly moving expanses of grass, blotted now and then by slabs of furry-backed stones, fenced and patched by hastening ranks of trees, and beyond that a colourless blur of sky, reddening now a little at the death of the sun, still with blue curls of smoke scrolled upon it.

If I must look at a landscape – and frankly, I am not an outdoors man – this is how I prefer to see it.

As I left the room, with Magdalen talking quietly at my side, I suddenly remembered the waltzing figures in the other room, and knew that they had reminded me of the beautifully carved pairs of candlesticks on the walls.

Magdalen said that she would show me the way to Ogden's study, and on the way we passed the door of the room which held Marion. For some reason, I felt impelled to look inside. However, I could not open the door fully – it was as if something was pressing against it from within. This was odd, because although the sounds and movements of children were as strong as ever, from the tiny glimpse I could gain of Marion's corner, she was no longer there.

Magdalen, too, peered over my shoulder, and uttered one of those soft, caressing murmurs which one associates with people who disturb young birds in a nest, or puppies or kittens nursing.

'Ah, dear Marion; I must go and tell Peregrine,' she whispered. '*How* pleased he will be – so soon, though we all expected it.'

And still the empty room, and the great pressures and sounds and movements, which gradually thrust the door shut, against my shoulder.

'Would you like—' Magdalen hesitated for a moment. 'You see, I should talk to Peregrine about this – technically, it is one of our major achievements. It may perhaps be dull for you and, of course, there are things he might wish to say to me about it that—' she hesitated again, but very gracefully.

'Oh, I can understand that quite easily,' I said immediately, 'a case history – that will need some discussion, I suppose. You won't need me there for a while. You must keep that coffee warm for me, though.'

'In the meantime, perhaps, you would like to look through our laboratories – Charley said you were interested, and

Peregrine told us something of your work, naturally. They are through here—' She began leading me towards the doors Charley had pulled me gently away from, before the meal.

'A passion of mine, a well-kept laboratory, properly equipped, waiting for work and its occupant,' I said, with pleasure.

'Oh, everyone here has a passion,' replied Magdalen lightly. 'Some more important than others. Yours, I would think, could only be a most important one. Your opinions will be most valuable to us.'

'Tell me, how do you help – if you won't think me rude?'

Magdalen shrugged expressively. 'There are so many ways of helping these people – drugs, the injections of the right chemicals, an operation, perhaps, to fit them for the right sphere. Even a humble anaesthetist – ' she curtseyed swiftly ' – is a necessary appendage. In some cases, I am called upon to keep certain patients under just the right amount of anaesthetic for really quite long periods. That can work marvels – perhaps you know?'

No, I hadn't known. 'So everyone has their own passion, and some their great and unattainable peculiarities. Even you?'

Magdalen laughed. 'Oh, this is the last place in which to say that there is such a thing as true normality. Everyone is a little mad, yes? What is that saying your people have about the method in madness? All one has to do is to find a little method, and then direct, in any of a number of ways. Don't be too sure of yourself, my friend – perhaps only poor Charley is one who has truly and unalterably graduated. But then he should have never been here, in the first place. Everyone is very kind to him, though, and he is so good, such a help, so full of intuitions and love.'

We walked slowly down the passages between the white-topped benches. The instruments, the burners, the beakers – great cupboards, full of glassware, gleaming through transparent doors – it all looked as though it had hardly been used. Where there were not windows, there were mirrors – a most pleasing prospect. The mirrors seemed to extend the laboratory serenely and infinitely. I saw a continuous motion of my own image, in many directions, and everywhere the tools of my trade, not smoke-blackened or acid-burned or dye-stained, as in the workshops I was used to, but pristine and virgin, worthy of the best uses.

The coffee would wait, and Magdalen had to have her chat with Ogden. There were journals on the shelves, whose numbers I hadn't yet looked into, though I had always promised myself—

'Well, this is certainly my weakness.' I sighed. 'Someone will have to come and fetch me, you know, Magdalen, or I shall be lost for ever in the immensities of my own researches. The whole place, the people, the atmosphere – there's something that almost demands one's attention and affection – perhaps devotion. You feel it, of course, more than I do, as a member of the staff.'

'Someone will come and help you,' said Magdalen practically. 'You'll need an assistant, even though I know you will find something to do without our aid. Yes, I am fortunate, as you say. In my world, where I was born, we have no such places as Peregrine has made. It was by pure chance that I found my way from my own world to this – and there, I think, no one would have recognized me.'

She was laughing, as she let herself out. A joke, of course, no wonder her clear amusement lingered in the air, after the doors had closed, and left me wrapped in the quietness of the laboratory. A strange joke – but the memory of it began to leave me as I looked around at the shelves, the containers, the inviting benches.

There was so much I could do here. And I had plenty of time – it was not as if I had to hurry. There is always plenty of time when great changes or great improvements are to be made, to things or to people or to life itself.

A cupboard to hand so obviously stood a little ajar, suggesting clean white overalls. As I eased my shoulders into one, I found myself hoping that perhaps Charley had had laboratory experience. It might perhaps be Charley whom they sent to help me.

Marc Laidlaw

Tissue

Marc Laidlaw was born in 1960, and I wish I could have written as well as that when I was eighteen, or have been half as energetic and professional. Many a writer trying for his first solo professional sale would have given up after the first rejection, yet when I rejected two stories (fine, but not right for this book) he bounced back with 'Tissue'. I couldn't resist that ending, but I wanted revisions elsewhere, which he sent almost by return of post. Although he is a student at the University of Oregon he manages to write scripts and to sell stories to Omni, Year's Best Science Fiction, The Future at War *and, I'm sure by the time this sees print, others. He has also written novels (*The Mistress of Shadows, The Minions of L'Thoa*) which will have reached a friendly editor by now, I hope.*

At the age of seventeen he played 'Son' in an educational film about divorce. His father was played by Hal Landon Junior, who is one of the more unnerving characters in Eraserhead, *the most nightmarish film ever made. A good start for a writer of nightmares like this one.*

'Here,' Daniel said, handing Paula the photograph. 'Take a look at this, then tell me you *still* want to meet my father.'

Paula hefted it in one hand; it was framed in dark wood, covered with a heavy rectangle of glass. A fringe of dust clung to the glass's edges, under the frame, blurring the borders of the photograph into a spidery haze.

'What is it? *Who* is it?'

'Us. My family.'

'But there's only . . .'

Paula's words faded away as she stared at the photograph, trying to understand. Squinting her eyes, polishing the glass – nothing seemed to resolve it. It was merely a simple figure, a

133

person, but as blotched and mottled as an old wall, with sharply ragged edges that unsettled Paula: she couldn't focus, it was like looking through a prism. There was a disturbing disparity within it, too; abrupt internal changes of tone and texture.

'Your *family*?' she repeated.

Daniel nodded, looking straight ahead at the road as he drove. The shadows were lengthening, the gloom descending. Through the endless stand of trees along the roadside, fields and hills were visible.

'It's a composite,' he said. 'You know, like a collage.' He glanced down at the photograph and pointed at the figure's left hand. 'That's my hand. The right one's my mother's.'

'*What?*'

'And the chin, there, is my sister's. That's my brother's . . . forehead, I think, yeah – and that's his nose, too. The clothes, I – I'm not sure.'

'And the eyes?'

'My father's.'

'Daniel, what is this? I mean, why?'

His hands tightened on the steering wheel. Paula found herself staring at his left hand. The one from the picture.

'Daniel, why?'

He shook his head. 'My father's a madman, that's why. No reason for it, he's just . . . Well, yeah, to *him* there's a reason. This, to him, shows us as a group – close-knit. "One optimally functioning individual organism," he used to say.'

Paula looked at the picture with apparent distaste, then slid it back into the briefcase from which Daniel had taken it.

'It's grotesque,' she said, rubbing dust from her hands.

'He sent that to me three years ago, when I had just moved away from home. Made it out of old photographs, begging me to come back. God, he must have worked on that thing for weeks – the joints are almost invisible.'

He fell silent, perhaps watching the road for their turn-off, perhaps just thinking. After a while he sighed, shook his head.

'I don't know,' he said. 'I don't know why I'm doing this – why I'm giving in and going back after all this time.'

Paula moved closer and put her hand on his arm. 'He's human – he's alone. Your mother just died. You didn't even go to the funeral, Daniel – I think this is the least you can do. It's only for a few days.'

Daniel looked resentfully thoughtful. 'Maybe that's the problem. Maybe that started the whole thing.'

'What?'

'Loneliness. He must be awfully lonely, though, to have come up with his obsessions. He used to play with a jigsaw puzzle, Paula, made entirely out of a shattered pane of glass. For hours. And then that . . . thing.' He gestured towards the briefcase, but Paula knew he meant what was in it.

'You'll survive,' she said.

'Yeah. To survive. That's the whole thing.'

There was another silence as he considered this.

'Funny,' he said presently. 'That's exactly what my father was always saying.'

The shadows had swallowed the old farmhouse by the time they found it, trapped in ancient trees at the end of a rough dirt road. The sun was gone, only a pale wash of orange light marking the direction in which it had sunk. Paula looked for a sign of light or life around the weathered building, but found only flooding blackness, shining where it was a window, splintered and peeling where it was the front door.

Daniel stopped the car and stretched back in his seat, yawning. 'I feel like I've been driving for a month.'

'You look it, too,' said Paula. 'I offered to drive . . .'

He shrugged. 'I'll get to sleep early tonight,' he said, pushing open the door. They got out of the car, into the quiet grey evening.

'Is anyone home?' Paula asked as Daniel came around the car.

'With my luck, yes. Come on.'

They walked through a fringe of dead grass, then carefully up the rotten steps. Daniel paused at the top, stepping back on the step beneath him. It creaked and thumped. Creaked and thumped. Daniel smiled nostalgically. Paula reminded herself that he had grown up in this house, out here in the middle of nowhere, far from the city and the campus where she had met him, where they were now living together. Daniel never spoke of his childhood or family, for reasons Paula was unsure of. He seemed bothered by his past, and perhaps somewhat afraid of it.

Across the porch, the door was a panel of emptiness, suddenly creaking as it opened. Paula tried to look through the widening gap; she jerked back as something pale came into view.

'Dad?'

The voice that replied was as worn and weathered as the house: 'Daniel, son, you've come. I knew you would.' The dim pale head bobbed and nodded in the darkness, coarse grey hair stirring. Something white fluttered into view, lower in the frame of darkness: a hand. Daniel's father was coming out.

'Um, I'm sorry I didn't make the funeral, dad. I was really busy with school and my job . . . uh . . .'

And here he came, swimming through the gloom, both white hands coming forward like fish, grasping Daniel. Paula saw the hunched dark figure of the old man only dimly; her eyes were fastened on those hands. They clutched, grabbed, prodded Daniel, exploring as if hungry. It was vaguely revolting. Daniel stood motionless; he had determined to be firm with his father, now he was faltering.

'Dad . . .'

Daniel pushed away one flabby hand but it was clever; it twisted, writhed, locked around his own. Paula gasped. The sluggish white fingers intertwined with Daniel's. He looked up at her, aghast, silently crying for help.

'Uh, hello,' Paula blurted, stepping towards them.

The hands jerked, stopped. The old man came around.

'Who are you? Daniel, who is this?'

'Dad, this is Paula, I told you about her. We're living together.'

Paula started to extend her hand. She remembered what might meet it, and drew away. 'Hello.'

'Living together?' Daniel's father said, watching him. 'Not married?'

'Uh, no, dad. Not yet, anyway.'

'Good . . . good. Good. It would weaken the bond, *break* the bond between us.' He did not even look at Paula again. His hands returned to Daniel, though not so frantically this time. They guided him forward into the house. Paula followed, shutting the door behind her, waiting for her eyes to adjust to the dark. When her vision had cleared, she could see Daniel and his father vaguely limned against a distant doorway; there was light beyond.

When she caught up, they were seating themselves on an antique sofa. It had been poorly kept; springs and padding spilled through in places. The room around them had been equally neglected; darkness lay upon it like soot. A single dull lamp glowed beside the sofa.

Daniel caught Paula's eye when she entered, warning her away from them. She sat in a nearby chair. Daniel was shrugging away the proddings of his father, fighting off the creeping fingers. But they kept coming, peering around the long shadows, then hurrying across Daniel while he sat at last unmoving, silent.

'We . . . we were terribly sorry to hear about your wife,' said Paula. The sound of her words muffled the rustling noises.

'Hm?' The old man sat up, leaving Daniel for a moment. His eyes were sharp, intense. 'Yes, it's bad . . . bad. She and I, we were – *close*, towards the end. Locked. Like this.' He clasped his two puffy hands together before his face, staring at them.

Daniel took this opportunity to move to a chair beside Paula, where his father could not follow. The old man hunched after him, hands straining, but didn't rise.

'Daniel, come back here. Sit beside me.'

'Uh, I think I'd better stay right here, dad.'

'Ah.' The old man hissed like a serpent. 'Stubborn. You were always stubborn – all of you. Your sister, your brother, they both resisted. Look what happened to them.'

Daniel looked nervously away from the old man's black stare. 'Don't talk about Louise like that, dad. It's all over now. And it had nothing to do with stubbornness.'

'Nothing? She ran away, Daniel, as you all did. She could not function, Daniel, she could not maintain herself. No more than the liver, the heart, the lungs, can function outside of the body. No more than the individual cells can function outside of the tissue that maintains them; even as this tissue is dependent on the organ it contributes to; as this organ in turn is dependent on all other organs to keep the whole intact.'

Paula had gone rigid in her chair, watching the old man speak. Suddenly that hanging black gaze turned to her.

'You,' he said. 'Do you know how an organism survives?'

'Pardon me?' she said weakly.

'It survives because its components work together, each one specialized towards its specific contribution to the organism. Specialization, yes. Louise was specialized; she did not survive.'

Daniel sighed, rubbing his forehead. 'Dad, it wasn't specialization. It was drugs. She made some mistakes.'

'And your brother?'

'What about him? He's doing fine. He has his own business now, he seems to be happy.'

'But he deserted us! He threatened the existence of us all. Your sister deteriorated. Your mother crumbled. And then you . . .'

'What about me?'

The old man shrugged. 'You returned. We still have a chance.'

Paula, through all this, said nothing. But she was thinking: *My God. My God.*

'I'm going to be going home, dad. I'm not staying very long.'

The old man snapped, 'What?'

'I told you that in my letter. I'm only staying for a day or two.'

'But you can't go back! You – you can't! Otherwise I have no chance – not alone. Nor you either, Daniel.'

'Look, dad—'

'Together we can survive, perhaps recover. And . . . and maybe your brother will return.'

'He's raising a family.'

'Ah, see?' He raised one pallid finger. 'He has learned!'

'Maybe we'd better not stay at all,' said Daniel, rising. His features had gone hard, faced with all this. Easier to run than worry about it.

'No!' This was a bleat, a plea, escaping from the old man as if he had been punctured. His expression, too, was wounded. 'Daniel, you can't . . .'

Paula rose and touched Daniel gently on the arm until he turned to her. Thank God he hadn't pulled away from *her* touch.

'Daniel,' she said, 'it's really getting late. I don't think you should do any more driving tonight.'

Daniel searched her expression, saw only concern. He nodded.

'We'll stay the night then, dad. But we're leaving in the morning.'

The old man started forward, then sank back in apparent despair. His breath was loud and laboured, wheezing; his hands crouched upon his knees, waiting for Daniel to stray near.

'You can't leave me, Daniel. I need you to survive, I *need* you!' His eyes glimmered, turning to Paula. '*You* know, don't you? That's why you're taking him from me . . . to strengthen yourself. Well you'll never have him. He's mine. Only mine.'

The words slid into Paula like a blade of ice, malevolent in their cold precision. She felt weak.

138

'I—' she began. 'Honestly, it's nothing like that. I don't want Daniel that way.'

The worm-white head rotated. 'Then you are a fool.'

'Paula,' Daniel repeated, 'maybe we'd better leave right now.'

'Haven't you heard what I've said? You mustn't leave!' Again, pain had replaced malicious insanity on the old man's pale features. Paula felt sorry for him.

'Daniel,' she said, 'just the night. It's really too late to leave.'

Daniel looked once at the poised hands of his father. Then he sighed, tensely, and nodded. 'But I don't want to hear any more of this, dad. One more word of it and we're going for sure.'

He turned back to Paula. 'Come on, I'll show you to your room. Hopefully there's something to eat around here.'

They started to leave, stepping towards another dark doorway.

'Daniel.' The voice was cold again, chilling. They stopped and looked back at the old man.

'You forget,' he said, eyes narrowing, face hardening. 'I'm stronger than you. I always was. You cannot resist the organism.'

Paula felt Daniel's muscles tighten beneath her hand.

'Good night, dad,' he said. They walked out.

Much later, in the darkened hallway upstairs, Daniel apologized again.

'He's gotten worse, Paula – worse than I had ever expected.' Daniel was nervous, his expression intensely bothered.

'It's all right, Daniel, really. Things happen to people as they get old.'

Daniel pulled her closer to him. It was cold in the draughty darkness, only the feeble grey moonlight trickling in through the window at the end of the hall. But the embrace was not warming; Daniel seemed to be protecting himself with Paula.

'It's as if he wants to swallow me – the way he keeps touching and grabbing. So . . . so *greedy!* I wouldn't have come back if I thought he'd be this way.'

'What did he used to be like?' Paula asked.

She looked up at Daniel, but he wasn't looking at her. His eyes were fixed on the door to his father's room, where a narrow fringe of light spread into the hall from under the door. His gaze seemed clouded, distant; he was remembering something. Something unpleasant.

'What is it, Daniel?'

He shook his head, slightly disgusted. It was the look he always got when she asked him about his childhood. She could feel his heart pounding against her breasts.

'*Daniel*, please, what's *wrong*?'

'I – I never told you. I never thought I'd tell anyone . . .'

She began to urge him on, but he continued without prompting.

'When I was a kid, I came out here one night – I'd had a nightmare, I think. It was late. I thought I heard noises in my parents' room; the light was coming out just like it is now. I knocked, but no one answered, so I opened the door – just a little, you know? – and started to go in.

'They were – they – just lying there, my mother and my father, wrapped around each other, and the light was so bright I wasn't sure that – that it was my mother there –

'I thought it was my *sister*, Paula!'

Paula caught her breath, then instantly relaxed. Daniel had been young – he'd seen his parents having sex. Such experiences often led to traumas, delusions. She could imagine it lurking in his mind all these years, breaking free now. Daniel was trembling.

'I yelled,' he continued. 'I remember yelling. But . . . *they didn't even move.* They just lay there until I ran away.'

He paused. Then, 'It wasn't my sister, of course. It *couldn't* have been, I can't believe it. She and my mother had the same colour of hair, and that was all I could see; the light was so bright, they were so close together . . . not moving. But I thought, for just a moment, that he . . .' Daniel looked towards the door and shuddered again.

'Daniel, do you want me to stay with you tonight?'

'What? Oh, no, that's all right.' He forced a laugh. 'Might be a little too hard on my dad. Maybe later, when he's asleep, you can sneak over . . .'

She yawned uncontrollably. 'Maybe. If I can stay awake.'

They kissed and said goodnight. Daniel parted with obvious reluctance, then went through the door into his room, closing it softly behind him. Paula looked down the hall, where light still spilled from beneath his father's door. Thank God she was on the other side of Daniel; he was between her and that old man. Daniel's story was ridiculous, of course: a childhood hallucination, magnified by the years. Things like that . . . incest . . . just didn't happen.

She slipped into her own room, and was somewhat dismayed to find that the lock didn't work. It needed a key that was nowhere to be found. Just another inconvenience among many. She was surprised, actually, that this place even had electricity. The room itself was dusty and suffocating, but she supposed she could stand it for one night.

In a minute she was in bed, trying to warm herself, the small table lamp shut off. When the sounds of her settling in had faded, the darkness swarmed around her uncomfortably, creaking and breathing in the manner of such old houses. She tried to ignore it, suddenly glad that they had stayed the night. Another nap in the car and she would have gone mad. At least she had been able to shower here. The old man was bearable when she didn't have to confront him directly.

Presently she drifted off, breathing with the house, her thoughts muffled by its thick atmosphere. But her sleep was restless, uncertain.

Paula was never positive she had slept at all when she realized that she was wide awake again. The stillness was incredible. The house was holding its breath. She sat up, certain that something had jarred her from sleep. A noise.

There. Perhaps from Daniel's room, perhaps from the hall. Perhaps trailing from the hall *into* Daniel's room . . .

Suddenly Paula was certain she'd heard a door shut. And – footsteps? But where were they going? Where had they been?

Those sounds were clear in the swollen darkness. But after a moment came less certain ones – rising and falling, always soft, as deceptive as the rush of blood in her ears. She was hearing things. No. Paula shook her head. She did *not* imagine things. Straining her ears, the sounds resolved themselves.

Voices. From Daniel's room.

They stopped.

Paula waited; heard nothing. A slight dragging sound that might have been the night passing through her mind. A dull footstep. And then, quite distinctly, three words, in the old man's voice:

'I need you!'

And creaking.

Paula was out of bed in an instant, hurrying quietly across the floor. She didn't trust that old man, not for a minute, not alone with Daniel. She found the door, jerked on the knob—

It was locked.

Paula remembered the sound that had awakened her; it returned very clearly now that she could place it. It had clicked, metallically. A lock engaging.

She pounded once on the door. Again, louder, tugging at the knob.

And still not a sound from the other room.

'Daniel, *Daniel!*' Paula began to sob, wishing that there would be another sound, Daniel's voice.

The door. Quieting, she returned her attention to it. The lock didn't seem terribly strong, it was old. For a minute she considered throwing herself against the door, but it opened the wrong way. Chanting Daniel's name, she wrenched at the knob, pulling it back with all her strength. It seemed to give a little. Paula glanced back into the room, hoping for something useful. Her hand mirror glimmered on the table, reflecting moonlight. It was heavy, had a sturdy handle.

In a moment she was cracking the doorframe with it, chipping away the splintered wood, ripping and tearing. There was a grinding, and she yanked on the doorknob and the door crashed open, stunning her. She stood for just a second, considering the darkened hall beyond, then moved forward, into it, the mirror dropping from her fingers.

No sound from Daniel's room. None at all. Not through all her screaming and pounding and thundering . . . nothing.

'Daniel?' she called softly. She stopped outside his door, listening. Everything was grey and dim, shrouded in shadows. 'Daniel?'

Before she could reason with herself, she had turned the knob, had found it unlocked, had opened the door and entered.

Entered.

'Daniel?'

On the bed, something grey, tangled in blankets, two shapes. God help her, she was going forward, approaching the bed.

'Please, Daniel, are you all right?' The words came as a whimper.

She was at the bedside, eyes squinted with fear, so that all she could see was the two of them, vaguely, Daniel and his father pressed close together as if . . . as if kissing, or making love, his father on top.

Down in the gloom, a huge spider, almost filling the bed.

Her eyes closed.

'Daniel—'

Her hand went forward, to touch. Gingerly.

'Please—'

And there, on top, was the back of the old man's head, his hair coarse around her fingers. She moved her hand down, consciously, forcing it to touch his ear, and pass around it, still down. Over a rough cheek, withered skin. Skin that abruptly smoothed; skin that continued, unbroken ...

Unbroken ...

Straight to another cheek, another ear, and the back of Daniel's head.

Peter Valentine Timlett

Without rhyme or reason

*Peter Valentine Timlett was born in London in 1933. He has
two daughters 'who are quite the most magnificent thing that
has ever happened to me'. He has worked as a jazz musician
and in the distribution department of Howard & Wyndham;
for several years he was a practising ritual magician, until he
became frustrated by the aims of the occult group of which he
was a member. His* Seedbearers *trilogy is based on his occult
experiences. His later work includes an Arthurian trilogy and
a novel based on the witchcraft trial of Father Urbain
Grandier,* Nor All Thy Tears – *none of which prepares us for
the following.*

It was a large house, far bigger than she had expected. Must
be five or six bedrooms at least. Not all that old, late Victorian
probably, and the gardens were superb. It was set well back off
a very minor road about a mile outside the village with not
another house in sight, and as a consequence it was beautifully
quiet and peaceful. She could be very happy here indeed.

She rang the bell and waited. After a couple of minutes she
rang again. There must be someone at home, surely. Her
appointment was for three o'clock, and she was punctual
almost to the second.

'Yes?' said a sharp voice behind her.

She spun round, startled. 'Oh, I'm sorry. I didn't hear you
come up.' The woman was in her late forties, tall and slimly
built, with clear grey eyes that studied her firmly, almost
fiercely. 'I am Miss Templeton – Deborah Templeton. The
agency sent me. Are you Mrs Bates?'

The woman nodded. 'You are punctual. I like that.' The
grey eyes swept her from head to foot. 'You are also very
pretty. I told the agency that you had to be pretty. I like to be
surrounded by beautiful things, including people. You are not

beautiful but you are very pretty. It's the dress, I think, and the hairstyle. Pretty but not beautiful.'

Miss Templeton's hand strayed involuntarily to her hair. 'I usually wear it down,' she said.

'Yes, you should. With your hair down, a decent eyeshadow, green I think, and a daring evening gown you could look quite stunning.'

The girl smiled. 'It's been a long time since I dressed like that. There has been no occasion.' Mrs Bates was no advertisement for her own philosophy. She wore patched and faded jeans, muddy at the knees, and a shapeless smock-like top that did little for her figure, and her hair was pushed up under an old hat that looked as though it might have begun life a decade earlier as a chic jockey-cap in a Chelsea boutique. But she had that classical facial bone structure that most women envy, giving her face that precious ageless look. Given the right clothes this woman could also look quite stunning, despite her age.

Mrs Bates was aware of her appraisal. 'One should dress to please oneself, not others,' she said firmly. 'When I am in the garden I dress like a gardener. In the evenings I dress like a woman, even when I'm alone.' She turned and walked away. 'Come into the house,' she said over her shoulder.

Miss Templeton followed her round the side of the house and into a sun-lounge through a pair of French windows. A curious woman, this Mrs Bates. The agency had been right to describe her as somewhat eccentric. But the room was beautiful. Each piece of furniture, as far as she could tell, was a genuine antique, and the woman waved her to a Victorian chaise-longue that alone would be worth a fortune by her own standards.

'As I am in my gardening clothes I will remain standing,' said Mrs Bates. 'I am a wealthy woman, Miss Templeton. The contents of this house are worth far more than the house itself, and for that reason alone I have to be careful whom I invite to live with me.'

'I understand.'

'And there is also the question of compatible personalities.' Again those grey eyes scanned her from head to toe. 'I imagine that the agency told you that I am an eccentric.'

'They said that you were a strongly individualistic person,' said Miss Templeton carefully.

'And so I am. This is my house and thus I have the right to determine how it shall be run.'

'Of course.'

'I am a fanatical gardener, Miss Templeton. Summer or winter I spend most of my time in the garden. I do not want a companion, let's be clear about that. I want someone to look after the house, leaving me free to tend the garden. Anything to do with the house, anything at all, will be your province.'

'So I understand. The agency gave me a list of all the duties and conditions and I find them very acceptable.'

'Good. As to meals, I see to myself during the week. You will be required to cook only one meal a week, on Saturday evening, for which I trust you will join me. I am a fanatic about the garden but not about the house. Providing it is kept reasonably clean and tidy you may come and go as you please. If you like walking you will find the countryside around here quite delightful. I am not a sociable woman, Miss Templeton. I can be quite charming when I put my mind to it but basically I prefer my own company. During the week, when you are not actually engaged upon work in the house, I would be grateful if you would remain in your rooms, but I would welcome your company on the Saturday evening.'

The girl nodded. 'You want the house to run smoothly without you being bothered about it, and I am to stay out of your way except on Saturdays.'

The woman smiled. 'Exactly. All this may sound a bit odd to you but I find that it suits me very well and I need someone who can fit in with that pattern, someone who is also quite happy with their own company most of the time. Your letter said that you are twenty-eight, an only child, and that your parents are dead. Any other attachments?'

'No, none, not even a romance.'

'I see. Sorry to ask these rather personal questions but the reasons are obvious. However, I think it is only fair that I reciprocate. So, Miss Templeton, I can tell you that I am forty-eight and do not give a damn who knows it. Like yourself, my parents also died when I was young, and like yourself, I am also an only child. Because of that I was already fairly wealthy in my own right even before I married, and my husband had money as well. We were married for ten years before he ran off with a younger woman.'

'Oh, I am sorry.'

'To be candid so was I. It was a good marriage, or so I thought, even though there were no children.'

'Why did he leave?'

For a brief moment a look of bleak hatred crossed her eyes. 'Let us say that the girl in question used her physical assets to good effect. So I, too, am quite alone with no attachments whatever. Did the agency tell you the salary?'

'Yes, the money is fine.'

'Good.' Again those grey eyes surveyed her critically. 'Well, Miss Templeton, I think we will get on very well indeed. I'll leave you for a few minutes to think about it. By all means have a look round the house. Your rooms are the first two on the right at the top of the stairs. There is a bedroom with your own bathroom attached, and a small sitting room with a connecting door. I'm sure you will be comfortable. When you are ready you'll find me in the garden,' and she turned and walked out on to the patio.

Deborah Templeton continued to sit there in the sun-lounge for a few moments. What a curious woman, she thought, and what an extraordinary interview. It was the sort of interview that a man might have conducted, not a woman. For a brief moment the thought crossed her mind that Mrs Bates might have unusual tastes, hence the reason perhaps why her husband had left her for a more normal woman and hence the reason perhaps why she was so insistent that her employee be young and attractive, but she dismissed the idea almost as soon as it arose. The woman might be odd but that oddness certainly didn't stem from Sappho.

She rose and walked through the house. She had not exactly come from penurious circumstances herself, but she had never lived in such luxurious surroundings as this. The kitchen was enormous and fitted with just about every labour-saving device on the market, and the main lounge was a superb room of elegance and grace. She walked up the main staircase and directly she entered what was to be her bedroom she knew that she simply had to have this position, for there was the most gorgeous four-poster bed curtained in woven tapestry of gold and red like something out of a fairy tale. It was silly, she knew, to let such a trivial thing as a bed clinch the decision, but it had always been a fantasy of hers to sleep in a four-poster.

She looked at herself in the tall cheval mirror and pulled a wry smile. Pretty but not beautiful. An accurate but deflating description. There had been a time, oh so many years ago now, when she had been stunningly attractive, in the days when she had deliberately dressed for that effect, but the image that stared back at her from the mirror was suburbanly 'mumsy' and hardly likely to stir the male libido.

She walked over to the window and stared down into the garden to where Mrs Bates was busy weeding the flowerbeds. The woman was certainly an autocrat, but if it was true that she would not see her for most of the time then that was no real problem. And yet there was still something odd about the whole thing. It was all too good to be true. Or perhaps the oddness was more to do with Mrs Bates herself than the position she was offering. Anyway, she would be a fool to turn it down.

The name on the list of duties that the agency had given her was Mary Elizabeth Bates, followed by an indecipherable signature. The name, Mary, was really quite apposite. 'Mary, Mary, quite contrary,' she murmured, 'how does your garden grow?' and the answer was that it grew very well, though Mary Bates herself was certainly contrary, contrary indeed.

The girl left the room and went downstairs into the garden. 'I think I will be very happy here,' she said simply.

The woman smiled. 'When I read your letter and saw your photograph I was already half certain, but when I saw you standing at the door I knew that you were going to be the one. When can you come?'

'Would Monday be too soon?'

Mrs Bates held out her hand. 'Monday will be fine. I'll see you then.'

Deborah had said Monday just to give herself the weekend should she wish to change her mind, but by Saturday lunch time she had given the landlady of her bedsit a week's rent in lieu of notice and was already packed and eager to go. Saturday evening and all day Sunday stretched to a seeming eternity but at last the Monday came and the taxi delivered her to her new home by noon.

Mrs Bates, still in the same old pair of jeans, welcomed her kindly but not effusively. 'You know where your rooms are. Use today to get settled in. Cook yourself a meal when you feel like it. I'll talk to you more fully, and go over the house accounts with you, tomorrow,' and she turned and went back into the garden. Deborah smiled wryly and lugged her suitcases up to her rooms, and by two o'clock she was unpacked and ready to explore the house.

Her mother had always said that you could know almost

everything there was to know about a woman's environment, temperament, and character by the contents of her kitchen cupboards, her wardrobe, and her laundry bin. The kitchen harboured no surprises, in view of the evidence of wealth in the rest of the house. The tins and jars and bottles in the cupboards revealed a highly expensive epicurean taste that promised a future of delightful cuisine, though no doubt it would prove a disaster to any calorie-controlled diet, and the wine rack contained a dozen or more bottles, mostly German hocks, though in amongst the array of white wine there were two bottles of Nuit St George. Mrs Bates obviously dined well.

The girl did not dare go into her employer's bedroom to see her wardrobe, but she did make a quick examination of the contents of the laundry bin and there met with a surprise that almost bordered on shock. There were two suspender belts, one of black and purple and one of black and scarlet, and five pairs of the scantiest briefs that she had ever seen, again in scarlet, black, and purple, and all of them lacy and highly revealing. And in addition there were two bras, one black and one red, so brief that they simply had to be quarter-bras that would make the point quite clear on any normally endowed woman. It was puzzling. These were the underclothes of a young Soho showgirl, not those of a forty-eight year old rural semi-recluse. Mrs Bates was proving to be something of an intriguing mystery.

At four o'clock it began to rain and Deborah rushed to her sitting room window to see what Mrs Bates would do. The woman hurried into the conservatory and emerged a few minutes later dressed in wellington boots, oilskin trousers, and a waterproof anorak with the hood pulled up over her head, and calmly went back to work. She really did look quite ridiculous bent over the flowerbeds with the rain drumming on her back. Being late June the weather was still quite warm despite the rain, and if you are suitably waterproofed then there was no logical reason why you should not work in the rain, and yet it seemed ludicrous. People didn't tend their gardens in the pouring rain. It simply wasn't *done*. And how on earth could you equate that comical and eccentric figure down there in the rain with the sort of woman that wore lurid and provocative underclothes? It was delightfully mysterious.

Deborah did not see Mrs Bates that evening, but on the following morning she found a note in the kitchen asking her to come into the library after breakfast to go over the house accounts. Well at last Deborah would see Mrs Bates in something other than jeans, but when she entered the library the result was oddly disappointing. She was dressed in pale blue slacks and a white high-necked blouse. The outfit was simple, tasteful, and hardly in keeping with the erotic contents of the laundry bin. And Mrs Bates proved to have a good brain, neat, precise, and logical. The house accounts were all neatly annotated and filed in alphabetical order in a proper filing cabinet in the library, and within half an hour the familiarization talk was over and Mrs Bates changed back into her jeans and returned to the garden.

In accordance with her instructions Deborah Templeton kept out of her employer's way for the rest of that Tuesday and all day Wednesday, though Mrs Bates in the garden was constantly in her view from the house. And it was this constant view of her employer that revealed yet another oddity. It was true that Mary Bates gave her attention to all parts of the garden, but again and again she returned to that same flowerbed where Deborah had first seen her. If she moved to another part of the garden it would only be a matter of minutes, ten at the most, before she returned to what was obviously her favourite spot.

The flowerbed was a low mound some twenty feet long and six feet wide, and it would have been called a rockery but for the fact that it had no rocks. Deborah Templeton was no gardener and could scarce put a name to any particular plant in that blaze of colour except for the tulips and the aubretia, and indeed to her untutored eye some of them seemed very unusual and thus probably quite rare, but it was certainly a beautiful bed and obviously thrived on the loving care that Mrs Bates lavished upon it. 'With silver bells and cockleshells,' she murmured as she saw Mrs Bates move back to her favourite spot for the umpteenth time.

On Thursday she went shopping in the village and there discovered yet another oddity, one that was rather disquieting. 'Well, I will say this for Mrs Bates,' said the butcher, an enormous man with fat red cheeks, 'she certainly knows how to pick 'em!'

'How do you mean?'

Fortunately the shop was empty, otherwise the man might not have been so forward and thus the oddity would have remained hidden a little longer. 'Well, you're a very attractive young lady, Miss Templeton, if I may say so, but then all of Mrs Bates' girls have been good lookers.'

From the later viewpoint of hindsight Deborah decided that it was at that precise moment that the first warning bell began to sound inside her. 'All of them?' she said. 'Why, how many have there been?'

The butcher pursed his lips. 'You're the seventh, I think.'

She signed the bill and was just about to leave when on impulse she said: 'Do you remember their names?'

'Of course,' he said, and rattled off six names, 'and you're the best looking one so far,' he added gallantly.

Once outside the shop she wrote the names in her pocket diary before she forgot them and then began the mile walk home, but before she left the village she placed a call from the public telephone box. It was not a call that she would have cared to make from the house.

The agency was polite and apologetic but not very forthcoming. Yes, she was indeed the seventh. Yes, the six names were correct. No, they had not told her about her predecessors because of Mrs Bates' instructions to that effect. As far as they understood, all the girls had quickly grown bored with the job, having little to do, and had left. No, they had not seen any of the girls after they had left. In each case they had not known that the girl had left until Mrs Bates had contacted the agency for a replacement. No, they did not think it particularly unusual.

Deborah did not see Mrs Bates to speak to that Thursday, nor the Friday. It was not until the Saturday morning that her employer sought her out. 'I do trust that you have not forgotten that today is Saturday.'

'No, of course not. Dinner will be at eight.'

At seven o'clock, with everything prepared and going nicely, Deborah went up to dress. She took a quick shower and then combed her hair down long and full. She then tried on her only full-length evening gown. She had not worn it for several years and it still fitted surprisingly well. She had not put on as much weight as she had feared. The gown was black with a simple flowing line. It was a cross-over halter-neck that left half her breasts exposed and all her midriff to below the navel. Not content with that the dress was slashed up the front to mid-thigh and fitted so tightly around her hips and bottom that any underclothing at all, even the merest wisp, always spoiled the line of it, and she wondered how on earth she had ever had the courage to wear it. She looked at herself critically in the cheval mirror and shook her head. It was a great dress, and she would love to wear it just to disprove that 'pretty but not beautiful' tag, but it really wasn't very suitable for this present occasion. Reluctantly she stripped and folded it away, put on under-clothes and a simple calf-length cocktail dress that did not reveal anything, and left the room to go downstairs.

As she was closing her bedroom door she saw her employer going down the stairs, and the sight almost made her gasp. Her own black evening gown would have been declared modest by comparison to the creation that Mrs Bates was wearing. It was a pure white gown cut in a Grecian style of a material so fine that she trailed wisps of it behind her as she moved, and it was quite staggering how little of Mrs Bates it covered. The con-trast to the wellington-booted figure in the garden was so start-ling that it was scarcely believable that it was the same woman.

Without even thinking about it Deborah went back into her bedroom, stripped off her cocktail dress and her underclothes, put on her evening gown, and went downstairs to serve dinner.

Neither gown was mentioned during dinner, indeed little was said at all. Mrs Bates made an appreciative comment about the prawn cocktail, was quite complimentary in respect to the Tournedos Rossini, and said that she found the lemon sorbet to be delicious. It was only when they withdrew to the main lounge for coffee that the first mention was made. 'An excel-lent meal, my dear,' said Mrs Bates, 'and I completely with-draw my earlier remark about being merely pretty. You look quite stunning. I doubt that any man could keep his hands off you.'

The girl smiled. 'With you in the room I doubt that he would even see me.'

Mrs Bates looked down at herself. 'Yes, men are quite stupidly physical. With a dress like this, or one like yours, a man's every instinct prompts him to reach out and remove what little there is. All female virtues are as nothing compared to the power of a revealing gown, as I know to my cost.'

Deborah sipped her coffee. 'The girl who took your hus-band?' she said softly.

The woman smiled grimly. 'We entertained a lot in those days, mostly business acquaintances of my husband's, and people from his office. I did not dress then as you see me now. I used to dress elegantly and tastefully, but never revealingly. An old-fashioned attitude, perhaps, in these days of blatant sexuality, but we all have our own particular tastes and stan-dards.'

'And the girl?'

'A personal assistant to one of my husband's directors. She came to one of our dinner parties dressed in a gown almost exactly like this one and made it perfectly obvious to my husband that he need only snap his fingers for her to remove it altogether.' Mrs Bates put her coffee cup on a side table and leant back in the armchair. 'Two weeks later he left me and went off with her.'

'I'm sorry,' said the girl quietly.

The woman was silent for a moment. 'He would have come back to me, you know, when the novelty had worn off, and I would have taken him. It was a good marriage. Men are so vulnerable to a really determined and blatant advance from an attractive woman. Few of them can resist. It is almost part of their nature, you might say.'

'What happened?'

'Three weeks after he left they were both killed in a car crash in southern France, and I hope she rots in hell for all time. And it was all so unnecessary. A discreet affair would have been far better. It would have satisfied the sexual attraction and preserved the marriage.'

The girl did not comment. Her sympathy was instinctively with the husband. An autocratic woman such as Mrs Bates would not be easy to live with from any aspect, sexual or otherwise. There was probably more than one reason why he had left her.

'And all because of a revealing evening gown,' said Mrs Bates bitterly. 'That girl had worked at that office for two years and I *know* that there had been nothing between them prior to that dinner party. It was the gown that did it.'

Deborah sipped at her coffee again. Possible, but not likely. If it had only been a question of sex then a discreet affair would indeed have satisfied the situation. There had to be more to it than that. The way this woman kept harping on that one particular aspect seemed to suggest that Mrs Bates felt very inadequate and inferior in that area.

'And so I went out and bought this gown, and some other clothing,' said Mrs Bates. 'And do you know why?'

Deborah shook her head. She didn't like the way this was going. The woman really did have a most peculiar expression in her eyes.

Mrs Bates stood up abruptly. 'Then I will show you. Come with me,' and she took the girl's hand and led her to the other end of the lounge to where a large mirror hung on the wall. 'That's why,' she said, pointing to the two reflections. 'Having come off second best on one notable occasion I wanted to see how I would compare if I were similarly dressed.'

The girl felt her spine begin to tingle. Not fear exactly, but that instinctive nervous apprehension that the sane sometimes feel in the company of the insane. By God, how long had this woman brooded on her misfortune to have produced this sort of crazy reaction? This obviously explained the long string of attractive girls. Mrs Bates was measuring herself against them, one after the other. And then what? If the measurement was in the older woman's favour then presumably that was an end of the matter, honour having been satisfied. But what if the comparison was unfavourable?

Deborah looked at the two reflections. Mary Bates really was an attractive woman. Her body was trim and taut, and her figure was still quite superb, even without a bra, and in that wisp of a gown she looked like a high priestess of a pagan cult, sensual, uninhibited, and devastatingly provocative. Few women her age could even begin to compare. But she was forty-eight years of age, and she looked it. Nothing could hide that difference in age between the two women reflected in that mirror, and ironically the two provocative gowns served only to reveal that difference more clearly. Deborah was not vain about her own looks, but she knew that if a choice had to be made at that precise moment then most men would choose herself. Mrs Bates simply did not compare.

The girl smiled nervously. 'There's no comparison,' she said lightly. 'If there were any men around I wouldn't stand a chance.' In the mirror she saw the woman's eyes narrow to an expression of cold hatred.

'Nonsense, my dear,' said Mrs Bates smoothly. 'You are far more attractive than I. If the whole situation occurred again my husband would undoubtedly go off with you.'

Deborah released her hand and walked away back to the coffee table. 'You underestimate yourself, Mrs Bates.' She picked up her shawl. 'I'm not attractive to men and never have been, no matter what I wear. Why do you think I live on my own? It's not by choice, I assure you.' She began to move towards the door. Oh God, she simply had to escape from this stupid insanity. 'Anyway, it's getting late, and the wine has given me a headache. If you'll excuse me I think I'll go to bed.'

The look of hatred had vanished from the woman's eyes. 'By

all means,' she said coldly. 'Thank you for a lovely dinner, and a most entertaining evening.'

The girl could not get to her room fast enough. Once inside the bedroom she leant back against the door and closed her eyes. Her hands were trembling, and sweat had broken out over her whole body. What a weird scene! No wonder the others had left in so much of a hurry. First thing tomorrow she would see if she could get her old bedsit back again. She was not going to stay in this house with that crazy woman a minute longer than absolutely necessary. She stripped off her gown, towelled herself dry, put on her nightdress, and lay down on the bed, but her mind was in too much of a turmoil for sleep.

It was about half past eleven when she heard Mrs Bates come up the stairs and go to her own bedroom, but an hour later Deborah was still fretfully awake. She went to the open window and stared down into the garden. It looked even more beautiful by moonlight, and the silver bells really did look silver. It was a warm night, and oppressively close. Perhaps a walk round the garden would calm her down.

Silently she opened the bedroom door and stood there listening, but all was quiet. That wretched woman must be fast asleep by now, dreaming whatever weird images would rise in such a neurotic as Mrs Bates. She slipped on her dressing gown over her nightdress and went downstairs and out into the garden.

It was a lovely night, and for the first time during that entire evening she was able to breathe more easily. It was in many ways a dreadful shame that she had to leave. On the surface it was an ideal job in ideal surroundings, but even from the beginning it had seemed too good to be true, and so it had proved. She sighed and meandered across the lawn. Such a beautiful garden, but such a weird gardener. Even here in the garden the behaviour of her employer had been decidedly odd, coming back again and again to this particular spot. Deborah looked down at the long low mound of Mrs Bates' favourite flower-bed. 'Mary, Mary, quite contrary,' she murmured, 'how does your garden grow? With silver bells and cockleshells, and pretty maids all in a row.'

And it was then, at that precise moment, that the earlier warning bells, the odd behaviour of Mrs Bates, and the fact of the missing girls, all came together in an explosion of realization in her mind. So sudden was the revelation, and so terrifying, that for a full minute she could not move at all even though every instinct in her screamed out for her to get away, and her whole body trembled with wave after wave of piercing coldness. Then slowly she began to back away. Oh dear God, it cannot be, surely!

'Admiring the flowers in the moonlight?' said a voice behind her.

Deborah spun round and there, just a few feet away, was Mrs Bates looking pale and ghostly in a flowing white dressing gown. This second shock, coming so close on the first, came near to causing a fatal heart attack, quite literally. The girl gave a piercing shriek of terror and fled in panic towards the house, bursting in through the French windows and flying up the stairs to her bedroom.

There was no key to the bedroom door, and no straight-backed chair to prop under the door handle. Frantically she dragged the dressing table across the carpet and rammed it against the door, and only just in time.

'What on earth is the matter, girl!' Mrs Bates called out from the corridor, rattling the handle and pushing against the door. 'Let me in. You frightened the life out of me, shrieking like that. What on earth is the matter? Let me in!'

Deborah said nothing. She picked up a pair of scissors and backed away to the middle of the room. Mrs Bates had shoved the door open a couple of inches but could move it no more, and Deborah saw her pale hand come snaking round the edge to identify the obstruction.

'This is ridiculous!' the woman shouted. 'Remove that thing and open this door!'

'Get out! Get out!' the girl shrieked.

The hand disappeared and then there was silence. Fifteen seconds passed, half a minute, and still there was no sound from the corridor.

'You forgot the connecting door,' said a calm voice behind her, and a hand descended on her shoulder.

Again that shriek of hysterical terror rang out. Deborah spun round and stabbed blindly with her scissors, again and again. She stabbed the woman's eyes, and her face, and her shoulders, and fell with her to the floor, and kept on stabbing again and again, at her arms, at her breast, and again and again and again at what was left of her face, and then she sprang clear, flung away the scissors, raced through the connecting door, through the sitting room and out into the corridor, and stumbled hysterically down the stairs to the telephone.

The police arrived twenty minutes later; an inspector, a

sergeant, two male constables, and a policewoman. Little sense had been made of the hysterical babble on the telephone and they had come prepared for almost anything, though hardly for what they actually found. The girl was covered in blood from head to foot, and at first they assumed that she had been attacked and savagely beaten, but as her story began bubbling out they began to realize that here was something far more grim. 'They're out there, I tell you, buried in the flowerbed, murdered by that crazy woman upstairs!' she finished. 'And I was to be next! If you don't believe me, go and look!' and she burst into great racking sobs.

Leaving the constables downstairs with the girl, the Inspector and the sergeant went up to the bedroom. They came out two minutes later and leant against the wall, fighting down the nausea. 'You knew Mrs Bates quite well,' said the inspector at last. 'Is that her?'

The sergeant wiped his brow. 'How the hell can I say! It doesn't even look human!'

Presently the two men came down the stairs and walked over to the open french windows. 'There should be a spade or a fork out there somewhere,' said the inspector. 'Take the two lads. Just dig enough to verify the story. The rest can wait.'

Thirty minutes later the sergeant returned and the two men exchanged a whispered conversation, and then the inspector came over to Deborah. 'Now let's take this again from the beginning.'

'What more do you want!' said the girl hysterically. 'You've seen what's upstairs and you've seen what's in the garden! For God's sake get me out of this place.'

'I've seen you, and certainly I've seen what's upstairs,' said the inspector grimly. 'It's the rest of the story I don't understand.'

The girl sprang to her feet. 'Good God, there are six dead girls buried in the flowerbed! I've told you why and how! What else is there to understand!'

The inspector shook his head. 'There is no one buried in the flowerbed, Miss Templeton,' he said quietly, 'no one at all. Now let's start right from the beginning – and take it very, very slowly.'

Bob Shaw
Love me tender

Bob Shaw was born in 1931 and educated in Belfast. He worked in structural engineering and aircraft design, then in 1958 he became a journalist. After three years on a daily newspaper he began to specialize in industrial public relations, but in 1975 he became a full-time author. In 1973 he and his wife Sadie and three children moved to Stan Laurel's birthplace in the English Lakes. All of which, apart from Stan Laurel, is an awfully po-faced introduction to this large shy man who can drink everyone else into a state so euphoric that they will laugh at his horrid jokes about koalas and Brighton Pier and a great deal else. He has been guest of honour at conventions in Sweden, USA, England, Scotland, Italy and Belgium, and is to be found at most British sf conventions. You can locate him by the groans at the end of the joke.

Among his novels are Night Walk, The Palace of Eternity, Who Goes Here?, The Shadow of Heaven, *and* Vertigo. *His short stories are collected as* Tomorrow Lies in Ambush *and* Cosmic Kaleidoscope. *The only joke in the following story is the grim pun of the title.*

It's a funny thing – I can think all right, but I can't think about the future. Tomorrow doesn't seem to exist for me any more. There's only today, and this drowsy, dreamy acceptance.

Most of the time it's cool here in the shack, the mosquito screens are holding together fairly well, and the bed is a whole lot better than some of the flea pits I've been in lately.

And she waits on me hand and foot. Couldn't be more attentive. Brings me food and drink – all I can stomach – and cleans me up afterwards. Even when I wake up during the night I can see her standing at the door of the room, always watching, always waiting.

But what's she waiting for? That's what I ask myself every so often, and when I do . . .

The swamp buggy had started off life as an ordinary Volkswagen, a beetle convertible, but somebody had extended the axles and fitted pudgy aircraft tyres which spread the vehicle's weight sufficiently to keep it from sinking in mud. Snow chains had been wrapped around the tyres to provide traction. The buggy was noisy, ungainly and uncomfortable, but it was able to negotiate the narrow tracks that ran through the Everglades, and Joe Massick felt it had been well worth the trouble he had taken to steal it.

He sat upright at the wheel, glancing over his shoulder every now and again as though expecting to see a police helicopter swooping down in pursuit, but the sky remained a featureless grey void. The air was hot and so saturated with water that it reminded him of the atmosphere inside the old-fashioned steam laundry where he had once worked as a boy. He did his best to ignore the sweat which rolled down his slab-like body, concentrating his attention on maintaining a north-westerly course in the general direction of Fort Myers.

His best chance of avoiding capture lay in making a quick crossing of the Florida peninsula without being seen, but it was beginning to dawn on him that the journey was not one to be undertaken lightly. The sloughs and swamps of the northern Everglades made up one of the last truly wild regions of the country, and as a confirmed town-dweller he felt threatened by every aspect of the flat and prehistoric landscape through which he was travelling. For the past thirty minutes he had been encountering stands of lifeless trees draped with Spanish moss, and now the intervals between the trees were growing so brief that he appeared to be entering a dead forest which provided a habitat for countless varieties of birds, insects and reptiles. The sound of the buggy's engine was almost drowned by the protests of the colonies of birds it disturbed, and on all sides there was a furtive agitation of other life forms, a sense of resentment, of being scrutinized and assessed by primeval eyes.

It was a feeling which Massick disliked intensely, prompting him to seek reassurance from the buggy's fuel gauge. The position of the needle showed that he still had three-quarters of a tank – more than enough, even allowing for forced detours, to take him to the far side of Big Cypress. He nodded, relaxing slightly into the burlap-covered seat, and had driven for perhaps another minute when a disturbing thought lodged itself like a pebble in the forefront of his mind.

According to the fuel gauge the tank had been three-quarters full when he first set out in the buggy almost an hour earlier. An optimist might have concluded that the vehicle's modest engine was using practically no gasoline, but Massick was beyond such naïvety. He tapped the gauge with his knuckles and saw that the needle was immovable, locked in place.

Doesn't prove a thing, he thought, vainly trying to sell himself the idea. *For all I know, the tank was filled right up.*

A mile further along the track, as he had known in his heart it was bound to do, the engine cut without even a preliminary cough. Massick turned the steering wheel and brought the buggy to rest in a thicket of saw grass and huge ferns. He sat for a moment with his head bowed, whispering the same swear word over and over again until it came to him that he was wasting precious time. The girl back in West Palm Beach might have died – he had been forced to hit her pretty hard to keep her quiet – but if she was still alive she would have given his description to the police and they would have connected him with the one in Orlando and the other one up in Fernandino. In any case, there was no time for sitting around feeling sorry for himself.

Massick picked up the plastic shopping bag which contained all his belongings, stepped down from the buggy, squelched his way back on to the trail and began walking. The surface was better for walking on than he had expected – probably owing its existence to the oil prospecting that had been carried out in the area some years earlier – but it soon became apparent that he was not cut out for trekking across swamps. He had been desperately tired to start off with, and before he had taken a dozen paces his clothes were sopping with perspiration, binding themselves to his well-larded body, maliciously hampering every movement. The air was so humid that he felt himself to be drinking with his lungs.

Now that he was proceeding without the roar of an engine and the clatter of chains, the swamp seemed ominously quiet and again he had the impression of being watched. The profusion of tree trunks and the curtains of hanging moss made it difficult to see far in any direction, and for all he knew he could have been accompanied by a stealthy army whose members were waiting until he collapsed with exhaustion before closing in. Childish though the fantasy was, he was unable to dismiss it completely from his mind and occasionally as he walked he fingered the massy solidity of the .38 pistol in his bag. The sky sagged close overhead, heavy with rain.

Two hours later he crossed one of the innumerable small concrete bridges which carried the track over dark streams and found that it forked in two directions, both of them uninviting to an equal degree. The sun had been invisible all along, and now that dusk was falling Massick's rudimentary trail sense was totally unable to cope with the task of identifying the branch which lay closest to the north-westerly course he wanted. He paused, breathing heavily, and looked around him in the tree-pillared gloom, suddenly understanding why in local Indian legend the big swamp was regarded as the home of ancestral spirits. It was easy to see the ghosts of dead men standing in slim canoes, drifting in silence through the endless colonnades and caverns.

The realization that he was going to have to spend the night in such surroundings jerked Massick out of his indecision. He chose the right-hand path and moved along it at an increased pace, looking out for a hillock of any description upon which he would have a reasonable chance of remaining dry while he slept. It was only when he recalled that snakes also had a preference for high ground, especially in the wet season, that he admitted to himself the seriousness of his situation. He had no real idea how far he was from the townships of the west coast, and even if he did succeed in making his way through Big Cypress on foot he was going to emerge looking conspicuously bearded and filthy – the sort of figure that any cop would want to interrogate on sight.

The thought of being caught and put back in prison after less than a month of freedom caused Massick to give an involuntary moan. He reached into the plastic bag, took out the bottle of rum he had acquired at the same time as the swamp buggy and drank the few ounces of neat liquor it contained. The rum was warm and had an aftertaste of burnt brown sugar which made him wish he had a full fifth for solace during the approaching night. He hurled the bottle away, heard it come down with a splash and on the instant a cicada began to chirp nearby as though he had startled it into life. Within seconds a hundred others had taken up the chorus, walling him in with sound, advertising his presence for the benefit of any creature – human or inhuman – which might be lurking in the encompassing darkness. Startled, prey to fears he was unable to acknowledge, he quickened his pace even though each passing minute made the track more difficult to see. He was beginning to contemplate retracing his steps to the last concrete bridge when a yellow glow sprang into existence some distance ahead and slightly to his left.

Convinced for the moment that he had seen the headlights of an approaching vehicle, Massick snatched his pistol out of the bag, then realized there were no mechanical sounds such as another swamp buggy would have made. Keeping the gun at the ready, he went forward until he reached a barely discernible side track which branched off to the left and seemed to lead straight towards the glimmer of light. All the indications were that, against the odds, he had found some kind of habitation in the heart of the swamp.

The pang of pleasure and relief Massick experienced was not quite enough to obliterate his natural wariness. The only reason he could envisage for people living in the waterlogged wilderness was that they were wardens for one of the area's wildlife sanctuaries – and, for him, walking into an official establishment which had radio equipment could be as disastrous as calling in at a police station. He threaded his way along the path, trying not to make any sound as he negotiated successive barriers of dark vegetation, and after several minutes reached a hummock upon which was perched a wooden shanty. The wan radiance which seeped from the windows and the screen door was swallowed up by the surrounding blackness, but there was enough refraction to show that the building had been constructed from second-hand timbers – which pretty well ruled out the possibility of it being an outpost of authority. Emboldened by what he had found thus far, Massick crossed a cleared area to the nearest window and cautiously looked through it.

The room beyond the smeared glass was lit by oil lanterns hanging from hooks in the ceiling. Much of the floor space was taken up with stacks of cardboard boxes, and in the centre of the room was a rough wooden table at which sat a small stoop-shouldered man of about sixty. He had cropped grey hair, a sprinkling of silver stubble around his chin, and tiny crumpled ears which gave the impression of being clenched like fists. He was dressed in well-worn slacks and a faded green beach shirt. On the table before him was a bottle of whisky and several glass jars containing what looked like small twists of coloured paper. He was preoccupied with removing the coloured objects from the jars and carefully placing them in individual plastic boxes, pausing now and then to swig whisky straight from the bottle.

The room had two interior doors, one of them leading into a

163

primitive kitchen. The other door was closed, but Massick guessed it led into a bedroom. He remained at the window long enough to assure himself that the occupant of the shanty was alone, then slipped the pistol into his side pocket, walked quietly to the screen door and tapped on it. The mosquito mesh made a noise like distant thunder. A few seconds later the small man appeared with a flashlight which he shone on Massick's face.

'Who's out there?' he growled. 'Whaddaya want?'

'I got stranded,' Massick explained, enduring the searching brilliance. 'I need shelter for the night.'

The man shook his head. 'I got no spare room. Go away.'

Massick opened the door and went inside, crowding the other man back. 'I don't need much room, and I'll pay you twenty dollars for the night.'

'What's the idea? What makes you think you can just walk in here?'

For a reply Massick used a trick he had perfected over a period of years. He smiled broadly and at the same time hardened his gaze and projected a silent message with all the conviction he could muster: *If you cross me up I'll tear your head right off your body.* The little man suddenly looked uncertain and backed further into the room.

'I got to be paid in advance,' he said, trying to retain some advantage.

'Fair enough. I tell you what I'll do, Pop. I could use a few drinks to make up some of the sweat I lost, so here's an extra ten for a share in that bottle. How's that?' Massick took his billfold from his pocket, counted out thirty dollars and handed them over.

'Okay, I guess.' The man took the money and, looking mollified, tucked it into his shirt pocket. 'The whole bottle didn't cost ten.'

'Consider it a reward for your hospitality to a weary traveller,' Massick said jovially, smiling again. He was prepared to be generous while armed with the knowledge that when he left he would be taking the money back, along with any other cash and valuables his host happened to have around. 'What's your name, Pop?'

'Ed. Ed Cromer.'

'Nice to meet you, Ed.' Massick went on into the room he had surveyed from the outside and picked up the whisky bottle from the table, observing as he did so that the small coloured objects his host had been packaging were dead butterflies and moths. 'Is this some kind of a hobby you've got here?'

'Business,' Cromer replied, squaring his thin shoulders importantly. 'Profession.'

'Is that a fact? Is there much demand for bugs?'

'Me and my partner supply lepidopterists – them's collectors – all over the state. All over the country.'

'Your partner?' Massick slid his hand into the pocket containing the pistol and glanced towards the closed door of the bedroom. 'Is he in there?'

'No!' The expression of pride vanished from Cromer's face and his eyes shuttled anxiously for a moment. 'That's my private room in there. There's nobody allowed in there bar me.'

Massick noted the reaction with mild interest. 'There's no need to get up tight, Ed. It was just when you mentioned your partner . . .'

'He runs the store up in Tampa. Only comes down one day a month to pick up the new catch.'

'He'll be here soon, will he?'

'Not for a couple of weeks. Say, mister, what's the third degree for? I mean, I could ask you who you are and where you're from and what you're doin' wanderin' around Big Cypress in the dark.'

'That's right,' Massick said comfortably. 'You could ask.'

He cleared some magazines from a wicker chair and sat down near the window, suddenly realizing how close he was to total exhaustion. His intention had been to press on towards the west coast in the morning, but unless Cromer had a swamp buggy parked out of sight nearby it might be best to wait until the partner arrived with transportation. It would be difficult to find a safer place to lie low and rest for a couple of weeks. Turning the matter over in his mind, he took off his sweat-stained jacket and draped it over the back of the chair, then settled back to drink whisky.

There followed fifteen minutes of almost total silence during which Cromer, who had returned to his meticulous sorting and mounting of butterflies, glanced expectantly at Massick each time he raised the bottle to his lips. At length, realizing there was going to be no taking of turns, he took a fresh bottle of Canadian Club from a cupboard in the corner and began drinking independently. After his initial querulousness he showed no sign of resenting his unexpected guest, but Massick noticed he was drinking somewhat faster than before and becoming less precise in his movements. Massick watched contentedly, enjoying his ability to cause apprehension in others simply by being near them, as Cromer fitted a jeweller's magnifier over his right eye and began examining a small heap of blue-winged insects one by one, using his flashlight to supplement the room's uncertain illumination.

'What are you doing now, Pop?' he said indulgently. 'Is it all that hard to tell the boys from the girls?'

'Checkin' for look-alikes,' Cromer mumbled. 'Mimics, they're called. You don't know nothin' about mimics, do you?'

'Can't say I do.'

Cromer sniffed to show his contempt. 'Didn't think you would somehow. Even them so-called experts up in Jacksonville with their fancy college degrees don't know nothin' about mimics. *Nobody* knows more about mimics than I do, and one of these days . . .' He broke off, his narrow face taut with sudden belligerence, and took a long drink of whisky.

'You're going to show them a thing or two, are you, Professor?' Massick prompted. 'Make them all sit up and take notice?'

Cromer glanced at the bedroom door, then selected two pale blue butterflies from the table and held them out on the palm of his hand. 'Whaddaya say about them? Same or different?'

Massick eyed the closed door thoughtfully before turning his attention to the insects. 'They look the same to me.'

'Want to bet on it?'

'I'm not a gambling man.'

'Just as well – you'da lost your money,' Cromer said triumphantly. 'This one on the left has a kinda blue glaze all over his wings and the birds leave him alone because he don't taste good. This other feller does taste good to birds, so he fools them by copyin' the same blue, but he does it by mixin' in blue bits and white bits on his wings. Of course, you need one of them microscopes to see it proper. I'm goin' to get me one of them microscopes real soon.'

'Very interesting,' Massick said, abstracted, noticing for the first time that the door to the room he had presumed to be a bedroom was secured by a farmhouse-type latch and that the latch was held down by a twist of wire. Was it possible, he wondered, that Cromer had something valuable hidden away? It was difficult to imagine what the shabby recluse might have, but it was a well-known fact that elderly people who lived in conditions of abject poverty often had large sums of money tucked into mattresses and under floorboards. In any case, there would be no harm in investigating the matter while he was actually on the premises. Deciding that no immediate action was required, he continued sipping whisky and pretending to listen to Cromer's rambling discourse on entomology.

The little man appeared to have an extensive though informal knowledge of his subject which he dispensed in an anecdotal folksy style, with frequent references to Seminole legends, but his words were becoming so slurred that it was almost impossible to follow his meaning at times. The practice of mimicry among insects, fish and animals seemed to fascinate him and he kept returning to it obsessively, drinking all the while, his face and clamped-down ears growing progressively redder as the level in his bottle went down.

'You ought to go easy on that stuff,' Massick told him with some amusement. 'I don't want to put you to bed.'

'I can handle it.' Cromer stood up, swaying even though he was holding the edge of the table, and gazed at Massick with solemn blue eyes. 'I gotta consult the head of the family.'

He lurched to the outer door and disappeared through it into the night, already fumbling with his trouser zip. Massick waited a few seconds, stood up and was surprised to discover that he too was unsteady on his feet. He had forgotten that exhaustion and hunger would enhance the effects of the liquor he had consumed. Blinking to clear his vision, he crossed the room to the locked door, pulled the wire away from the latch and dropped it on the floor. He opened the door, took one step into the room beyond and froze in mid-stride, his jaw sagging in surprise.

There was a young woman lying on the narrow bed, her body covered by a single sheet.

At the sound of Massick's entrance she raised herself on one elbow – a strangely languid movement, as though she was weakened by illness – and he saw that she had smooth, swarthy skin and black hair. His impression that she was an Indian was strengthened by the fact that she had three dots tattooed in a triangle on her forehead, although he had never seen that particular marking before. She stared at him in silence for a moment, showing no signs of alarm, and began to smile. Her teeth were white, forming a flawless crescent.

'I'm sorry,' Massick said. 'I didn't know . . .' He backed out of the room, pulling the door closed, trying to understand why the sight of the woman had been so disconcerting. Was it the sheer unexpectedness of her presence in Cromer's bedroom? Was it that the circumstances suggested she was being held captive? Massick picked up his bottle, gulped some whisky and was wiping his mouth with the back of his hand when the answer to his questions stole quietly into his mind. She had looked at him – and had smiled.

He could not remember a single occasion in the twenty-odd years of his adult life on which a woman had set eyes on him for the first time and had reacted by smiling. As a youth he had spent hours before the mirror trying to decide what it was about his appearance that made all the girls in his age group avoid his eyes and refuse point blank to date him. There had been a two-year period in which he had done his best to conform to the same image as the sexually successful young men in the neighbourhood – trying to put a twinkle into the slate pellets that were his eyes, trying to smile when every muscle in his face wanted to scowl, trying to crack jokes, to be lean-hipped, to be a good dancer – but the net result had been that the girls had shunned him more assiduously than before. After that he had simply begun taking them, whether they liked it or not. And none of them had liked it.

Over the years Massick had grown accustomed to the arrangement, so much so that he found real stimulation in the sudden look of mingled terror and disgust on a woman's face as she realized what was going to happen to her. Underneath it all, however, imprisoned far down in buried layers of his mind-body complex, there still lived a boyish Joe Massick who yearned for another kind of encounter, one in which there was gentleness in place of force, gladness in place of revulsion, in which soft arms welcomed as the world flowed out and away until there was nothing to see anywhere except eyes that shone with a special warm lustre and lips that smiled . . .

'That's better,' Cromer said, coming in through the screen door. He went straight to his chair at the table, executed a lateral shuffle which showed he was quite drunk, and sat down before the assortment of insects and plastic boxes.

Massick returned to his own seat and gazed at Cromer with speculative eyes. Was it possible that the little man, in spite of his scrawny and dried-up appearance, had a taste for hot-blooded Indian girls? The notion inspired Massick with a sharp pang of jealousy. He had seen enough of the girl's body to know that she was strong-breasted, lush, ripe – and that she would be totally wasted on a miserable old stick like Cromer. If anybody was to bed down with her that night it ought to be Joe Massick, because he was the one who had been going through hell and needed relief from the tensions that racked his body, he was the one who had the size and strength to give the chick what she deserved, and because he was in that kind of a mood. Besides, she had smiled at him . . .

'The Calusas was the ones who knew this swamp,' Cromer was muttering, staring down at a moth in its tiny crystal coffin. 'They were here long before the Seminoles ever even *seen* the place, and they knew all about it, that's for sure . . . knew when the nymphs was turnin' into imagos . . . knew when it was time to pull up stakes and move on.'

'You're a wily old bird, aren't you?' Massick said. 'You've got this place stocked up with everything you need.'

'Hear them cicadas out there?' Cromer, apparently unaware that Massick had spoken, nodded towards the black rectangle of the door. 'Seventeen years they live under the ground, gettin' ready to come up and breed. It stands to reason there must be other critturs that takes longer – maybe thirty years, maybe fifty, maybe even a . . .'

'I'm a bit disappointed in you, Ed. I just didn't think you were the selfish type.'

'Selfish?' Cromer, looking puzzled and hurt, attempted to focus his gaze on Massick. 'What's this selfish?'

'You didn't introduce me to your friend.'

'Friend? I got no . . .' Cromer's flushed, narrow face stiffened with consternation as he turned to look at the bedroom door. He threw himself forward on to his hands and knees, picked up the piece of wire Massick had discarded, and wrapped it around the latch, snorting with urgency as his clumsiness protracted an operation that should have been instantaneous.

Massick watched the performance with good humour. 'Do you generally keep your lady friends locked up?'

'She . . . She's sick.' Cromer got to his feet, breathing audibly, his eyes nervous and pleading. 'Best left alone in there.'

'She didn't look all that sick to me. What's her name?'

'Don't know her name. She wandered in here a couple of days ago. I'm lookin' after her, that's all.'

Massick shook his head and grinned. 'I don't believe you, Ed. I think you're a horny old goat and you're keeping that young piece in there for your own amusement. Shame on you!'

'You don't know what you're talkin' about. I tell you she's sick, and I'm looking after her.'

Massick stood up, bottle in hand. 'In that case we'll give her a drink – best medicine there is.'

'No!' Cromer darted forward, grabbing for Massick's arm. 'Listen, if you want to know the . . .'

Massick swung at him more out of irritation than malice, intending merely to sweep the little man out of his way, but Cromer seemed to fall on to his fist, magnifying the effect of the blow. The force of the impact returning along his forearm told Massick he had done some serious damage, and he stepped back. Cromer went down into a collision with the table, his eyes reduced to blind white crescents, and dropped to the floor with a slapping thud which could have been produced by a side of bacon. The sound alone was as good as a death certificate to Massick.

'You stupid old bastard,' he whispered accusingly. He stared down at the body, adjusting to the new situation, then knelt and retrieved his money from Cromer's shirt pocket. A search of the dead man's personal effects yielded only a cheap wrist-watch and eleven extra dollars in single bills. Massick put the watch and money away in his pocket. He took a firm grip on Cromer's collar, dragged the body to the screen door and out into the raucous darkness of the swamp. The chorus of insect calls seemed to grow louder as he moved away from the shanty, again creating the impression of an all-pervading sentience. In spite of the stifling heat Massick felt a crawling coldness between his shoulderblades. Suddenly appreciating the futility of trying to dispose of the body before daylight, he released his burden and groped his way back towards the sallow glimmers of the hurricane lamps.

Once inside the building, he bolted the outer door and went around the main room twitching curtains into place across the windows. As soon as he felt safe from the pressures of the watchful blackness he picked up the whisky bottle and drank from it until his throat closed against the rawness of the liquor. Somewhat restored by the alcohol, he allowed his thoughts to return to the bedroom door and there was a stirring of warmth low down in his belly as he remembered what lay beyond.

It's cosier this way, he thought. *Three always was a crowd.*

He put the bottle aside, went to the door and removed the wire from the latch. The door swung open easily, allowing a swath of light to fall across the bed, revealing that the black-haired girl was still lying down, apparently undisturbed by any commotion she may have heard. As before, she raised herself on one elbow to look up at him. Massick stood in the doorway and scanned her face, waiting for the change of expression to which he was so accustomed, the clouding of the eyes with fear and loathing, but – exactly as before – the girl began to smile. He bared his own teeth in a manufactured response, scarcely able to believe his luck.

'What's your name, honey?' he said, moving closer to the bed.

She went on smiling at him, her gaze locked into his, and there was nothing anywhere in her face to show that she had heard the question.

'Don't you have a name?' Massick persisted, a new idea beginning to form at the back of his mind. *Never had a deaf-mute before!*

The girl reacted by sitting up a little further, a movement which allowed the sheet to slip down from her breasts. They were the most perfectly formed that Massick had ever seen – rounded, almost pneumatic in their fullness, with upright nipples – and his mouth went dry as he advanced to the side of the bed and knelt down. The girl's dark eyes remained fixed on his, bold and yet tender, as he put out his hand and with his fingertips gently traced a line from the three dots on her forehead, down her cheek and neck and on to the smooth curvature of her breast. His hand lingered there briefly and was moving on towards the languorous upthrust of her hip – taking the edge of the sheet with it – when she made a small, inarticulate sound of protest and caught his wrist.

Thwarted and tantalized, Massick gripped the sheet with the intention of ripping it away from the lower part of her body, then he saw that the girl was still smiling. She let go of his wrists, raised her hands to his chest and began to undo his shirt, fumbling in her eagerness.

'You raunchy little so-and-so,' Massick said in a gratified whisper. He got to his feet, tearing at his clothing and in a few seconds was standing naked beside the bed. The girl relaxed on to her pillow, waiting for him. He lowered his thick torso on to the bed beside her and brought his mouth down on hers. She returned his kiss in a curiously inexpert manner which served only to heighten his pleasure. Giving way to his impatience, he propped himself up on one elbow and used his free hand to throw back the sheet, his eyes hungering for the promised magical concourse of hip and belly and thigh unique to woman.

The ovipositor projecting from the she-creature's groin was

a tapering, horny spike. Transparent eggs were already flowing from the aperture at its tip, bubbling and winking, sliming its sides, adding to the jellied mass of spawn which had gathered on her distended abdomen.

Massick had time for a single whimper of despair, then the she-creature was on him, bearing down with an inhuman strength which was scarcely necessary. The first probing stab from the ovipositor had hurt for only an instant, then ancient and merciful chemistries had taken over, obliterating all pain, inducing a flaccid paralysis which gripped his entire frame. He lay perfectly still, hushed and bemused, as his lover worked on him, stabbing again and again, skilfully avoiding vital organs, filling his body cavities with the eggs which would soon produce a thousand hungry larvae.

It's a pity she had to change. I liked her better the other way — before those dots on her forehead changed into watchful black beads, before her eyes developed the facets and began to drift to the side of her head, before those magnificent breasts began reshaping themselves into a central pair of legs.

But she's kind to me, and that counts for a lot. Waits on me hand and foot, like an attentive lover. Even when I wake up during the night I can see her standing at the door of the room, always watching, always waiting.

But what's she waiting for? That's what I ask myself every so often, and when I do . . .

Gene Wolfe
Kevin Malone

Gene Wolfe was born in Brooklyn in 1931 and sent me a biographical essay as engrossing as his stories. 'Here it is,' he wrote at the top. 'Good luck.' I'm tempted to run it complete, but this book is already longer than it was supposed to be. Soon he was in Poeria, where little Rosemary Dietch lived next door, but by the late thirties he was established in Houston, where he attended Edgar Allan Poe elementary school (read 'Masque of the red death' in fifth grade, learned 'The Raven' in sixth, enviably – I had to make do with Jane Austen and Matthew Arnold). Five blocks away from home was the Richmond Pharmacy, where he read Famous Fantastic Mysteries *behind the candy case. High school led by a devious route to the National Guard, whence he landed at Texas A & M ('an all-male land-grant university specializing in animal husbandry and engineering – only Dickens could have done justice to A & M as I knew it, and he would not have been believed'). The GI Bill eventually got him to the University of Houston. He married Rosemary Dietch five months after taking a job in engineering development. After sixteen years he joined the staff of Plant Engineering. The Wolfe children are Roy II, Madeleine, Therese, and Matthew.*

Soon after the marriage he began to write 'in the hope of making enough money to buy furniture'. Since then he has published more than eighty stories. 'The death of Doctor Island' (not to be confused with 'The island of Doctor Death' or 'The doctor of Death Island') won a Nebula Award for best novella, his contemporary novel Peace *won the Chicago Foundation for Literature Award. Other novels are the fantasy* Devil in a Forest, Operation Ares, *and* The Fifth Head of Cerberus, *one of the subtlest of science fiction novels. His approach to the tale of terror is subtle too, as you will see.*

Marcella and I were married in April. I lost my position with Ketterly, Bruce & Drake in June, and by August we were desperate. We kept the apartment – I think we both felt that if we lowered our standards there would be no chance to raise them again – but the rent tore at our small savings. All during July I had tried to get a job at another brokerage firm, and by August I was calling fraternity brothers I had not seen since graduation, and expressing an entire willingness to work in whatever businesses their fathers owned. One of them, I think, must have mailed us the advertisement.

> Attractive young couple, well educated and well connected, will receive free housing, generous living allowance for minimal services.

There was a telephone number, which I omit for reasons that will become clear.

I showed the clipping to Marcella, who was lying with her cocktail shaker on the chaise-longue. She said, 'Why not,' and I dialled the number.

The telephone buzzed in my ear, paused, and buzzed again. I allowed myself to go limp in my chair. It seemed absurd to call at all; for the advertisement to have reached us that day, it must have appeared no later than yesterday morning. If the position were worth having—

'The Pines.'

I pulled myself together. 'You placed a classified ad. For an attractive couple, well educated and the rest of it.'

'I did not, sir. However, I believe my master did. I am Priest, the butler.'

I looked at Marcella, but her eyes were closed. 'Do you know, Priest, if the opening has been filled?'

'I think not, sir. May I ask your age?'

I told him. At his request, I also told him Marcella's (she was two years younger than I), and gave him the names of the schools we had attended, described our appearance, and mentioned that my grandfather had been a governor of Virginia, and that Marcella's uncle had been ambassador to France. I did not tell him that my father had shot himself rather than face bankruptcy, or that Marcella's family had disowned her – but I suspect he guessed well enough what our situation was.

'You will forgive me, sir, for asking so many questions. We are almost a half day's drive, and I would not wish you to be disappointed.'

I told him that I appreciated that, and we set a date – Tuesday of the next week – on which Marcella and I were to come out for an interview with 'the master'. Priest had hung up before I realized that I had failed to learn his employer's name.

During the teens and twenties some very wealthy people had designed estates in imitation of the palaces of the Italian Renaissance. The Pines was one of them, and better preserved than most – the fountain in the courtyard still played, the marbles were clean and unyellowed, and if no red-robed cardinal descended the steps to a carriage blazoned with the Borgia arms, one felt that he had only just gone. No doubt the place had originally been called *La Capana* or *Il Eremitaggio*.

A serious-looking man in dark livery opened the door for us. For a moment he stared at us across the threshold. 'Very well . . .' he said.

'I beg your pardon?'

'I said that you are looking very well.' He nodded to each of us in turn, and stood aside. 'Sir. Madame. I am Priest.'

'Will your master be able to see us?'

For a moment some exiled expression – it might have been amusement – seemed to tug at his solemn face. 'The music room, perhaps, sir?'

I said I was sure that would be satisfactory, and followed him. The music room held a Steinway, a harp, and a dozen or so comfortable chairs; it overlooked a rose garden in which old remontant varieties were beginning that second season that is more opulent though less generous than the first. A kneeling gardener was weeding one of the beds.

'This is a wonderful house,' Marcella said. 'I really didn't think there was anything like it left. I told him you'd have a john collins – all right? You were looking at the roses.'

'Perhaps we ought to get the job first.'

'I can't call him back now, and if we don't get it, at least we'll have had the drinks.'

I nodded to that. In five minutes they arrived, and we drank them and smoked cigarettes we found in a humidor – English cigarettes of strong Turkish tobacco. A maid came, and said that Mr Priest would be much obliged if we would let him know when we would dine. I told her that we would eat whenever it was convenient, and she dropped a little curtsy and withdrew.

'At least,' Marcella commented, 'he's making us comfortable while we wait.'

*

Dinner was lamb in aspic, and a salade, with a maid – another maid – and footman to serve while Priest stood by to see that it was done properly. We ate at either side of a small table on a terrace overlooking another garden, where antique statues faded to white glimmerings as the sun set.

Priest came forward to light the candles. 'Will you require me after dinner, sir?'

'Will your employer require us; that's the question.'

'Bateman can show you to your room, sir, when you are ready to retire. Julia will see to madame.'

I looked at the footman, who was carrying in fruit on a tray.

'No, sir. That is Carter. Bateman is your man.'

'And Julia,' Marcella put in, 'is my maid, I suppose?'

'Precisely.' Priest gave an almost inaudible cough. 'Perhaps, sir – and madame – you might find this useful.' He drew a photograph from an inner pocket and handed it to me.

It was a black and white snapshot, somewhat dogeared. Two dozen people, most of them in livery of one kind or another, stood in brilliant sunshine on the steps at the front of the house, men behind women. There were names in India ink across the bottom of the picture: James Sutton, Edna DeBuck, Lloyd Bateman . . .

'Our staff, sir.'

I said, 'Thank you, Priest. No, you needn't stay tonight.'

The next morning Bateman shaved me in bed. He did it very well, using a straight razor and scented soap applied with a brush. I had heard of such things – I think my grandfather's valet may have shaved him like that before the First World War – but I had never guessed that anyone kept up the tradition. Bateman did, and I found I enjoyed it. When he had dressed me, he asked if I would breakfast in my room.

'I doubt it,' I said. 'Do you know my wife's plans?'

'I think it likely she will be on the South Terrace, sir. Julia said something to that effect as I was bringing in your water.'

'I'll join her then.'

'Of course, sir.' He hesitated.

'I don't think I'll require a guide, but you might tell my wife I'll be with her in ten minutes or so.'

Bateman repeated his, 'Of course, sir,' and went out. The truth was that I wanted to assure myself that everything I had carried in the pockets of my old suit – car keys, wallet, and so on – had been transferred to the new one he had laid out for me; and I did not want to insult him, if I could prevent it, by doing it in front of him.

Everything was where it should be, and I had a clean handkerchief in place of my own only slightly soiled one. I pulled it out to look at (Irish linen) and a flutter of green came with it – two bills, both fifties.

Over eggs Benedict I complimented Marcella on her new dress, and asked if she had noticed where it had been made.

'Rowe's. It's a little shop on Fifth Avenue.'

'You know it, then. Nothing unusual?'

She answered, 'No, nothing unusual,' more quickly than she should have, and I knew that there had been money in her new clothes too, and that she did not intend to tell me about it.

'We'll be going home after this. I wonder if they'll want me to give this jacket back.'

'Going home?' She did not look up from her plate. 'Why? And who are "they"?'

'Whoever owns this house.'

'Yesterday you called him *he*. You said Priest talked about *the master*, so that seemed logical enough. Today you're afraid to deal with even presumptive masculinity.'

I said nothing.

'You think he spent the night in my room – they separated us, and you thought that was why, and you just waited there – was it under a sheet? – for me to scream or something. And I didn't.'

'I was hoping you had, and I hadn't heard you.'

'Nothing happened, dammit! I went to bed and went to sleep; but as for going home, you're out of your mind. Can't you see we've got the job? Whoever he is – wherever he is – he likes us. We're going to stay here and live like human beings, at least for a while.'

And so we did. That day we stayed on from hour to hour. After that, from day to day; and at last from week to week. I felt like Klipspringer, the man who was Jay Gatsby's guest for so long that he had no other home – except that Klipspringer, presumably, saw Gatsby from time to time, and no doubt made agreeable conversation, and perhaps even played the piano for him. Our Gatsby was absent. I do not mean that we avoided him, or that he avoided us; there were no rooms we were forbidden to enter, and no times when the servants seemed eager that we should play golf or swim or go riding. Before the good weather ended, we had two couples up for a weekend; and when Bette Windgassen asked if Marcella had inherited the place, and then if we were renting it, Marcella said, 'Oh, do you like it?' in such a way that they left, I think, convinced that it was ours, or as good as ours.

And so it was. We went away when we chose, which was seldom, and returned when we chose, quickly. We ate on the various terraces and balconies, and in the big, formal dining room, and in our own bedrooms. We rode the horses, and drove the Mercedes and the cranky, appealing old Jaguar as though they were our own. We did everything, in fact, except buy the groceries and pay the taxes and the servants; but someone else was doing that; and every morning I found one hundred dollars in the pockets of my clean clothes. If summer had lasted for ever, perhaps I would still be there.

The poplars lost their leaves in one October week; at the end of it I fell asleep listening to the hum of the pump that emptied the swimming pool. When the rain came, Marcella turned sour and drank too much. One evening I made the mistake of putting my arm about her shoulders as we sat before the fire in the trophy room.

'Get your filthy hands off me,' she said. 'I don't belong to you.'

'Priest, look here. He hasn't said an intelligent word to me all day or done a decent thing, and now he wants to paw me all night.'

Priest pretended, of course, that he had not heard her.

'Look over here! Damn it, you're a human being, aren't you?'

He did not ignore that. 'Yes, madame, I am a human being.'

'I'll say you are. You're more a man than he is. This is your place, and you're keeping us for pets – is it me you want? Or him? You sent us the ad, didn't you. He thinks you go into my room at night, or he says he does. Maybe you really come to his – is that it?'

Priest did not answer. I said, 'For God's sake, Marcella.'

'Even if you're old, Priest, I think you're too much of a man for that.' She stood up, tottering on her long legs and holding on to the stonework of the fireplace. 'If you want me, take me.

If this house is yours, you can have me. We'll send him to Vegas – or throw him on the dump.'

In a much softer tone than he usually used, Priest said, 'I don't want either of you, madame.'

I stood up then, and caught him by the shoulders. I had been drinking too, though only half or a quarter as much as Marcella; but I think it was more than that – it was the accumulated frustration of all the days since Jim Bruce told me I was finished. I outweighed Priest by at least forty pounds, and I was twenty years younger. I said: 'I want to know.'

'Release me, sir, please.'

'I want to know who it is; I want to know now. Do you see that fire? Tell me, Priest, or I swear I'll throw you in it.'

His face tightened at that. 'Yes,' he whispered, and I let go of his shoulders. 'It was not the lady, sir. It was you. I want that understood this time.'

'What the hell are you talking about?'

'I'm not doing this because of what she said.'

'You aren't the master, are you? For God's sake tell the truth.'

'I have always told the truth, sir. No, I am not the master. Do you remember the picture I gave you?'

I nodded.

'You discarded it. I took the liberty, sir, of rescuing it from the wastecan in your bedroom. I have it here.' He reached into his coat and pulled it out, just as he had on the first day, and handed it to me.

'It's one of these? One of the servants?'

Priest nodded and pointed with an impeccably manicured forefinger to the figure at the extreme right of the second row. The name beneath it was *Kevin Malone*.

'Him?'

Silently, Priest nodded again.

I had examined the picture on the night he had given it to me, but I had never paid special attention to that particular half-inch-high image. The person it represented might have been a gardener, a man of middle age, short and perhaps stocky. A soft, sweat-stained hat cast a shadow on his face.

'I want to see him.' I looked towards Marcella, still leaning against the stonework of the mantel. 'We want to see him.'

'Are you certain, sir?'

'Damn you, get him!'

Priest remained where he was, staring at me; I was so furious that I think I might have seized him as I had threatened and pushed him into the fire.

Then the french windows opened, and there came a gust of wind. For an instant I think I expected a ghost, or some turbulent elemental spirit. I felt that pricking at the neck that comes when one reads Poe alone at night.

The man I had seen in the picture stepped into the room. He was a small and very ordinary man in worn khaki, but he left the windows wide behind him, so that the night entered with him, and remained in the room for as long as we talked.

'You own this house,' I said. 'You're Kevin Malone.'

He shook his head. 'I am Kevin Malone – this house owns me.'

Marcella was standing straighter now, drunk, yet still at that stage of drunkenness in which she was conscious of her condition and could compensate for it. 'It owns me too,' she said, and walking almost normally she crossed the room to the baronial chair Malone had chosen, and managed to sit down at his feet.

'My father was the man-of-all-work here. My mother was the parlour maid. I grew up here, washing the cars and raking leaves out of the fountains. Do you follow me? Where did you grow up?'

I shrugged. 'Various places. Richmond, New York, three years in Paris. Until I was sent off to school we lived in hotels, mostly.'

'You see, then. You can understand.' Malone smiled for a moment. 'You're still recreating the life you had as a child, or trying to. Isn't that right? None of us can be happy any other way, and few of us even want to try.'

'Thomas Wolfe said you can't go home again,' I ventured.

'That's right, you can't go home. There's one place where we can never go – haven't you thought of that? We can dive to the bottom of the sea and some day NASA will fly us to the stars, and I have known men to plunge into the past – or the future – and drown. But there's one place where we can't go. We can't go where we are already. We can't go home, because our minds, and our hearts, and our immortal souls are already there.'

Not knowing what to say, I nodded, and that seemed to satisfy him. Priest looked as calm as ever, but he made no move to shut the windows, and I sensed that he was somehow afraid.

'I was put into an orphanage when I was twelve, but I never forgot The Pines. I used to tell the other kids about it, and it got bigger and better every year; but I knew what I said could never equal the reality.'

He shifted in his seat, and the slight movement of his legs sent Marcella sprawling, passed out. She retained a certain grace still; I have always understood that it is the reward of studying ballet as a child.

Malone continued to talk. 'They'll tell you it's no longer possible for a poor boy with a second rate education to make a fortune. Well, it takes luck; but I had it. It also takes the willingness to risk it all. I had that too, because I knew that for me anything under a fortune was nothing. I had to be able to buy this place – to come back and buy The Pines, and staff it and maintain it. That's what I wanted, and nothing less would make any difference.'

'You're to be congratulated,' I said. 'But why . . .'

He laughed. It was a deep laugh, but there was no humour in it. 'Why don't I wear a tie and eat my supper at the end of the big table? I tried it. I tried it for nearly a year, and every night I dreamed of home. That wasn't home, you see, wasn't The Pines. Home is three rooms above the stables. I live there now. I live at home, as a man should.'

'It seems to me that it would have been a great deal simpler for you to have applied for the job you fill now.'

Malone shook his head impatiently. 'That wouldn't have done it at all. I had to have control. That's something I learned in business – to have control. Another owner would have wanted to change things, and maybe he would even have sold out to a subdivider. No. Besides, when I was a boy this estate belonged to a fashionable young couple. Suppose a man of my age had bought it? Or a young woman, some whore.' His mouth tightened, then relaxed. 'You and your wife were ideal. Now I'll have to get somebody else, that's all. You can stay the night, if you like. I'll have you driven into the city tomorrow morning.'

I ventured, 'You needed us as stage properties, then. I'd be willing to stay on those terms.'

Malone shook his head again. 'That's out of the question. I don't need props, I need actors. In business I've put on little shows for the competition, if you know what I mean, and sometimes even for my own people. And I've learned that the only actors who can really do justice to their parts are the ones who don't know what they are.'

'Really—' I began.

He cut me off with a look, and for a few seconds we stared at one another. Something terrible lived behind those eyes.

Frightened despite all reason could tell me, I said, 'I understand,' and stood up. There seemed to be nothing else to do. 'I'm glad, at least, that you don't hate us. With your childhood it would be quite natural if you did. Will you explain things to Marcella in the morning? She'll throw herself at you, no matter what I say.'

He nodded absently.

'May I ask one question more? I wondered why you had to leave and go into the orphanage. Did your parents die or lose their places?'

Malone said, 'Didn't you tell him, Priest? It's the local legend. I thought everyone knew.'

The butler cleared his throat. 'The elder Mr Malone – he was the stableman here, sir, though it was before my time. He murdered Betty Malone, who was one of the maids. Or at least he was thought to have, sir. They never found the body, and it's possible he was accused falsely.'

'Buried her on the estate,' Malone said. 'They found bloody rags and the hammer, and he hanged himself in the stable.'

'I'm sorry . . . I didn't mean to pry.'

The wind whipped the drapes like wine-red flags. They knocked over a vase and Priest winced, but Malone did not seem to notice. 'She was twenty years younger and a tramp,' he said. 'Those things happen.'

I said, 'Yes, I know they do,' and went up to bed.

I do not know where Marcella slept. Perhaps there on the carpet, perhaps in the room that had been hers, perhaps even in Malone's servants' flat over the stables. I breakfasted alone on the terrace, then – without Bateman's assistance – packed my bags.

I saw her only once more. She was wearing a black silk dress; there were circles under her eyes and her head must have been throbbing, but her hand was steady. As I walked out of the house, she was going over the Sévres with a peacock-feather duster. We did not speak.

I have sometimes wondered if I were wholly wrong in

anticipating a ghost when the french windows opened. How did Malone know the time had come for him to appear?

Of course I have looked up the newspaper reports of the murder. All the old papers are on microfilm at the library, and I have a great deal of time.

There is no mention of a child. In fact, I get the impression that the identical surnames of the murderer and his victim were coincidental. *Malone* is a common enough one, and there were a good many Irish servants then.

Sometimes I wonder if it is possible for a man – even a rich man – to be possessed, and not to know it.

Joan Aiken
Time to laugh

*Joan Aiken is the daughter of Conrad Aiken, author of at
least two minor classics of the macabre (*Mr Arcularis *and*
Silent Snow, Secret Snow). *Her mother educated her at home
until she was twelve, when she went to a small progressive
boarding school in Oxford. She worked for the BBC and the
United Nations, and was features editor for* Argosy *for five
years before, in the early sixties, she began to write full time.
By now she has written about fifty books, three of which won
the Guardian Award for children's literature; one (*The Wolves
of Willoughby Chase) *also won the Lewis Carroll Award,
while* Nightfall *was honoured by the Mystery Writers of
America. She is married to the American painter Julius
Goldstein.*

*Does she also get an award for the greatest number of title
changes? In America,* Trouble with Product X *became* Beware
of the Bouquet; Hate Begins at Home *became* Dark Interval;
The Ribs of Death *turned into* The Crystal Crow; The Butterfly
Picnic *ended up as* A Cluster of Separate Sparks, *and yet some
of us would be content to invent just one title as striking. Here
is more of her originality.*

When Matt climbed in at the open window of The Croft, it had
been raining steadily for three days – August rain, flattening
the bronze-green plains of wheat, making dim green jungles of
the little woods round Wentby, turning the motorway which
cut across the small town's southern tip into a greasy nightmare on which traffic skidded and piled into crunching heaps;
all the county police were desperately busy trying to clear up
one disaster after another.

If there had been a river at Wentby, Matt might have gone
fishing instead, on that Saturday afternoon . . . but the town's
full name was Wentby Waterless, the nearest brook was twenty

185

miles away, the rain lay about in scummy pools on the clay, or sank into the lighter soil and vanished. And if the police had not been so manifestly engaged and distracted by the motorway. chaos, it might never have occurred to Matt that now would be the perfect time to explore The Croft; after all, by the end of three days' rain, what else was there to do? It had been ten years since the Regent Cinema closed its doors for the last time and went into liquidation.

A grammar-school duffelcoat would be too conspicuous and recognizable; Matt wore his black plastic jacket, although it was not particularly rainproof. But it was at least some protection against the brambles which barred his way.

He had long ago worked out an entry into The Croft grounds, having noticed that they ended in a little triangle of land which bit into the corner of a builder's yard where his father. had once briefly worked; Matt had a keen visual memory, never forgot anything he had once observed and, after a single visit two years ago to tell his father that Mum had been taken off to hospital, was able to pick his way without hesitation through cement mixers, stacks of two-by-two, and concrete slabs, to the exact corner, the wattle palings and tangle of elderberry bushes. Kelly never troubled to lock his yard, and, in any case, on a Saturday afternoon, no one was about; all snug at home, watching telly.

He bored his way through the wet greenery and, as he had reckoned, came to the weed-smothered terrace at the foot of a flight of steps; overgrown shoots of rambler rose half blocked them, but it was just possible to battle upwards, and at the top he was rewarded by a dusky, triangular vista of lawn stretching away on the left towards the house, on the right towards untended vegetable gardens. Amazingly – in the very middle of Wentby – there were rabbits feeding on the lawn, who scattered at his appearance. And between him and the house two aged, enormous apple trees towered, massive against the murky sky, loaded down with fruit. He had seen them in the aerial photograph of the town, recently exhibited on a school noticeboard; that was what had given him the notion of exploring The Croft; you could find out a few things at school if you kept your eyes open and used your wits. And he had heard of The Croft before that, of course, but it was nowhere to be seen from any of the town streets: a big house, built in the mid nineteenth century on an inaccessible plot of land, bought subsequently, after World War Two, by a rich retired actress and her company director husband, Lieutenant-Colonel and Mrs Jordan. They were hardly ever seen; never came out, or went anywhere; Matt had a vague idea that one of them – maybe both? – had died. There was a general belief that the house was haunted; also full of treasures; also defended by any number of burglar alarms inside the building, gongs that would start clanging, bells that would ring up at the police station, not to mention mantraps, spring guns, and savage alsatians outside in the grounds.

However the alsatians did not seem to be in evidence – if they had been, surely the rabbits would not have been feeding so peacefully? So, beginning to disbelieve these tales, Matt picked his way, quietly but with some confidence, over the sodden tussocky grass to the apple trees. The fruit, to his chagrin, was far from ripe. Also they were wretched little apples, codlins possibly, lumpy and misshapen, not worth the bother of scrumping. Even the birds appeared to have neglected them; numbers of undersized windfalls lay rotting already on the ground. Angrily, Matt flung a couple against the wall of the house, taking some satisfaction from the squashy thump with which they spattered the stone.

The house had not been built of local brick like the rest of Wentby, but from massive chunks of sombre, liver-coloured rock, imported, no doubt at great expense, from farther north; the effect was powerful and ugly; dark as blood, many-gabled and frowning, the building kept guard over its tangled grounds. It seemed deserted; all the windows were lightless, even on such a pouring wet afternoon; and, prowling round to the front of the house, over a carriage sweep pocked with grass and weeds, Matt found that the front doorstep had a thin skin of moss over it, as if no foot had trodden there for months. Perhaps the back—? but that was some distance away, and behind a screen of trellis work and yellow-flecked ornamental laurels. Working on towards it, Matt came to a stop, badly startled at the sight of a half-open window, which, until he reached it, had been concealed from him by a great sagging swatch of untrimmed winter jasmine, whose tiny dark-green leaves were almost black with wet. The coffin-shaped oblong of the open window was black too; Matt stared at it, hypnotized, for almost five minutes, unable to decide whether to go in or not.

Was there somebody inside, there, in the dark? Or had the house been burgled, maybe weeks ago, and the burglar had left the window like that, not troubling to conceal evidence of his entry, because nobody ever came to the place? Or? – unnerving thought – was there a burglar inside now, at this minute?

Revolving all these different possibilities, Matt found that he had been moving slowly nearer and nearer to the wall with the window in it; the window was about six feet above ground, but so thickly sleeved around with creeper that climbing in would present no problem at all. The creeper seemed untouched; showed no sign of damage.

Almost without realizing that he had come to a decision, Matt found himself digging toes into the wet mass and pulling himself up – showers of drops flew into his face – until he was able to lean across the windowsill, bracing his elbows against the inner edge of the frame. As might have been expected, the sill inside was swimming with rainwater, the paint starting to crack; evidently the window had been open for hours, maybe days.

Matt stared into the dusky interior, waiting for his eyes to adjust to the dimness. At first, all he could see was vague masses of furniture. Slowly these began to resolve into recognizable forms: tapestried chairs with high backs and bulbous curving legs, side tables covered in ornaments, a standard lamp with an elaborate pleated shade, dripping tassels, a huge china pot, a flower-patterned carpet, a black shaggy hearthrug, a gold-framed portrait over the mantel. The hearth was fireless, the chair beside it empty, the room sunk in silence. Listening with all his concentration, Matt could hear no sound from anywhere about the house. Encouraged, he swung a knee over the sill, ducked his head and shoulders under the sash, and levered himself in; then, with instinctive caution, he slid the sash down behind him, so that, in the unlikely event of another intruder visiting the garden, the way indoors would not be so enticingly visible.

Matt did not intend to close the window completely, but the sash cord had perished and the heavy frame, once in motion, shot right down before he could stop it; somewhat to his consternation, a little catch clicked across; evidently it was a burglar-proof lock, for he was unable to pull it open again; there was a keyhole in the catch, and he guessed that it could not now be opened again without the key.

Swearing under his breath, Matt turned to survey the room. How would it ever be possible to find the right key in this cluttered, dusky place? It might be in a bowl of odds and ends on the mantelpiece – or in a desk drawer – or hanging on a nail – or in a box – no casual intruder could hope to come across it. Nor – he turned back to inspect the window again – could he hope to smash his way out. The windowpanes were too small, the bars too thick. Still, there would be other ways of leaving the house, perhaps he could simply unlock an outside door. He decided that before exploring any farther he had better establish his means of exit, and so took a couple of steps towards a doorway that he could now see on his right. This led through to a large chilly dining room where a cobwebbed chandelier hung over a massive mahogany dining table, corralled by eight chairs, and reflecting ghostly grey light from a window beyond. The dining room window, to Matt's relief, was a casement; easy enough to break out of that, he thought, his spirits rising; but perhaps there would be no need, perhaps the burglar catch was not fastened; and he was about to cross the dining room and examine it closely when the sound of silvery laughter behind him nearly shocked him out of his wits.

'Aha! Aha! Ha-ha-ha-ha-ha-ha!' trilled the mocking voice, not six feet away. Matt spun round, his heart almost bursting out through his rib cage. He would have been ready to swear there wasn't a soul in the house. Was it a spook? Were the stories true, after all?

The room he had first entered still seemed empty, but the laughter had certainly come from that direction, and as he stood in the doorway, staring frantically about him, he heard it again, a long mocking trill, repeated in exactly the same cadence.

'Jeeez!' whispered Matt.

And then, as he honestly thought he was on the point of fainting from fright, the explanation was supplied: at exactly the same point from which the laughter had come, a clock began to chime in a thin silvery note obviously intended to match the laughter: *ting, tong, ting, tong.* Four o'clock.

'Jeez,' breathed Matt again. 'What do you know about that? A laughing clock!'

He moved over to inspect the clock. It was a large, elaborate affair, stood on a kind of bureau with brass handles, under a glass dome. The structure of the clock, outworks, whatever you call it, was all gilded and ornamented with gold cherubs who were falling about laughing, throwing their fat little heads back, or doubled up with amusement.

'Very funny,' muttered Matt sourly. 'Almost had me dead of heart failure, you can laugh!'

Over the clock, he now saw, a big tapestry hung on the wall, which echoed the theme of laughter: girls in frilly tunics this time, and a fat old guy sitting on a barrel squashing grapes into his mouth while he hugged a girl to him with the other arm, all of them, too, splitting themselves over some joke, probably a rude one to judge from the old chap's appearance.

Matt wished very much that the clock would strike again, but presumably it would not do that till five o'clock – unless it chimed the quarters; he had better case the rest of the house in the meantime, and reckon to be back in this room by five. Would it be possible to pinch the clock? he wondered. But it looked dauntingly heavy – and probably its mechanism was complicated and delicate, might go wrong if shifted; how could he ever hope to carry it through all those bushes and over the paling fence? And then there would be the problem of explaining its appearance in his father's council flat; he could hardly say that he had found it lying on a rubbish dump. Still he longed to possess it – think what the other guys in the gang would say when they heard it! Maybe he could keep it in Kip Butterworth's house – old Kip, lucky fellow, had a room of his own and such a lot of electronic junk all over it that one clock more or less would never be noticed.

But first he would bring Kip here, at a time just before the clock was due to strike, and let *him* have the fright of his life . . .

Sniggering to himself at this agreeable thought, Matt turned back towards the dining room, intending to carry out his original plan of unfastening one of the casement windows, when for the second time he was stopped dead by terror.

A voice behind him said, 'Since you are here, you may as well wind the clock.' And added drily, 'Saturday is its day for winding, so it is just as well you came.'

This time the voice was unmistakably human; trembling like a leaf, Matt was obliged to admit to himself that there was no chance of its being some kind of electronic device – or even a spook – it was an old woman's voice, harsh, dry, a little shaky, but resonant; only, where the devil *was* she?

Then he saw that what he had taken for wall beyond the fireplace was, in fact, one of those dangling bamboo curtains, and beyond it – another bad moment for Matt – was this motionless figure sitting on a chair, watching him; had been watching him – must have – all the time, ever since he had climbed in, for the part of the room beyond the curtain was just a kind of alcove, a big bay window really, leading nowhere. She must have been there all the time . . .

'Go on,' she repeated, watching Matt steadily from out of her black triangles of eyes, 'wind the clock.'

He found his voice and said hoarsely, 'Where's the key, then?'

'In the round bowl on the left side.'

His heart leapt; perhaps the window key would be there too. But it was not; there was only one key: a long heavy brass shaft with a cross-piece at one end and a lot of fluting at the other.

'Lift the dome off; carefully,' she said. 'You'll find two key-holes in the face. Wind them both. One's for the clock, the other for the chime.'

And, as he lifted off the dome and began winding, she added thoughtfully, 'My husband made that clock for me, on my thirtieth birthday. It's a recording of my own voice – the laugh. Uncommon, isn't it? He was an electrical engineer, you see. Clocks were his hobby. All kinds of unusual ones he invented – there was a Shakespeare clock, and a barking dog, and one that sang hymns – my voice again. I had a beautiful singing voice in those days – and my laugh was famous of course. ' "Miss Langdale's crystalline laugh", the critics used to call it . . . My husband was making a skull clock just before he died. There's the skull.'

There it was, to be sure, a real skull, perched on top of the big china jar to the right of the clock.

Vaguely now, Matt remembered reports of her husband's death; wasn't there something a bit odd about it? Found dead of heart failure in the underpass below the motorway, at least a mile from his house; what had he been *doing* there, in the middle of the night? Why walk through the underpass, which was not intended for pedestrians anyway?

'He was going to get me some cigarettes when he died,' she went on, and Matt jumped; had she read his thought? How could she know so uncannily what was going through his head?

'I've given up smoking since then,' she went on. 'Had to, really . . . They won't deliver, you see. Some things you can get delivered, so I make do with what I can get. I don't like people coming to the house too often, because they scare the birds. I'm a great bird person, you know—'

Unless she has a servant, then, she's alone in the house, Matt

thought, as she talked on, in her sharp, dry old voice. He began
to feel less terrified – perhaps he could just scare her into letting him leave. Perhaps, anyway, she was mad?

'Are you going to phone the police?' he asked boldly. 'I
wasn't going to pinch anything, you know – just came in to
have a look-see.'

'My dear boy, I don't care *why* you came in. As you *are* here,
you might as well make yourself useful. Go into the dining
room, will you, and bring back some of those bottles.'

The rain had abated, just a little, and the dining room was
some degrees lighter when he walked through it. All along the
window wall Matt was amazed to see wooden wine racks filled
with bottles and half-bottles of champagne. There must be
hundreds. There were also, in two large log baskets beside the
empty grate, dozens of empties. An armchair was drawn close
to an electric bar fire, not switched on; a half-empty glass and
bottle stood on a silver tray on the floor beside the armchair.

'Bring a glass too,' Mrs Jordan called.

And when he returned with the glass, the tray, and several
bottles under his arm, she said,

'Now, open one of them. You know how to, I hope?'

He had seen it done on television; he managed it without
difficulty.

'Ought to be chilled, of course,' she remarked, receiving the
glass from him. One of her hands lay limply on the arm of her
chair – she hitched it up from time to time with the other hand
when it slipped off; and, now that he came near to her for the
first time, he noticed that she smelt very bad; a strange, fetid
smell of dry unwashed old age and something worse. He began
to suspect that perhaps she was *unable* to move from her chair.
Curiously enough, instead of this making him fear her less, it
made him fear her more. Although she seemed a skinny, frail
old creature, her face was quite full in shape, pale and puffy
like underdone pastry. It must have been a handsome one long
ago – like a wicked fairy pretending to be a princess in a fairytale illustration; now she just looked spiteful and secretive,
grinning down at her glass of bubbly. Her hair, the colour of
old dry straw, was done very fancy, piled up on top of her head.
Perhaps it was a wig.

'Get a glass for yourself, if you want,' she said. 'There are
some more in the dining-room cupboard.'

He half thought of zipping out through the dining-room window while he was in there; but still, he was curious to try the

fizz, and there didn't seem to be any hurry, really; it was pretty plain the old girl wasn't going anywhere, couldn't be any actual danger to him, although she did rather give him the 'gooeys'. Also he did want to hear that chime again.

As he was taking a glass out from the shimmering ranks in the cupboard, a marvellous thought struck him: why not bring all the gang here for a banquet? Look at those hundreds and hundreds of bottles of champagne – what a waste, not to make use of them! Plainly *she* was never going to get through them all – not in the state she was in. Maybe he could find some tinned stuff in the house too – but anyway, they could bring their own grub with them, hamburgers and crisps or stuff from the Chinese Takeaway; if the old girl was actually paralysed in her chair, she couldn't stop them; in fact it would add to the fun, the excitement, having her there. They could fetch her in from the next room, drink her health in her own bubbly; better not leave it too long, though, didn't seem likely she could last more than a few days.

Candles, he thought, we'd have to bring candles; and at that point her voice cut into his thoughts, calling,

'Bring the two candles that are standing on the cupboard.'

He started violently – but it was only a coincidence, after all; picked up the candles in their tall cut-glass sticks and carried them next door with a tumbler for himself.

'Matches on the mantel,' she said.

The matches were in a fancy enamel box. He lit the candles and put them on the little table beside her. Now he could see more plainly that there was something extremely queer about her: her face was all drawn down one side, and half of it didn't seem to work very well.

'Electricity cut off,' she said. 'Forgot to pay bill.'

Her left hand was still working all right, and she had swallowed down two glasses in quick succession, refilling them herself each time from the opened bottle at her elbow. 'Fill your glass,' she said, slurring the words a little.

He was very thirsty – kippers and baked beans they always had for Saturday midday dinner, and the fright had dried up his mouth too. Like Mrs Jordan he tossed down two glasses one after the other. They fizzed a bit – otherwise didn't have much taste.

'Better open another bottle,' she said. 'One doesn't go anywhere between two. Fetch in a few more while you're up, why don't you.'

She's planning, he thought to himself; knows she can't move from that chair, so she wants to be stocked up for when I've gone. He wondered if in fact there was a phone in the house. Ought he to ring for doctor, police, ambulance? But then he would have to account for his presence. And then he and the gang would never get to have their banquet; the windows would be boarded up for sure, she'd be carted off to the Royal West Midland geriatric ward, like Auntie Glad after her stroke.

'There isn't a phone in the house,' said Mrs Jordan calmly. 'I had it taken out after Jock died; the bell disturbed the birds. That's right, put them all down by my chair, where I can reach them.'

He opened another bottle, filled both their glasses, then went back to the other room for a third load.

'You like the clock, don't you,' she said, as he paused by it, coming back.

'Yeah. It's uncommon.'

'It'll strike the quarter in a minute,' she said, and soon it did – a low, rather malicious chuckle, just a brief spurt of sound. It made the hair prickle on the back of Matt's neck, but he thought again – Just wait till the rest of the gang hear that! A real spooky sound.

'I don't want you making off with it, though,' she said. 'No, no, that would never do. I like to sit here and listen to it.'

'I wasn't going to take it!'

'No, well, that's as maybe.' Her triangular black eyes in their hollows laughed down at him – he was squatting on the carpet near her chair, easing out a particularly obstinate cork. 'I'm not taking any chances. Eight days – that clock goes for eight days. Did you wind up the chime too?'

'Yeah, yeah,' he said impatiently, tipping more straw-coloured fizz into their glasses. Through the pale liquid in the tumbler he still seemed to see her eyes staring at him shrewdly.

'Put your glass down a moment,' she said. 'On the floor – that will do. Now, just look here a moment.' She was holding up her skinny forefinger. Past it he could see those two dark triangles. 'That's right. Now – watch my finger – you are very tired, aren't you? You are going to lie down on the floor and go to sleep. You will sleep – very comfortably – for ten minutes. When you wake, you will walk over to that door and lock it. The key is in the lock. Then you will take out the key and push it under the door with one of the knitting needles that are lying on the small table by the door. Ahhh! You are so sleepy.'

She yawned, deeply. Matt was yawning too. His head flopped sideways on to the carpet and he lay motionless, deep asleep.

While he slept it was very quiet in the room. The house was too secluded in its own grounds among the builders' yards for any sound from the town to reach it; only faintly from far away came the throb of the motorway. Mrs Jordan sat impassively listening to it. She did not sleep; she had done enough sleeping and soon would sleep even deeper. She sat listening, and thinking about her husband; sometimes the lopsided smile crooked down one corner of her mouth.

After ten minutes the sleeping boy woke up. Drowsily he staggered to his feet, walked over to the door, locked it, removed the key and, with a long wooden knitting needle, thrust it far underneath and out across the polished dining-room floor.

Returning to the old lady he stared at her in a vaguely bewildered manner, rubbing one hand up over his forehead.

'My head aches,' he said in a grumbling tone.

'You need a drink. Open another bottle,' she said. 'Listen: the clock is going to strike the half-hour.'

On the other side of the room the clock gave its silvery chuckle.

Kit Reed
Chicken soup

Kit Reed lives in Connecticut, and there isn't much more I can say about her. Her science fiction novels are Magic Time *and* Armed Camps, *but she also writes novels outside that field (for example,* The Ballad of T. Rantula). *Her play* The Bathyscape *was produced on American public radio. I get the impression that she likes her work to speak for her, and so it does, not least in the collections* Mr Da V. *and* The Killer Mice. *So does this one, a fine example of (among other things) the retrospectively horrific title.*

When he was little Harry loved being sick. He would stay in bed with his books and toys spread out on the blankets and wait for his mother to bring him things. She would come in with orange juice and aspirin at midmorning; at lunchtime she always brought him chicken soup with Floating Island for dessert, and when he had eaten she would straighten the pillow and smooth his covers and settle him for his nap. As long as he was sick he could stay in this nest of his own devising, safe from schoolmates' teasing and teachers who might lose their tempers, and falling down and getting hurt. He could wake up and read or drowse in front of the television, perfectly content. Some time late in the afternoon, when his throat was scratchy and boredom was threatening his contentment, he would start watching the bedroom door. The shadows would be long by that time and Harry restless and perhaps faintly threatened by longer shadows that lurked outside his safe little room: the first intimations of anxiety, accident and risk. Finally he would hear her step on the stair, the clink of ice in their best glass pitcher, and she would come in with cookies and lemonade. He would gulp the first glass all at once and then, while she poured him another, he would feel his own forehead in hopes it would be hot enough to entitle him to another day. He

197

would say: I think my head is hot. What do you think? She would touch his forehead in loving complicity. Then the two of them would sit there together, Harry and Mommy, happy as happy in the snug world they had made.

Harry's father had left his widow well fixed, which meant Mommy didn't have to have a job, so she had all the time in the world to make the house pretty and cook beautiful meals for Harry and do everything he needed even when he wasn't sick. She would wake him early so they could sit down to a good hot breakfast together, pancakes with sausage and orange juice, after which they would read to each other out of the paper until it was time for Harry to go. They always talked over the day when he came home from school and then, being a good mother, she would say, Don't you want to play with a little friend? She always made cookies when his friends came over, rolling out the dough and cutting it in neat circles with the rim of a wine glass dusted with sugar. She sat in the front row at every violin and flute recital, and when Harry had trouble with a teacher, any kind of trouble at all, she would go up to the grammar school and have it out with him. Harry's bed was made for him and his lunches carefully wrapped and, although nobody would find out until they reached middle school and took communal showers, Harry's mother ironed his underwear. In return Harry emptied the garbage and made the phone calls and did most of the things the man of the house would have done, if he had been there.

Like all happy couples they had their fights, which lasted only an hour or two and cleared the air nicely. Usually they ended with one of them apologizing and the other saying, with admirable largess, I forgive you. In fact the only bad patch they had came in the spring of the year Harry was twelve, when Charles appeared with a bottle of wine and an old college yearbook in which he and Harry's father were featured. Naturally Mommy invited him to dinner and Harry was shocked to come out of the kitchen with the bottle opener just in time to hear his mother saying, 'You don't know what a relief it is to have an adult to talk to for a change.'

Didn't Harry get asthma that night, and wasn't he home sick for the rest of the week? He did not spend his usual happy sick time because his mother seemed distracted almost to the point of being neglectful, and he was absolutely astonished at lemonade time that Friday. There were two sets of footsteps on the stairs.

Mommy came in first. 'Oh Harry, I have a surprise for you.'

'I'm too sick.'

She managed to keep the smile in her voice. 'It's Charles. He's brought you a present.'

'I don't want it.' He flopped on his stomach and put the pillows over his head.

'Oh Harry.'

'Let me handle this.' There was Charles's voice in his bedroom, his bedroom, that had always been sacrosanct. Harry wanted to rage and drive him out, he might even brain him with a bookend, but that would involve showing himself, and as long as he stayed under the pillows there was the chance Charles would give up and go away.

There was something wriggling on his bed.

'Help. What's that?'

'It's a puppy.'

'Go away.'

'Charles has brought you a lovely puppy.'

'A puppy?'

There it was. He was so busy playing with it that he only half-heard when Mommy said the puppy's name was Ralph and Ralph was going to keep him company while she and Charles went out for a little while. Wait, Harry said, or tried to, but the puppy was warm under his hands and he couldn't keep his mind on what he was saying. It had already wet the blanket, and Harry was riveted by the experience. The wet was soaking right through the blanket and the sheet and into Harry's pyjama leg, and by the time he had responded to the horror and the wonder of it, Mommy had already kissed him and she and Charles were gone.

For the first hour or two he and the puppy were happy together, but just as he began to take it into his confidence, convincing himself that it was company enough, the puppy flopped on its side and slept like a stone, leaving Harry alone in the room, jabbering to the gathering shadows. He clutched the covers under his chin and kept on talking, but the empty house was terrifying in its silence, so that Harry too fell silent, certain that both he and the house were listening.

She took for ever to come home. When she did come in she was voluble and glowing, absently noting that she had forgotten to leave him anything for supper, passing it off with a halfhearted apology and a long recital of everything Charles had said and thought. She approached the bed with the air of a jeweller unveiling his finest creation and proffered a piece of Black Forest cake she had wrapped carefully right there in the restaurant and brought halfway across town cradled in her lap.

Harry did the only logical thing under the circumstances. He started wheezing. The puppy woke and blundered across the blanket to butt him with its head. He picked it up, murmuring to it between wheezes.

'Harry, Harry, what's the matter?'

He said, to the puppy, 'I told you I was sick.'

'Harry, please!' She proffered cough medicine and he spurned it; she held out the inhaler and he knocked it away.

He said, not to her, but to the puppy, 'Mommy left me alone when I was sick.'

'Harry, please.'

'Right, puppy?'

'Oh Harry, please take your medicine.'

'It's you and me, puppy. You and me.'

Harry and the puppy were thick as thieves for the next couple of days. They refused to read the paper with his mother when she came in with breakfast and they wouldn't touch anything on any of her trays. Instead they bided their time and sneaked down to raid the kitchen when she was asleep. They talked only to each other, refusing all her advances, brooking no excuses and no apologies.

On the third day she cracked. She came to Harry's room empty-handed and weeping. 'All right, what do you want me to do?'

He answered in a flash. 'Never leave me alone when I'm sick.'

'Is that all?'

'I don't like that guy.'

'Charles?'

'I don't like him.'

Her face was a study: whatever she felt for Charles in a tug-of-war with the ancient, visceral pull. After a pause she said, 'I don't like him either.'

Harry smiled. 'Mommy, I'm hungry.'

'I'll bring you a nice bowl of chicken soup.'

That was the end of Charles.

After that Harry and his mother were closer than ever. If it cost her anything to say goodbye to romance she was gallant about it and kept her feelings well hidden. There was Harry to think about. She was the one who argued with his teachers

200

over that last quarter of a point and prepped him for tests and sent the coach packing when he suggested that, with his build, Harry was a natural for basketball; and if Harry seemed at all reluctant to give up the team trips, boys and girls together on a dark and crowded bus, his mother pointed out that it would be the worst possible thing for his asthma. It was his mother who badgered the dean of admissions until Harry was enrolled in the college of his choice, located three convenient blocks from their house. They were both astonished when, at the end of the first term, the dean suggested that he take a year off because he needed to mature. Harry and his mother talked about it privately and concluded that, for whatever reasons, the administration objected to the presence of a middle-aged woman, however attractive, at the college hangout and in various seminars and waiting with Harry on the bench outside the dean's office until it was his turn to go in.

'Who needs college?' she said.

Harry thought, but did not say: Hey, wait.

'After all,' she was saying. 'We both know you're going to be an artist.'

Harry was not so sure. His mother had enrolled him in the class because she had always wanted art lessons and so she assumed he would want them too, and Harry dutifully went to the Institute on Tuesday to do still lifes of fruit of the season with the same old clay wine bottle, in pencil, charcoal, pastels and acrylics. His colours all ran together and the shapes were hideous, but his mother admired them all the same.

'Oh Harry,' she would say, promiscuous in her approval, 'that's just beautiful.'

'That's what you always say.' It irritated him because it meant nothing, so that he was both flattered and fascinated when the cute girl from the next class came in just as he was finishing a depressing oil of that same old wine bottle, with dead leaves and acorns this time, and said, in hushed tones:

'Gee, that really stinks.'

'Do you really think so?'

'Sorry, I just . . .'

'You're the first person who's ever told the truth. What's your name?'

'Marianne.'

Harry fell in love with her.

It was around this time that his mother began to get on his nerves. If he lingered after class to talk to Marianne or buy her a cup of coffee, his mother would spring out the front door before he put his key in the lock. She would be a one-woman pageant of anxiety: Where have you been? What kept you? I thought you'd been hit by a taxi or run over by a truck, oh Harry, don't frighten me like that again. He would say, Aw, Ma, but she would already be saying: The least you could do is call when you're going to be late. She managed to be in the hall every time he used the phone, and when he began to go out with Marianne she could not keep herself from asking where he was going, how long he would be; it didn't matter whether he came home at ten or twelve or two or four a.m., she would be rattling in the kitchen, her voice would take on the high hum of hysteria: I couldn't sleep.

He should have known better than to bring Marianne home to meet her. She didn't do much; she didn't say much, but she brought in his puppy, which was no longer a puppy but instead was ageing, balding, with broken, rotting teeth. When Harry squatted to pet the dog his mother looked at Marianne over his head. 'That's the only thing Harry has ever loved. Can't sleep without him.'

Marianne looked at her in shock. 'What?'

'Right next to him on the pillow, too. Head to head. I tried to get him to put that thing in the cellar, but all I have to do is mention it and Harry starts to wheeze.'

'Harry wheezes?'

'Oh all the time,' his mother said cheerfully, opening the front door for her.

When she was gone, Harry turned on his mother in a rage, but she managed to stop him in his tracks. 'I only do these things because I love you. Think of what I have given up for you.' She was wheezing herself, as she confronted him with their whole past history in her face.

'Oh Mother. I—'

'I don't like Marianne.'

All their years together accumulated and piled into him like the cars of a fast express. 'I don't like her either,' he said.

At the same time he knew he could not stand the force of his mother's love, wanted to leave her because he was suffocating; did not know how. He didn't know whether he would ever find another girl who loved him but, if he did, he was going to handle it differently.

His first vain thought was to marry his mother off, but she would not even accept a date. 'You might need me,' she said, in spite of all his protests that he was grown now, would do fine without her. 'I wouldn't do that to you.'

It was implied that he wouldn't do that to her, either, but he would in a flash. if he could only figure out how. It was around this time that he started going into the library in the evenings, and it was natural that he should find himself attracted to one of the librarians. She liked him too, and they had a nice thing going there in the stacks, late-night sandwiches and hurried kisses. But one night Harry heard a distinct rustling in the next aisle, and when he came around the end of Q-S and into T-Z he found his mother crouching, just as the girl he had been fondling saw her and began to scream . . .

When he stamped into the house that night she greeted him with a big smile and an apple pie.

'Mother, how could you?'

'Look, Harry, I baked this for you. Your favourite.'

'How could you do a thing like that?'

'Why Harry, you know I would do anything for you.'

'But you . . . damn . . . ruined . . .' He was frothing, raging and inarticulate. He looked into that face suffused by blind mother love and in his fury took desperate measures to dramatize his anger and frustration. 'You . . .' He snatched the pie from her, ignoring her craven smile. 'Have . . .' He raised it above his head, overriding her hurried 'It's-your-favourite', and screamed: 'Got to stop.' He took the fruit of her loving labour and dashed it to the floor.

There.

He was exhausted, quivering and triumphant. He had made her understand. She had to understand.

When the red film cleared and he could see again she was on her hands and knees in front of him, scraping bits of pie off the rug as if nothing could make her happier. 'Oh Harry,' she said, imperturbable in her love, 'you know I would do anything for you.'

A less determined son would have given up at that point, sinking into the morass of mother love, but two things happened to Harry around that time, each peculiarly liberating. First his puppy died. Then they began life classes at the Institute and Harry, who up to that point had seen only selected fragments of his mother, saw his first woman nude.

Her name was Coral and he fell in love with her. They began to stay after class, Harry pretending to keep sketching, Coral pretending to pose, until the night their hands met as he pretended to adjust her drape, and Coral murmured into his ear and Harry took her home. He may have been aware of rustling in the bushes outside the studio, or of somebody following as they went up the drive to Coral's bungalow; he may have sensed a determined, feral presence under Coral's bedroom window, but he tried to push back the awareness, to begin what Coral appeared to be so ready to begin. He would have, too, kissing her as he took off his shirt, but as he clasped her to him Coral went rigid and began to scream. He turned quickly to see what had frightened her and although he caught only a glimpse of the face in the window it was enough.

'Harry, what is it?'

He lied. 'Only a prowler. I think it's gone.' He knew it wasn't.

'Then kiss me.'

'I can't.' He just couldn't.

'Please.'

'I can't – yet. There's something I have to take care of.'

'Don't go.'

'I have to.'

'When will you come back?'

'As soon as I can. It may not be until tomorrow.'

'Tomorrow, then.' Gradually, she let go. 'Tomorrow or never, Harry. I don't wait.'

'I promise.' He was buttoning his shirt. 'But right now there's something I have to do.'

She was waiting for him at the end of the driveway, proffering something. He didn't know how she had got there because he had taken the car; he had the idea she might have run the whole way because she was breathing hard and her clothes were matted with brambles; her stockings were torn and muddy at the knees. Her face was a confusing mixture of love and apprehension, and as he came towards her she shrank.

'I thought you might need your sweater.'

He looked at her without speaking.

'I only do these things because I love you.'

He opened the car door.

'Harry, you know I'd do anything for you.'

He still did not speak.

'It you're mad at me, go ahead and get good and mad at me. You know I'll forgive you, no matter what you do.'

'Get in.'

She made one more stab. 'It's raining, Harry. I thought you might be cold.'

Later, when they made the turn away from their house and up the road into the foothills, she said, 'Harry, where are we going? Where are you taking me?'

His response was dredged from millennia of parent–child dialogues. He leaned forward, taking the car into rocky, forbidding country, up an increasingly sharp grade. He said, 'We'll see.'

Maybe he only planned to frighten her, but at that last terrible moment she said, blindly, 'I'll always be there when you need me.'

He got rid of her by pushing her into Dumbman's Gorge. She got right out of the car when he told her to – she would have done anything to keep on his right side – and when he pushed her she looked back over her shoulder with an inexorable motherly smile. There were dozens of jagged tree stumps and sharp projecting rocks and she seemed to ricochet off every single one of them going down but, in spite of that and perhaps because of the purity of the air and the enormous distance she had to tumble, he thought he heard her calling to him over her shoulder, I forgive you – the words trailing behind her in a dying fall.

He didn't know whether it was guilt or the simple result of going all the way to the peak above Dumbman's Gorge and standing out there arguing in such rotten weather, but he was sick by the next evening, either flu or pneumonia, and there was no going to Coral's house that evening to take his reward. He telephoned her instead and she came to him, looking hurried and distracted and shying off when he began to cough and sneeze.

'I really want to, Harry, but right now you're too contagious.'

'But Coral.' He could hardly breathe.

'As soon as you get better.' She closed the bedroom door behind her.

When he tried to get up to plead with her he found he was too weak to stand. 'But Coral,' he said feebly from his bed.

'I'll lock the front door behind me,' she said, her voice rising behind her as she descended the stairs. 'Do you want some chicken soup?'

His voice was thin but he managed to say, 'Anything but that.'

He heard the thump as she closed the front door.

Despairing, he fell into a fevered sleep.

It may have been partly the depression of illness, the frustration of having his triumph with Coral postponed, it may have been partly delirium and partly the newly perceived flickering just beyond the circle of his vision: the gathering shadows of mortality. It may only have been a sound that woke him. All Harry knew was that he woke suddenly around midnight, gasping for breath and sitting bolt upright, swaying in the dark. He was paralysed, trembling in the fearful certainty that something ominous was approaching, coming slowly from a long way off. When he found that his trunk could not support itself and his legs would no longer move he sank back into the pillows, bloating with dread.

There had been a sound: something on the walk, sliding heavily and falling against the front door.

I came as soon as I could.

'What?' Why couldn't he sit up?

He did not know how much time passed but, whatever it was, it was in the house now. It seemed to be dragging itself through the downstairs hall. Was that it in the kitchen? In his terror and delirium he may have blacked out. He came to, returning from nowhere, thought he might have been hallucinating, tried to slow his heart. Then he heard it again. It was on the stairs leading to his room, mounting tortuously.

You're sick.

'My God.' He tried to move.

The sound was in the hall outside his room now, parts of whatever it was were thumping or sliding wetly against his bedroom door in a travesty of a knock. In another second it would start to fumble with the knob. He cried out in terrible foreknowledge: 'Who's there?'

Harry, it's Mother.

James Wade
The pursuer

James Wade was born in 1930 in Illinois, but lives now in Korea, where he works as a journalist and translator. The death of his wife in 1973 (the circumstances of which were incorporated into his friend Fritz Leiber's novel Our Lady of Darkness *to prevent that novel from becoming uncomfortably autobiographical) has stopped him, alas, from writing fiction since then. His stories are collected as* Such Things May Be, *but he is best known as a composer: his operas include* A Wicked Voice, *based on Vernon Lee's ghost story, and* The Martyred, *highly praised by the conductor Fritz Mahler.*

In Such Things May Be *he describes horror fiction as 'further and subtler variations on ever more familiar, and archaic, themes'. I think this tells us more about his attitude to his work than about the field. The best macabre fiction is timeless; 'The pursuer' was written in 1951 and rejected by* Weird Tales *and* Magazine of Fantasy, *both of which folded soon after. Urban horror fiction is more plentiful now, but this story has not been left behind by the field.*

He has been following me for longer than I dare to remember. And it scares me to think how long he may have been following me before I noticed him.

He follows me when I go to work in the morning, and when I come home at night. He follows me when I am alone, and when I date a girl or go out with friends – although I've almost stopped doing those things because it's no fun to be with people while he's around.

I can't say to my friends, or to the police or anyone, 'That man there – he's following me! He's been following me for months!' They'd think I was crazy. And if I tried to point him out to them another time, somewhere else far away from the first place, to prove it, why – he just wouldn't be there. I'm sure of that.

I think I know now what he wants.

I remember when I first noticed him – noticed that he was following me, that is. I was down in the Loop on a Saturday night, just messing around, planning to take in a few of the cheaper bars and lounges. Saturday night is a pretty big night in Chicago.

I was getting some cigarettes in a drug store, and when I turned around he was there standing right next to me: small and seedy-looking, in a long brown overcoat and a brown hat pulled low. His face was long and leathery, with a thin nose and wide, wet lips. He didn't seem to be looking at me or at anything in particular.

I recognized him as the little guy I'd seen around my neighbourhood a lot, in stores and on the street. I didn't know who he was, and I'd never talked to him, but I started to open my mouth and say something in a conversational way about running into him down here. Then I looked closer at his face and for some reason I didn't say anything. I just edged past him and left the store. He followed.

Every bar. Every lounge. Every joint.

As I fled from him, one spot to another, I kept remembering other unlikely times and places I'd seen him in the last few days, and longer ago than that, it seemed to me. Maybe I imagined a few of them, but there were plenty I could be pretty sure about.

And I began to get scared. I didn't know what he wanted; I thought he might be planning to rob me or kill me (why, I didn't know; I had little enough). I couldn't face him, I couldn't look at him.

He would come into a place like he always does, just a little after me – very quiet, very unnoticeable – and stay just a medium distance away from me. Nothing suspicious. And he wouldn't leave just when I did, he was too clever for that; but soon after I left a spot, I'd know that he was coming on behind me.

I have never heard him speak.

The last place I went to that night, I must have been pretty shook up. I couldn't take my eyes away from the door, but I couldn't stand to keep looking at it, either. The barkeep, a big bald-headed guy, leaned forward and squinted at me through the foggy neon light.

''S matter, buddy, you expecting somebody?'

I got up and went out.

It took a lot of courage to go through that door; I was deadly afraid of meeting him coming in.

I didn't, and I didn't see him on the street, either, but right away I knew he was behind me.

I was pretty drunk by that time, with all the doubles I had knocked back in the bars I'd visited, and it was like some crazy nightmare, staggering along Randolph Street under all the glaring neon signs, with the loudspeakers blaring music from inside the lounges, and the crowds pushing in every direction. I felt sick, and scared enough almost to cry. People looked at me, but I guess they thought I was just drunk. Naturally, no one ever noticed him.

After a while I threw up in an alley, and then I felt a little calmer and headed for home. I knew he was on the street car with me, and I knew he got off at my stop. I went down the street as fast as I could, hardly able to tell my rooming house from all the others just like it.

At last I found it and staggered upstairs, groped open my door, and threw the bolt behind me. I went to the window and looked down, peering intently through the darkness towards the splashes of light from the street lamps, but I didn't see him below on the street; it was dark and quiet and empty. (I never do see him down there, in fact; but somehow he's always after me as soon as I come out.)

I went over to the mirror and stood there, as if for company. If only I'd had some family, or anyone that cared enough to believe such a crazy story! But there was no one.

I was very scared; at that time I believed he wanted to hurt me. I know better now.

I went over and lay down on the bed, trembling. After a while I fell asleep, and slept all the next day.

When I went out that evening, he was standing on the corner.

That's how it's been ever since: day or night, anywhere, everywhere, I can always spot him if I dare look. I've tried every way to dodge or elude him, even made a sort of grim game out of it, but nothing is any good.

All this time I couldn't think of anything to do about him.

I knew that I couldn't prove a thing, that there was no way to get any witnesses without making people think I was crazy. I knew that even if I took a train or plane and went a thousand miles, he'd be there, if he wanted to be, as soon as I was there or sooner, and it would start all over.

After a while I began almost to get used to it. I became convinced he wouldn't try to hurt me; he'd had too many chances to do that already. The only thing I could think of to do was to keep working, to act as if nothing was the matter, and to ignore him. Maybe some day he wouldn't be there.

I started staying in, not seeing anyone, pretending to be sick if friends called. Gradually they stopped calling. I tried to read magazines all the time I was off work.

Lately I find that I can't stand that any more. I can't sit in my room and do nothing, and not know where he is. As bad as it is, it's better to know that he's walking behind me, or standing at the end of the bar, or waiting on the corner outside – better than imagining all sorts of things.

So I walk.

I walk in all kinds of weather, in all kinds of places. I walk at any time of the day or night. I walk for hours and if I get tired I get on a street car or a bus, and when I get off I walk some more.

I walk along shabby streets of lined-up flats and brownstones, where the prostitutes stand under the street lights after dark and writhe their bodies when you pass by. I walk in the park during afternoon rains, when no one is there but us and the thunder. I walk on the lake-front breakwater at midnight, while the cold wind sends waves slithering inland to shatter into nets of spray.

I walk in suburban neighbourhoods; the sun bakes the brick and concrete, cars are parked in neat rows under shade trees. I walk in the snow and slush along Skid Row, where legless beggars and awful cripples and drunks and degenerates sprawl on the sidewalks. I walk through market day on Maxwell Street, with all the million-and-one things in stalls and booths, with the spicy food smells and the crazy sales *spiels* and the jabbering crowds of every kind of people on earth.

I walk by the university campuses, and the churches, and the blocks and blocks of stores and bars, stores and bars. And I know that whenever I look behind, I'll be able to see his small shuffling form, that brown hat and overcoat, that long expressionless face – never looking at me, but knowing I'm there.

And I know what he wants.

He wants me, some night on a dark street (or in the neon glow outside a tavern, or in a park at noon, or by a church while they're holding services inside and you can hear the hymn singing) – he wants me to turn around and wait for him. No – he wants me to walk back and come up to him.

He wants more than that. He doesn't expect me to ask what he's doing, why he's following me. The time is long past for that. He wants me – he is inviting me to come up to him in blind rage and attack him; to try to kill him in any way I'm able.

And that I must not do. I don't know why, but the thought of doing that – as satisfying as it should be after all I've been through – makes me run cold with a sweat of horror beyond any revulsion I felt for him up to now.

I must not, I dare not approach him. Above all, I must not touch him, or try to injure him in any way. I can't imagine what would happen if I did, but it would be very awful.

I must continue not to pay him any heed at all.

And yet I know, if he keeps on following me, some time, somewhere, I'll not be able to help myself; I will turn back on him with insane fury and try to kill him. And then . . .

Graham Masterton

Bridal suite

*Graham Masterton was born in 1947, and sends me a
mysterious paragraph about himself. He and his wife and
three children divide their time between Epsom Downs in
England and Key West in Florida. He is a skilled underwater
swimmer and a collector of rare umbrellas. Eh? Maybe living
in Philip Marlowe territory does things to a man.*

His novels include The Manitou *(filmed by the late William
Girdler),* The Sphinx, The Djinn, *and* Charnel House. *He
specializes in visiting myths from the past on the present. If
'Bridal suite' is in some ways more traditional, nevertheless
until recently it could hardly have been published.*

They arrived in Sherman, Connecticut, on a cold fall day when
the leaves were crisp and whispery, and the whole world seemed
to have crumbled into rust. They parked their rented Cordoba
outside the front steps of the house, and climbed out. Peter
opened the trunk and hefted out their cases, still new, with
price tags from Macy's in White Plains, while Jenny stood in
her sheepskin coat and smiled and shivered. It was a Saturday,
mid-afternoon, and they had just been married.

The house stood amongst the shedding trees, white weather-
boarded and silent. It was a huge old colonial, 1820 or there-
abouts, with black-paint railings, an old coach lamp over the
door, and a flagged stone porch. All around it stretched silent
leafless woods and rocky outcroppings. There was an abandoned tennis court, with a sagging net and rusted posts. A
decaying roller, overgrown with grass, stood where some gardener had left it, at some unremembered moment, years and
years ago.

There was utter silence. Until you stand still in Sherman,
Connecticut, on a crisp fall day, you don't know what silence
is. Then suddenly a light wind, and a scurry of dead leaves.

213

They walked up to the front door, Peter carrying the suitcases. He looked around for a bell, but there was none.

Jenny said: 'Knock?'

Peter grinned. 'With that thing?'

On the black-painted door was a grotesque corroded brass
knocker, made in the shape of some kind of howling creature,
with horns and teeth and a feral snarl. Peter took hold of it
tentatively and gave three hollow raps. They echoed inside the
house, across unseen hallways and silent landings. Peter and
Jenny waited, smiling at each other reassuringly. They had
booked, after all. There was no question but they had booked.

There was no reply.

Jenny said: 'Maybe you ought to knock louder. Let me try.'

Peter banged louder. The echoes were flat, unanswered. They
waited two, three minutes more. Peter, looking at Jenny, said:
'I love you. Do you know that?'

Jenny stood on tippy-toes and kissed him. 'I love you, too.
I love you more than a barrelful of monkeys.'

The leaves rustled around their feet and still nobody came
to the door. Jenny walked across the front garden to the living-
room window and peered in, shading her eyes with her hand.
She was a small girl, only five-two, with long fair hair and a
thin oval face. Peter thought she looked like one of Botticelli's
muses, one of those divine creatures who floated two inches off
the ground, wrapped in diaphanous drapery, plucking at a harp.
She was, in fact, a *sweet* girl. Sweet-looking, sweet-natured,
but with a slight sharpness about her that made all that sweetness palatable. He had met her on an Eastern Airlines flight
from Miami to La Guardia. He had been vacationing, she had
been visiting her retired father. They had fallen in love, in
three months of beautiful days that had been just like one of
those movies, all out-of-focus swimming scenes and picnics in
the grass and running in slow motion across General Motors
Plaza while pigeons flurried around them and passing pedestrians turned and stared.

He was an editor for Manhattan Cable TV. Tall, spare, given
to wearing hand-knitted tops wih floppy sleeves. He smoked
Parliament, liked Santana and lived in the village amidst a
thousand LPs, with a grey cat that liked to rip up his rugs,
plants and wind chimes. He loved Doonesbury and never knew
how close it got to what he was himself.

Some friends had given them a polythene bag of grass and a
pecan pie from the Yum-Yum Bakery for a wedding present.

214

Her father, dear and white-haired, had given them three thousand dollars and a water-bed.

'This is crazy,' said Peter. 'Did we book a week at this place or did we book a week at this place?'

'It looks deserted,' called Jenny, from the tennis court.

'It looks more than deserted,' complained Peter. 'It looks run down into the ground. *Cordon bleu* dining, they said in *Connecticut*. Comfortable beds and all facilities. It looks more like Frankenstein's castle.'

Jenny, out of sight, suddenly called: 'There's someone here. On the back terrace.'

Peter left the cases and followed her around the side of the house. In the flaking trees, black-and-white wood warblers flurried and sang. He walked around by the tattered tennis-court nets, and there was Jenny, standing by a deck chair. In the chair, asleep, was a grey-haired woman, covered by a blanket of dark green plaid. On the grass beside her was a copy of the New Milford newspaper, stirred by the breeze.

Peter bent over the woman. She had a bony, well-defined face, and in her youth she must have been pretty. Her mouth was slightly parted as she slept, and Peter could see her eye-balls moving under her eyelids. She must have been dreaming of something.

He shook her slightly, and said: 'Mrs Gaylord?'

Jenny said: 'Do you think she's all right?'

'Oh, she's fine,' he told her. 'She must have been reading and just dozed off. Mrs Gaylord?'

The woman opened her eyes. She stared at Peter for a moment with an expression that he couldn't understand, an expression that looked curiously like suspicion, but then, abruptly, she sat up and washed her face with her hands, and said: 'Oh, dear! My goodness! I think I must have dropped off for a while.'

'It looks that way,' said Peter.

She folded back her blanket, and stood up. She was taller than Jenny, but not very tall, and under a grey plain dress she was as thin as a clothes horse. Standing near her, Peter detected the scent of violets, but it was a strangely closeted smell, as if the violets had long since died.

'You must be Mr and Mrs Delgordo,' she said.

'That's right. We just arrived. We knocked, but there was no reply. I hope you don't mind us waking you up like this.'

'Not at all,' said Mrs Gaylord. 'You must think that I'm

awful . . . not being here to greet you. And you just married, too. Congratulations. You look very happy with each other.'

'We are,' smiled Jenny.

'Well, you'd better come along inside. Do you have many bags? My handyman is over at New Milford this afternoon, buying some glass fuses. I'm afraid we're a little chaotic at this time of year. We don't have many guests after Rosh Hashanah.'

She led the way towards the house. Peter glanced at Jenny and shrugged, but Jenny could only pull a face. They followed Mrs Gaylord's bony back across the untidy lawn and in through the door of a sun room, where a faded billiard table mouldered, and yellowed framed photographs of smiling young men hung next to yachting trophies and varsity pennants. They passed through a set of smeary french doors to the living room, dark and musty and vast, with two old screened fireplaces, and a galleried staircase. Everywhere around there was wood panelling, inlaid flooring and dusty drapes. It looked more like a neglected private house than a '*cordon bleu* weekend retreat for sophisticated couples'.

'Is there . . . anybody else here?' asked Peter. 'I mean, any other guests?'

'Oh, no,' smiled Mrs Gaylord. 'You're quite alone. We are very lonely at this time of year.'

'Could you show us our room? I can always carry the bags up myself. We've had a pretty hard day, what with one thing and another.'

'Of course,' Mrs Gaylord told him. 'I remember my own wedding day. I couldn't wait to come out here and have Frederick all to myself.'

'You spent your wedding night here too?' asked Jenny.

'Oh, yes. In the same room where you will be spending yours. I call it the bridal suite.'

Jenny said: 'Is Frederick – I mean, is Mr Gaylord—?'

'Passed over,' said Mrs Gaylord. Her eyes were bright with memory.

'I'm sorry to hear that,' said Jenny. 'But I guess you have your family now. Your sons.'

'Yes,' smiled Mrs Gaylord. 'They're all fine boys.'

Peter took his luggage from the front doorstep and Mrs Gaylord led them up the staircase to the second-floor landing. They passed gloomy bathrooms with iron claw-footed tubs and amber windows. They passed bedrooms with unslept-in beds and drawn blinds. They passed a sewing room, with a silent pedal sewing machine of black enamel and inlaid mother-of-pearl. The house was faintly chilly, and the floorboards creaked under their feet as they walked towards the bridal suite.

The room where they were going to stay was high-ceilinged and vast. It had a view of the front of the house, with its driveway and drifts of leaves, and also to the back, across the woods. There was a heavy carved-oak closet, and the bed itself was a high four-poster with twisting spiral posts and heavy brocade drapes. Jenny sat on it, and patted it, and said: 'It's kind of hard, isn't it?'

Mrs Gaylord looked away. She seemed to be thinking about something else. She said: 'You'll find it's most comfortable when you're used to it.'

Peter set down the cases. 'What time do you serve dinner this evening?' he asked her.

Mrs Gaylord didn't answer him directly, but spoke instead to Jenny. 'What time would you like it?' she asked.

Jenny glanced at Peter. 'Around eight would be fine,' she said.

'Very well. I'll make it at eight,' said Mrs Gaylord. 'Make yourself at home in the meanwhile. And if there's anything you want, don't hesitate to call me. I'm always around someplace, even if I am asleep at times.'

She gave Jenny a wistful smile and then, without another word, she left the room, closing the door quietly behind her. Peter and Jenny waited for a moment in silence until they heard her footsteps retreating down the hall. Then Jenny flowed into Peter's arms, and they kissed. It was a kiss that meant a lot of things: like, I love you, and thank you, and no matter what everyone said, we did it, we got married at last, and I'm glad.

He unbuttoned her plain wool going-away dress. He slipped it from her shoulder and kissed her neck. She ruffled his hair with her fingers and whispered: 'I always imagined it would be like this.'

He said: 'Mmh.'

Her dress fell around her ankles. Underneath, she wore a pink gauzy bra through which the darkness of her nipples showed and small gauzy panties. He slipped his hand under the bra and rolled her nipples between his fingers until they knurled and stiffened. She opened his shirt, and reached around to caress his bare back.

217

The fall afternoon seemed to blur. They pulled back the covers of the old four-poster bed and then, naked, scrambled between the sheets. He kissed her forehead, her closed eyelids, her mouth, her breasts. She kissed his narrow muscular chest, his flat stomach.

From behind the darkness of her closed eyes, she heard his breathing, soft and urgent and wanting. She lay on her side, with her back to him, and she felt her thighs parted from behind. He was panting harder and harder, as if he was running a race, or fighting against something, and she murmured: 'You're worked up. My God, but I love it.'

She felt him thrust inside her. She wasn't ready, and by his unusual dryness, nor was he. But he was so big and demanding that the pain was a pleasure, too, and even as she winced she was shaking with pleasure. He thrust and thrust and thrust, and she cried out, and all the fantasies she'd ever dreamed of burst in front of her closed eyes – fantasies of rape by brutal Vikings with steel armour and naked thighs, fantasies of being forced to show herself to prurient emperors in bizarre harems, fantasies of being assaulted by a glossy black stallion.

He was so fierce and virile that he overwhelmed her, and she seemed to lose herself in a collision of love and ecstasy. It took her whole minutes to recover, minutes that were measured out by a painted pine wall clock that ticked and ticked, slow as dust falling in an airless room.

She whispered: 'You were fantastic. I've never known you like that before. Marriage must definitely agree with you.'

There was no answer. She said: 'Peter?'

She turned, and he wasn't there. The bed was empty, apart from her. The sheet was rumpled, as if Peter had been lying there, but there was no sign of him.

She said, in a nervous voice: 'Peter? Where are you?'

There was silence, punctuated only by the clock.

She sat up. Her eyes were wide. She said, so softly that nobody could have heard: 'Peter? Are you there?'

She looked across the room, to the half-open door that led to the bathroom suite. Late sunlight fell across the floor. Outside, in the grounds, she could hear leaves shifting and the faint distant barking of a dog.

'Peter – if this is supposed to be some kind of a game—'

She got out of bed. She held her hand between her legs and her thighs were sticky with their lovemaking. She had never known him fill her with such a copious flow of semen. It was so much that it slid down the inside of her leg on to the rug. She lifted her hand, palm upwards, and frowned at it in bewilderment.

Peter wasn't in the bathroom. He wasn't under the bed, or hiding under the covers. He wasn't behind the drapes. She searched for him with a pained, baffled doggedness, even though she knew that he wasn't there. After ten minutes of searching, however, she had to stop. He had gone. Somehow, mysteriously, gone. She sat on the end of the bed and didn't know whether to giggle with frustration or scream with anger. He must have gone someplace. She hadn't heard the door open and close, and she hadn't heard his footsteps. So where was he?

She dressed again, and went to look for him. She searched every room on the upper landing, including the bureaux and the closets. She even pulled down the ladder from the attic and looked up there, but all Mrs Gaylord had stored away was old pictures and a broken-down baby carriage. Up there, with her head through the attic door, she could hear the leaves rustling for miles around. She called: 'Peter?' anxiously; but there was no reply, and so she climbed down the ladder again.

Eventually, she came to one of the sun rooms downstairs. Mrs Gaylord was sitting in a basketwork chair reading a newspaper and smoking a cigarette. The smoke fiddled and twisted in the dying light of the day. On the table beside her was a cup of coffee with a wrinkled skin forming on the top of it.

'Hallo,' said Mrs Gaylord, without looking around. 'You're down early. I didn't expect you till later.'

'Something's happened,' said Jenny. She suddenly found that she was trying very hard not to cry.

Mrs Gaylord turned around. 'I don't understand, my dear. Have you had an argument?'

'I don't know. But Peter's gone. He's just disappeared. I've looked all around the house and I can't find him anywhere.'

Mrs Gaylord lowered her eyes. 'I see. That's most unfortunate.'

'Unfortunate? It's terrible! I'm so worried! I don't know whether I should call the police or not.'

'The police? I hardly think that's necessary. He's probably gotten a case of cold feet, and he's gone out for a walk on his own. Men do feel like that sometimes, when they've just been wed. It's a common complaint.'

'But I didn't even hear him leave. One second we were – well, one second we were resting on the bed together, and the next thing I knew he wasn't there.'

Mrs Gaylord bit at her lips as if she was thinking.

'Are you sure you were on the bed?' she asked.

Jenny stared at her hotly, and blushed. 'We are married, you know. We were married today.'

'I didn't mean that,' said Mrs Gaylord, abstractedly.

'Then I don't know what you *did* mean.'

Mrs Gaylord looked up, and her momentary reverie was broken. She gave Jenny a reassuring smile, and reached out her hand.

'I'm sure it's nothing terrible,' she said. 'He must have decided to get himself a breath of fresh air, that's all. Nothing terrible at all.'

Jenny snapped: 'He didn't open the door, Mrs Gaylord! He just vanished!'

Mrs Gaylord frowned. 'There's no need to bark at me, my dear. If you're having a few complications with your new husband, then it's most certainly not my fault!'

Jenny was about to shout back at her, but she put her hand over her mouth and turned away. It was no good getting hysterical. If Peter had simply walked out and left her, then she had to know why; and if he had mysteriously vanished, then the only sensible thing to do was search the house carefully until she found him. She felt panic deep inside her, and a feeling which she hadn't felt for a very long time – loneliness. But she stayed still with her hand against her mouth until the sensation had passed, and then she said quietly to Mrs Gaylord, without turning around: 'I'm sorry. I was frightened, that's all. I can't think where he could have gone.'

'Do you want to look around the house?' asked Mrs Gaylord. 'You're very welcome.'

'I think I'd like to. That's if you don't mind.'

Mrs Gaylord stood up. 'I'll even help you, my dear. I'm sure you must be feeling most upset.'

They spent the next hour walking from room to room, opening and closing doors. But as darkness gathered over the grounds and the surrounding woods, and as the cold evening wind began to rise, they had to admit that wherever Peter was, he wasn't concealed or hiding in the house.

'Do you want to call the police?' asked Mrs Gaylord. They were standing in the gloomy living room now. The log fire in the antique hearth was nothing more than a heap of dusty white ashes. Outside, the wind whirled in the leaves, and rattled at the window frames.

'I think I'd better,' said Jenny. She felt empty, shocked, and hardly capable of saying anything sensible. 'I think I'd like to call some of my friends in New York, too, if that's okay.'

'Go ahead. I'll start preparing dinner.'

'I really don't want anything to eat. Not until I know about Peter.'

Mrs Gaylord, her face half-hidden in shadow, said softly: 'If he's really gone, you're going to have to get used to it, my dear; and the best time to start is now.'

Before Jenny could answer her, she had walked out of the living room door and along the corridor to the kitchen. Jenny saw an inlaid mahogany cigarette box on a side table, and for the first time in three years she took out a cigarette and lit it. It tasted flat and foul, but she took the smoke down, and held it, her eyes closed in anguish and isolation.

She called the police. They were courteous, helpful, and they promised to come out to see her in the morning if there was still no sign of Peter. They had to warn her, though, that he was an adult, and free to go where he chose, even if it meant leaving her on her wedding night.

She thought of calling her mother, but after dialling the number and listening to it ring, she set the phone down again. The humiliation of Peter having left her was too much to share with her family or her close friends right now. She knew that if she heard her mother's sympathetic voice, she would only burst into tears. She crushed out the cigarette and tried to think who else to call.

The wind blew an upstairs door shut, and she jumped in nervous shock.

Mrs Gaylord came back after a while with a tray. Jenny was sitting in front of the dying fire, smoking her second cigarette and trying to keep back the tears.

'I've made some Philadelphia pepper soup, and grilled a couple of New York steaks,' said Mrs Gaylord. 'Would you like to eat them in front of the hearth? I'll build it up for you.'

Throughout their impromptu dinner, Jenny was silent. She managed a little soup, but the steak caught in her throat, and she couldn't begin to swallow it. She wept for a few minutes, and Mrs Gaylord watched her carefully.

'I'm sorry,' said Jenny, wiping her eyes.

'Don't be. I understand what you're going through only too well. I lost my own husband, remember.'

Jenny nodded, dumbly.

221

'I think it would better if you moved to the small bedroom for tonight,' suggested Mrs Gaylord. 'You'll feel more comfortable there. It's a cosy little room, right at the back.'

'Thank you,' Jenny whispered. 'I think I'd prefer that.'

They sat in front of the fire until the fresh logs were burned down, and the long-case clock in the hallway began to strike two in the morning. Then Mrs Gaylord cleared away their plates, and they mounted the dark, creaking staircase to go to bed. They went into the bridal suite to collect Jenny's case, and for a moment she looked forlornly at Peter's case, and his clothes scattered where he had left them.

She suddenly said: '*His clothes.*'

'What's that, my dear?'

She flustered: 'I don't know why I didn't think about it before. If Peter's gone, then what's he wearing? His suitcase isn't open, and his clothes are lying right there where he left them. He was *naked*. He wouldn't go out on a cold night like this, naked. It's insane.'

Mrs Gaylord lowered her gaze. 'I'm sorry, my dear. We just don't know what's happened. We've looked all over the house, haven't we? Maybe he took a robe with him. There were some robes on the back of the door.'

'But Peter wouldn't—'

Mrs Gaylord put her arm around her. 'I'm afraid you can't say what Peter would or wouldn't do. He *has*. Whatever his motive, and wherever he's gone.'

Jenny said quietly: 'Yes. I suppose you're right.'

'You'd better go get some sleep,' said Mrs Gaylord. 'Tomorrow, you're going to need all the energy you can muster.'

Jenny picked up her case, paused for a moment, and then went sadly along the landing to the small back bedroom. Mrs Gaylord murmured: 'Goodnight. I hope you sleep.'

Jenny undressed, put on the frilly rose-patterned nightdress she had bought specially for the wedding night, and brushed her teeth at the small basin by the window. The bedroom was small, with a sloping ceiling, and there was a single bed with a colonial patchwork cover. On the pale flowery wallpaper was a framed sampler, reading, 'God Is With Us'.

She climbed into bed and lay there for a while, staring up at the cracked plaster. She didn't know what to think about Peter any more. She listened to the old house creaking in the darkness. Then she switched off her bedside lamp and tried to sleep.

Soon after she heard the long-case clock strike four, she

thought she detected the sound of someone crying. She sat up in bed and listened again, holding her breath. Outside her bedroom window the night was still utterly dark, and the leaves rattled like rain. She heard the crying noise again.

Carefully, she climbed out of bed and went to the door. She opened it a little way, and it groaned on its hinges. She paused, her ears straining for the crying sound, and it came again. It was like a cat yowling, or a child in pain. She stepped out of her room and tippy-toed halfway along the landing, until she reached the head of the stairs.

The old house was like a ship out at sea. The wind shook the doors and sighed between the shingles. The weathervane turned and grated on its mounting, with a sound like a knife being scraped on a plate. At every window, drapes stirred as if they were being touched by unseen hands.

Jenny stepped quietly along to the end of the landing. She heard the sound once more – a repressed mewling. There was no doubt in her mind now that it was coming from the bridal suite. She found she was biting at her tongue in nervous anxiety, and that her pulse rate was impossibly quick. She paused for just a moment to calm herself down, but she had to admit that she was afraid. The noise came again, clearer and louder this time.

She pressed her ear against the door of the bridal suite. She thought she could hear rustling sounds, but that may have been the wind and the leaves. She knelt down and peered through the keyhole, although the draught made her eyes water. It was so dark in the bridal suite that she couldn't see anything at all.

She stood up. Her mouth was parched. If there was someone in there – who was it? There was so much rustling and stirring that it sounded as if there were two people there. Maybe some unexpected guests had called by while she was asleep; although she was pretty sure that she hadn't slept at all. Maybe it was Mrs Gaylord. But if it was her, then what was she doing, making all those terrifying noises?

Jenny knew that she had to open the door. She had to do it for her own sake and for Peter's sake. It might be nothing at all. It might be a stray cat playing around in there, or an odd downdraught from the chimney. It might even be latecoming guests and, if it was, then she would wind up embarrassed. But being embarrassed had to be better than not knowing. There was no way she could go back to her small bedroom and sleep soundly without finding out what those noises were.

She put her hand on the brass doorknob. She closed her eyes tight, and took a breath. Then she turned the knob and jerkily opened the door.

The noise in the room was horrifying. It was like the howl of the wind, only there was no wind. It was like standing on the edge of a clifftop at night, with a yawning chasm below, invisible and bottomless. It was like a nightmare come true. The whole bridal suite seemed to be possessed by some moaning, ancient sound; some cold magnetic gale. It was the sound and the feel of fear.

Jenny, shaking, turned her eyes towards the bed. At first, behind the twisted pillars and drapes, she couldn't make out what was happening. There was a figure there, a naked woman's figure, and she was writhing and whimpering and letting out sighs of strained delight. Jenny peered harder through the darkness, and she saw that it was Mrs Gaylord, as thin and nude as a dancer. She was lying on her back, her claw-like hands digging into the sheets, her eyes closed in ecstasy.

Jenny stepped into the bridal suite, and the wind gently blew the door shut behind her. She crossed the rug to the end of the bed, her mind chilled with fright, and stood there, looking down at Mrs Gaylord with a fixed and mesmerized stare. All around her, the room whispered and moaned and murmured, an asylum of spectres and apparitions.

With complete horror, Jenny saw why Mrs Gaylord was crying out in such pleasure. *The bed itself, the very sheets and under-blankets and mattress, had taken on the shape of a man's body, in white linen relief, and up between Mrs Gaylord's narrow thighs thrust an erection of living fabric. The whole bed rippled and shook with hideous spasms, and the man's shape seemed to shift and alter as Mrs Gaylord twisted around it.*

Jenny screamed. She didn't even realize that she'd done it until Mrs Gaylord opened her eyes and stared at her with wild malevolence. The bed's heaving suddenly subsided and faded, and Mrs Gaylord sat up, making no attempt to cover her scrawny breasts.

'*You!*' said Mrs Gaylord, hoarsely. 'What are you doing here?'

Jenny opened her mouth but she couldn't speak.

'You came in here to spy, to pry on my private life, is that it?'

'I – I heard—'

Mrs Gaylord climbed off the bed, stooped, and picked up a

green silk wrap, which she loosely tied around herself. Her face was white and rigid with dislike.

'I suppose you think you're a clever girl,' she said. 'I suppose you think you've discovered something momentous.'

'I don't even know what—'

Mrs Gaylord tossed her hair back impatiently. She didn't seem to be able to keep still, but kept on pacing around the bridal suite, loaded with tension. Jenny, after all, had interrupted her lovemaking, however weird it had been, and she was still frustrated. She gave a sound like a snarl, and paced back around the room again.

'I want to know what's happened to Peter,' said Jenny. Her voice was shaky but for the first time since Peter's disappearance, her intention was firm.

'What do you think?' said Mrs Gaylord, in a caustic voice.

'I don't know what to think. That bed—'

'This bed has been here since this house was built. This bed is the whole reason this house was built. This bed is both a servant and a master. But more of a master.'

'I don't understand it,' said Jenny. 'Is it some kind of mechanism? Some kind of trick?'

Mrs Gaylord gave a sharp, mocking laugh. 'A trick?' she asked, fidgeting and pacing. 'You think what you saw just now was a trick?'

'I just don't see how—'

Mrs Gaylord's face was sour with contempt. 'I'll tell you how, you witless girl. This bed was owned by Dorman Pierce, who lived here in Sherman in the 1820s. He was an arrogant, dark, savage man, with tastes that were too strange for most people. He took a bride, an innocent girl called Faith Martin, and after they were married he led her up to his bridal suite and *this* bed.'

Jenny heard the wind moaning again. The cold, old wind that stirred no drapes nor aroused any dust.

'What Dorman Pierce did to his new bride on this bed that first night – well, God only knows. But he used her cruelly and broke her will, and made her a shell of the girl she once was. Unfortunately for Dorman, though, the girl's godmother got to hear of what had happened, and it was said that she had connections with one of the most ancient of Connecticut magic circles. She may even have been a member herself. She paid for a curse to be put upon Dorman Pierce, and it was the curse of complete submission. In future, *he* would have to serve women, instead of women serving *him*.'

Mrs Gaylord turned towards the bed, and touched it. Its sheets seemed to shift and wrinkle by themselves.

'He lay in this bed one night and the bed absorbed him. His spirit is in the bed even now. His spirit, or his lust, or his virility, or whatever it is.'

Jenny frowned. 'The bed did what? *Absorbed* him?'

'He sank into it like a man sinking into quicksand. He was never seen again. Faith Martin stayed in this house until she was old, and every night, or whenever she wished it, the bed had to serve her.'

Mrs Gaylord pulled her wrap tighter. The bridal suite was growing very cold. 'What nobody knew, though, was that the enchantment remained on the bed, even after Faith's death. The next young couple who moved here slept on this bed on their wedding night, and the bed again claimed the husband. And so it went on, whenever a man slept on it. Each time, that man was absorbed. My own husband, Frederick was— Well, he's in there, too.'

Jenny could hardly stand to hear what Mrs Gaylord was going to say next.

She said: 'And *Peter*?'

Mrs Gaylord touched her own face, as if to reassure herself that she was real. She said, ignoring Jenny's question: 'The women who decided to stay in this house and sleep on this bed all made the same discovery. For each man who was absorbed, the bed's strength and virility grew that much greater. That's why I said that it's more of a master than a servant. Right now, with all the men that it has claimed, it is sexually powerful to an enormous degree.'

She stroked the bed again, and it shuddered. 'The more men it takes,' she whispered, 'the more demanding it becomes.'

Jenny whispered: 'Peter?'

Mrs Gaylord smiled vaguely, and nodded, her fingers still caressing the sheets.

Jenny said: 'You knew what was going to happen, and you actually let it? You actually *let* my Peter—'

She was too shocked to go on. She said: 'Oh, God. Oh, my God.'

Mrs Gaylord turned to her. 'You don't have to *lose* Peter, you know,' she said, cajolingly. 'We could both share this bed if you stayed here. We could share all of the men who have been taken by it. Dorman Pierce, Peter, Frederick, and all the dozens of others. Have you any idea what it's like to be taken by twenty men at once?'

Jenny, feeling nauseous, said: 'Yesterday afternoon, when we—'

Mrs Gaylord bent forward and kissed the sheets. They were snaking and folding with feverish activity, and to Jenny's horror, they were beginning to rise again into the form of a huge, powerful man. It was like watching a mummified being rise from the dead; a body lifting itself out of a starched white shroud. The sheets became legs, arms and a broad chest, and the pillow rose into the form of a heavy-jawed masculine face. It wasn't Peter, it wasn't any man; it was the sum of *all* the men who had been caught by the curse of the bridal suite, and dragged into the dark heart of the bed.

Mrs Gaylord pulled open her wrap, and let it slither to the floor. She looked at Jenny with glittering eyes, and said: 'He's here, your Peter. Peter and all his soulmates. Come and join him. Come and give yourself to him . . .'

Skinny and naked, Mrs Gaylord mounted the bed, and began to run her fingers over the white shape of the sheets. Jenny, with rising panic, crossed the room and tried the door handle, but the door seemed to be wedged firmly shut. The windless wind rose again, and an agonized moaning filled the room. Now Jenny knew what that moaning was. It was the cries of those men trapped for ever within the musty substance of the bridal bed, buried in its horsehair and its springs and its sheets, suffocatingly confined for the pleasure of a vengeful woman.

Mrs Gaylord seized the bed's rising member, and clutched it in her fist. 'See this?' she shrieked. 'See how strong it is? How proud it is? We could share it, you and I! Come share it!'

Jenny tugged and rattled at the door, but it still refused to open. In desperation she crossed the room again and tried to pull Mrs Gaylord off the bed.

'Get away!' screeched Mrs Gaylord. 'Get away, you sow!'

There was a tumultuous heaving on the bed, and Jenny found herself struck by something as heavy and powerful as a man's arm. She caught her foot on the bed's trailing sheets, and fell. The room was filled with ear-splitting howls and bays of fury, and the whole house was shuddering and shaking. She tried to climb to her feet, but she was struck again, and she knocked her head against the floor.

Now Mrs Gaylord had mounted the hideous white figure on

the bed, and was riding it furiously, screaming at the top of her voice. Jenny managed to pull herself up against a pine bureau, and seize an old glass kerosene lamp which was standing on top of it.

'*Peter!*' she shouted, and flung the lamp at Mrs Gaylord's naked back.

She never knew how the kerosene ignited. The whole of the bridal suite seemed to be charged with strange electricity, and maybe it was a spark or a discharge of supernatural power. Whatever it was, the lamp struck Mrs Gaylord on the side of the head and burst apart in a shower of fragments, and then there was a soft *woofff* sound, and both Mrs Gaylord and the white figure on the bed were smothered instantly in flames.

Mrs Gaylord screamed. She turned to Jenny with staring eyes and her hair was alight, frizzing into brownish fragments. Flames danced from her face and her shoulders and her breasts, shrivelling her skin like a burning magazine.

But it was the bed itself that was most horrifying. The blazing sheets struggled and twisted and churned, and out of the depths of the bed came an echoing agonized roar that was like a choir of demons. The roar was the voice of every man buried alive in the bed, as the fire consumed the material that had made their spirits into flesh. It was hideous, chaotic, unbearable and, most terrible of all, Jenny could distinguish Peter's voice, howling and groaning in pain.

The house burned throughout the rest of the night, and into the pale cold dawn. By mid-morning it was pretty much under control, and the local firemen trod through the charred timbers and wreckage, hosing down the smouldering furniture and collapsed staircases. Twenty or thirty people came to stare, and a CBS news crew made a short recording for television. One old Sherman citizen, with white hair and baggy pants, told the newsmen that he'd always believed the place was haunted, and it was better off burned down.

It wasn't until they moved the fallen ceiling of the main bedroom that they discovered the charred remains of seventeen men and one woman, all curled up as small as monkeys by the intense heat.

There had been another woman there, but at that moment she was sitting in the back of a taxi on the way to the railroad station, wrapped tightly in an overcoat, her salvaged suitcase resting on the seat beside her. Her eyes, as she watched the brown-and-yellow trees go past, were as dull as stones.

Dennis Etchison and Mark Johnson

The spot

*Dennis Etchison was born in California in 1943 and is getting
tired of being described as a young Californian writer. 'Do you
suppose that one of these days I'll pass an invisible peak and
suddenly become middle aged without ever having gone
through my prime?' he wonders. I suspect that blurb writers
and such folk don't quite know how else to describe him, since
so many of his stories are uncompromisingly subtle and
original. They have appeared in* Frights, Orbit, Whispers, The
Year's Best Horror Stories, Shadows, *and* Nightmares, *as well
as in many magazines. His first novel* Red Dreams *(a kind of
sequel to 'The spot') was published recently.*

*Mark Johnson is a cartoonist and illustrator, and a collector
of movie memorabilia. Their collaboration is more allegorical
than most of the tales in the book, but the allegory by no means
explains away the tale.*

The van crept up Elevado Way, its headlights stabbing like ice
picks at the encroaching darkness.

Martin kicked at the debris on the floorboard, but the cans
and paper bags were all empty; he tried to put the thought of
food out of his mind. He rolled down the window and peered
out at the old Spanish-style houses, at the sun as it disappeared
like a tired eye behind the tops of the palm trees that rimmed
the horizon of the city below.

'Better step on it, Rog,' he said. 'The Old Man doesn't like
it when we get in after seven, remember?'

'I guess he doesn't have much of a choice, does he?' said
Roger, bulldogging the wheels around a steep curve. 'He gave
us three buildings to do today – and overtime is overtime.
We're the best team he's got, aren't we? If he doesn't like it
we can always go back on unemployment, right, Jackie? Am I
right?'

Martin leaned his chin on his hand and watched the flickering tile roofs, which glowed now with a deep ochre stain from the setting sun, as he kept track of the house numbers with one half-closed eye.

He was thinking of the time he and Kathy had bought a map to the stars' homes, that first week in California. Now he felt that he might be following the endless bifurcations of one of those same winding streets with pretentious, foreign-sounding names. The only thing they had found that seemed alive that Sunday, however, was an old man with an Indian blanket over his legs, his wheelchair planted in the sun on the other side of an enormous lawn fronting a house that looked suspiciously like a misplaced Southern mansion. They hadn't got close enough to be sure, but he could not help wondering if there had been more to it than a false front, an old movie set installed around a modest house with a view, perhaps to improve the land value. They had waited there under a shade tree, eating their picnic lunch in the car, but the old man had never moved. For all they could tell, he might have been nothing more than a made-up skeleton set out as a prop on the too perfect grass.

Martin heard his stomach growl. He gave up. 'Hey,' he said, 'you don't have any more of that Kentucky Fried Chicken stashed in back, do you, Rog?'

Roger glanced reflexively at the equipment in the rear of the van. 'Aw, tighten your belt. We'll be able to cop something when we get inside – this neighbourhood's full of fat cats, I can tell. Anyway, I hear it's supposed to be good for people in our profession to stay a little bit hungry.'

Martin recalled the rotten stench from the refrigerator in the last place they had cleaned, and shuddered.

Our profession, he thought. And what profession is that, Roger? If you do that sort of thing you become that sort of animal, don't you, Rog?

He remembered to check the numbers. He blinked and turned his head, almost missing one.

'Hey, I think that was it,' he said, and then Roger was downshifting and swinging around a gravel circle and braking with a noisy ratcheting in front of the Carlton Arms.

It was another of those buildings taped and glued together back in the fifties around an indeterminate number of crackerbox apartments, somehow always more than you would guess from the outside. Martin thought of the architects for these quiet horrors, all right-angles of powdering stucco and rust from hidden drain pipes, as the ballpoint pen boys: they could be relied upon to make an infinite number of copies, but no originals.

The manager, a pale, nervous man who treated everyone as a potential process server, scrutinized the work order as they stood shifting their weight from foot to foot, as they studied their shoes and said nothing, and directed them at last to the elevator.

They passed an overweight housekeeper in a white uniform on her way out of the building. She picked her teeth and watched them suspiciously, as if they were in some strange way competitors. They ignored her and unloaded the wet-and-dry vac, the buckets and mops and cart full of cleansers and disinfectants from the van, clattered it all through the garage and up to the third floor, to what were undoubtedly still described in rental ads as penthouse apartments.

The tenant had probably moved out within the last couple of days, possibly within the last few hours; Martin noticed a half-loaf of not yet mouldy bread on top of an old copy of *Variety*, a can of crystallized honey and a plastic bag full of Blue Chip stamps. Martin pocketed the stamps as Roger screwed a 250 watt bulb into the kitchen ceiling, and they set to work to make the place habitable for the next occupant, whoever that might be.

Who knows what else got left behind? he wondered. In closets and back rooms, in cupboards and under sinks, on top shelves and in forgotten drawers, so much overlooked or perhaps simply and conveniently disremembered by those on the move, as though on purpose, as a way of shedding the collected burdens of a life gone on too long in one place. Like snakeskins, he thought, or the dead casings of gypsy moths. Still, when he thought of it at all, it always surprised him just how much they left behind, some of it inexplicably valuable.

There was a lingering smell about the room that Martin could not quite place. Another housekeeper or maid in a tight white uniform passed by outside. From time to time as they worked muffled sounds penetrated the paper-thin plaster, the echo of delicate movements as of mice busy under the linoleum or behind the peeling latex paint on the walls.

Martin had just begun cleaning the chipped metal grooves of the sliding windows with a toothbrush, when a door on the opposite landing swung slowly open. A beam of dingy light cut through the twilight, tracing faint yellow streaks across the discoloured bottom of the empty swimming pool in the courtyard below.

'I think we're being watched,' he said, pausing between strokes.

The window frame had not been cleaned in years; a residue of soot and unidentifiable particles from the air had settled along with piles of sharp, corroded filings like insect droppings within the cracks. It was difficult to get rid of, even with the large wire brush and the chemical solvent.

'How much longer do you figure, Rog? We only have one unit to do in this building, don't we, and that's it?'

'Two more,' said Roger.

'You've got to be kidding.'

Martin swore under his breath, aware of the woman in the opposite doorway. Her features were lost in darkness, but he could see jagged points of hair sticking out from her head in the backlight like the spokes of a broken wheel.

'Get a load of that pose,' said Roger, mixing the rug shampoo. 'I wonder what she's waiting for.'

Martin made a quick mental note of the proportions, of the odd cant of the limbs. 'Do you remember *The Bride of Frankenstein*?' he said.

'I worked with Elsa Lanchester once,' said Roger. 'Did I ever tell you—?'

'You did.' Many times, he thought. 'Listen,' he said abruptly, dropping the brush. 'Will you tell me something? What in hell are we doing here?'

'About three-thirty an hour,' said Roger.

'Seriously.'

'Seriously,' said Roger, 'it's my latest role – it's called "paying the rent". Do you know that the average SAG member makes like seven hundred dollars a year?'

'But you didn't decide to be an actor for the bucks,' said Martin impatiently. 'You couldn't have. You'd have been a fool.'

Hell, he thought, the average guys I went to school with, the jocks, are all managing supermarkets or selling Porsches now. I could have had a piece of that. So why didn't I? Why did I turn my back on Kathy, a house, kids? There must be a reason. Or maybe I'm just a fool. Maybe that's all there is to it, after all.

Roger unwound the cord and tried to find an outlet. 'You

may not believe this, Jack,' he said, 'but there are times when I'm glad to be pushing a broom for a living. Like right now.' He groaned and stretched. Martin heard bones crack in the empty room. 'My mind's still my own, you know? I mean, when we leave here, we're through. And I'm my own man. Till my agent calls me for another reading. A commercial, anything, I'm not particular, so long as I have the chance to practise my craft.'

That's crap, thought Martin, but didn't say it. Because he didn't know why. But there was something basically wrong with the equation, though it had sounded reasonable enough for him to take this job himself until his next commission, until . . .

Roger was staring across the courtyard. The woman had left the doorway and was now making her way tenuously towards them, one hand on the railing for support.

'That one's about ready for the bone orchard, if you ask me,' said Roger. He backed up and fumbled with the cord reel, as if he recognized her, as if he did not want to. His hands were shaking. Why is he so upset? wondered Martin.

'Did I ever tell you about my next project, Jack? It's a real departure for me. I've been working on the treatment in my head.' He was talking too fast, rattling through the words as if they were beads. '*The Adventures of Reggae Rat.* It's a children's story. Bet you didn't know I could write, too, did you? My agent's been after me for years to put together a property of my own. Naturally there'll be a part in it for me, so that when I sell the film rights – I'll need an illustrator for the book first, of course. Why don't you see what you can come up with? When you have the time. I know you're doing that other thing on spec right now, what's it called – *Pipe Dreams*? That's it, isn't it, Jackie? Am I right?'

Roger stopped talking as the woman arrived at their door. Martin stood to one side to let it happen, whatever it would be.

'How's it going, ma'am?' said Roger. 'Nice evening, isn't it?'

'Young man,' began the woman.

Martin stifled a laugh. How many more years can we get away with it? *Young men on the way up. Promising talents. Ageing enfants terribles,* he thought. Very rapidly ageing.

'You simply must help me. I have a terrible, terrible problem!'

Roger reached for the work order. 'Let me see here,' he said. 'What apartment was that now?'

'Number twenty-six,' she said. 'I'm only staying between engagements, you understand, until I can find more suitable quarters. But you must come at once.'

'I don't see it,' said Roger, scanning the clipboard. 'Are you sure—?'

'Oh, the coloured girls come in and clean around me once a week, or is it once a month? I've so much on my mind these days, you know. But you really must help me. Why, I've called and called to complain, but it never does any good!'

Roger exchanged glances with Martin. He seemed to be forcing himself to a decision.

'Now just you calm down, ma'am. We'll see what we can do, all right? I'll be over in a jiffy.'

The old lady wandered away, clutching her housecoat, muttering to herself.

'What . . . ?'

'It's good PR,' said Roger, grabbing a boxful of cleansers and sponges. 'See, we spend five minutes with Baby Jane here. She tells the manager, the manager tells the Old Man. The Old Man gets a lock on the building. She's satisfied – and we get a raise. That's called "priming the pump", my boy. "Greasing the pig".' He shouldered a broom and started out. 'Do what you can with this dump in the meantime, but don't knock yourself out. I'll be right back.'

Martin watched as Roger disappeared into the opposite apartment, ahead of the old lady, holding the screen door for her.

He shook his head. Great, he thought. Who knows when we'll get out of here now? He withdrew to a corner of the living room and leaned against the wall.

He looked around at the floor polisher, the scrub brushes, the plastic jugs of cleaning solution and germ killer and the packet of paper bands for the toilets that said SANITIZED in cheerful script.

He sighed.

He sank down so that he was sitting on the floor and took out his sketch pad and a Pilot Fineliner pen. He opened to a blank page. The sketches he had been working up for his *Red Dreams* concept were all grotesques; she would fit in nicely. Altogether they would form the core of a fantastic one-man show, if anybody in the La Cienega galleries were into that sort of thing yet.

He was trying to reproduce the lumpy outline of her coat

when a scream sounded from the other apartment.

He tapped the cap of his pen on his teeth. He squinted into the darkness and started to get up. At that instant the other door opened and Roger came running with his supplies, looking like a Fuller Brush man who has just been bitten by the family dog.

He stumbled in, out of breath. 'Jesus Christ,' he said with a wild look in his eyes. 'I feel more like I do now than when we got here!'

Martin put away his notebook. 'That bad, huh?' She had seemed like a candidate for the cackle factory, all right. 'What happened?'

'The usual. She wanted me to kill the rug.'

'What?'

'The lint, rather. On the rug. She says it's really bugs – cockroaches or something.'

'Is it?'

'Are Donny and Marie Osmond sisters?'

'I don't know.'

'My point exactly! I tell you, man, I had to get out of there. I thought I could handle her – I'm used to dealing with people. But I should have trusted my instincts. There's something about that old bird that gives me the creeps. Another minute and I wouldn't have known my own hole from an ass on the ground.'

Martin considered Roger's face. He was trying to make sense of his partner's overreaction, when the screen door slammed open across the way and the old woman staggered out, making unintelligible sounds in her throat.

'Here we go again,' said Roger. 'I can't do it, Jack. You try if you want to. Hey, maybe you can bring us back some eats. She's got something cooking in there, I could smell it. Just don't take too long, okay?'

Martin tried in vain to get a good look at her. Probably just an old Hollywood crank, he thought. There must be a lot of them around here. Maybe the whole building's full of them, who knows? Some sort of retirement set-up. There were no children visible, no pets, no tricycles. Now that he thought of it, the manager down below had had a certain thespian fussiness about him.

'I can pay you,' she said as she came up.

'Don't worry,' said Martin, stepping forward, feeling sorry for her in spite of himself. 'A regular service of the Sunshine

Cleaning Company. It's all free and it won't hurt a bit.'

He left Roger, walking behind her at a respectful distance. As he followed her into her apartment, he was finally able to see her bright orange hair and the eyes that bulged like poached eggs through flesh caked with accumulated make-up. There was something vaguely familiar about her, even under the wan light that filtered through the dusty tassels of the lamp, but he still could not place her.

She collapsed on to an overstuffed sofa, reupholstered in purple crushed velvet, as if the exertion had been more than she could bear. She was silent for a moment. Then her eyelids unfolded, twitching thickly as she caught him staring at her.

'It's there, by the table,' she said, pointing a long arm that would have been graceful if not for the arthritis.

He felt himself bow slightly.

Her hand retracted to cover her eyes, shielding them from the light that came through the burnt lampshade. Her chest began to rise and fall, as if she were sinking into a deep slumber.

He went to the table, realizing after a few steps that he was on tiptoe.

It was a fine old Chippendale with years of wax rubbed into the surface, but with an incongruous sample of frayed pink velvet thrown haphazardly over the top. There was a small open box of tarnished antique jewellery, a copy of *TV Guide*, and a framed photograph of what appeared to be a flying saucer.

His attention drifted automatically to other photographs and certificates on the wall, glossies gone sepia with age and news clippings and hand-lettered commendations. He recognized one of the faces, that of a young actor who had been killed tragically in a car crash when Martin himself was a teenager.

'It moves,' she said.

He turned, startled. 'I beg your pardon?'

'It goes away and then it comes back. I've told them to clean it, I've pleaded and begged, but they won't do anything about it. It always comes back. Small in the afternoons and then larger in the evenings, but it always comes back. I used to clean it twice a week with the carpet sweeper, but lately I've been so terribly, terribly tired, I don't know why . . .'

Her voice failed. Even now as Martin watched her, the last of her strength seemed to leave her body and seep into the cushions and pillows.

What was she talking about?

He heard the clinking of silver on dishes and low voices from the next room. He took another step and saw a doorway that led to the kitchen.

The old woman moaned and got to her feet. He felt her brush past him, trailing an aura of cheap perfume.

'Why, it's as plain as the nose on your face,' she said. With a crooked finger she directed his eyes to the floor, holding the door frame with her other hand. 'Will you help me? If you won't, I don't know what I'll do.'

'Of course I'll help you,' he said quickly. 'That's what I'm here for.'

That seemed to pacify her. She nodded shakily and went on into the kitchen.

Martin turned his attention to the carpet at his feet. It was a worn Oriental design with bone-white threads showing through. In the middle, extending outwards from the legs of the table, was a long, spider-like spot. It ended at a dark, oval outline in the shape of a stomach sac.

He knelt and suspended his hand above the pile of the carpet, as if trying to detect something from the feel of it, the texture.

The spot flowed over and covered his knuckles.

He drew back.

The spot returned to the carpet.

He stood up and stepped carefully around it. As he did so the spot enlarged, bleeding off the carpet and on to the floor.

Suddenly he let out a chuckle.

He looked at the lampshade, the curtained window behind it, the end of the sofa between the lamp and the table.

That was all there was to it, then.

The spot? It was only a shadow, growing as the sun went down, disappearing and then reappearing when the lamp was snapped on. A shadow. Nothing more.

He shook his head.

He walked around the room, strangely relieved, and again heard voices from the kitchen.

'None of the dead has been identified . . .'

It was a radio or television set, he realized.

He found himself back at the table. He noticed signed photographs on the wall of a man in a grey suit shaking hands with various minor celebrities. One of them was an old-time actor who had appeared in most of the cheapjack science fiction films of the fifties. Martin had seen them all, or most of them, either in theatres at the time or on the 'Late, Late Show' in the years since. One of the certificates was inscribed, 'To Albert Zugman From The Baron Frankenstein Society in recognition of his Contribution to the Genre'.

That was it: the man in the grey suit was none other than the late Albert Zugman, king of the 'B' Pictures. His movies had been Martin's absolute favourites as a boy. Perhaps they had even been the original source of his taste for the bizarre. How many times had he sneaked into the old Rialto Theatre on Saturday afternoons to see them over and over again?

He traced the edges of the publicity stills with genuine affection. *Robot Invaders*, *circa* 1953, if he remembered correctly. And *I Was a Teenage Dracula*, about 1958. Even *Hippie High School* from 1967. That one had been Zugman's last attempt at another kind of exploitation picture; it had failed. So, apparently, had Zugman. As nearly as Martin could recall, Zugman had died quietly in the early seventies, all but forgotten.

The flying saucer? That would be from *Mars vs Earth*. Of course.

And the old woman would be Mrs Zugman herself, the former model and actress. In person.

My God, he thought.

There must be something he could do for her, some way of repaying even a small part of the hours of pleasure he had received.

Then he remembered.

He lifted the end of the sofa and moved it twelve or fourteen inches and set it down so that there was no longer a direct line between it and the lamp. There. Now there will be no more shadows to bother her, he thought.

It seemed so little.

Well, wasn't there something more he could do before he left, some other detail, perhaps, further to ease her mind?

He waited, but she did not come out of the kitchen.

He circled the room, a patternless array of objects and *memorabilia*, a sad mixture of quality furnishings and the dreariest chintz. For the first time he noticed cardboard cartons along one wall, some of them containing odds and ends of statuary, vases, pictures. She – or someone – was in the process of moving her things in or out, he couldn't tell which.

He turned into the small hall.

It was a crackerbox apartment, all right, with two tiny

rooms, a kitchen and a bath. He flicked on the bathroom light.

The imitation-porcelain basin was coated with layers of spilled face powder, hardened into cement over the years.

He switched off the light.

In the bedroom was a transparent mask attached to an oxygen tank. Rays of light from a streetlamp outside slanted through the adjustable louvered panels of the window, casting sharp vertical shadows over her bed.

He heard a sound somewhere behind him. Feeling like a trespasser, he turned back to the living room.

She was standing by the table.

'Oh!' she cried. 'Oh, my dear! What have you done?'

'Excuse me,' he said hurriedly. 'I was just wondering if there was anything more I could . . .'

'You mustn't touch my things!' She pressed her hands to her face, her watery eyes fixed on the sofa. 'This is all I have left of the estate. I hear them coming in at all hours like thieves in the night, like ants. Oh, you're one of them, aren't you? You're just like the rest!'

She lunged unsteadily to the kitchen.

'Ma'am?' he called, following her. 'I was only trying to help, please believe me. Mrs Zugman?'

He saw another person with her in the kitchen, a woman in a white uniform.

'Don't make me hurt you,' one of them was saying. He couldn't tell which one.

He rapped on the door jamb. 'Ma'am, if you'll let me explain . . .'

She spotted him and hobbled out in a near-panic. He heard her closing the door to her bedroom and her bony fingers struggling with a lock that would not catch.

The other woman remained seated at the kitchen table. She leaned forward on her elbows, squeezing something in her fat hands. She might have been Mexican or middle-European, he could not be sure. A portable television set was propped across from her. Patiently her lidded eyes returned to it.

They must be cooks, he thought, all of them in their white dresses. That would explain why they're so well fed, their uniforms taut and bursting at the seams.

A huge kettle simmered on the stove. He smelled a familiar lingering odour and recognized it at last as a mixture of heavy spices about to boil, as if held in readiness for a long time. But why? The refrigerator stood open, the racks inside picked clean. It looked as if it had been empty for days, perhaps longer.

He took a tentative step forward, trying to think of something to say. There were questions taking shape in his mind, but he did not yet know how to frame them.

Her hands flexed almost imperceptibly in the white light, and he saw that she held nothing in them, after all. It had been only the fleshiness of her own hands, cupped expectantly around each other.

She glanced up at him, her jaws grinding in a steady, regular rhythm. Her lips fell open. There was nothing in her mouth, not yet.

And a sudden dread began to overtake him, creeping up the back of his neck and spreading across his scalp. It was like nothing he had ever felt before.

Her jaws clenched and unclenched, a trickle of colourless fluid starting already from the sides of her mouth, dripping from the corners of her faint but unmistakable moustache. She made no move to wipe it away.

'Was that trip really necessary?' Roger was saying. He had been muttering for several blocks, but this was the first of his quasi-observations to register. Martin let it go and tried to lose himself in the rush of foliage outside the van.

Can't you step on it? he thought.

Roger tore open a package of Mickey Banana Dreams with his teeth, devoured one and set the other on the dashboard. He pushed it towards Martin.

'Found 'em in one of the drawers,' Roger said. 'You know, it blows my mind sometimes, the stuff they leave behind when they go.' He tried to laugh but it didn't come out right. He licked his fingers and let the wrapper fly out the window. 'Anyway, I just hope the Old Man doesn't find out about those other two units, at least not till we get paid for the week. If the manager complains, we'll say one of us got sick and had to split. Which is true, right?' Roger eyed his partner in the semi-darkness. 'She really got to you, didn't she?'

'You recognized her before I did,' said Martin. Say it, he thought.

The van shook, turning downhill.

Roger took a long time to answer. 'She was Lylah Lord,' he said wonderingly. '*The* Lylah Lord. I wasn't sure at first.' He

240

adjusted the rearview mirror, his eyes glassy. 'But you saw her. That was what got to you, too, wasn't it?'

'I saw her,' Martin said. He saw her now, in fact, saw her no matter how hard he tried not to: the tattered robe, the spindly wrists, the veins and age spots on her legs. A tired, starved old woman, living with death and waiting helplessly for the end; it was her final, hysterical role, one in which she had awakened to find herself trapped and from which she could not escape. He tried, but he could not put her out of his mind.

'You want to get drunk?' said Roger.

'It's late.'

'That it is. And we have a big, new apartment complex over on the east side first thing tomorrow morning. I saw the order. But I just thought, when we get back to the valley, away from here—'

Unexpectedly Roger's voice, the trained instrument that it was, failed him.

'I know,' said Martin.

'I used to wonder what happens to old actors in this town. Now I wish I'd never found out. Did I ever tell you, Jackie, that I had quite a crush on her? She was the love of my life for years. I collected her pictures on trading cards. Even carried one around in my wallet. I wonder if it's still there? Lylah Lord! Jesus Christ.'

They approached the base of the foothills, where Elevado Way merged and become one with the plain of jewel-like streets and traffic signals and dimly lighted windows, each the tired eye of another private residence within which one more sad melodrama was playing itself out, alone, to the end. And among the lights, Martin knew, were the bright, cold flowers of theatre marquees and television screens where the faces of people long dead and forgotten spoke and gestured from another time and place, and where they would continue to do so, for ever perhaps, or until even the last remaining record of their lives would itself break and decompose into remnants to be carted away with the rest. Like the actors whose photographs were even now curling and disintegrating on the walls of her apartment. He reached for the pack of cigarettes on the seat.

'I didn't know you smoke, Jackie.'

'I don't.'

Martin lit up and sat watching the cigarette flare in the darkness and then subside to an ember. He inhaled deeply but it did no good. Cars passed them on either side, taillights braking and then growing weak in the distance. Once a huge truck roared by, rattling the van from a great height, as if it meant to run them off the road, as if it did not even see them. The vibration knocked the ash from Martin's cigarette. He watched the burning continue the length of the cigarette, converting it all to ashes.

'Maybe we're in the wrong profession,' said Roger.

Martin looked over at him, trying to see his eyes.

'I don't just mean Sunshine Cleaning,' said Roger. 'I mean—' He cut the wheel sharply and they mounted an on-ramp. 'Look, the first thing I had to learn as an actor was to eat shit. Unsalted. You know? And it isn't much better in your field, am I right?'

Martin thought: Why is consensus so important to him?

'So what are we breaking our balls for? Can you tell me that? I mean, being an artist is fine if you get the breaks. But why should we waste our whole lives waiting for some kind of – I don't know—' Roger's hands trembled on the steering wheel, under the strobing of lights that passed above. 'I'm sure as hell not going to let myself end up like her. I know that now. The way I see it, we've just been fooling ourselves.'

What, then? wondered Martin.

'Let's get it together, Jackie. Who do you think hires those maids or whatever the hell they are, for example? Somebody, right? He must be raking in the dough, enough to make some kind of a life, you know? I bet he has guys who do nothing but haul them out in the morning, pick them up at the end of the day. You figure he needs more drivers? That's what we ought to be into, something with a future. What do you think?'

Martin was thinking about what he had seen at the Carlton Arms. Whether it was true or not in its particulars didn't really matter; the sense of it was the same. It was big fishes eating little fishes, consuming and being consumed, just as we feed and are fed upon in turn by the Old Man. And so on.

The feeling returned then. The feeling that had made him want to be out of there. I have to break the chain, he thought. And, feeling an even greater fear, he thought: *It stops here.*

They were nearing the end. The cigarette had burned down to the filter and was sputtering dangerously close to his fingers, but he was not aware of it. For some reason he was thinking of the young actor who had been killed in the car crash when he himself was only a boy. He felt pain; and his eyes filled with tears.

A shadow passed over them as an illuminated roadsign swept by overhead.

'I want out,' he heard himself say.

Roger smiled at him. 'I know. Believe me. I've got to get home and get something to eat myself. But, hey, I think there's a Bob's Big Boy coming up. If you don't want a drink, maybe we could grab a bite before we go back. Man, I sure wouldn't mind having one of those maids' jobs right now, let me tell you. I'll bet they sneak whatever they want right out from under those old birds' noses. Am I right, Jackie?'

'My name's Jack,' said Martin.

Roger drove on in silence. They left the freeway and headed along the main street, the restaurant logo becoming clearer until it dominated the night sky.

'You sure you don't want to stop?'

Martin did not answer.

'Well,' said Roger, 'you give the idea some thought, okay? This racket's for losers. Now, port-a-maid or whatever they call it, that's the kind of scam we should be into, I'm telling you. One thing about it – we'd never go home hungry. At least see if you can find out who they work for. You can do that, can't you?'

No, thought Martin. No, I can't. He was hungry, all right. But not that hungry.

Cherry Wilder

The gingerbread house

*Cherry Wilder was born and educated in New Zealand but
lived in New South Wales for many years. She now lives in
Germany with her husband Horst Grimm and their two
daughters Cathie and Louisa.*

She began both reading and writing at six. The Auckland
Herald *bought a Santa Claus story from her when she was
eleven. 'I was bound to get back to speculative fiction,' she
says and, in 1974, after publishing 'literary and other short
stories' (eh?) and reviews in Australia, she decided to follow up
the success of her first sf story in a Ken Bulmer anthology.
Since then she has appeared in anthologies edited by Terry
Carr, Lee Harding, Virginia Kidd, Maxim Jakubowski and
others, and there is a sequel to her novel* The Luck of Brins
Five.

*'Germans do not think their country particularly haunted or
haunting . . . they tend to believe that all the best ghosts live
in England. On the other hand, as a newcomer, I see ghosts
and ghost stories looming everywhere.' This is her first
published ghost story, but will certainly not be her last.*

Amanda stood in the road for a few minutes after the taxi had
driven off. Then she walked back the way they had come, re-
crossed the rustic bridge and began to approach the cottage
through the woods. It was early afternoon; the mist had begun
to lift but under the tall canopy of beech trees there was a chill
that reached through the layers of pale mohair that swathed
Amanda and seeped in at the soles of her suede thigh boots.

She soon became aware that she had taken on too much; the
pigskin bag was too heavy; the carpet of crisp leaves was uneven. She leaned against a tree; a woodpecker tapped, high up,
against the golden roof of the forest. All around the leaves fell,
with a light damp sound; at her feet she saw mushrooms of a

smooth pale lilac. The trees were widely spaced but even at a short distance the ranks of tall, green-scurfed trunks blurred and wavered. The profound stillness of the woods settled on Amanda; she drew the folds of her ridiculous model gear around her thin frame and walked on slowly.

She was not quite alone. A lady in a tailored gabardine raincoat and matching hat of Tyrolean shape walked her dog, a long-haired miniature dachshund. Amanda staggered on, past an inviting yellow bench, and saw the cottage.

It was small and greyish but not unbearably picturesque. The tilted roof dipped quaintly at the eaves; in the peak of the gable was an open window, with bedding set to air. The fence was of crumbling wooden slats and new wire; the garden was planted with potatoes, asters, chrysanthemums. Amanda stared; it really did not look like Douglas at all. She noticed with alarm a cream Volkswagen parked in the old, mossy garage on the far side of the house.

She was pressing on but suddenly the little dog, the dachshund, scuffed leaves at her feet; she saw its mistress hurrying towards her.

'Ein Moment, bitte!'

The woman had an inaccessibly ordinary, firm, plain face and sharp blue eyes. No trace of regional accent; not a scrap of make-up; gold studs in her ears. An Englishwoman of similar vintage . . . Amanda thought of her mother . . . would have worn tweeds, a pale lipstick, might have addressed Amanda as 'My dear . . .'

'Are you going to the cottage?' asked the woman in English.

'Yes,' said Amanda, 'my brother . . .'

It was out before she had time to think but the woman did not seem to notice her moment of panic. She stuck out her hand.

'Luisa Schneider.'

'Amanda King.' Amanda shook hands.

'An English lady rented this house,' said Frau Schneider. 'I was her friend.'

She turned her head and spoke to her dog, then turned back to Amanda with decision.

'Frau Winter was not happy about the house. There were things which . . . baffled her understanding . . .'

Frau Schneider said 'beffled' and Amanda caught it as an echo of the English lady's own voice. She realized what she was being told and what it must have cost the woman to speak up.

'We will be all right,' she said. 'I'm sure we will be all right.'

'I hope you will forgive me. Frau Winter would have wished me to speak to the next people . . .'

'Thank you, Frau Schneider.'

'Nickie!' Frau Schneider called her dog to heel.

'He would never enter the place,' she whispered suddenly, 'not even to eat meat!'

She snapped the lead on to Nickie who waved his golden plume of a tail and looked up at Amanda with melting eyes.

'He is a dear little dog!' she said.

'He is like a child,' said Frau Schneider wearily.

As she turned to go she established her kinship with Amanda's mother.

'You must help yourself to the garden vegetables,' she said. 'It is in the contract. You are too thin, Fräulein King . . . you must round yourself out. I have had daughters myself . . .'

Amanda felt her smile growing fixed; Frau Schneider let Nickie lead her away through the columns of beech trees. A well-worn path led Amanda to the side gate and she could not struggle round to the front of the house. She stared at a kitchen window with white net curtains and a box of geraniums on the sill. Her heart thumped; someone behind the curtains vanished.

She dragged her suitcase a little further down the path, the gate slammed shut behind her; she stood still and called:

'Douglas!'

The back door, half glass with white net covering the panels, swung open without a sound.

'Douglas . . . can you come?'

She looked at the garden beds on either side of the path; they were unweeded but still flourishing. A trowel and a single gardening glove lay by an old crock of parsley, half buried in the dark earth. She had been standing on the path for half a minute; Douglas was not coming out. She left her suitcase where it was, gripped the strap of her shoulder bag and stooped down unnecessarily to enter the doorway.

Douglas King slammed the door shut behind his sister and wiped his face with a checked tea towel.

'Christ,' he said, 'you take your time. Was someone watching you?'

'No,' said Amanda.

She backed into the kitchen to get a look at him; the sink was still full of warm suds. Douglas had been watching through the window and had ducked down out of sight when she appeared at the back gate.

Douglas was seven years older than Amanda and a few inches shorter; a muscular man, handsome, his hair black as a raven's wing. She had been taught to envy his hair and his long eyelashes . . . 'wasted on a man' her mother said. At this moment, in shirt sleeves, he looked paunchy; Amanda felt sure that his appetite was as large as ever.

The thought of eating overwhelmed her with desire and revulsion; must take something . . . it has been twelve hours, no, fourteen. She stumbled into the sitting room and folded into a chair.

'You idiot,' said her brother, 'you really shouldn't have . . .'

She bit her lip to stave off the wretched faintness and prepared to repel his kind inquiries. Even he could not refrain from urging his sister to eat.

'I'm all right,' she said. 'I'll have a brandy.'

Douglas was not making kind inquiries; she moved her head and saw him crouched down at the back door, lifting aside the white curtains.

'Idiot!' he said again. 'To leave that bloody great suitcase on the path.'

'Douglas, come and tell me what this is all about.'

Douglas came into the sitting room still clutching the tea towel and sat on the edge of a green velvet armchair. He looked like a hen-pecked husband.

'What did Helen tell you?' he demanded.

'Nothing,' lied Amanda. 'I haven't seen her. You know I've been at the clinic for weeks.'

'In Zurich?'

'Of course. Douglas, I want you to tell me. What is the matter?'

'Just the divorce.'

'*Tell* me . . .'

He shook his head; it was an admission that there was more to tell. It satisfied her for the moment. Douglas smiled at last.

'You do look all in . . .' he said.

He strode off into the kitchen and she heard the tinkle of glass; he would fetch her brandy. Amanda gazed slowly around the room taking in the narrow grate, the handsome old chairs and the dining table, the lamps. Surely it was unusual in this part of the world for a house to be let fully furnished. Douglas had not bothered with flowers and there were no ornaments except a pink and green shepherdess in Staffordshire pottery. It put Amanda in mind of the English lady.

The door to the kitchen and the back hallway closed slowly and she heard the click of the lock. The room was darker now but more evenly lit with a pale autumn light from the window. The door into the front hall moved six inches, remained ajar. Amanda extended long fingers into her handbag and brought out a packet of bitter Swiss chocolate. She ate two squares doggedly, then leaned back and closed her eyes; presently she must unzip the damned boots . . .

She fell into a light uncomfortable sleep, the kind of sleep she might have on a plane. Just beyond the boundaries of her sleep there was bustle and movement. She saw Douglas with a terrible expression on his face stumping past with her suitcase. She slept more deeply and began to dream.

She was on a picnic in the woods with a man, a man of her dreams, tall and warm, bearing only a superficial resemblance to her 'lost love', her old no-love-lost Roger Mallett. They ate raspberries, the taste was tart and clean and cured her of her disease. Between one tree and the next she lost him, she was lost, she wandered among the trees . . . fir trees . . . with a growing anxiety.

She knew in her dream that this was one of her usual anxiety dreams but suddenly it became much worse. The tang of the fir trees turned dank and sour like old water in a flower vase. She saw the cottage, shrunken and dark, in the distance, and a figure kneeling at the base of a tree, digging deeply into the thick leaf mould. The scene was flavoured with an old, aching fear, half out of mind. She nibbled on something from her pocket and it had an awful taste, stale, dead, peppery sweet.

Amanda woke up shuddering, her lips drawn back in a grimace. It was dark outside the room now and the lamps had been switched on. Her glass of brandy stood beside her chair on a little table, golden in the lamplight. She sipped it eagerly, savouring the relief of her escape from the dream. She called lazily:

'Douglas . . .'

There was a rattle of pots and pans from the kitchen. When she turned her head she could see her reflection in the glass front of a cupboard. She floated, incorporeal, the thin essence of Amanda. *I am transparent, I am made of spun glass, every-*

thing gross has been purged away. I will do what I want to do. I will have my way. She was thinking of Jane, thirty kilos, the fat nurse shrieking aloud and the scent of the fir trees in the grounds of the clinic. Jane would have her way.

There was a crash of glass from the kitchen. The sound went through her head like jagged lightning and Amanda cried out. The silence rolled back; she was not even sure that she had heard the crash at all. Her gaze returned to her own reflection; she altered her pose, rearranged a billowing sleeve.

The door of the cupboard swung open without a sound; Amanda's reflection became distorted and hideous. She felt cold, cold, the carpet under her feet was chill and damp as the forest floor. A whiff of foul air had entered the room.

Amanda felt for the cologne in her handbag but she was too late. The stench filled the room in a choking cloud. It was carrion, decay, a suppurating foulness. She rose up, gagging helplessly, and stumbled into the front hall. She tried to call her brother and could not. A light was switched on in the hall; she realized that Douglas had gone out, he was not there. She was, more or less, alone in the house.

She turned and raced up the stairs; Douglas had been careful to leave on some lights. She paused at the top landing. Two small bedrooms, a bathroom, a yard or so of corridor: the air sweet and clean, not a mouse stirring. She went to the window at the end of the corridor and looked down at the garage. Lights blinked through the trees; Douglas drove into the garage with a characteristic roar from the Volkswagen.

She went into the bedroom where her suitcase leaned drunkenly against the foot of the bed. The window was still wide open but the featherbed and the huge soft pillow had been taken in and set in place. Her tartan travelling rug trailed out of the straps on the pigskin bag; she picked it up and slung it around her shoulders. She closed the window. Down, far down in the reaches of the house, there was another rending crash of glass and crockery.

Amanda went quickly and quietly down as far as the first landing. The door into the sitting room was moving backwards and forwards; she heard little thumps and taps at the skirting board as if someone were sweeping behind the door. She knew, with deep resentment, that she was very much afraid. Steps sounded on the path, a key grated in the lock of the front door, and Douglas came in cheerfully with a plastic sack of groceries.

'Did you hear a noise?' Amanda heard her own voice shake.

Douglas stared at his sister and began to grin.

'*I heard the owl scream and the crickets cry,*' he intoned. '*Did you not speak?*'

Amanda drew the folds of the tartan rug about her and strode down the stairs.

'*Hark!*' she said. '*Who lies in the second chamber?*'

'*Donalbain!*' they cried in chorus.

Macbeth had cleared the air. They sat on the third step; there was just room for the pair of them.

'You're skin and bone,' said Douglas. 'Sorry I was strung up. Helen has been playing merry hell. I had to get away for a while.'

'The school . . .'

'I tossed it in at the end of last term,' he said with a touch of the old nonchalance. 'I've been doing some writing.'

'Why did you send for me?'

'Lonely,' he said, 'and I needed someone to improve the set-up. Helen could be having this place watched.'

'Douglas, this house . . .'

She drew back. The house was quiet and sweet smelling. A cuckoo clock chirred beside the coat rack. The cuckoo sprang out seven times but did not speak . . . it had been silenced. Don't speak, warned the silent cuckoo.

'Yes, this place is a marvellous find,' said Douglas defensively. 'Most flats don't have a stove, let alone all this furniture and crockery.'

'How did you find it?'

'Pure luck. Got talking to the agent in a train. They have trouble letting the place . . . something to do with a deceased estate.'

He helped her up and they strolled into the kitchen. Douglas began stowing food into the small, inadequate refrigerator. Amanda looked about for shards of glass and china knowing she would find none.

'Do most of the shopping in the evenings,' he said. 'I drive out to a huge supermarket . . . sells everything from bread to benzine.'

'Did you have trouble renting the car?'

'Of course not!'

He could not look her in the eye; she could not say any more. Douglas piled wrappers into the pedal bin.

'I had better have something to eat,' said Amanda.

'Good kid,' he said jovially. 'Did you finish that washing up or did I?'

They took their plates into the sitting room which was warm and wholesome in the lamplight.

'I've got the ordinary central heating going,' said Douglas, 'but in the winter I'll have an open fire as well.'

Amanda ate two tangerines, a cup of blueberry yoghourt, a slice of crispbread with cheese; she kept her eyes averted from her brother's laden plate. Douglas had rented an elegant, small colour television; they watched *Einsatz in Manhattan*. A policeman had his wife handcuffed to the bed because she was a heroin addict.

'Surely that's Lynn Redgrave,' said Douglas.

'She seems to have lost weight,' said Amanda.

'What's it called in English anyway?'

'*Kojak.*'

Amanda went up to bed and left her brother pottering about tidying up. She took two of her strongest capsules, curled up in the short wooden bed and fell into a deep, dreamless sleep.

In the darkness of early morning she half woke, then lay in a strange dreaming state. The feather quilt was hot and heavy; she was fat, her legs ached, her ankles were swollen. She was restless, she must get up and sweep the stairs, make them all clean, hide what must be hidden. Amanda woke up fully for a few seconds and dragged one skinny arm out from under the covers. *I am Amanda . . . like spun glass . . .* She flung off the clinging discomfort of the dream and slept again.

Next time she woke it was half-past nine; the mist outside was giving way to cool autumn sunshine. There were two tangerines on her bedside table. Amanda smelled coffee and remembered a time when she enjoyed the smell of coffee, even the smell of bacon frying. From the bathroom window she thought she saw Frau Schneider and Nickie, taking their walk.

She was adjusting the shawl collar of the pink sweater when she caught a look of panic on her own face in the glass. A regular sound of tapping . . . someone was sweeping the stairs. She peered through the bathroom door expecting to see nothing . . . the noise continuing and nothing else, no one. But what she saw was worse – a woman, a strange woman in a shapeless raincoat and headscarf, sweeping the stairs.

Amanda died of terror there on the spot, then rallied. The woman was solid as a tree trunk, not an apparition. She worked away, tap-tapping with her dustpan and brush, then raised her head to stare at the bathroom door with an expression of ferocious ill-will. And this was the worst of all. Amanda's stomach tightened into a knot, she had to clutch at the door frame. She went into all the old anti-fainting tricks, bit her lips, lowered her head, held tight to the door frame. She gulped air and let it out in a scream:

'*Douglas!*'

She flung open the bathroom door. Douglas was hanging up the raincoat and scarf.

'What's the matter now?' he asked gruffly.

'You gave me a terrible fright!'

'What ... this old coat? There was a shower ...'

'You were wearing a headscarf ...'

'No umbrella.'

Douglas picked up his dustpan and brush from the little chest of drawers.

'Come and have some breakfast.'

He went into the kitchen. As she walked down into the coffee smell he called:

'There is that wretched woman with the dog ...' Amanda went straight out of the front door and down the path.

'*Guten Morgen*, Frau Schneider!'

'*Guten Morgen!*'

Nickie sat down in the leaves and had to be dragged along on his bottom towards the garden gate.

'How have you found the house?'

'Not very nice. There *are* things ... What did your friend ...?'

'Frau Winter was kind and friendly. Yet she changed, she would not let me in ... she spoke dreadful things, things I would never have believed she could say ... in German at any rate.'

'Who lived here before she came?'

'I don't know, I could not ask,' said Frau Schneider. 'Some poor woman. Frau Winter was found out of doors on a winter's night, half-frozen. Mud and leaves were frozen to her fingers. She never recovered.'

Amanda wiped her hands against her trousers.

'At first she loved the house,' said Frau Schneider. 'She said it was from a fairytale ... her *Lebkuchenhaus*.'

'Her gingerbread house,' said Amanda.

She remembered the dreadful taste in her dream ... old and stale and peppery sweet. Nickie was dragging Frau Schneider off again. Amanda walked slowly back down the path, fumbling in her pocket for imaginary crumbs.

Gingerbread houses, the real ones, could be rather nasty because they were seldom eaten up. The beautiful frosted eaves and windows encrusted with jujubes were put away until next year. It was enough to make her shudder . . . it was her dream all over again, a dream that she might have had before. Old things, dead things, filthy dusty places that would never come clean. Sweetness gone stale, food left to moulder and rot, mad Miss Havisham's terrible 'bride cake', the haunt of mice and spiders. She looked up and saw Douglas at her bedroom window; she had to wait some time before he came downstairs and let her in.

When he did come down he was so much himself again that she put off any confrontation. Douglas settled down at the coffee table in the sitting room and typed with his maddening slowness. Amanda wandered about. Writing had been so much his thing at one time. She sat on the first landing of the stairs and looked up and down at the dimensions of the small house.

There was nothing to say how old it was, none of the bulging paintwork or uneven walls which suggested that a house was several hundred years old. She would guess that the place was built in about 1930, but perhaps the site was already old. Perhaps there had always been some sort of house here in the woods.

She put her head on her knees and thought of her friend Jane, who had looked a little like Snow White, and of the English lady. Really one could not escape a witch, if she were determined . . . either she came after you, snug in your cottage, armed with a poisoned apple, or she lured you inside her gingerbread house. Yet what else was here but an old cry of pain, the remains of some guilty ritual? She and Douglas were not children, left wandering in the woods.

Amanda laughed aloud. Because that was exactly what they were. She went down the stairs singing a little song and she did not recognize it until she came to the door of the sitting room.

Brother come and dance with me,
Both my hands I offer thee . . .

'Douglas,' she said, 'please take a break. I want to talk to you.'

'Fine,' said Douglas, 'but you must have something to eat.'

If he hoped to put her off it did not work. They went into the kitchen and Amanda selected a square of cheese, a tomato, a slice of *gelbwurst*.

'How is your friend Jane?' asked Douglas.

Amanda tightened her hold on the thin white plate.

'Jane had her way,' she said. 'She did what she wanted to do.'

She carried her plate into the sitting room; the cupboard door hung open a few inches.

'Jane was the most languid female I ever set eyes on,' chuckled Douglas, following with her glass of buttermilk. 'She never wanted to do anything except starve herself to death.'

He broke off, appalled.

'Yes,' said Amanda.

He sat on the couch and stared at his sister. She quickly bit into the tomato, nibbled a morsel of cheese, consumed a fragment of sausage. *Forgive me, Jane, I am not spun glass . . . I am skin and bone.*

Douglas stared until she was embarrassed. At last he said:

'You've got it too, I hope you admit that, Amanda. You've got this wretched thing, this *anorexia nervosa.*'

'I admit it,' said Amanda.

She choked on the tomato, felt the seeds crawl down her throat, sipped quickly at the buttermilk . . . tiny sips, a bird drinking. She wanted to eat as much as she could, get it down before he put her off her food.

'You've nearly killed Mummy with this starvation carry-on,' said Douglas. 'I hope you face up to the truth.'

'Mummy is tough,' said Amanda, finishing her cheese, 'but I admit that it must have been a bit of a strain.'

'You've ruined your life,' said Douglas. 'The modelling is too much for you; Roger didn't want to marry a skeleton. Helen thinks you're completely round the bend and doesn't want you to have anything to do with the children.'

'In case they don't eat their veggies?' asked Amanda.

She pushed away the plate and glass with a feeling of clearing the decks.

'I admit all this,' she said, 'and I'm trying to improve.'

'You take it far too calmly. I want you to face facts!'

'Douglas, will *you* face facts? You're five thousand pounds in debt.'

'Rubbish, I made some payments!'

'I didn't see Helen but she wrote to me in Switzerland. You worked a swindle over the car insurance. You were sacked from the school. But the worst thing of all, the thing you must go back for, is the hit and run . . . the boy in Hammersmith . . .'

'Do you believe this bullshit?' said Douglas in a trembling voice.

'Interpol believe it. They came to the clinic.'

'What did you tell them?'

'That I had no idea where you were. I said you had friends in Italy . . .'

'You probably led them right to this doorstep!'

'Now you're talking nonsense,' said Amanda. 'They are only an information bureau.'

'You left a trail a mile wide . . . staggering about like some bloody spectre . . .'

She could feel the room stirring into life; the cold came seeping up from the floor like mist. The hall door slammed and Douglas jumped. Something inexplicable was happening to the carpet, a heaving and wrinkling as if something crawled beneath it at the edges of the room. The cupboard door moved gently back and forth; the smell of corruption sidled out. Amanda felt a firm pressure on her shoulder; as she turned her head her glass bounced across the room and smashed. The butttermilk made a thick white pool among the jagged slivers of glass.

Douglas came up from the couch with his eyes blazing, his mouth pouting and twisted. He marched into the kitchen with an odd flat-footed walk and came back instantly with the dustpan and a cloth.

'Filthy . . .' he said thickly, 'a filthy liar . . .'

He wiped the fragments of glass into the pan and went back to the kitchen; she heard the clang of the pedal bin, the running tap. He came back with the rinsed cloth and wiped at the table with bent head. Douglas was muttering some words which she could not catch . . . or did not believe . . . and she saw that in his left hand he still held the base of the glass, broken off into long jagged teeth. The foul smell had become very strong; his hand began to come up in a long curve.

Amanda screamed and struggled to her feet. He made a long inaccurate swipe and Amanda felt the glass brush the hand she had flung up to shield her face. Then, heavy-footed, he was at the mantelpiece, wiping it down, wiping the wooden arms of the couch. He came to the cupboard and stood stock still, arms hanging by his sides; his whole body sagged. The hall door rattled briefly, the stairs creaked; the room still wavered, unsettled.

Douglas glared at her.

'Don't stand there gawping as if your throat was cut,' he said. 'What am I doing with this damned glass?'

Amanda's hand stung; she saw for the first time that it had been cut by the glass and was oozing fine beads of blood.

'Doug,' she said, 'is there anything in that cupboard?'

'No,' he said, 'no, it's empty. Mandy . . . what's wrong? You mustn't take any notice of the draughts in this place.'

He edged away from the cupboard and flung the broken glass into the fireplace among the crumpled newspaper and kindling wood. Amanda watched him and licked the blood from her hand. *Why does the taste of blood not revolt me?* Immediately it did revolt her, the whole room reeked of blood. She pressed a hand to her mouth and went to the casement window. Sunlight came in and a smell of roses; the house was a good creature again, quite docile. Douglas was sitting on the couch, his mouth still twisted; she thought: *He will be taken again; he will go so far away that I will never be able to get him back!*

'Doug . . . we must get out of this house . . .'

Horribly he began to cry. He covered his face with his hands and sobbed aloud.

'Doug, please . . .'

She knelt beside him while the room chirruped and rattled.

'Ran right under the wheels,' sobbed Douglas. 'Oh God, Mandy . . . it's in my head, I can't think of anything else. I killed the poor little beggar . . .'

'Douglas, listen to me . . .'

'Don't know what I'm doing half the time . . .'

'Douglas, the boy in Hammersmith is not dead . . . not even badly hurt!'

He took in great gulps of air and fumbled for his handkerchief.

'Is that a fact? I didn't kill . . .'

'Truly,' she said. 'You must go back. You must stop running away.'

'So must you,' he said, with a reassuring touch of the old self-righteousness.

'Yes,' she said, 'yes, I promise. I'll eat . . . I'll put on ten pounds, twelve. Only we must leave this house.'

'There is two weeks' rent paid.'

'Douglas, this is a rotten place. It plays tricks.'

His eyes swivelled nervously in the direction of the cupboard.

'You may be right,' he whispered.

'My things are still packed,' she said. 'Let me pack yours.'

'You mean now, at once?'

'I don't want to spend another night in this house.'

Douglas ran a hand through his black hair in what his mother had deplored as an artistic gesture.

'All right,' he said. 'I'll tidy up a bit down here.'

Amanda went up the stairs whistling. She stripped the beds and cleared the bathroom and packed. Douglas had been living neatly out of a suitcase: had he tried to leave the house? She paused, kneeling beside his bed and heard the distant roar of the vacuum cleaner. She felt for her watch, worn on a chain round her neck, and found that it was past midday.

Amanda, she asked herself quietly, *why do you wear your watch on a chain?* She felt the links of the chain run between her fingers; a chain of lies and evasions; the disease dominated her life. She could not wear a wristwatch, her wrist was a bird's bone, the bands slipped and chafed. Long sleeves and buttoned cuffs to hide her arms. No more dressing rooms, bedroom and bathroom doors always locked: no one must see Amanda stripped to the bone.

Years of lying about food; almost second nature now to say, 'I've just had something'; to pretend dietary quirks: 'I don't eat meat'; 'I can't digest eggs.' The silly stratagems to make her eat. 'Finish this ice cream, pet, so that I can wash the bowl.' The Swedish *au pair*, who was really a nurse. She cracked much sooner than Mummy; seized Amanda bodily and forced custard into her mouth. Amanda leaned forward on to the folded featherbed and tenderly felt the spot where her rib had been broken.

A bitter childish hatred engulfed her; she was drowning in their care, it was like vile nourishing mush sliding down the back of her throat. She had endured force feeding more than once but at Zurich it was never permitted. But what was the secret? She knew, she must know somewhere inside herself, the reason for it. She was not Jane, she had her own reasons. She closed her eyes and tried to look for the secret. When she opened them again the darkness remained, the room had grown dark.

She sprang up awkwardly and thunder crashed overhead. As she closed the window huge drops of rain warm as blood fell on her hand; the black clouds had rolled up in an instant over the woods. Through the sparse raindrops she could see the misty fields, the ruined watchtower and the tall apartment blocks of the little town still in a shaft of sunlight. But the house was dark and wracked with thunder.

She called into the shadowy hall: 'Douglas.' There was no

answer. Amanda sagged against the banister and began to go down one step at a time, her long legs trembling with fear. Douglas had gone, had been taken again, but *she* could escape. Fragile Amanda could snatch a coat from the rack and rush off into the rainy garden. She called more loudly, 'Douglas,' hearing her voice shake. It was oddly familiar, it sounded like her mother's voice. And as she came to the foot of the stairs pale lightning flashed and the thunder spoke and she regained her courage. Amanda looked down some dusty corridor of time and saw another self, a sturdy, yes, even a fat little girl – a tomboy, enormously stubborn and strong willed. Strong willed to the point of madness, to the point of death; no one, nothing was a match for her.

She flung herself against the sitting-room door shouting her brother's name. It came open then was slammed against her; a voice, hoarse and unrecognizable, came out from under the door. The German was thick and sibilant with a heavy Hessian accent; she could not understand a word. Amanda ran into the kitchen, seized a broom and let it fall, looked about for a weapon to drive out evil. Cold iron, water, sunlight . . . then the lightning flashed again and gave her the answer. She scrabbled in the cupboard under the sink looking for paraffin or cleaning fluid and found something better, a jerry-can of petrol. She took the box of giant kitchen matches and went through the narrow box of the kitchen into the back hallway. She burst into the sitting room through its back door.

The room was pitch dark and the switch for the overhead light did not work, but Amanda knew that she had not miscalculated. Douglas or that other was still crouched by the far door. Amanda struck a match and saw the horror turning to face her. Wrapped in the tartan rug, face pudgy, lined, transformed, the face of a madwoman, yet inexplicably her brother's face.

'Let him go!' shouted Amanda.

The creature came for her, slow and clumsy, as if its feet hurt, its joints were stiff from years of housecleaning. The room was icy cold beyond the flame of the long match and it stank of death and corruption. The cupboard opened with a little scratching sound. Amanda moved towards the cupboard, she deliberately flung the doors wide and looked inside. She had been ready to cry out that the cupboard was empty, but it was not. She made out the small folded limbs, the head like a doll's head, waxy and putrescent, with a fluff of baby hair on the peeling scalp; the little corpse seemed to give off its own light. The match burned Amanda's fingers and she flung it aside with a cry. Heavy steps came towards her in the darkness. The voice panted:

...'... *Muss graben* ... have to bury it ...'

Amanda blundered away towards the fireplace and struck another match. The madwoman ... Douglas ... leaned against the couch, arms outstretched, the hands crooked into claws for digging, for scratching. Some object came hurtling across the room from another direction right at Amanda's forehead and her anger was rekindled. She dropped the jerry-can and caught the china shepherdess in mid-air. She set it down carefully on the mantelpiece and unscrewed the cap of the jerry-can; she spilled petrol on the paper in the grate.

'Let him go!' she said again, hearing a furious malevolence in her own voice. '*Lass ihn los* ... let him go or I will burn this house!'

She threw the lighted match into the fireplace and the flames roared up.

This time, perhaps, she *had* miscalculated horribly. The jerry-can was half full of petrol, a spark would send it up like a Molotov cocktail. The firelight reflected in the dark window pane showed thin Amanda among flames, she could feel them in her hair, could feel the room grow into an inferno, with the crouching figure of Douglas burning like a Buddhist monk.

Suddenly the casement window burst open; wind and rain blew cleanly into the dark room. There was a long cry that sprang first from the contorted lips of Douglas then left him and echoed from the very walls of the house. The house was wracked with sobs and Amanda read them as an endless, an age-old sorrow, a female sorrow, that told of blood and filth and drudgery and hatred of one's own body and a useless grief for children dead. She ran to the window and flung the jerry-can far out into the wet garden. The rain struck at her face and mingled with her own tears.

'Please . . .' she said aloud. 'Please . . . I understand.'

Then she was talking to the empty air; the house was still, really still at last. The only sounds were heavy drops of rain on the sill or hissing down the chimney into the ashes of the fire. Douglas heaved himself up from the carpet and sat shivering on the couch with the tartan rug around his shoulders.

'The cupboard,' he said hoarsely. 'Did you see . . . ?'

'There's nothing in the cupboard now,' said Amanda firmly.

She went and ran her hands over the empty shelves. She almost wished for some token . . . a scrap of cloth or paper that she could take out and bury. She wondered what might be found if the house were pulled down, if anyone took a spade to the forest floor.

'The packing is done,' she said. 'Douglas, I think we should . . .'

'Yes,' he said. 'Yes . . . as soon as possible. There's nothing to keep us here.'

The rain had stopped when they left but the sky was still overcast. As her brother got out the car Amanda walked through the trees to the bridge and met Frau Schneider.

'You think it best, Fräulein King?'

'I don't trust the place,' said Amanda, 'and Douglas has to go back to London.'

She reached into her bag and brought out the china shepherdess.

'Frau Schneider, I wish you would keep this. It will get broken if it stays in the house.'

Frau Schneider looked puzzled.

'It belongs to Frau Winter,' she said. 'All her things were packed up. This must have been left out.'

'Please keep it,' said Amanda, 'in memory of Frau Winter.'

Nickie began to bark at the base of an oak tree beyond the bridge and the two women saw a squirrel, two squirrels, whisking along the upper branches. The Volkswagen came roaring up and parked; Douglas and Frau Schneider exchanged a nod.

'But Fräulein King,' she said softly, 'the English lady is not dead. Frau Winter is not dead.'

'I thought . . .'

Frau Schneider reached out and patted Amanda's hand, holding the shepherdess, with her own gloved hand.

'You take it,' she said kindly. 'It is of no use if I bring it to the sanatorium. The poor woman would not know it.'

They turned together, as if at a command, and stared at the house, framed among the autumn trees.

'She has never recovered,' said Frau Schneider. 'She cannot even keep herself clean.'

Amanda could not speak. She stowed the pink and green figure in her handbag. Nickie began to give tongue even more loudly among the oak trees and Frau Schneider went to fetch him. Amanda walked briskly towards the car, her boot heels breaking through the crust of the fallen leaves as if the ground were already half frozen.

Russell Kirk

Watchers at the strait gate

*Russell Kirk was born in Michigan in 1918, and is the only
living writer to challenge (or, better, to complement) Robert
Aickman's supremacy among living writers of the ghostly tale;
yet hardly a story of his can be found in print in Britain, let
alone a collection. A selection from his superb book* The Surly
Sullen Bell *is included in his Arkham House collection* The
Princess of all Lands, *and his novels are* A Creature of the
Twilight *(a political fantasy) and* Old House of Fear. *He has
received the Ann Radcliffe Award for his Gothic fiction, and
his story 'There's a long, long trail a-winding' won the World
Fantasy Award. He lives with his wife, Annette Yvonne Cecile
Courtemanche, and four daughters in a house which 'is
crowded with Vietnamese refugees [ten of them], reformed
hobos, university students, young mothers with babies, and a
congeries of fugitives from Progress'.*

*He is regarded as one of America's leading conservative
thinkers, as which he has published several influential books,
including* The Conservative Mind, The Roots of American
Order, Decadence and Renewal in the Higher Learning, *and*
Eliot and his Age *(which was given the Christopher Award).
In his essay which concludes* The Surly Sullen Bell *he writes,
'I venture to suggest that the more orthodox is a writer's
theology, the more convincing, as symbols and allegories, his
uncanny tales will be.' Here is a fine example of what he meant.*

> 'I am for the house with the narrow gate,
> which I take to be too little for pomp to
> enter. Some that humble themselves may,
> but the many will be too chill and tender,
> and they'll be for the flow'ry way that leads
> to the broad gate and the great fire.'

> > – *All's Well That
> > Ends Well*

The rectory at St Enoch's, Albatross, was in poor repair. That did not much matter to Father Justin O'Malley, who felt in poor repair himself, and meant to leave the money-grubbing for a new rectory to the New Breed pastor who would succeed him here.

No doubt the New Breed types at the chancery would insist upon erecting a new church, as well as a new rectory, once Justin O'Malley was put out to pasture conveniently. They had succeeded in exiling him to the remotest parish in the diocese – to Albatross, away north among the pines and birches. The handsome simple old boulder church of St Enoch, built with their own hands by the early farmers of this infertile parish, could have stood with little repair for another two or three centuries; but the New Breed meant to pull it down 'to facilitate the new liturgy' once Justin O'Malley was disposed of. Meanwhile St Enoch's bell, at Father O'Malley's insistence, still was rung daily.

No, Justin O'Malley did not much heed the shutter that banged at his study window in this night's high wind, nor even the half-choked chimney that sent an occasional streamer of smoke towards his desk from the oak-limb fire flickering in the fireplace. He sat writing his sermon at three in the morning, or almost that, a decanter of whiskey on the corner of the desk, a handful of cigars beside it, and five battered volumes of Cardinal Newman stacked precariously before him. Now and again he hummed wryly when the shutter gave a particularly ferocious crack, mumbling the lyrics:

This old house once rang with laughter,
This old house knew many shouts;
Now it trembles in the darkness
When the lightning walks about . . .

He wasn't sure he had those lines quite right, but it was better to mangle lyrics than to mutilate dogmata. Sister Mary Ruth had called him a 'dogmatist' before she had shaken the dust of Albatross from her sandals – as if heterodoxy were ordained of God. Sister Mary Ruth had demanded that she be permitted to exhort from the pulpit of St Enoch's, and Father O'Malley had said her nay, dogmatically; so she had gone away to the world – and, he suspected, to the flesh and the devil. St Enoch's Elementary School had only two nuns left now, and he supposed that the next pastor would close it.

On Father O'Malley's study wall hung a Hogarth engraving,

'The Bathos', concerned with the end of all things. Father Time himself lay expiring in the foreground, amidst cracked bells and burst guns, and the word *Finis* was written upon the tobacco smoke that issued from Time's dying lips. A broken tower rather like the tower of St Enoch's hulked in the background. If only Hogarth had drawn also a torn-up missal and a roofless schoolhouse, the relevance to St Enoch's Parish would have been perfect. From the sublime to the ridiculous! So the Church, or at least this diocese, had descended in some fifteen years.

Father O'Malley sipped his whiskey and drew long on his thick cigar. He *must* stick to only one cigar an evening; otherwise the angina would come on worse than before. He had fought as best he could in this diocese, had been thrashed, and now lay eyeless in Gaza, otherwise Albatross. Defeat in the battle against innovation had left him a wreck – to mix metaphors – stranded on the barren shingle of the world. Perhaps, just conceivably, the Church might come to know better days; but he would not behold them. On he hummed:

> Got no time to fix the shingles or to mend the windowpane;
> Ain't gonna need this house no longer . . .

Oh, come now, Justin! You've got a sermon to finish; put the nonsense out of your head. Should he blast the New Breed one more time? *Come one, come all, this rock shall fly from its firm base as soon as I* . . . Yes: give them a dose of Newman, whom they never had read, actually.

He took up his copy of Newman's *Dream of Gerontius*. In Newman's spirit, very nearly, Vatican II had been conceived and convened; but that council had led, vulgarized, to much that Newman would have found anathema. Like Newman's Gerontius, the Reverend Justin O'Malley bent 'over the dizzy brink of some sheer infinite descent'. He asked now for little but to depart in peace.

Well, what should he call this comminatory sermon of his, here at the back of beyond, to his little congregation of ageing faithful? Should it be 'Prospect of the Abyss'? Would they be shocked, or would they notice at all – especially those among them who were in the habit of slipping out the church door right after the Sacrament? What would they think if he should quote certain chilling lines from *Gerontius*:

> And, crueller still,
> A fierce and restless fright begins to fill

> *The mansion of my soul. And, worse and worse,*
> *Some bodily form of ill*
> *Floats on the wind, with many a loathsome curse,*
> *Tainting the hallowed air, and laughs, and flaps*
> *Its hideous wings,*
> *And makes me wild with horror and dismay.*

Rather a strong dose for the old ladies who frequently confessed the great sin that their thoughts wandered at mass? Father O'Malley put the slim volume *Gerontius* aside and took up the fat *Development of Doctrine*. But the words blurred before his eyes. How he could use a cat nap! Nevertheless he persisted, covering half a page of paper with notes. He should have commenced this job earlier in the evening, and have abstained from even one whiskey. He ought to get outdoors more often, he knew, even in a winter so fierce as this, for the sake of his circulation. Why didn't he fetch those snowshoes out of the cellar? An hour or two of following a woods trail would put him in a better temper.

Once upon a time, he recollected, somebody had said that O'Malley was the one priest in the diocese who had a joke for every occasion. Had it been the bishop before this one? Well, why not laugh?

> *Life is a jest, and all things shew it;*
> *I thought so once, but now I know it.*

Should he put it in his will that they were to cut John Gay's epitaph on O'Malley's gravestone? But here, what was he scribbling on his sheet of sermon notes? 'O'Malley's a jest, and all things . . .' And he couldn't read half the sentences he had scrawled above that remark. Really, he must have a five-minute nap.

It required some force of will to remove the glass, the bottle, and the ash tray to a side table, sleepily, and to pile the books on the floor. Then Father O'Malley laid his face on his forearms, there on the old mahogany desk, and closed his eyes. High time it was for the nap, he reflected as consciousness drifted away: the pain in his chest had been swelling as he grew fatigued, but now it must ebb. The blessed dark . . .

Was it a really tremendous bang of the loose shutter that woke him? He could have slept only for a few minutes, but he felt rested. Then why was he uneasy? He glanced round his study;

the desk lamp showed him that nothing had changed. Getting up, he went to the window. Indeed that shutter was being torn loose altogether by the storm outside, the blizzard had increased, so that the snowflakes postively billowed against the panes. Why was he so uneasy? He had lived alone in this rectory for decades. Newman's line crept back into his mind: *Some bodily form of ill* . . . He crossed himself.

Then something rattled and fell in the little parlour, adjacent to the study, where usually he had parishioners wait if he was busy when they came to talk with him. In that parlour was an umbrella stand, and presumably some stick or umbrella had fallen. But what had made it fall, at this hour? Some strong draught?

With a certain reluctance, he opened the parlour door. The light from the desk lamp did not show him much. Was that a bulk in the further armchair?

'Father,' said a deep voice, 'I didn't mean to disturb you. I can just sit here till you're ready, Father. Ah, it's a blessing to be off that long, long trail and snug indoors this night. This chair of yours is like a throne, Father O'Malley . . .

> *'Up from Earth's Centre through the Seventh Gate*
> *I rose, and on the Throne of Saturn sate,*
> *   And many a Knot unravel'd by the Road,*
> *But not the Master-knot of Human Fate.'*

Justin O'Malley had sucked in his breath when the bulk in the tall chair stirred, but now he knew who it was: Frank Sarsfield, no other, with his quoting of the *Rubaiyat*. Frank had not come to him for more than a year. Now he would be wanting a bed, a meal, and a few dollars before he set out again. Oh, Frank was an old client, he was. Father O'Malley crossed himself again; this visitant could have been a different type. Only last month two priests had been hacked to death in their beds, at a house in Detroit.

'Frank,' he said, 'you gave me a turn. Come into my study and I'll see what I can do for you.'

'I think I was dozing off myself, Father, and my foot touched that umbrella stand, and something fell, I'm sorry. A little while ago I peeked in and saw you resting at your big desk, and I said to myself, "Nobody deserves his rest more than Father O'Malley," so I took the liberty of occupying that throne-chair of yours till you should wake. I'm not asking anything, Father, it's just that I came out of the blizzard, thinking we both might profit from a few words together. I know what I owe you already, Father Justin O'Malley, having kept track of it in my stupid head, year in, year out: it's a long-standing debt, most of it, coming altogether to the sum of four hundred and ninety-seven dollars and eleven cents. Is that the right sum, Father? Well, as the bums say when they're hauled before the bar of justice: *Jedge, I've had a run o' hard luck*. My ship didn't come in, Father, and none of my lottery tickets won big. But I know what I owe you, more than I owe anybody else in this world, and I've come here to square accounts, if that's all right with you, Father O'Malley.'

Perhaps Frank was careful with his diction when addressing the clergy; but his speech must be very good for a tramp, in any company. What damaged his polished address was the accent – and the intonation. There was a strong salt flavour of 'down east' – Sarsfield had been born on the Maine coast, O'Malley knew – blended with flop-house accents. ('Bird' became 'boid'.) The man had been a tramp since he was fifteen years or younger, Father O'Malley had found out, and he must be past sixty now. When not on the road during those weary decades, he had been in prisons chiefly. He must have slept here in the rectory nearly a dozen times, on his endless aimless peregrinations. Sarsfield professed to be a Catholic of sorts: if he should pilfer church poor-boxes, he preferred Catholic poor-boxes.

'Settle up?' Father O'Malley offered Sarsfield whiskey, as he always did; and as always Sarsfield declined the glass. 'Settle up, Frank? I'll believe that when you settle down, which you won't do until Judgment Day, I suppose. Have a cigar, then.'

'Get thee behind me,' Sarsfield answered, chuckling at his own wit. 'You know I never did smoke, Father, and only once I drank a bottle of wine – Million Bell it was – and it made me sick, as my mother said it would; so I'm not tempted, thank you.' At O'Malley's gesture, Sarsfield resumed his seat in the tall chair he had called a throne; apparently he did not intend to enter the pastor's study. It took a strong great chair to sustain Frank. For Sarsfield was a giant, almost, with a great Viking head, carrying more weight than was good for him. Yet he had a good colour now, Father O'Malley noticed, and seemed less elephantine in his movements than he had the last time he called at St Enoch's.

'Then you'll be wanting to raid the refrigerator, Frank? Mrs Syzmanski left some cold chicken there, I know. And you must be worn out, afoot on a night like this. There's a bed for you – the little room with the yellow wallpaper, if you're ready to turn in. How far did you come today – or yesterday, rather?'

'Far, Father, farther than ever – and found your door unlocked, as if you'd been expecting some tramp or other. Begging your pardon, Father Justin, I wouldn't leave the rectory open to all comers at night. Nowadays there's desperate characters on the move everywhere. You heard what was done to those two priests in Detroit, Father? And I could tell you about other cases . . . But I guess you're like that French bishop – *nisi Dominus custodierit domum, in vanum vigilant qui custodiunt eam*. What good are watchers, unless the Lord guards the house?'

Frank Sarsfield had succeeded several times in startling Father O'Malley with his scraps of learning and his faculty for quotation, which ran to whole long poems; yet this Latin, wretchedly pronounced though it was, staggered his host. He knew that this strange man, whose hair was perfectly white now, has been subjected to only four or five years of schooling; his knowledge of books came from public libraries in little towns, Christian Science reading rooms, prison libraries. 'Frank, I've told you before that you'd have made a good monk, but it's late for that.'

'Ah, Father, too late for that or for anything else, or nearly anything. Yet there's one thing, Father Justin O'Malley, that you've urged me to do, time and time again, and I've not done it, but I'll do it now, if you say it's not too late. If it pleases you, Father, it's one way of paying you back. It's this: will you hear my confession?'

What had come over this man? What had he done lately? During the several years of their intermittent acquaintance, Sarsfield had sat through masses at St Enoch's, but never had taken communion or gone to confession. 'At this hour, Frank? Right here?'

'As for the hour, Father, I know you're a night person; and I never sleep well, whatever the hour. As for the place – well, no, Father, I'd rather confess to you in that handsome old walnut confessional in the church. You'll know who I am – that can't be helped – but I won't see your face, nor you mine, and that'll make things easier, won't it? I hear that nowadays they call it "reconciliation", Father, and sometimes they just sit face to face with the priest, talking easy like this, but that's not what I want. I want you to hear everything I did and then absolve me, if you can. What's the old word for it, out of King Arthur and such? You know – *shriven*, that's it. I want to be shriven.'

Father O'Malley never had expected this. He supposed that a psychiatrist might call Frank Sarsfield an 'autistic personality'; certainly Frank was a loner, an innocent of sorts, sometimes shrewd, sometimes very like a small boy, indolent, unmachined, guilt ridden, as weak of will as he was strong of body. Like Lady Macbeth, Sarsfield was forever washing himself, using up the rectory's rather scanty hot water, as if there were immaterial stains not to be washed away; he was every day clean shaven, his thick hair well-brushed, his clothes neat and clean. Sarsfield had been concentred all in self, turned in upon himself, his seeming joviality a mere protective coloration that helped him to beg his way through the world. He had been no solipsist, the priest judged, but had withdrawn ever since childhood within a shell – a mollusc of a man. *This* one was ready to confess to him at half-past three in the morning?

'It'll be cold in the church, Frank . . .'

'Why, this coat of mine is warm, Father – I bought it with my dish-washing pay, never fear – and you can put on your overcoat, if it's not too much trouble, and your gloves, and we needn't go outside, for there's that passage between the rectory here and the church that I scrubbed for you three years and seven months ago. You don't mind going into your own church, do you, Father, with a man who looks rougher than Jean Valjean, in the dead of night?'

Suddenly Father O'Malley did mind. There had come into his memory of this man a recollection of a certain evening – yes, about three years and seven months ago – when he had invited Frank Sarsfield to confess, and the man had declined, and he had given Frank a piece of advice. Some intuition then had told Father O'Malley that Frank, despite all his repressing of his impulses, despite his accustomed humbling of himself, despite his protestations of having been always 'non-violent' – well, that Frank Sarsfield potentially was a very dangerous man. A hint of madness, he had noticed then, lingered in Frank's light blue eyes that were forever furtively peeking out of their own corners. And that evening he had said bluntly to Sarsfield, 'Look out you don't turn berserker, Frank.'

Just what impelled this great hulking fellow to confess at last? What had he done – in Detroit, perhaps?

Some bodily form of ill floats on the wind . . .

It wasn't that Sarsfield seemed distraught; on the contrary, that strange giant seemed more easy in manner than ever O'Malley had known him before, more confident, all diffidence gone – as if a tension within him had been relaxed – or as if, perhaps, something within him had snapped at last.

Yet how could he refuse Sarsfield's request? Would it have been safe to refuse? Those Detroit priests – what face had they seen in the wee hours?

'Give me a moment to tidy my papers in the study, Frank, and then . . .'

'Now, Father, don't put me off.' That was said with a smile, but Father O'Malley watched Sarsfield narrowly, and did not smile back. 'Let your study tidy itself, and come along into the church with me, while the mood is on me. It was you that told me I ought to confess my sins, and told me ten times over. Here I am for you, Father O'Malley; come straight along, for Christ's sake.'

Frank at his heels, then, Father O'Malley went downstairs, willynilly, and opened the sticky door that gave entrance to the short passage between rectory and church. Why had Sarsfield prevented him from returning to the study? Had he guessed that there was a loaded revolver, never used, in one of the desk drawers?

He led the way along the chilly corridor to the yet colder Church of St Enoch. Something O'Malley had read in a book about the Mountain Men came into his mind: *Never walk the trail ahead of Hank Williams in starving time.* Frank Sarsfield, potential or actual berserker, was just behind him, silent except for the squeaking of one of his boots.

Father O'Malley reached for the light switch in the church, but Sarsfield said, 'We know the way, Father; the confessional's just over there; and we don't want any folks wondering what's up in the church at three in the morning.' So they made their way along the aisle of a musty church lighted only by some nocturnal candles in the choir, the wind flinging itself savagely against the tall painted windows, to the antique carved walnut confessional. There the two of them parted momentarily, the priest to his station, the penitent to his stool within the massive box; and then they sat invisible, facing each other, a black curtain between their faces.

'Forgive me, Father, for I have sinned,' said Frank Sarsfield. He was very rusty at this business. He was still for a moment; then, 'How shall I tell you, Father? Do I go through all my life since I was confirmed, or is there some other way?' The huge man was desperately embarrassed, Father O'Malley sensed.

'If you like,' the invisible confessor murmured, 'begin with the greatest sins, the biggest mortal sins, and then go on to the lesser, the venial ones.'

'All right, Father. I've thought about this many a time. Maybe the worst is this: one day or another, one year or another, I robbed seven churches.'

'That is sacrilege. How much money did you take?'

'Altogether, I reckon, three hundred and eighteen dollars and twenty-four cents, Father. And altogether I got fifteen years' imprisonment for it, and more the two times I tried to escape and was caught.'

'Why did you commit such sins?'

'Well, Father, most of those times I was up against it, in big towns where nobody would give me anything, and so I broke open the poor boxes.'

'What did you do with the money?'

'Oh, I spent it right off for meals and lodging and some better clothes, Father; and once I bought presents for two little kids with part of the loot.'

This was Sarsfield's greatest sin? He had paid for it ten times over, in prisons. He was an enormous boy, never grown up.

'After these robberies of churches, what was your next greatest sin, my son?'

There came a heavy pause. The deep voice at length murmured, 'Running away from home, I guess, when I was an ungrateful kid. I never saw Mother again, or Dad.'

'Why did you run away?'

'Well, Dad drank a lot – that's why Mother made me promise not to drink, and I never did, except for that one bottle of Mission Bell – and then he'd beat me up. One day he took to licking and kicking me out in the field. I couldn't take it, and I went down on my knees to beg Dad to stop, and I put my arms around his legs, begging, and that made him fall over, and he hurt himself on an old plough. Then I knew that when he got up he'd kill me – really beat me until I was dead, Father, beat me with anything handy, beat me over the head – so I ran for it. As Providence would have it, there was a rail line next to that field of ours, and there was a freight passing, and I got aboard before Dad could catch me, and I never went back, not while Dad was alive, not while Mother was alive. My Mother was a saint—'

Was the giant sobbing there in the dark?

The catalogue of mortal sins ran on; Father O'Malley was astonished at their triviality, though he kept his peace on that point. This man who had passed through some of the worst prisons in the land was almost untouched by such experiences. As if a little child, clearly he was guiltless of sexual offences. He fought only in self-defence – or for five or ten dollars, against professional pugs at county fairs, where he was beaten invariably. He never had destroyed property wantonly, or stolen without need. He had been arrested for mere vagrancy, on most occasions; and his long sentences had been imposed because he had tried to escape from serving his short sentences. Frank Sarsfield was a fool: a medieval fool, that is; one of Shakespeare's half-wise clowns; one of those fools who, the Moslems say, lie under God's particular protection.

They passed on to venial sins, there in the deathly cold of St Enoch's. Father O'Malley grew weary of the recital, but Sarsfield was so earnest! 'And is there anything fairly recent?' the confessor inquired at last, hoping that the ordeal was nearly over.

'Something that may have been recent, Father, though I'm not sure: it might have been last night, or it might have been sixty years ago. Let me tell you, Father, this was a scary thing, and I paid for it. I killed six men in one house.'

'*What was that you said?*'

'I killed six men in one house, Father – almost as good, I guess, as the Brave Little Tailor, "Seven at one blow!" ' Here the confessional shook, as if a heavy shudder had run through the man's great body. 'I kept yelling, "All heads off but mine!" and off they came. I used an axe that one of them had tried to use on me.'

Father O'Malley sat stupefied in the dark. Was Sarsfield a maniac? Had he really done this atrocity – and perhaps not in one house only? And having confessed this so fully, would Sarsfield spare the confessor? He managed to gasp, 'You classify this as a *venial* sin?' It sounded absurd – both the offence and the interrogation.

'Oh, the classifying's up to you, Father. I don't know if it was a sin at all. I hadn't much choice about it. Those were the worst men that had broken out of prison, killers and worse than killers, and they were after a young mother and her three little daughters. After I butted in, it was either those six or yours truly. It turned out to be both, Father. It was the only time in my life I didn't behave like a coward, so you know better than I do whether I sinned. Maybe I took Heaven by storm.'

Father O'Malley, trying frantically to form some plan of action, played for time. 'You don't know whether you did this yesterday or sixty years ago?'

'No, Father, it's all mixed up in my head; and usually, as you know, my memory is good – the one thing I was proud of. Probably it's because so much has happened to me since that bloody fight, since I stood in that room like a slaughterhouse.'

The shudder came again.

'What do you mean, *something happened to you*?'

'Why, Father, being shot, and bleeding like a pig on the stairs and in the snow, and then the great long journey – all alone, except for the Watchers. But it turned out better than I deserved, Father. There's a poem by somebody named Blake, William Blake. I can't put into words most of what happened to me after I died, but these lines give you a notion of it:

> *'I give you the end of a golden string,*
> *Only wind it into a ball,*
> *It will lead you in at Heaven's gate*
> *Built in Jerusalem's wall.'*

Justin O'Malley had been a voluble priest, sometimes jocular. But at what Sarsfield had just said, he was struck dumb. The silence grew so intense that Father O'Malley could hear his pocket watch, a good venerable quiet watch, ticking enormously in the empty church; but he dared not draw that watch to find out the time; perhaps this lunatic, this vast overwhelming lunatic Sarsfield, might think he was reaching for something else.

For his part, the madman sat silent also, as if awaiting the imposition of a salutary penance. Father O'Malley shook where he sat. Could Sarsfield detect his dread? Yes, yes, he was supposed to impose a penance now. What penance should a priest impose for the real or imaginary crimes of a homicidal maniac who thinks himself already dead? Father O'Malley could not collect himself. He began to babble hurriedly whatever came into his imperilled head:

'For your grave sins, say ten Hail Marys . . .'

What trivial rubbish was he uttering? Ten Hail Marys for murdering a half-dozen men? Yet the brute on the other side of the curtain was murmuring, like a small boy, 'Yes, Father; I'll do that, Father . . .'

As if in a nightmare, Father O'Malley dashed from the insufficient penance to the implausible pardon. How much free will had this Frank ever been able to exercise, as boy or as man? Had he ever been perfectly sane? But put that aside, Justin: you've no time just now for casuistry.

'May the almighty and merciful Lord grant you pardon, absolution . . .' Had he gone mad himself? What impelled him to absolve so casually such a sinner as this? Yet Father O'Malley rushed through the old formula. Then Frank Sarsfield interrupted:

'Father, would you say the rest in Latin, please? They used it all the time when I was a boy. Maybe the words count for more if they're Latin, my mother, rest her, would have said so.'

'If you like,' O'Malley told his monstrous penitent – rather gratified, even in this dreadful moment, to encounter an Old Breed sinner. He hastened on:

'*Passio Domini nostri Iesu Christi, merita beatae Mariae Virginis, et omnium Sanctorum* . . .' Father O'Malley stumbled a little; it had been long since he had run through the Latin for a penitent; but he finished: '. . . *et praemium vitae aeternae. Amen.*'

'Amen!' Sarsfield responded, his stentorian voice echoing through the high-vaulted church. 'Doesn't that mean *reward of everlasting life*? I heard those Latin words for years and years, Father, and never thought about them.'

O'Malley muttered some banality; he was more immediately concerned at this moment for his own aged mortal envelope, at the mercy of this night visitor. Sarsfield seemed to expect something more, here in the confessional. '*Pax vobiscum!*' Father O'Malley breathed.

'*Et cum spiritu tuo,*' Sarsfield responded, and then rose, bumping against the wooden wall of the confession box as he blundered his way out. Father O'Malley wished dearly that he might have remained in the confessional, for his part, until dawn should have come and this grim wanderer should have left St Enoch's. But that was not to be. He too groped his way to the aisle.

A baker's dozen of votive candles burned near the high altar, the only illumination of the church this fierce night; their flames wavered in the draught.

'Father,' the voice was saying right beside him, 'there's some prayer for somebody dying or dead. Could we go down on our knees and say that together?' He must mean the Recommendation for a Departing Soul.

'*Kyrie, eleison,*' Father O'Malley commenced, kneeling at the nearest bench. To his horror, Sarsfield knelt very close beside him, shoulder to shoulder, in this spreading empty church – as if there were happy contagion in sanctity.

'It will be all right to do this in English, Father,' Sarsfield muttered, 'begging your pardon, because I want to understand all of it.'

'Holy Abel, all ye choirs of the just, Holy Abraham . . .' Father O'Malley rattled through the calendar – John the Baptist, Joseph, patriarchs and prophets, Peter, Paul, Andrew, John, apostles and evangelists, innocents, Stephen, Lawrence, martyrs, Sylvester, Gregory, Augustine, bishops and confessors, Benedict, Francis, Camillus, John of God, monks and hermits, Mary Magdalen, Lucy, virgins and widows, saints. 'From Thy wrath, from the peril of death, from an evil death, from the pains of hell, from all evil, from the power of the devil, through Thy birth, through Thy cross and passion, through Thy death and burial, through Thy glorious resurrection . . .' Where was he? Where was he, indeed? 'In the day of judgment, we sinners beseech thee, hear us . . . O Lord, deliver him . . . *Libera eum, Dominie.*'

'*Libera nos,*' Sarsfield put in, as if responding. 'Lord, have mercy, Christ, have mercy; Lord, have mercy.'

On and on Father O'Malley ran, the killer right against him in the dark, shifting from English to Latin, from Latin to English, as the spirit moved him, Sarsfield now and again responding irregularly or joining the priest in some passage that he seemed to recall. What a memory! Abruptly Sarsfield's voice drowned out O'Malley's:

'Mayest thou never know aught of the terror of darkness, the gnashing of teeth in the flames, the agonies of torment. May Satan most foul, with his wicked crew, give way before us; may he tremble at our coming with the Angels that attend us, and flee away into the vast chaos of eternal night. Let God arise, and let His enemies be scattered; and let them that hate Him flee from before His face. As smoke vanisheth, so let them vanish away; as wax melteth before the fire, so let the wicked perish at the presence of God; and let the just feast and rejoice before God. May, then, all the legions of hell be confounded and put to shame, nor may the ministers of Satan dare to hinder our way.'

Then Father O'Malley was permitted to resume. The recommendation seemed to eat up hours, though really only minutes could be elapsing. At length he thought they had finished, and fell silent with a final 'Amen'. Would this killer make an end of him now? But Sarsfield said, 'I think, Father, there's a prayer to Our Lord Jesus Christ that a dying man says himself, if he can, and it won't do any harm for the pair of us to say that too.'

With fear and trembling, Father O'Malley began to utter that prayer, and Sarsfield joined him. Sarsfield's voice grew louder and louder as they approached the end:

'Do Thou, O Lord, by these Thy most holy pains, which we, though unworthy, now call to mind, and by Thy holy cross and death, deliver Thy servants praying here from the pains of hell, and vouchsafe to lead us whither Thou didst lead the good Thief who was crucified with Thee.' A few more words, and this second prayer was done.

Father O'Malley could not run away; for Sarsfield sat between him and the aisle, and the other end of their bench ended against the stone wall. To have tried to clamber over the bench-back in front of them would have been too conspicuous, perhaps inviting violence. Sarsfield remained upon his knees, as if sunk in a long silent prayer, but presently sat back on the bench.

'You must have read about those people that claim to have come back from death, Father,' Sarsfield told him, rather hesitantly. Father O'Malley scarcely could make out Sarsfield's face at all. 'You know – there's some woman doctor wrote a book about cases like that, and there's other books, too. Most of them tell about some long tunnel, and at the end of it everything's hunkydory.'

Justin O'Malley murmured acknowledgement. Did this fellow mean to experiment in that fashion with his confessor?

'Well, Father, it isn't like that – not like that at all.' Sarsfield bent to lift up the kneeler, giving more room down below for his big boots. 'Once a man's dead, Father O'Malley, he stays dead; he doesn't come back in the flesh and walk around, not unless Jesus Christ does for him what he did for Lazarus. Those tunnel people were *close* to death, that's all: they never went over the edge. Just being close isn't the same condition. 'It's my experience, Father, that when you cross over there's a hesitation and lingering, for a little while. Then you move on out, and that's scary, because you don't know where you're going; you've got no notion whatsoever. It's not that happy little tunnel with light at the end. Why, it's more like a *darkling plain*, Father. And you're all alone, or seem to be, except where those ignorant armies clash by night. On and on you go. And when you think or feel that at last you've arrived at the strait gate *which leadeth unto life* – well, then you meet the Watchers.'

The Sleepless Ones, the Watchers! Into Father O'Malley's awareness flashed some lines from *Gerontius*:

Like beasts of prey, who, caged within their bars,
In a deep hideous purring have their life,
And an incessant pacing to and fro.

'Understand, Father,' Sarsfield went on, 'I'm trying to put into words for you some experiences that words don't fit. Somebody said, didn't he, that all life is an allegory, and we can understand it only in parable? So when I tell you about the darkling plain, and about the Sleepless Ones, those Watchers, you're not supposed to take me literally, not all the way. I'm just giving you an approximation, in words, of what you feel at your core. That's the best I can do; I'm no philosophist and no poet.

'But sure as hell's a mantrap, it's no Tunnel of Love you find yourself in when you cross over, Father O'Malley. Even if the Watchers don't have claws literally, you sure know they're after you, and they sure know your weakness. I suppose I got past them, almost to the destination, because I'm a fool who took Heaven by storm.'

'But you tell me that you've come back amongst us living, Frank,' Father O'Malley ventured. Just conceivably he might be able to draw this mad Frank Sarsfield, this berserker, back towards some degree of right reason – if he were very cautious in the endeavour. Would that he could recollect his Thomistic syllogisms at this hour! 'So how can that be, Frank, when not long ago you told me that once a man's dead, so far as this world of flesh is concerned, he stays dead?'

From Sarsfield, almost invisible, there came something like a chuckle. 'Ah, I died right enough, Father; they shot me twice, and maybe three times. The thing is, I haven't returned to the land of the living. I've come just far enough back to meet you in shadow land.'

Had this thing returned seeking whom he might devour? But Father O'Malley said aloud, 'Why come back at all, Frank?'

'I give you the end of a golden string, Father. I'd gone down the narrow way, as they call it in those old books, until I'd almost forgotten about what I'd left undone. Then I thought of you.

'I can't ever pay you that four hundred and ninety-seven dollars and eleven cents, not now, Father O'Malley. But that doesn't much matter, not where rust doesn't tarnish nor moth corrupt. All the same, I might pay you back some of your friendship.

'Father Justin, I couldn't think of any friend but you, as I slowed down there on the narrow way. The Watchers had my scent, but I stood still and thought about you. Nobody else ever gave me a meal without being asked for it, or lent me over a hundred dollars without much chance of getting it back, or – that was best of all, Father – ever talked with me for hours as if I had a mind and was worth passing the time with. So there on the narrow way, when it seemed as if the end would be just around the corner, I turned back towards St Enoch's and you. I could do it because after I took up that axe in that lonely old house against those six men, I wasn't a coward any longer.

'I came back here, or maybe was sent back here, to lend you a hand on your journey, Father Justin. I know the way to the little gate, so to speak, fool though I am. It's fearsome, Father, groping that way when the Watchers are purring in the dark. But the two of us together . . .'

O'Malley's dread of this madman had diminished a little, though a little only. Sarsfield might mean to take his confessor with him down to dusty death, but his mood of the moment was not hostile. If he could persuade Frank to settle himself down in the bed in the guest room, the poor crazy giant might sleep off his present frantic delusion. Frank must have footed it through the blizzard all the way to Albatross, from God knew where; perhaps extreme weariness had snapped Frank's uncertain grip upon reality. Or if Frank Sarsfield actually had killed six men, only yesterday – why, Justin O'Malley could telephone the sheriff once Frank was abed, and check that out. The sheriff and his boys could take Frank sleeping, without harming him.

'Come back into the rectory, Frank,' Father O'Malley contrived to tell him, 'before I take the end of that golden string of yours. Surely we've time enough to tidy my desk and have a cold chicken sandwich apiece, before we start rolling string into balls.'

'We may blow off like tumbleweeds any moment now, Father,' Frank answered. They returned to the passage between church and rectory. 'Go on ahead, Frank,' his confessor told him, dissimulating. 'You know the way.'

Sarsfield laughed. 'Don't you want me at your back, Father? I always was non-violent, till the last. It's not Frank Sarsfield you have to worry about: keep an eye peeled for the Watchers. After you, Father.'

So it was Father O'Malley who led the way back to the rectory, and up the stairs to his study. Every step of the way he had to nerve himself to keep from shuddering. Once, years ago – it came to him now – he had told Frank Sarsfield that some folk work out their Purgatory in this life, conceivably – and that he, Frank, might be one such. On another occasion, he had instructed Frank that for the Lord all time is eternally present; and that, knowing the heart, the Lord might have something especial in store for Frank Sarsfield, his failings notwithstanding.

He might as well have preached in Mecca. Indeed the Lord did seem to have reserved something for Frank Sarsfield, heavy vessel for dishonour: the slaying of six men – and now perhaps the murder of the pastor of St Enoch's. Why was this cup thrust upon Justin O'Malley? This came of leaving doors open to all comers. The Lord had dozed.

The two of them entered the study. Someone was sitting at Father O'Malley's desk – or rather, had relaxed there with his head resting upon his forearms.

Justin O'Malley started back, pale as a ghost. Frank Sarsfield caught him before he could fall.

'Ah, Father, it gave me such a twist myself, the first moment of awareness. I was looking at myself all blood, head to foot . . . Now don't be afraid of what's in that chair, Father. Look at it for the last time. We shall be changed.'

Screwing his courage to the sticking place, Justin O'Malley looked fixedly at that silent old husk. The body slumped there had perished during sleep, without pain, the old heart ceasing to pump. The face had been his own.

'We're off to the gate built in Jerusalem's wall,' Frank was telling him. 'Few there be that find it, they say; but if we humble ourselves, Father, we'll evade those pacing Sleepless Ones. I was sent to be your clown along the narrow way. Here, Father, take hold on yourself, we're going . . .'

The walls of the rectory fell away, and the winter landscape disintegrated, and for a moment Father O'Malley knew himself all fractured atoms.

Then the two of them were upon what seemed a darkling plain, and a path led through the marshes. It was all far more real than Albatross, and more perilous, and more promising. There was no pain at O'Malley's heart. Across the fens, drifting in the night breeze, corpse candles glimmered here and there. But the two of them could make out the high ground far beyond the bogs.

'Let's have no gnashing of teeth now, Father,' Frank was crying, with a wild sort of laugh. 'It's the faint-hearted that the Watchers catch.'

They strode forward as if they wore seven-league boots. At their backs, the sensual world which could be understood only in parable faded to the shadow of a shade.

Karl Edward Wagner

·220 Swift

*Karl Edward Wagner was born in 1945 in Knoxville,
Tennessee, and is a red-bearded giant who looks as if he should
be flinging his wench aside as Kirk Douglas calls the Vikings
to battle. In fact he was a psychiatrist before becoming a
full-time writer and publisher, and he and his wife are two of
the reasons (the others are the Wellmans and the Drakes) why
you could die of hospitality in Chapel Hill. His sword-and-
sorcery novels read like Robert E. Howard on LSD, though
Wagner created his character Kane ('an effort to go back to
the hero-villain of the Gothic novels') before he read Howard.
His work has all the energy and power of the best pulp fiction,
but is more intelligent than almost any of its predecessors.*

His books include Darkness Weaves *(originally altered by
the copy editor so that Kane would look like the cover!),* Death
Angel's Shadow, Bloodstone, Dark Crusade, Night Winds *and*
In the Wake of the Night. *He has also written of an occult
investigator* (Sign of the Salamander) *and of Robert E.
Howard's* Conan *and* Bran Mak Morn. *Nevertheless it was
a horror story, 'Sticks', which won him the British Fantasy
Award.*

*' "·220 Swift" has its beginnings in the summer I spent (1969)
living in an old log cabin in Haywood County, NC (on the NC
side of the Smokies, National Park that is, and not the fuzz).
According to my notes I started writing it in May 1973. Locales
are authentic, as are place names and the bits of data (legends,
place names, archaeological curiosa, etc). I wanted to develop
the material into something more than the old dodge: Here's
an old legend – arrgh! it got me!*

*I must say I began to wonder if I was ever going to see this
story, but it was worth the wait.*

I

Within, there was musty darkness and the sweet-stale smell of
damp earth.

Crouched at the opening, Dr Morris Kenlaw poked his head into the darkness and snuffled like a hound. His spade-like hands clawed industriously, flinging clods of dirt between his bent knees. Steadying himself with one hand, he wriggled closer to the hole in the ground and craned his neck inward.

He stuck out a muddy paw. 'Give me back the light, Brandon.' His usually overloud voice was muffled.

Brandon handed him the big flashlight and tried to look over Kenlaw's chunky shoulder. The archaeologist's blocky frame completely stoppered the opening as he hunched forward.

'Take hold of my legs!' came back his words, more muffled still.

Shrugging, Brandon knelt down and pinioned Kenlaw's stocky legs. He had made a fair sand-lot fullback not too many years past, and his bulk was sufficient to anchor the over-balanced archaeologist. Thus supported, Kenlaw crawled even farther into the tunnel. From the way his back jerked, Brandon sensed he was burrowing again, although no hunks of clay bounced forth.

Brandon pushed back his lank white hair with his forearm and looked up. His eyes were hidden behind mirror sunglasses, but his pale eyebrows made quizzical lines towards Dell Warner. Dell had eased his rangy denim-clad frame on to a limestone knob. Dan made a black-furred mound at his feet, tail thumping whenever his master looked down at him. The young farmer dug a crumpled pack of cigarettes out of his shirt pocket, watching in amused interest.

'Snake going to reach out, bite his nose off,' Dell ventured, proffering the cigarettes to Brandon, selecting one himself when the other man declined.

The cool mountain breeze whisked his lighter flame, whipped the high weeds that patchworked the sloping pasture. Yellow grass and weed – cropped closely here, there a verdant blotch to mark a resorbed cow-pie. Not far above them dark pines climbed to the crest of the ridge; a good way below, the slope levelled to a neat field of growing corn. Between stretched the steep bank of wild pasture, terraced with meandering cow-paths and scarred with grey juts of limestone. The early summer breeze had a cool, clean taste. It was not an afternoon to poke one's head into dank pits in the ground.

Kenlaw heaved convulsively, wriggling back out of the hole. He banged down the flashlight and swore; dirt hung on his black moustache. 'Goddamn hole's nothing but a goddamn groundhog burrow!' Behind his smudged glasses his bright-black eyes were accusing.

Dell's narrow shoulders lifted beneath his blue cotton work shirt. 'Groundhog may've dug it out, now – but I remember clear it was right here my daddy told me Granddad filled the hole in. Losing too much stock, stepping off into there.'

Kenlaw snorted and wiped his glasses with a big handkerchief. 'Probably just a hole leading into a limestone cave. This area's shot through with caves. Got a smoke? Mine fell out of my pocket.'

'Well, my dad said Granddad told him it was a tunnel mouth of some sort, only all caved in. Like an old mine shaft that's been abandoned years and years.'

Ill-humouredly snapping up his host's cigarette, Kenlaw scowled. 'The sort of story you'd tell to a kid. These hills are shot through with yarns about the mines of the ancients, too. God knows how many wild goose chases I've been after these last couple days.'

Dell's eyes narrowed. 'Now all I know is what I was told, and I was told this here was one of the mines of the ancients.'

Puffing at his cigarette, Kenlaw wisely forbore to comment.

'Let's walk back to my cabin,' Brandon suggested quickly. 'Dr Kenlaw, you'll want to wash up, and that'll give me time to set out some drinks.'

'Thanks, but I can't spare the time just now,' Dell grunted, sliding off the rock suddenly. The Plott hound scrambled to its feet. 'Oh, and Ginger says she's hoping you'll be down for supper this evening.'

'I'd like nothing better,' Brandon assured him, his mind forming a pleasant image of the farmer's copper-haired sister.

'See you at supper then, Eric. So long, Dr Kenlaw. Hope you find what you're after.'

The archaeologist muttered a goodbye as Warner and his dog loped off down the side of the pasture.

Brandon recovered his heavy Winchester Model 70 in ·220 Swift. He had been looking for woodchucks when he'd come upon Dell Warner and his visitor. From a flap pocket of his denim jacket he drew a lens cover for the bulky Leupold 3X9 telescopic sight.

'Did you say whether you cared for that drink?'

Kenlaw nodded. 'Jesus, that would be good. Been a long week up here, poking into every groundhog hole some hillbilly thinks is special.'

'That doesn't happen to be one there,' Brandon told him, hefting the rifle. 'I've scouted it several times for chucks – never anything come out.'

'You just missed seeing it – or else it's an old burrow,' Kenlaw judged.

'It's old,' Brandon agreed, 'or there'd be fresh dug earth scattered around. But there's no sign of digging, just this hole in the hillside. Looks more like it was dug out from below.'

II

The cabin that Eric Brandon rented stood atop a low bluff about half a mile up a dirt road from the Warner farmhouse. Dell had made a show of putting the century-old log structure into such state of repair that he might rent it out to an occasional venturesome tourist. The foot-thick poplar logs that made its rough-hewn walls were as solid as the day some *ante bellum* Warner had levered them into place. The grey walls showed rusty streaks where Dell had replaced the mud chinks with mortar, made from river sand hauled up from the Pigeon as it rushed past below the bluff. The massive river-rock fireplace displayed fresh mortar as well, and the roof was bright with new galvanized sheet metal. Inside was one large puncheon-floored room, with a low loft overhead making a second half-storey. There were no windows, but a back door opened on to a roofed porch overlooking the river below.

Dell had brought in a power line for lighting, stove and refrigerator. There was cold water from a line to the spring on the ridge above, and an outhouse farther down the slope. The cabin was solid, comfortable – but a bit too rustic for most tourists. Occasionally someone less interested in heated pools and colour tv found out about the place, and the chance rent helped supplement the farm's meagre income. Brandon, however, had found the cabin available each of the half-dozen times over the past couple of years when he had desired its use.

While the archaeologist splashed icy water into the sink at the cabin's kitchen end, Brandon removed a pair of fired cartridges from the pocket of his denim jacket. He inspected the finger-sized casings carefully for evidence of flowing, then dropped them into a box of fired brass destined for reloading.

Towelling off, Kenlaw watched him sourly. 'Ever worry about ricochets, shooting around all this rock like you do?'

'No danger,' Brandon returned, cracking an icetray briskly.

'Bullet's moving too fast – disintegrates on impact. One of the nice things about the ·220 Swift. Rum and coke OK?' He didn't care to lavish his special planter's punch on the older man.

Moving to the porch, Kenlaw took a big mouthful from the tall glass and dropped on to a ladderback chair. The Jamaican rum seemed to agree with him; his scowl eased into a contemplative frown.

'Guess I was a little short with Warner,' he volunteered.

When Brandon did not contradict him, he went on. 'Frustrating business, though, this trying to sort the thread of truth out of a snarl of superstition and hearsay. But I guess I'm not telling you anything new.'

The woven white oak splits of the chair bottom creaked as Kenlaw shifted his ponderous bulk. The Pigeon River, no more than a creek this far upstream, purled a cool, soothing rush below. Downstream the Canton papermills would transform its icy freshness into black and foaming poison.

Brandon considered his guest. The archaeologist had a sleek roundness to his frame that reminded Brandon of young Charles Laughton in *Island of Lost Souls*. There was muscle beneath the pudginess, judging by the energy with which he moved. His black hair was unnaturally sleek, like a cheap toupee, and his bristly moustache looked glued on. His face was round and innocent; his eyes, behind round glasses, round and wet. Without the glasses, Brandon thought they seemed tight and shrewd; perhaps this was a squint.

Dr Morris Kenlaw had announced himself the day before with a peremptory rap at Brandon's cabin door. He had started at Brandon's voice behind him – the other man had been watching from the ridge above as Kenlaw's dusty Plymouth drove up. His round eyes had grown rounder at the thick-barrelled rifle in Brandon's hands.

Dr Kenlaw, it seemed, was head of the Department of Anthropology at some southern college, and perhaps Brandon was familiar with his work. No? Well, they had told him in Waynesville that the young man staying at the Warners' cabin was studying folklore and Indian legends and such things. It seemed Mr Brandon might have had cause to read this or that article by Dr Kenlaw . . . No? Well, he'd have to send him a few reprints, then, that might be of interest.

The archaeologist had appropriated Brandon's favourite seat and drunk a pint of his rum, before he finally asked about the lost mines of the ancients. And Brandon, who had been given little chance before to interrupt his visitor's rambling discourse, abruptly found the other's flat stare fixed attentively on him.

Brandon dutifully named names, suggested suggestions; Kenlaw scribbled notes eagerly. Mission accomplished, the archaeologist pumped his hand and hustled off like a hound on a scent. Brandon had not expected to see the man again. But Dell Warner's name was among those in Kenlaw's notes, and today Brandon had run into them – Kenlaw, having introduced himself as a friend of Brandon, had persuaded Dell to show him his family's version of the lost mines. And that trail, it would seem, had grown cold again.

The chunky reddish-grey squirrel – they called them boomers – that had been scrabbling through the pine needle sod below them, suddenly streaked for the bushy shelter of a Virginia pine. Paying no attention, Dan romped around the corner of the cabin and bounded on to the porch. Brandon scratched the Plott hound's black head and listened. After a moment he could hear the whine and rattle as a pick-up lurched up the dirt road.

'That'll be Dell,' he told Kenlaw. 'Dan knew he was headed here and took the shortcut up the side of the ridge. Dog's one of the smartest I've seen.'

Kenlaw considered the panting black hound. 'He's a bear hound, isn't he?'

'A damn good one,' Brandon asserted.

'A bear killed young Warner's father, if I heard right,' Kenlaw suggested. 'Up near where we were just now. How dangerous are the bears they have up here?'

'A black bear doesn't seem like much compared to a grizzly,' Brandon said, 'but they're quite capable of tearing a man apart – as several of these stupid tourists find out every summer. Generally they won't cause trouble, although now and then you get a mean one. Trouble is, the bears over in the Smokies have no fear of man, and the park rangers tend to capture the known troublemakers and release them in the more remote sections of the mountains. So every now and then one of these renegades wanders out of the park. Unafraid of man and unaccustomed to foraging in the wild, they can turn into really nasty stock killers. Probably what killed Bard Warner that night. He'd been losing stock and had the bad sense to wait out with a bottle and his old 8 mm Mannlicher. Bolt on the Mannlicher is too damn slow for close work. From what I was told, Bard's first shot didn't do it, and he never got off his second.

Found what was left pulled under a rock ledge the next morning.'

Dell's long legs stuck out from the battered door of his old Chevy pick-up. He emerged from the cab balancing several huge tomatoes in his hands; a rolled newspaper was poked under one arm.

'These'll need to go into the refrigerator, Eric,' he advised. 'They're dead ripe. Get away, Dan!' The Plott hound was leaping about his legs.

Brandon thanked him and opened the refrigerator. Finger-combing his windblown sandy hair, Dell accepted his offer of a rum and coke. 'Brought you the Asheville paper,' he indicated. 'And you got a letter.'

'Probably my adviser wondering what progress I've made on my dissertation,' Brandon guessed, setting the letter with no return address carefully aside. He glanced over the newspaper while his friend uncapped an RC and mixed his own drink. Inflation, Africa, the Near East, a new scandal in Washington, and in New York a wave of gangland slayings following the sniping death of some syndicate kingpin. In this century-old cabin in the ancient hills, all this seemed distant and unreal.

'Supper'll be a little late,' Dell was saying. 'Faye and Ginger took off to Waynesville to get their hair done.' He added: 'We'd like to have you stay for supper too, Dr Kenlaw.'

The redhead's temper had cooled so that he remembered mountain etiquette. Since Kenlaw was still here, he was Brandon's guest, and a supper invitation to Brandon must include Brandon's company as well – or else Brandon would be in an awkward position. Had Kenlaw already left, there would have been no obligation. Brandon sensed that Dell had waited to see if the archaeologist would leave, before finally driving up.

'Thanks, I'd be glad to,' Kenlaw responded, showing some manners himself. Either he felt sheepish over his brusque behaviour earlier, or else he realized he'd better use some tact if he wanted any further help in his research here.

Brandon refilled his and Kenlaw's glasses before returning to the porch. Dell was standing uncertainly, talking with the archaeologist, so Brandon urged him to take the other porch chair. Taking hold with one hand of the yard-wide section of white oak log that served as a low table, he slid it over the rough planks to a corner post and sat down. He sipped the drink he had been carrying in his free hand and leaned back.

It was cool and shady on the porch, enough so that he would have removed his mirror sunglasses had he been alone. Brandon, a true albino, was self-conscious about his pink eyes.

As it was, Kenlaw was all but gawking at his host. The section of log that Brandon had negligently slewed across the uneven boards probably weighed a couple of hundred pounds. Dell, who had seen the albino free his pick-up from a ditch by the straightforward expedient of lifting the mired rear wheel, appeared not to notice.

'I was asking Dr Kenlaw what it was he was looking for in these mines,' Dell said.

'If mines they are,' Brandon pointed out.

'Oh, they're mines, sure enough,' the archaeologist asserted. 'You should be convinced of that, Brandon.' He waved a big hand for emphasis. Red clay made crescents beneath untrimmed nails.

'Who were the *ancients* who dug them?' Dell asked. 'Were they the same Indians who put up all those mounds you see around here and Tennessee?'

'No, the mound builders were a lot earlier,' Kenlaw explained. 'The mines of the ancients were dug by Spaniards – or more exactly, by the Indian slaves of the *conquistadores*. We know that de Soto came through here in 1540 looking for gold. The Cherokees had got word of what kind of thieves the Spaniards were, though, and while they showed the strangers polite hospitality, they took pains not to let them know they had anything worth stealing. De Soto put them down as not worth fooling with, and moved on. But before that he sank a few mine shafts to see what these hills were made of.'

'Did he find anything?' Dell wanted to know.

'Not around here. Farther south along these mountains a little ways, though, he did find some gold. In northern Georgia you can find vestiges of their mining shafts and camps. Don't know how much they found there, but there's evidence the Spaniards were still working that area as late as 1690.'

'Must not have found much gold, or else word would have spread. You can't keep gold a secret.'

'Hard to say. They must have found something to keep coming back over a century and a half. There was a lot of gold coming out of the New World, and not much of it ever reached Spain in the hands of those who discovered it. Plenty of reason to keep the discovery secret. And, of course, later on this area produced more gold than any place in the country before the

Western gold rush. But all those veins gave out long before the Civil War.'

'So you think the Spaniards were the ones that dug the mines of the ancients,' Dell said.

'No doubt about it,' stated Kenlaw, bobbing his head fiercely.

'Maybe that's been settled for northern Georgia,' Brandon interceded, 'although I'd had the impression this was only conjecture. But so far as I know, no one's ever proved the *conquistadores* mined this far north. For that matter, I don't believe anyone's ever made a serious study of the lost mines of the ancients in the North Carolina and Tennessee hills.'

'Exactly why I'm here,' Kenlaw told him impatiently. 'I'm hoping to prove the tie-in for my book on the mines of the ancients. Only, so far I've yet to find proof of their existence in this area.'

'Well, you may be looking for a tie-in that doesn't exist,' Brandon returned. 'I've studied this some, and my feeling is that the mines go back far beyond the days of the *conquistadores*. The Cherokees have legends that indicate the mines of the ancients were here already when the Cherokees migrated down from the north in the thirteenth century.'

'This is the first I've heard about it, then,' Kenlaw scoffed. 'Who do you figure drove these mines into the hills, if it wasn't the *conquistadores*? Don't tell me the Indians did it. I hardly think they would have been that interested in gold.'

'Didn't say it was the Indians,' Brandon argued.

'Who was it then?'

'The Indians weren't the first people here. When the Cherokees migrated into the Tellico region not far from here, they encountered a race of white giants – fought them and drove the survivors off, so their legends say.'

'You going to claim the Vikings were here?' Kenlaw snorted.

'The Vikings, the Welsh, the Phoenicians, the Jews – there's good evidence that on several occasions men from the Old World reached North America long before Columbus set out. Doubtless there were any number of pre-Columbian contacts of which we have no record, only legends.'

'If you'll forgive me, I'll stick to facts that are on record.'

'Then what about the Melungeons over in Tennessee? They're not Indians, though they were here before the first pioneers, and even today anthropologists aren't certain of their ancestry.'

Brandon pressed on. 'There are small pockets of people all

across the country – not just in these mountains – whose ethnic origins defy pinning down. And there are legends of others – the Shonokins, for example . . .'

'Now you're dealing with pure myth!' Kenlaw shut him off. 'That's the difference between us, Brandon. I'm interested in collecting historical fact, and you're a student of myths and legends. Science and superstition shouldn't be confused.'

'Sometimes the borderline is indistinct,' Brandon countered.

'My job is to make it less so.'

'But you'll have to concede there's often a factual basis for legend,' Brandon argued doggedly. 'And the Cherokees have a number of legends about the caves in these mountains, and about the creatures who live within. They tell about giant serpents, like the Uktena and the Uksuhi, that lair inside caves and haunt lonely ridges and streams, or the intelligent panthers that have townhouses in secret caves. Then there's the Nunnehi, an immortal race of invisible spirits that live beneath the mounds and take shape to fight the enemies of the Cherokee – these were supposedly seen as late as the Civil War. Or better still, there's the legend of the Yunwi Tsunsdi, the Little People who live deep inside the mountains.'

'I'm still looking for that *factual basis*,' Kenlaw said with sarcasm.

'Sometimes it's there to find. Ever read John Ashton's *Curious Creatures in Zoology*? In his chapter on pygmies he quotes from three sources that describe the discovery of entire burying grounds of diminutive stone sarcophagi containing human skeletons under two feet in length – adult skeletons, by their teeth. Several such burial grounds – ranging upwards to an acre and a half – were found in White County, Tennessee, in 1828, as well as an ancient townsite near one of the burials. General Milroy found similar graves in Smith County, Tennessee, in 1866, after a small creek had washed through the site and exposed them. Also, Weller in his *Romance of Natural History* makes reference to other such discoveries in Kentucky as well as Tennessee. Presumably a race of pygmies may have lived in this region before the Cherokees, who remember them only in legend as the Yunwi Tsunsdi. Odd, isn't it, that there are so many Indian legends of a pygmy race?'

'Spare me from Victorian amateur archaeology!' Kenlaw dismissed him impatiently. 'What possible bearing have these half-baked superstitions on the mines of the ancients? I'm talking about archaeological realities, like the pits in Mitchell

County, like the Sink Hole mine near Bakersville. That's a pit forty feet wide and forty feet deep, where the stone shows marks of metal tools and where stone tools were actually uncovered. General Thomas Clingman studied it right after the Civil War, and he counted three hundred rings on the trees he found growing on the mine workings. That clearly puts the mine back into the days of the *conquistadores.* There's record of one Tristan de Luna, who was searching for gold and silver south of there in 1560; the Sink Hole mine contained mica, and quite possibly he was responsible for digging it and the other mines of that area.'

'I've read about the Sink Hole mine in Creecy's *Grandfather's Tales,*' Brandon told him. 'And as I recall the early investigators there were puzzled by the series of passageways that connected the Sink Hole with other nearby pits – passageways that were only fourteen inches wide.'

The archaeologist sputtered in his drink. 'Well, Jesus Christ, man!' he exploded after a moment. 'That doesn't have anying to do with Indian legends! Don't you know anything about mining? They would have driven those connecting tunnels to try to cut across any veins of gold that might have lain between the pits.'

Brandon spread his big hands about fourteen inches apart. He said: 'Whoever dug the passageways would have had to have been rather small.'

III

Afternoon shadows were long when Dell drove the other two men down to the house in his pick-up. The farmhouse was a two-storey board structure with stone foundation, quite old but in neat repair. Its wide planks showed the up-and-down saw marks that indicated its construction predated the more modern circular sawmill blade. The front was partially faced with dark mountain stone, and the foundation wall extended to make a flagstone veranda, shaded and garlanded by bright-petalled clematis.

Another truck was parked beside Kenlaw's Plymouth – a battered green 1947 Ford pick-up that Brandon recognized as belonging to Dell's father-in-law, Olin Reynolds. Its owner greeted them from the porch as they walked up. He was a thin, faded man whose bony frame was almost lost in old-fashioned overalls. His face was deeply lined, his hair almost as white as

Brandon's. Once he had made the best moonshine whisky in the region, but his last stay in Atlanta had broken him. Now he lived alone on his old homestead bordering the Pisgah National Forest. He often turned up about dinner time, as did Brandon.

'Hello, Eric,' Olin called in his reedy voice. 'You been over to get that chuck that's been after my little girl's cabbages yet?'

'Hi, Olin,' Brandon grinned. 'Shot him yesterday morning from over across by that big white pine on the ridge.'

'That's near a quarter-mile,' the old man figured.

Brandon didn't say anything because Ginger Warner just then stepped out on to the porch. Dell's younger sister was recently back from finishing her junior year at Western Carolina in nearby Cullowhee. She was tall and willowy, green-eyed and quick to smile. Her copper hair was cut in a boyish shag instead of the unlovely *bouffant* most country women still clung to. Right now she had smudges of flour on her freckled face.

'Hi, Eric,' she grinned, brushing her hands on her jeans. 'Supper'll be along soon as the biscuits go in. You sure been keeping to yourself lately.'

'Putting together some of my notes for the thesis,' he apologized, thinking he'd eaten dinner here just three nights ago.

'Liar. You've been out running ridges with Dan.'

'That's relaxation after working late at night.'

Ginger gave him a sceptical look and returned to her biscuits.

With a ponderous grunt, Dr Kenlaw sank on to one of the wide-armed porch rockers. He swung his feet up on to the rail and gazed thoughtfully out across the valley. Mist was obscuring the hills beyond now, and the fields and pasture closer at hand filled with hazy shadow. Hidden by trees, the Pigeon River rushed its winding course midway through the small valley. Kenlaw did not seem at ease with what he saw. He glowered truculently at the potted flowers that lined the porch.

'What the hell!' Kenlaw suddenly lurched from his rocker. The other three men broke off their conversation and stared. Balancing on the rail, the archaeologist yanked down a hanging planter and dumped its contents into the yard.

'Where the hell did this come from!' he demanded, examining the rusted metal dish that an instant before had supported a trailing begonia.

Dell Warner bit off an angry retort.

'For God's sake, Kenlaw!' Brandon broke the stunned reaction.

'Yeah, for God's sake!' Kenlaw was too excited to be nonplussed. 'This is a Spanish *morion*! What's it doing hanging here full of petunias?'

Ginger stepped on to the porch to announce dinner. Her freckled face showed dismay. 'What on earth . . . ?'

Kenlaw was abashed. 'Sorry. I forgot myself when I saw this, Please excuse me – I'll replace your plant if it's ruined. But, where did you get this?'

'That old bowl? It's lain around the barn for years. I punched holes along the rim, and it made a great planter for my begonia.' She glanced over the rail and groaned.

'It's a *morion* – a *conquistador*'s helmet!' Kenlaw blurted in disbelief. Painstakingly he studied the high-crested bowl of rusted iron with its flared edges that peaked at either end. 'And genuine, too – or I'm no judge. Show me where this came from originally, and I'll buy you a pick-up full of begonias.'

Ginger wrinkled her forehead. 'I really don't know where it came from – I didn't even know it was anything. What's a Spanish helmet doing stuck back with all Dad's junk in our barn? There's an old iron pot with a hole busted in it where I found this. Want to look at it and tell me if it's Montezuma's bulletproof bathtub?'

Kenlaw snorted. 'Here, Brandon. You look at this and tell me I'm crazy.'

The albino examined the helmet. It was badly pitted, but solid. It could not have lain outside, or it would have rusted entirely away centuries ago. 'It's a *morion*, of course,' he agreed. 'Whether it dates to *conquistador* days or not, I'm not the one to tell. But it does seem equally unlikely that a careful reproduction would be lying around your barn.'

'Hell, I know where that come from,' Olin cut in, craning his long neck to see. 'I was with your-all's daddy time he found it.'

Kenlaw stared at the old mountainman – his eyes intent behind thick glasses. 'For God's sake – where?'

Olin worked his pointed chin in a thoughtful circle, eyeing Dell questioningly. The younger man shrugged.
Tanasee Bald in what's now Pisgah National Forest. There's a
'Place up on Old Field Mountain,' Olin told him, 'near sort of cave there, and I guess it won't do no harm now telling

you a couple of old boys named Brennan used to make a little blockade from a still they'd built back inside. Me and Bard used to stop up there times and maybe carry wood and just set around. Well, one time Bard goes back inside a ways, and we worried some because he'd had a little – and after a while he comes back carrying that thing there and calling it an Indian pot cause he found it with a lot of bones way back in there. He liked to keep arrowheads and axeheads and such like when he found them, and so he carried that there back and put it with some other stuff, and I guess it's all just laid there and been scattered around the barn since.'

'You can find the place still?' Kenlaw pounced. 'Can you take me there tomorrow? Who else knows about this?'

'Why, don't guess there's nobody knows. The Brennans is all out of these parts now and gone – never did amount to much. Hardin Brennan got hisself shot one night arguing with a customer, and they said his brother Earl busted his head in a rock fall back there in the cave. Earl's wife had left him, and there was just his boy Buck and a daughter Laurie. She was half wild and not right in the head; young as she was, she had a baby boy they said must've been by her own kin, on account everybody else was half afraid of her. They all went up north somewheres – I heard to live with their mother. There's other Brennans still around that might be distant kin, but far as I know nobody's gone around that cave on Old Field Mountain since Buck and his sister left there better than twenty years back.'

Kenlaw swore in excitement. 'Nobody knows about it, then? Fantastic! What time tomorrow do you want to go? Better make it early. Seven?'

'Say about six instead,' Olin suggested. 'You'll need the whole day. How about coming up to the cabin – if that's all right with you, Eric? Shouldn't go back in there by yourself, and Lord knows my old bones are too brittle for scrambling around such places.'

'Sure, I'll go along,' Brandon agreed. 'Sounds interesting.'

'No need to,' Kenlaw told him. 'I've done my share of spelunking.'

'Then you know it's dangerous to go in alone. Besides, I'm intrigued by all this.'

'You all coming in to eat?' Faye Warner pushed open the screen. 'Ginger, I thought you'd gone to call them. Everything's ready.'

296

IV

There was chicken and ham, cornbread and gravy, tomatoes and branch lettuce, bowls of field peas, snap beans, corn and other garden vegetables. Kenlaw's scowl subsided as he loaded his plate a second time. Shortly after dinner the archaeologist excused himself. 'Been a long day, and we'll be up early enough tomorrow.'

Olin drove away not long after, and when Dell went off to see to some chores, Brandon had the porch to himself. He was half asleep when Ginger came out to join him.

'Did I startle you?' she apologized, sliding on to the porch swing beside him. 'You're jumpy as a cat. Is that what living in the city does to your nerves?'

'Keeps you alert, I guess,' Brandon said sheepishly.

Coppery hair tickled his shoulder. 'Then you ought to get out of New York after you finish your project or whatever it is. Sounds like you must spend most of your time travelling around from one place to another as it is.'

'That's known as field research.'

'Ha! Dell says you don't do anything but laze around the cabin, or go out hunting. No wonder you still don't have your doctorate. Must be nice to get a government grant to run around the country studying folklore.'

'Well, part of the time I'm organizing my notes, and part of the time I'm relaxing from the tension of writing.'

'I can see how lugging that cannon of a rifle around would be exercise. Why don't you use that little air pistol instead?'

'What air pistol?'

'You know. You use it sometimes, because once I saw you shoot a crow with it that was making a fuss in the apple tree in front of the cabin. I saw you point it, and there wasn't a sound except the crow gave a squawk, and then feathers everywhere. My cousin has an air pistol too, so I knew what happened.'

'Little spy.' His arm squeezed her shoulder with mock roughness.

'Wasn't spying,' Ginger protested, digging her chin into his shoulder. 'I was walking up to help Dell chop tobacco.'

When Brandon remained silent, she spoke to break the rhythmic rasp of the porch swing. 'What do you think of Dr Kenlaw?'

'A bit too pigheaded and pushy. They raise them that way up north.'

'That's one, coming from a New Yorker! Or are you from New York originally? You have less accent than Dr Kenlaw.'

'Hard to say. I grew up in a foster home; I've lived a lot of places since.'

'Well, folks around here like you well enough. They don't much like Dr Kenlaw.'

'I expect he's too aggressive. Some of these obsessive researchists are like that.'

Ginger lined her freckles in a frown. 'You're a researcher. Is Dr Kenlaw?'

Brandon went tense beneath her cheek. 'What do you mean?'

'I mean, have you ever heard of him? If you're both studying the same subjects pretty much . . . ?'

'I don't know his work, if that's what you mean.' Brandon's muscles remained steel tight. 'But then, he knows his subject well enough. Why?'

'He seems to be more interested in gold than in archaeology,' Ginger told him. 'At least, that's the way his questions strike most folks he talks to.'

Brandon laughed and seemed to relax again. 'Well, there's more acclaim in discovering a tomb filled with gold relics than in uncovering a burial of rotted bones and broken pot shards, regardless of the relative value to archaeological knowledge. That's why King Tutankhamen's tomb made headlines, while the discovery of a primitive man's jawbone gets squeezed in with the used car ads.'

'There was a curse on King Tut's tomb,' Ginger reminded him dourly.

'Even better, if you're fighting for a grant.'

'Grants!' Ginger sniffed. 'Do you really mean to get that degree, or do you just plan to make a career of living off grants?'

'There's worse ways to make a living,' Brandon assured her.

'Somehow I can't see you tied down to some university job. That's what you'll do when you get your doctorate, isn't it? Teach?'

'There's a lot of PhDs out there looking for jobs once the grants dry up,' Brandon shrugged. 'If there's an opening somewhere, I suppose so.'

'There might be an opening at Western Carolina,' Ginger hinted.

'There might.'

'And why not? You like it down here – or else you wouldn't

keep coming back. And people like you. You seem to fit right in – not like most of these loud New York types.'

'It does feel like coming home again when I get back here,' Brandon acknowledged. 'Guess I've never stayed in one place long enough to call it home. Would you like for me to set up shop in Cullowhee?'

'I just might.'

Brandon decided she had waited long enough for her kiss, and did something about it. Shadows crept together to form a misty darkness, and the cool mountain breeze carried the breath of entwined clematis and freshly turned earth. The creak of the porch swing measured time like an arthritic grandfather's clock, softened by the rustle of the river. A few cows still lowed, and somewhere a Chuck Will's Widow called to its mate. The quiet was dense enough so that they could hear Dan gnawing a bone in the yard below.

Ginger finally straightened, stretched cosily from her cramped position. 'Mmmm,' she purred; then: 'Lord, what is that dog chewing on so! We didn't have more than a plate of scraps for him after dinner.'

'Maybe Dan caught himself a rabbit. He's always hunting.'

'Oh! Go see! He killed a mother rabbit last week, and I know her babies all starved.'

'Dan probably saw that they didn't.' Brandon rose to go look. 'What you got there, boy?'

Ginger saw him stiffen abruptly. 'Oh, no! Not another mamma bunny!'

She darted past Brandon's arm before he could stop her.

Dan thumped his tail foolishly and returned her stare. Between his paws was a child's arm.

V

Olin Reynolds shifted his chaw reflectively. 'I don't wonder Ginger came to carry on such a fit,' he allowed. 'What did you figure it was?'

'Certainly not a child's arm,' Brandon said. 'Soon as you got it into good light you could see it was nothing human. It had to have been some type of monkey, and the resemblance gave me a cold chill at first glance, too. Pink skin with just a frost of dirty white fur, and just like a little kid's arm except it was all muscle and sinew instead of baby fat. And it was a sure enough hand, not a paw, though the fingers were too long and

299

sinewy for any child's hand, and the nails were coarse and pointed like an animal's claws.'

'Wonder where old Dan come to catch him a monkey,' Olin put in.

'Somebody's pet. Tourists maybe – they carry everything they own in those damn campers. Thing got away; or more likely, died and they buried it, and Dan sniffed it out and dug it up. He'd been digging, from the look of him.'

'What did you finally do with it?'

'Dell weighted it down in an old gunny sack and threw it into a deep hole in the river there. Didn't want Dan dragging it back again to give the ladies another bad start.'

'Just as well,' Olin judged. 'It might have had somebody coming for to see what come of it. I suspect that'll be Dr Kenlaw coming up the hill now.'

Kenlaw's Plymouth struggled into view through the pines. Brandon glanced at his watch, noted it was past seven. He stretched himself out of Olin's ladderback chair and descended the porch steps to greet the archaeologist.

'Had a devil of a time finding the turn-off,' Kenlaw complained, squeezing out from behind the wheel. 'Everything set?'

'Throw your stuff in my pick-up, and we'll get going,' Olin told him. 'Where we're headed, ain't no kind of road any car can follow up.'

'Will that old bucket make it up a hill?' Kenlaw laughed, opening his trunk to take out a coil of rope and two powerful flashlights.

'This here old Ford's got a Marmon-Herrington all-wheel-drive conversion,' Olin said coldly. 'She can ride up the side of a bluff and pull out a cedar stump while your feet are hanging straight out the back window of the cab.'

Kenlaw laughed easily, shoving spare batteries and a geologist's pick into the ample pockets of the old paratrooper's jacket he wore. Brandon help him stow his gear into the back of the truck, then climbed into the cab beside Reynolds.

It was a tight squeeze in the cab after Dr Kenlaw clambered in, and once they reached the blacktop road the whine of the gears and fan made conversation like shouting above a gale. Olin drove along in moody silence, answering Kenlaw's occasional questions in few words. After a while they left the paved roads, and then it was a long kidney-bruising ride as the dual-sprung truck attacked rutted mountain paths that bore ever upwards through the shouldering pines. Kenlaw cursed and braced himself with both arms. Brandon caught a grin in Olin's faded eyes.

The road they followed led on past a tumbledown frame house, lost within a yard that had gone over to first growth pine and scrub. A few gnarled apple trees made a last stand, and farther beneath the encroaching forest, Brandon saw the hulking walls of a log barn – trees spearing upwards past where the roof had once spread. He shivered. The desolation of the place seemed to stir buried memories.

Beyond the abandoned farmhouse the road deteriorated into little more than a cowpath. It had never been more than a timber road, scraped out when the lumber barons dragged down the primeval forest from the heights half a century or more ago. Farm vehicles had kept it open once, and now an occasional hunter's truck broke down the young trees that would otherwise have choked it.

Olin's pick-up strained resolutely upwards, until at length they shuddered into an overgrown clearing. Reynolds cut the engine. 'Watch for snakes,' he warned, stepping down.

The clearing was littered beneath witch's broom and scrub with a scatter of rusted metal and indistinct trash. A framework of rotted lumber and a corroded padlock faced against the hillside. Several of the planks had fallen inwards upon the blackness within.

Olin Reynolds nodded. 'That's the place. Reckon the Brennans boarded it over before they moved on to keep stock from falling in. Opening used to just lie hidden beneath the brush.'

Dr Kenlaw prodded the eroded timbers. The padlock hasp hung rusted nails over the space where the board had rotted away. At a bolder shove, the entire framework tore loose and tumbled inwards.

Sunlight spilled in past the dust. The opening was squeezed between ledges of rock above and below, wide enough for a man to stoop and drop through. Beyond was a level floor, littered now with the debris of boards.

'Goes back like that a ways, then it narrows down to just a crack,' Olin told them.

Kenlaw grunted in a self-satisfied tone and headed back for the pick-up to get his equipment.

'Coming with us?' Brandon asked.

Olin shook his head firmly. 'I'll just wait here. These old bones are too eat up with arthuritis to go a-crawling through that snaky hole.'

'Wait with him, Eric, if you like,' Kenlaw suggested. 'I probably won't be long about this. No point you getting yourself all dirty messing around on what's likely to be just another wild goose chase.'

'I don't mind,' Brandon countered. 'If that *morion* came out of this cave, I'm curious to see what else lies hidden back there.'

'Odds are, one of those Brennans found it someplace else and just chucked it back in there. Looks like this place has been used as a dump.'

Kenlaw cautiously shined his light across the rubble beneath the ledge. Satisfied that no snakes were evident, the archaeologist gingerly squeezed his corpulent bulk past the opening and lowered himself to the floor of the cavern. Brandon dropped nimbly beside him.

Stale gloom filled a good-sized antechamber. Daylight trickled in from the opening, and a patch of blackness at the far end marked where the cavern narrowed and plunged deeper into the side of the mountain. Brandon took off his mirror sunglasses and glanced about the chamber – the albino's eyes were suited to the dank gloom.

The wreckage of what had once been a moonshine still cluttered the interior of the cavern. Copper coil and boiler had long ago been carried off, as had anything else of any value. Broken barrels, rotted mounds of sacks, jumbles of firewood, misshapen sculptures of galvanized metal. Broken bits of Mason jars and crockery shards crunched underfoot; dead ashes made a sodden raisin pudding. Kenlaw flung his light overhead and disclosed only sooty rock and somnolent bats.

'A goddamn dump,' he muttered petulantly. 'Maybe something farther back in.'

The archaeologist swung his light towards the rear of the chamber. A passage led farther into the mountain. Loose stones and more piled debris half blocked the opening. Pushing his way past this barricade, Kenlaw entered the narrow tunnel.

The passage was cramped. They ducked their heads, twisted about to avoid contact with the dank rock. Kenlaw carefully examined the walls of the cavern as they shuffled on. To Brandon's eye, there was nothing to indicate that man's tools had shaped the shaft. After a time, the sunlight from behind them disappeared, leaving them with their flashlights to guide them. The air grew stale with a sourness of animal decay, and as the passage seemed to lead downwards, Brandon wondered whether they might risk entering a layer of noxious gases.

'Hold on here!' Kenlaw warned, stopped abruptly.

Darkness met their probing flashlight beams several yards ahead of their feet, as the floor of the passage disappeared. Kenlaw wiped his pudgy face and caught his breath, as they shined their lights down into the sudden pit that confronted them.

'Must be thirty–forty feet to the bottom,' Kenlaw estimated. 'Cavern's big enough for a highschool gym. The ledge we're standing on creeps on down that fault line towards the bottom. We can make it if you'll just watch your step.'

'Is the air OK?' Brandon wondered.

'Smells fresh enough to me,' Kenlaw said. He dug a crumpled cigarette pack from his pocket, applied his lighter. The flame fanned outwards along the direction they had come. It fell softly through the blackness, showering sparks as it hit the floor.

'Still burning,' the archaeologist observed. 'I'm going on down.'

'Nice if that was natural gas down there,' Brandon muttered.

'This isn't a coal mine. Just another natural cavern, for my money.'

Clinging to the side of the rock for support, they cautiously felt their way down the steep incline. Although an agile climber could negotiate the descent without ropes, the footing was treacherous, and a missed step could easily mean a headlong plunge into the darkness.

They were halfway down, when Kenlaw paused to examine the rock wall. Switching hands with his flashlight, he drew his geologist's pick and tapped against the stone.

'Find something?' Brandon turned his light on to the object of the archaeologist's scrutiny, saw a band of lighter stone running along the ledge.

'Just a sample of stratum,' Kenlaw explained, hastily breaking free a specimen and shoving it into one of his voluminous pockets. 'I'll have to examine it back at my lab – study it for evidence of tool marks and so on.'

The floor of the pit appeared little different from the chamber through which they had entered the cavern, save that it lacked the accumulated litter of human usage. The air was cool and fresh enough to breathe, although each lungful carried the presence of a sunless place deep beneath the mountains.

'Wonder when the last time was anyone came down here?'

Brandon said, casting his light along the uneven floor. The bottom was strewn with broken rock and detritus, with a spongy paste of bat *guano* and dust. Footprints would be hard to trace after any length of time.

'Hard to say,' Kenlaw answered, scooping up a handful of gravel and examining it under his light. 'Sometimes the Confederates worked back into places like this after saltpetre. Maybe Bard Warner came down here, but I'm betting that *morion* was just something some dumb hillbilly found someplace else and got tossed on to the dump.'

'Are these bones human?' Brandon asked.

Kenlaw stuffed the gravel into a jacket pocket and scrambled over to where Brandon crouched. There was a fall of broken rock against the wall of the pit opposite their point of descent. Interspersed with the chunks of stone were fragments of mouldering bone. The archaeologist dug out a section of rib. It snapped easily in his hand, showing whiteness as it crumbled.

'Dead a long time,' Kenlaw muttered, pulling more of the rocks aside. 'Maybe Indian.'

'Then it's a human skeleton?'

'Stone burial cairn, at a guess. But it's been dug up and the bones scattered about. These long bones are all smashed apart.'

'Maybe he was killed in a rockslide.'

Kenlaw shook his head. 'Look how this femur is split apart. I'd say more likely something broke open the bones to eat the marrow.'

'An animal?'

'What else would it have been?'

Kenlaw suddenly bent forward, clawed at the detritus. His thick fingers locked on to what looked to be the edge of a flat rock. Grunting, he hauled back and wrenched forth a battered sheet of rusted iron.

'Part of a breastplate! Damned if this isn't the original skeleton in armour! Give me a hand with the rest of these rocks.'

Together they dragged away the cairn of rubble – Kenlaw puffing energetically as he flung aside the stones and fragments of bone. Brandon, caught up in the excitement of discovery himself, reflected with a twinge that this was hardly a careful piece of excavation. Nonetheless, Kenlaw's anxious scrabbling continued until they had cleared a patch of bare rock.

The archaeologist squatted on a stone and lit a cigarette. 'Doesn't tell me much,' he complained. 'Just broken bones and chunks of rust. Why was he here? Were there others with him?

Who were they? What were they seeking here?'

'Isn't it enough that you've found the burial of a *conquistador*?'

'Can't prove that until I've run some tests,' Kenlaw grumbled. 'Could have been a colonial – breastplates were still in use in European armies until this century. Or an Indian buried with some tribal heirlooms.'

'There's another passage back of here,' Brandon called out.

He had been shining his light along the fall of rock, searching for further relics from the cairn. Behind where they had cleared away some of the loose rocks, a passageway pierced the wall of the pit. Brandon rolled aside more of the stone, and the mouth of the passage took shape behind the crest of the rock pile.

Kenlaw knelt and peered within. 'Not much more than a crawl space,' he announced, 'but it runs straight on for maybe twenty or thirty feet, then appears to open on to another chamber.'

Brandon played his flashlight around the sides of the pit, then back to where they stood. 'I don't think this is just a rock slide. I think someone piled all these rocks here to wall up the tunnel mouth.'

'If they didn't want it found, then they must have found something worth hiding,' the archaeologist concluded. 'I'll take a look. You wait here in case I get stuck.'

Brandon started to point out that his was the slimmer frame, but already Kenlaw had plunged headfirst into the tunnel – his thick buttocks blocking Brandon's view as he squeezed his way through. Brandon thought of a fat old badger ducking down a burrow. He kept his light on the shaft. Wheezing and scuffling, the other man managed to force his bulk through the passage. He paused at the far end and called back something, but his words were too muffled for Brandon to catch.

A moment later Kenlaw's legs disappeared from view, and then his flushed face bobbed into Brandon's light. 'I'm in another chamber about like the one you're standing in,' he called back. 'I'll take a look around.'

Brandon sat down to wait impatiently. He glanced at his watch. To his surprise, they had been in the cavern some hours. The beam of his flashlight was yellowing; Brandon cut the switch to save the batteries, although he carried spares in his pockets. The blackness was as total as the inside of a grave, except for an occasional wan flash as Kenlaw shined his light past the tunnel mouth from the pit beyond. Brandon held his hand before his face, noted that he could dimly make out its outline. The albino had always known he could see better in the dark than others could, and it had seemed a sort of recompense for the fact that bright light tormented his pink eyes. He had read that hemeralopia did not necessarily coincide with increased night vision, and his use of infrared rifle scopes had caused him to wonder whether his eyes might not be unusually receptive to light from the infrared end of the spectrum.

Kenlaw seemed to be taking his time. At first Brandon had heard the sharp tapping of his geologist's pick from time to time. Now there was only silence. Brandon flipped his light back on, consulted his watch. It had been half an hour.

'Dr Kenlaw?' he called. He thrust his shoulders into the passage and called again, louder. There was no reply.

Less anxious than impatient, Brandon crawled into the tunnel and began to wriggle forward, pushing his light ahead of him. Brandon was stocky, and it was a tight enough squeeze. The crawl space couldn't be much more than two feet square at its widest point. Brandon reflected that it was fortunate that he was not one of those bothered by claustrophobia.

Halfway through the tunnel, Brandon suddenly halted to study its walls. No natural passage; those were tool marks upon the stone – not even Kenlaw could doubt now. The regularity of the passage had already made Brandon suspicious. Cramped as it was, it reminded him of a mine shaft, and he thought again about the mention in Creecy's *Grandfather's Tales* of the interconnecting tunnels found at the Sink Hole pits.

The tunnel opened into another chamber much like the one he had just quitted. It was a short drop to the floor, and Brandon lowered himself headfirst from the shaft. There was no sign of Kenlaw's light. He stood for a moment uneasily, swinging his flash about the cavern. Perhaps the archaeologist had fallen into a hidden pit, smashed his light.

'Dr Kenlaw?' Brandon called again. Only echoes answered.

No. There was another sound. Carried through the rock in the subterranean stillness. A sharp tapping. Kenlaw's geologist's pick.

Brandon killed his flash. A moment passed while his eyes adjusted to the blackness, then he discerned a faint haze of light – visible only because of the total darkness. Switching his own light back on, Brandon directed it towards the glimmer.

It came from the mouth of yet another passageway cut against the wall opposite.

He swung his light about the pit. Knowing what to look for now, Brandon thought he could see other such passages, piercing the rock face at all levels. It came to him that they began to run a real risk of losing their way if they were able to progress much farther within these caverns. Best to get Kenlaw and keep together after this, he decided.

The new shaft was a close copy of the previous one – albeit somewhat more cramped. Brandon scraped skin against its confines as he crawled towards the sound of Kenlaw's pick.

The archaeologist was so engrossed in what he was doing that he hadn't noticed Brandon's presence, until the other wriggled out on to the floor of the pit and hailed him. Spotlighted by Brandon's flash, Kenlaw glowered truculently. The rock face where he was hammering threw back a crystalline reflection.

'I was worried something had happened,' Brandon said, approaching.

'Sorry. I called to you that I was going on, but you must not have heard.' Kenlaw swept up handfuls of rock samples and stuffed them into the already bulging pockets of his paratrooper's jacket. 'We'd best be getting back before we get lost. Reynolds will be wondering about us.'

'What *is* this place? Don't tell me all of this is due to natural formation!' Brandon swept his light around. More diminutive tunnels pierced the sides of this pit also. He considered the broken rock that littered the floor.

'This is a mine of some sort, isn't it. Congratulations, Dr Kenlaw – you really have found one of the lost mines of the ancients! Christ, you'll need a team of spelunkers to explore these pits if they keep going on deeper into the mountain!'

Kenlaw laughed gruffly. 'Lost mines to the romantic imagination, I suppose – but not to the trained mind. This is a common enough formation – underground streams have forced their way through faults in the rock, hollowed out big chambers wherever they've encountered softer stone. Come on, we've wasted enough time on this one.'

'Soft rock?' Brandon pushed past him. 'Hell, this is quartz!'

He stared at the quartz dike where Kenlaw had been working. Under the flashlight beam, golden highlights shimmered from the chipped matrix.

'Oh my God,' Brandon managed to whisper.

These were good words for a final prayer, although Kenlaw probably had no such consideration in mind. The rush of motion from the darkness triggered some instinctive reflex. Brandon started to whirl about, and the pick of the geologist's hammer only tore a furrow across his scalp instead of plunging into his skull.

The glancing blow was enough. Brandon went down as if pole-axed. Crouching over him, Kenlaw raised the hammer for the *coup de grâce*.

When Brandon made no move, the murderous light in the other man's eyes subsided to cunning. Brandon was still breathing, although bare bone gleamed beneath the blood-matted hair. Kenlaw balanced the geologist's pick pensively.

'Got to make this look like an accident,' he muttered. 'Can't risk an investigation. Tell them you took a bad fall. Damn you, Brandon! You would have to butt in the one time I finally found what I was after! This goddamn mountain is made out of gold, and that's going to be my secret until I can lock up the mining rights.'

He hefted a rock — improvising quickly, for all that his attack had been born of the moment. 'Just as well the pick only grazed you. Going to have to look like you busted your head on the rocks. Can't have it happen in here though — this has to be kept hidden. Out there on the ledge where we first climbed down — that's where you fell. I'll block the tunnel entrance back up again. All they'll know is that we found some old bones in a cave, and you fell to your death climbing back up.'

He raised the rock over Brandon's head, then threw it aside. 'Hell, you may never wake up from that one there. Got to make this look natural as possible. If they don't suspect now, they might later on. Push you off the top of the ledge headfirst, and it'll just be a natural accident.'

Working quickly, Kenlaw tied a length of rope to Brandon's ankles. The man was breathing hoarsely, his pulse erratic. He had a concussion, maybe worse. Kenlaw debated again whether to kill him now, but considered it unlikely that he would regain consciousness before they reached the ledge. An astute coroner might know the difference between injuries suffered through a fatal fall and trauma inflicted upon a lifeless body — they always did on television.

Brandon was heavy, but Kenlaw was no weakling for all his

fat. Taking hold of the rope, he dragged the unconscious body across the cavern floor – any minor scrapes would be attributed to the fall. At the mouth of the tunnel he paused to pay out his coil of rope. Once on the other side, he could haul in Brandon's limp form like a fish on a line. It would only take minutes to finish the job.

The tunnel seemed far more cramped as he wriggled into it. The miners must have had small frames, but then people were smaller four centuries ago. Moreover, the Spaniards, who almost certainly would have used slave labour to drive these shafts, weren't men to let their slaves grow fat.

It *was* tighter, Kenlaw realized with growing alarm. For a moment he attempted to pass it off to claustrophobia, but as he reached a narrower section of the tunnel, the crushing pressure on his stout sides could not be denied. Panic whispered through his brain, and then suddenly he understood. He had crammed his baggy jacket pockets with rock samples and chunks of ore from the quartz dike; he was a good twenty pounds heavier and inches bulkier now than when he had crawled through before.

He could back out, but to do so would lose time. Brandon might revive; Reynolds might come looking for them. Gritting his teeth against the pressure on his ribs, Kenlaw pushed his light on ahead and forced his body onwards. This was the tightest point, and beyond that the way would be easier. He sucked in his breath and writhed forward another foot or more. His sides ached, but he managed yet another foot with all his strength.

No farther. He was stuck.

His chest aching, Kenlaw found scant breath to curse. No need to panic. Just back out and take off the jacket, push it in ahead of him and try again. He struggled to work his corpulent body backwards from the tunnel. The loose folds of his paratrooper's jacket rolled up as he wriggled backwards, bunching against the bulging pockets. Jammed even tighter against his flesh and against the rock walls, the laden coat bunched up into a wedge. Kenlaw pushed harder, setting his teeth against the pain, as rock samples gouged into his body.

He couldn't move an inch farther. Backwards or forwards.

He was stuck midway in the tunnel.

Still Kenlaw fought down his panic. It was going to cost him some bruises and some torn skin, no doubt, but he'd work his way free in good time. He must above all else remain calm, be patient. A fraction of an inch forwards, a fraction of an inch backwards. He would take his time, work his way loose bit by bit, tear free of the jacket or smooth out its bunched-up folds. At worst, Reynolds would find him, bring help. Brandon might be dead by then, or have no memory of the blow that felled him; he could claim he was only trying to drag his injured companion to safety.

Kenlaw noticed that the light from his flash was growing dim. He had meant to replace the batteries earlier; now the spares were part of the impedimenta that pinioned him here. No matter; he didn't need light for this – only to be *lighter*. Kenlaw laughed shakily at his own joke, then the chuckle died.

The flashlight was fast dwindling, but its yellowing beam was enough to pick out the pink reflections of the many pairs of eyes that watched him from the mouth of the tunnel –barely glimpsed shapes that grew bolder as the light they feared grew dim.

And then Kenlaw panicked.

VI

The throbbing ache in his skull was so intense that it was some time before Brandon became aware that he was conscious. By gradual increments, as one awakens from a deep dream, he came to realize that something was wrong, that there was a reason for the pain and clouded state of awareness. An elusive memory whispered of a treacherous attack, a blow from behind . . .

Brandon groaned as he forced himself to sit up, goaded to action as memory returned. His legs refused to function, and after a moment of confusion, he realized that his ankles were tied together. He almost passed out again from the effort to lean forward and fumble with the knots, and more time dragged past as he clumsily worked to free his ankles.

His brain refused to function clearly. He knew that it was dark, that he could see only dimly, but he could not think where his flashlight might be, nor marvel that his albino eyes had so accommodated to give him preternatural vision in a lightless cavern. Remembering Kenlaw's attack, he began to wonder where the other man had gone; only disjointedly did he understand the reasons behind the archaeologist's actions and the probable consequences of his own plight.

The knots at last came loose. Brandon dully considered the rope – his thoughts groping with the fact that someone had tied it to his ankles. Tied him to what? Brandon pulled on the rope, drew coils of slack through the darkness, until there was tension from the other end. He tugged again. The rope was affixed to something beyond. With great effort, Brandon made it to his feet, staggered forward to lean against the rock face beneath which he had lain. The rope was tied to the wall. No, it entered the wall, into the tunnel. It was affixed to something within the narrow passage.

Brandon knelt forward and followed the rope into the crawl space. Dimly he remembered that this was the shaft by which he had entered – or so he hoped. He had hardly crawled forward for more than a body length, when his fingers clawed against boots. Brandon groped and encountered damp cloth and motionless legs – the rope pressing on beneath their weight.

'Kenlaw?' he called out in a voice he scarcely recognized. He shook the man's feet, but no response came. Bracing himself against the narrow passage, Brandon grasped the other man's ankles and hauled back. For a moment there was resistance, then the slack body slid backwards under his tugging. Backing out of the tunnel, Brandon dragged the archaeologist's motionless form behind him. The task was an easy one for him, despite that the pain in his skull left Brandon nauseated and weak.

Emerging from the shaft, he rested until the giddiness subsided. Kenlaw lay where he had released him, still not moving. Brandon could only see the man as a dim outline, but vague as that impression was, something seemed wrong about the silhouette. Brandon bent forward, ran his hands over the archaeologist's face, groping for a pulse.

His fingers encountered warm wetness across patches of slick hardness and sticky softness, before skidding into empty eye sockets. Most of the flesh of Kenlaw's face and upper body had been stripped from the bone.

Brandon slumped against the wall of the cavern, trying to comprehend. His brain struggled drunkenly to think, but the agony of his skull kept making his thoughts tumble apart again just as understanding seemed to be there. Kenlaw was dead. He, Brandon, was in a bad way. This much he could hold in his mind, and with that, the recognition that he had to get out of this place.

That meant crawling back through the narrow shaft where Kenlaw had met his death. Brandon's mind was too dazed to feel the full weight of horror. Once again he crawled into the tunnel and inched his way through the cramped darkness. The rock was damp, and now he knew with what wetness, but he forced himself to wriggle across it.

His hands encountered Kenlaw's flashlight. He snapped its switch without effect, then remembered the fresh batteries in his pockets. Crawling from the tunnel and on to the floor of the chamber beyond, he fumbled to open the flashlight, stuff in new batteries. He thumbed the switch, again without result. His fingers groped across the lens, gashed against broken glass. The bulb was smashed, the metal dented; tufts of hair and dried gore caked the battered end. Kenlaw had found service from the flashlight as a club, and it was good for little else now. Brandon threw it away from him with a curse.

The effort had taxed his strength, and Brandon passed from consciousness to unconsciousness and again to consciousness without really being aware of it. When he found himself capable of thought once again, he had to remember all over again how he had come to this state. He wondered how much time had passed, touched his watch, and found that the glare from the digital reading hurt his eyes.

Setting his teeth against the throbbing that jarred his skull, Brandon made it to his feet again, clutching at the wall of the pit for support. Olin, assuming he was getting anxious by now, might not find the passage that led from the first pit. To get help, Brandon would have to cross this cavern, crawl through the shaft back into the first pit, perhaps climb up along the ledge and into the passageway that led to the outer cavern. In his condition it wouldn't have been easy even if he had a light.

Brandon searched his pockets with no real hope. A non-smoker, he rarely carried matches, nor did he now. His eyes seemed to have accommodated as fully to the absence of light as their abnormal sensitivity would permit. It was sufficient to discern the shape of objects close at hand as shadowy forms distinct from the engulfing darkness – little enough, but preferable to total blindness. Brandon stood with his back to the shaft through which he had just crawled. The other tunnel had seemed to be approximately opposite, and if he walked in a straight line he ought to strike the rock face close enough to grope for the opening.

With cautious steps, Brandon began to cross the cavern. The floor was uneven, and loose stones were impossible for him to see. He tried to remember if his previous crossing had revealed any pitfalls within this chamber. A fall and a broken leg would leave him helpless here, and slowly through his confused brain was creeping the shrill warning that Kenlaw's death could hardly have been from natural causes. A bear? There were persistent rumours of mountain lions being sighted in these hills. Bobcats, which were not uncommon, could be dangerous under these circumstances. Brandon concentrated on walking in a straight line, much like a drunk trying to walk a highway line for a cop, and found that the effort demanded his entire attention.

The wall opposite loomed before him – Brandon was aware of its darker shape an instant before he blundered into it. He rested against its cool solidity for a moment, his knees rubbery, head swimming after the exertion. When he felt stronger once again, he began to inch his way along the rock face, fumbling for an opening in the wall of the pit.

There – a patch of darkness less intense opened out of the stone. He dared not even consider the possibility that this might not be the shaft that was hidden behind the cairn. Brandon fought back unconsciousness as it surged over him once more, forced his muscles to respond. Once through this passage, Olin would be able to find him. He stooped to crawl into the tunnel, and the rock was coated with a musty stickiness.

Brandon wriggled forward across the moist stone. The sensation was already too familiar, when his out-thrust fingers clawed against a man's boot. Kenlaw's boot. Kenlaw's body. In the shaft ahead of him.

Brandon was too stunned to feel terror. His tortured mind struggled to comprehend. Kenlaw's body lay in the farther chamber, beyond the other passage by which he had returned. And Brandon knew a dead man when he came upon one. Had he circled the cavern, gone back the way he had come? Or was he delirious, his injured brain tormented by a recurring nightmare?

He clutched the lifeless feet and started to haul them back, as he had done before, or thought he had done. The boots were abruptly dragged out of his grasp.

Brandon slumped forward on his face, pressing against the stone to hold back the waves of vertigo and growing fear. Kenlaw's body disappeared into the blackness of the tunnel. How serious was his head injury? Had he imagined that Kenlaw was dead? Or was it Kenlaw ahead of him now in this narrow passage?

Brandon smothered a cackling laugh. It must not be Kenlaw. Kenlaw was dead, after all. It was Olin Reynolds, or some-one else, come to search for him.

'Here I am!' Brandon managed to shout. 'In here!'

His lips tasted of blood, and Brandon remembered the wet-ness he had pressed his face against a moment gone. It was too late to call back his outcry.

New movement scurried in the tunnel, from either end. Then his night vision became no blessing, for enough consciousness remained for Brandon to know that the faces that peered at him from the shaft ahead were not human faces.

VII

Olin Reynolds was a patient man. Age and Atlanta had taught him that. When the sun was high, he opened a tin of Vienna sausages and a pack of Lance crackers, munched them slowly, then washed them down with a few swallows from a Mason jar of blockade. Sleepy after his lunch, he stretched out on the seat and dozed.

When he awoke, the sun was low, and his joints complained as he slid from the cab and stretched. Brandon and Kenlaw should have returned by now, he realized with growing unease. Being a patient man, he sat on the running board of his truck, smoked two cigarettes and had another pull from the jar of whisky. By then dusk was closing, and Reynolds decided it was time for him to do something.

There was a flashlight in the truck. Its batteries were none too fresh, but Reynolds dug it out and tramped towards the mouth of the cave. Stooping low, he called out several times, and, when there came no answer to his hail, he cautiously let himself down into the cavern.

The flashlight beam was weak, but enough to see that there was nothing here but the wreckage of the moonshine still that had been a going concern when he last set foot within the cavern. Reynolds didn't care to search farther with his uncer-tain light, but the chance that the others might have met with some accident and be unable to get back was too great for him to ignore. Still calling out their names, he nervously picked his way along the passage that led from the rear of the antecham-ber.

His batteries held out long enough for Reynolds to spot the sudden drop-off before he blundered across the edge and into space. Standing as close to the brink as he dared, Reynolds pointed his flashlight downwards into the pit. The yellow beam was sufficient to pick out a broken heap of a man on the rocks below the ledge. Reynolds had seen death often enough before, and he didn't expect an answer when he called out into the darkness of the pit.

As quickly as his failing light permitted, Reynolds retraced his steps out into the starry darkness of the clearing. Breathing a prayer that one of the men might have survived the fall, he sent his truck careening down the mountain road in search of help.

Remote as the area was, it was well into the night before rescue workers in four-wheel-drive vehicles were able to converge upon the clearing before the cavern. Men with lights and emergency equipment hurried into the cave and climbed down into the pit beyond. There they found the broken body of Dr Morris Kenlaw – strangely mutilated, as if set upon by rats after he fell to his death. They loaded his body on to a stretcher, and continued to search for his companion.

Eric Brandon they never found.

They searched the cavern and the passageway and the pit from corner to crevice. They found the wreckage of an old still and, within the pit, Kenlaw's body – and that was all. Later, when there were more lights, someone thought he saw evidence that a rock fall against the far wall of the pit might be a recent one; but after they had turned through this for a while, it was obvious that only bare rock lay underneath.

By morning, news of the mystery had spread. One man dead, one man vanished. Local reporters visited the scene, took photographs, interviewed people. Curiosity seekers joined the search. The day wore on, and still no sign of Brandon. By now the State Bureau of Investigation had sent men into the area in addition to the local sheriff's deputies – not that foul play was suspected so much, but a man had been killed and his companion had disappeared. And since it was evident that Brandon was not to be found inside the cavern, the mystery centred upon his disappearance – and why.

There were many conjectures. The men had been attacked by a bear, Brandon's body carried off. Brandon had been injured, had crawled out for help after Olin Reynolds had driven off; had subsequently collapsed, or become lost in the forest, or was out of his mind from a head injury. Some few suggested that Kenlaw's death had not been accidental, although no motive was put forward, and that Brandon had fled in panic while Reynolds was asleep. The mountainside was searched, and searched more thoroughly the next day. Dogs were brought in, but by now too many people had trampled over the site.

No trace of the missing man was discovered.

It became necessary that Brandon's family and associates be notified, and here the mystery continued. Brandon seemed to have no next of kin, but then, he had said once that he was an orphan. At his apartment in New York, he was almost unknown; the landlord could only note that he paid his rent promptly – and often by mail, since he evidently travelled a great deal. The university at which he had mentioned he was working on his doctorate (when asked once) had no student on record named Eric Brandon, and no one could remember if he had ever told them the name of the grant that was supporting his folklore research.

In their need to know *something* definite about the vanished man, investigators looked through the few possessions and personal effects in his cabin. They found no names or addresses with which Brandon might be connected – nothing beyond numerous reference works and copious notes that showed he had indeed been a serious student of regional folklore. There was his rifle, and a handgun – a Walther PPK in ·380 ACP – still nothing to excite comment (the Walther was of pre-war manufacture, its serial number without American listing), until someone forced the lock on his attaché case and discovered the Colt Woodsman. The fact that this ·22 calibre pistol incorporated a silencer interested the SBI and, after fingerprints had been sent through channels, was of even greater interest to the FBI.

'They were manufactured for the OSS,' the agent explained, indicating the Colt semi-automatic with its bulky silencer. 'A few of them are still in use, although the Hi-Standard HD is more common now. There's no way of knowing how this one ended up in Brandon's possession – it's illegal for a private citizen to own a silencer of any sort, of course. In the hands of a good marksman, it's a perfect assassination gun – about all the sound it makes is that of the action functioning, and a clip of ·22 hollow points placed right will finish about any job.'

'Eric wouldn't have killed anyone!' Ginger Warner protested angrily. The FBI agent reminded her of a too scrubbed bible salesman. She resented the high-handed way he and the others had appropriated Brandon's belongings.

'That's the thing about these sociopathic types; they seem perfectly normal human beings, but it's only a mask.' He went on: 'We'll run ballistics on this and see if it matches with anything on file. Probably not. This guy was good. Real good. What we have on him now is purely circumstantial, and if we turn him up, I'm not sure we can nail him on anything more serious than firearms violations. But putting together all the things we know and that won't stand up in court, your tenant is one of the top hitmen in the business.'

'Brandon – a hitman!' scoffed Dell Warner.

'Brandon's not his real name,' the agent went on, ticking off his information. 'He's set up other identities too, probably. We ran his prints; took some looking, but we finally identified him. His name was Ricky Brennan when he was turned over to a New York State foster home as a small child. Father unknown; mother one Laurie Brennan, deceased. Records say his mother was from around here originally, by the way – maybe that's why he came back. Got into a bit of trouble in his early teens; had a fight with some other boys in the home. One died from a broken neck as a result, but since the others had jumped Brennan, no charges were placed. But out of that, we did get his prints on record – thanks to an institutional blunder when they neglected to expunge his juvenile record. They moved him to another facility, where they could handle his type; shortly after that, Brennan ran away, and there the official record ends.'

'Then how can you say that Eric is a hired killer!' Ginger demanded. 'You haven't any proof! You've said so yourself.'

'No proof that'll stand up in court, I said,' the agent admitted. 'But we've known for some time of a high-priced hitman who likes to use a high-powered rifle. One like this.'

He hefted Brandon's rifle. 'This is a Winchester Model 70, chambered for the ·220 Swift. That's the fastest commercially loaded cartridge ever made. Factory load will move a forty-eight-grain bullet out at a velocity of over 4,100 feet per second on a trajectory flat as a stretched string. Our man has killed with headshots from distances that must have been near three hundred yards, in reconstructing some of his hits. The bullet virtually explodes on impact, so there's nothing left for ballistics to work on.

'But it's a rare gun for a hitman to use, and that's where Brandon begins to figure. It demands a top marksman, as well as a shooter who can handle this much gun. You see, the ·220 Swift has just too much power. It burned out the old nickel steel barrels when the cartridge was first introduced, and it's said that the bullet itself will disintegrate if it hits a patch of turbulent air. The ·220 Swift may have fantastic velocity, but it also has a tendency to self-destruct.'

'Eric used that as a varmint rifle,' Dell argued. 'It's a popular cartridge for varmint shooters, along with a lot of other small calibre high-velocity cartridges. And as for that silenced Colt, Eric isn't the first person I've heard of who owned a gun that's considered illegal.'

'As I said, we don't have a case – yet. Just pieces of a puzzle, but more pieces start to fall into place once you make a start. There's more than just what I've told you, you can be sure. And we'll find out a lot more once we find Brandon. At a guess, he killed Kenlaw – who may have found out something about him – then panicked and fled.'

'Sounds pretty clumsy for a professional killer,' Dell commented.

The agent frowned, then was all official politeness once more. These hillbillies were never known for their cooperation with federal agents. 'We'll find out what happened when we find Brandon.'

'If you find him.'

VIII

Brandon seemed to be swirling through pain-fogged delirium – an endless vertigo in which he clutched at fragments of dream as a man caught in a maelstrom is flung against flotsam of his broken ship. In rare moments his consciousness surfaced enough for him to wonder whether portions of the dreams might be reality.

Most often, Brandon dreamed of limitless caverns beneath the mountains, caverns through which he was borne along by partially glimpsed dwarfish figures. Sometimes Kenlaw was with him in this maze of tunnels – crawling after him, his face a flayed mask of horror, a bloody geologist's pick brandished in one fleshless fist.

At other times Brandon sensed his dreams were visions of the past, visions that could only be born of his obsessive study of the folklore of this region. He looked upon the mountains of a primeval age, when the boundless forest was untouched by the iron bite and poisoned breath of white civilization. Copper-hued savages hunted game along these ridges, to come upon a race of diminutive white-skinned folk who withdrew shyly into the shelter of hidden caverns. The Indians were in awe of these little people, whose origins were beyond the mysteries of their oldest legends, and so they created new legends to explain them.

With the successive migrations of Indians through these mountains, the little people remained in general at peace, for they were wise in certain arts beyond the comprehension of the red man – who deemed them spirit-folk – and their ways were those of secrecy and stealth.

Then came a new race of men: white skins made bronze by the sun, their faces bearded, their flesh encased in burnished steel. The *cònquistadores* enslaved the little folk of the hills as they had enslaved the races of the south, tortured them to learn the secrets of their caves beneath the mountains, forced them to mine the gold from pits driven deep into the earth. Then followed a dream of mad carnage, when the little people arose from their tunnels in unexpected force, to entrap their masters within the pits, and to drive those who escaped howling in fear from that which they had called forth from beneath the mountains.

Then came the white settlers in a wave that never receded, driving before them the red man, and finally the game. Remembering the *conquistadores*, the little people retreated farther into their hidden caverns, hating the white man with his guns and his settlements. Seldom now did they venture into the world above, and then only by night. Deep within the mountains, they found sustenance from the subterranean rivers and the beds of fungoid growths they nourished, feeding as well upon other cave creatures and such prey as they might seek above on starless nights. With each generation, the race slipped farther back into primordial savagery, forgetting the ancient knowledge that had once been theirs. Their stature became dwarfish and apelike, their faces brutish as the regression of their souls; their flesh and hair assumed the dead pallor of creatures that live in eternal darkness, even as their vision and hearing adapted to their subterranean existence.

They remembered their hatred of the new race of men. Again and again Brandon's dreams were red with visions of stealthy ambush and lurid slaughter of those who trespassed upon their hidden domain, of those who walked mountain trails upon nights when the stars were swallowed in cloud. He saw children snatched from their blankets, women set upon in lonely places. For the most part, these were nightmares from previous centuries, although there was a recurrent dream in which a vapid-faced girl gave herself over willingly to their obscene lusts, until the coming of men with flashlights and shotguns drove them from her cackling embrace.

These were dreams that Brandon through his comatose delirium could grasp and understand. There were other visions that defied his comprehension.

Fantastic cities reeled and shattered as the earth tore itself apart, thrusting new mountains towards the blazing heavens, opening vast chasms that swallowed rivers and spat them forth as shrieking steam. Oceans of flame melted continents into leaden seas, wherein charred fragments of a world spun frenziedly upon chaotic tides and whirlpools, riven by enormous bolts of raw energy that coursed like fiery cobwebs from the cyclopean orb that filled the sky.

Deep within the earth, fortress cities were shaken and smashed by the hell that reigned miles above. From out of the ruins, survivors crept to attempt to salvage some of the wonders of the age that had died and left them exiles in a strange world. Darkness and savagery stole from them their ideals, even as monstrous dwellers from even greater depths of the earth drove them from their buried cities and upward through caverns that opened on to an alien surface. In the silent halls of vanished greatness, nightmarish shapes crawled like maggots, while the knowledge of that godlike age was a fading memory to the degenerate descendants of those who had fled.

How long the dreams endured, Brandon could not know. It was the easing of the pain in his skull that eventually convinced Brandon that he had passed from dream into reality, although it was into reality no less strange than that of delirium.

They made a circle about where he lay – so many of them that Brandon could not guess their number. Their bodies were stunted, but lacking the disproportion of torso to limbs of human dwarves. The thin white fur upon their naked pink flesh combined to give them something of the appearance of lemurs. Brandon thought of elves and of feral children, but their faces were those of demons. Broad nostrils and out-thrust tusked jaws stopped just short of being muzzles, and within overlarge red-pupilled eyes glinted the malign intelligence of a fallen angel.

They seemed in awe of him.

Brandon slowly raised himself on one arm, giddy from the effort. He saw that he lay upon a pallet of dried moss and crudely cured furs, that his naked body seemed thin from long fever. He touched the wound on his scalp and encountered old scab and new scar. Beside him, water and what might be broth or emollients filled bowls which might have been formed by human hands, or perhaps not.

Brandon stared back at the vast circle of eyes. It occurred to him to wonder that he could see them; his first thought was that there must be a source of dim light from somewhere. It then came to him to wonder that these creatures had spared him; his first thought was that as an albino they had mistakenly accepted him as one of their race. In the latter, he was closer to the truth than with the former.

Then slowly, as his awakening consciousness assimilated all that he now knew, Brandon understood the truth. And, in understanding at last, Brandon knew who he was, and why he was.

IX

There was only a sickle of moon that night, but Ginger Warner, feeling restless, threw on a wrap and slipped out of the house.

On some nights sleep just would not come, although such nights came farther apart now. Walking seemed to help, although she had forgone these nocturnal strolls for a time, after once when she realized someone was following her. As it turned out, her unwelcome escort was a federal agent – they thought she would lead them to where her lover was hiding – and Ginger's subsequent anger was worse than her momentary fear. But in time even the FBI decided that the trail was a cold one, and the investigation into the disappearance of a suspected hired killer was pushed into the background.

It was turning autumn, and the thin breeze made her shiver beneath her dark wrap. Ginger wished for the company of Dan, but her brother had taken the Plott hound off on a weekend bear hunt. The wind made a lonely sound as it moved through the trees, chattering the dead leaves so that even the company of her own footsteps was denied her.

Only the familiarity of the tone let her stifle a scream, when someone called her name from the darkness ahead.

Ginger squinted into the darkness, wishing now she'd brought a light. She whispered uncertainly: 'Eric?'

And then he stepped out from the shadow of the rock outcropping that overhung the path along the ridge, and Ginger was in his arms.

She spared only a moment for a kiss, before warning him in one breathless outburst: 'Eric, you've got to be careful! The police – the FBI – they've been looking for you all summer! They think you're some sort of criminal!'

In her next breath, she found time to look at him more closely. 'Eric, where have you been? What's happened to you?'

Only the warm pressure of his arms proved to her that Brandon was not a phantom of dream. The wind whipped through his long white hair and beard, and there was just enough moonlight for her to make out the streak of scar that creased his scalp. He was shirtless; his only attire a ragged pair of denim jeans and battered boots. Beneath his bare skin, muscles bunched in tight masses that were devoid of fleshy padding. About his neck he wore a peculiar amulet of gold, and upon his belt hung a *conquistador*'s sword.

'I've been walking up and down in the earth,' he said. 'Is summer over, then? It hadn't seemed so long. I wonder if time moves at a different pace down there.'

Both his words and his tone made her stare at him anew. 'Eric? God, Eric! What's happened to you?'

'I've found my own kind,' Brandon told her, with a laugh that gave her a chill. 'But I was lonely among them as well, and so I came back. I knew there must be an open passageway somewhere on your land here, and it didn't take me long to find it.'

'You've been hiding out in some caves?' Ginger wondered.

'Not hiding out. They recognized me for who I am, don't you understand! They've forgotten so much over the ages, but not all of the old wisdom has left them. They're not quite beasts yet!'

Ginger considered the scar on his head, and remembered that he must have been wandering in some undiscovered system of caverns for many weeks, alone in the darkness.

'Eric,' she said gently, 'I know you've been hurt, that you've been alone for a long time. Now I want you to come back with me to the house. You need to have a doctor look at your head where you hurt it.'

'It's certain to sound strange to you, I realize,' Brandon

322

smiled. 'I still sometimes wonder if it isn't all part of my dreams. There's gold down there – more gold than the *conquistadores* ever dreamed – and hoards of every precious stone these mountains hold. But there's far greater treasure than any of this. There's a lost civilization buried down below, its ruins guarded by entities that transcend any apocalyptic vision of hell's demons. It's been ages since any of my people have dared to enter the hidden strongholds – but I've dared to enter there, and I've returned.'

Ginger compressed her lips and tried to remember all she'd learned in her psychology course last year.

'Eric, you don't have to be worried about what I said about the police. They know you weren't to blame for Dr Kenlaw's death, and they admitted to us that they didn't have any sort of evidence against you on all that other nonsense.'

She hoped that was all still true. Far better to have Eric turn himself in and let a good lawyer take charge, than to allow him to wander off again in this condition. They had good doctors at the centre in Morganton who could help him recover.

'Come back?' Brandon's face seemed suddenly satanic. 'You'd have me come back to the world of men and be put in a cell? I think instead I'll rule in hell!'

Ginger did not share in his laughter at his allusion. There were soft rustlings among the leaves alongside the trail, and the wind was silent.

She cried out when she saw their faces, and instinctively pressed against Brandon for protection.

'Don't be afraid,' he soothed, gripping her tightly. 'These are my people. They've fallen far, but I can lead them back along the road to their ancient greatness.

'*Our* people,' Brandon corrected himself, 'Persephone.'

Ramsey Campbell
The fit

Ramsey Campbell – for a full biography, see page one. Most, if not all, fears begin in early life, and many are sexually based. Though this story isn't autobiographical, it felt as if it was.

I must have passed the end of the path a hundred times before I saw it. Walking into Keswick, I always gazed at the distant fells, mossed by fields and gorse and woods. On cloudy days shadows rode the fells; the figures tramping the ridges looked as though they could steady themselves with one hand on the clouds. On clear days I would marvel at the multitude of shades of green and yellow, a spectrum in themselves, and notice nothing else.

But this was a dull day. The landscape looked dusty, as though from the lorries that pulverized the roads. I might have stayed in the house, but my Aunt Naomi was fitting; the sight of people turning like inexperienced models before the full-length mirror made me feel out of place. I'd exhausted Keswick – games of Crazy Golf, boats on the lake or strolls round it, narrow streets clogged with cars and people scaffolded with rucksacks – and I didn't feel like toiling up the fells today, even for the vistas of the lakes.

If I hadn't been watching my feet trudging I would have missed the path. It led away from the road a mile or so outside Keswick, through a gap in the hedge and across a field overgrown with grass and wild flowers. Solitude appealed to me, and I squeezed through the gap, which was hardly large enough for a sheep.

As soon as I stepped on the path I felt the breeze. That raised my spirits; the lorries had half-deafened me, the grubby light and the clouds of dust had made me feel grimy. Though the grass was waist high I strode forward, determined to follow the path.

325

Grass blurred its meanderings, but I managed to trace it to the far side of the field, only to find that it gave out entirely. I peered about, blinded by smouldering green. Elusive grasshoppers chirred, regular as telephones. Eventually I made my way to the corner where the field met two others. Here the path sneaked through the hedge, almost invisibly. Had it been made difficult to follow?

Beyond the hedge it passed close to a pond, whose surface was green as the fields; I slithered on the brink. A dragonfly, its wings wafers of stained glass, skimmed the pond. The breeze coaxed me along the path, until I reached what I'd thought was the edge of the field, but which proved to be a trough in the ground, about fifteen feet deep.

It wasn't a valley, though its stony floor sloped towards a dark hole ragged with grass. Its banks were a mass of gorse and herbs; gorse obscured a dark green mound low down on the far bank. Except that the breeze was urging me, I wouldn't have gone close enough to realize that the mound was a cottage.

It was hardly larger than a room. Moss had blurred its outlines, so that it resembled the banks of the trough; it was impossible to tell where the roof ended and the walls began. Now I could see a window, and I was eager to look in. The breeze guided me forward, caressing and soothing, and I saw where the path led down to the cottage.

I had just climbed down below the edge when the breeze turned cold. Was it the damp, striking upwards from the crack in the earth? The crack was narrower than it had looked, which must be why I was all at once much closer to the cottage – close enough to realize that the cottage must be decaying, eaten away by moss; perhaps that was what I could smell. Inside the cottage a light crept towards the window, a light pale as marsh gas, pale as the face that loomed behind it.

Someone was in there, and I was trespassing. When I tried to struggle out of the trough, my feet slipped on the path; the breeze was a huge cushion, a softness that forced me backward. Clutching at gorse, I dragged myself over the edge. Nobody followed, and by the time I'd fled past the pond I couldn't distinguish the crack in the earth.

I didn't tell my aunt about the incident. Though she insisted I call her Naomi, and let me stay up at night far later than my parents did, I felt she might disapprove. I didn't want her to think that I was still a child. If I hadn't stopped myself brooding about it I might have realized that I felt guiltier than the incident warranted; after all, I had done nothing.

Before long she touched on the subject herself. One night we sat sipping more of the wine we'd had with dinner, something else my parents would have frowned upon if they'd known. Mellowed by wine, I said, 'That was a nice meal.' Without warning, to my dismay which I concealed with a laugh, my voice fell an octave.

'You're growing up.' As though that had reminded her, she said, 'See what you make of this.'

From a drawer she produced two small grey dresses, too smartly cut for school. One of her clients had brought them for alteration, her two small daughters clutching each other and giggling at me. Aunt Naomi handed me the dresses. 'Look at them closely,' she said.

Handling them made me uneasy. As they drooped emptily over my lap they looked unnervingly minute. Strands of a different grey were woven into the material. Somehow I didn't like to touch those strands.

'I know how you feel,' my aunt said. 'It's the material.'

'What about it?'

'The strands of lighter grey – I think they're hair.'

I handed back the dresses hastily, pinching them by one corner of the shoulders. 'Old Fanny Cave made them,' she said as though that explained everything.

'Who's Fanny Cave?'

'Maybe she's just an old woman who isn't quite right in the head. I wouldn't trust some of the tales I've heard about her. Mind you, I'd trust her even less.'

I must have looked intrigued, for she said: 'She's just an unpleasant old woman, Peter. Take my advice and stay away from her.'

'I can't stay away from her if I don't know where she lives,' I said slyly.

'In a hole in the ground near a pond, so they tell me. You can't even see it from the road, so don't bother trying.'

She took my sudden nervousness for assent. 'I wish Mrs Gibson hadn't accepted those dresses,' she mused. 'She couldn't bring herself to refuse, she said, when Fanny Cave had gone to so much trouble. Well, she said the children felt uncomfortable in them. I'm going to tell her the material isn't good for their skin.'

I should have liked more chance to decide whether I wanted

to confess to having gone near Fanny Cave's. Still, I felt too guilty to revive the subject or even to show too much interest in the old woman. Two days later I had the chance to see her for myself.

I was mooching about the house, trying to keep out of my aunt's way. There was nowhere downstairs I felt comfortable; her sewing machine chattered in the dining room, by the table spread with cut-out patterns; dress forms stood in the lounge, waiting for clothes or limbs. From my bedroom window I watched the rain stir the fields into mud, dissolve the fells into mounds of mist. I was glad when the doorbell rang; at least it gave me something to do.

As soon as I opened the door the old woman pushed in. I thought she was impatient for shelter; she wore only a grey dress. Parts of it glistened with rain – or were they patterns of a different grey, symbols of some kind? I found myself squinting at them, trying to make them out, before I looked up at her face.

She was over six feet tall. Her grey hair dangled to her waist. Presumably it smelled of earth; certainly she did. Her leathery face was too small for her body. As it stooped, peering through grey strands at me as though I was merchandise, I thought of a rodent peering from its lair.

She strode into the dining room. 'You've been saying things about me. You've been telling them not to wear my clothes.'

'I'm sure nobody told you that,' my aunt said.

'Nobody had to.' Her voice sounded stiff and rusty, as if she wasn't used to talking to people. 'I know when anyone meddles in my affairs.'

How could she fit into that dwarfish cottage? I stood in the hall, wondering if my aunt needed help and if I would have the courage to provide it. But now the old woman sounded less threatening than peevish. 'I'm getting old. I need someone to look after me sometimes. I've no children of my own.'

'But giving them clothes won't make them your children.'

Through the doorway I saw the old woman glaring as though she had been found out. 'Don't you meddle in my affairs or I'll meddle in yours,' she said, and stalked away. It must have been the draught of her movements that made the dress patterns fly off the table, some of them into the fire.

For the rest of the day I felt uneasy, almost glad to be going home tomorrow. Clouds oozed down the fells; swaying curtains of rain enclosed the house, beneath the looming sky. The grey had seeped into the house. Together with the lingering smell of earth it made me feel buried alive.

I roamed the house as though it was a cage. Once, as I wandered into the lounge, I thought two figures were waiting in the dimness, arms outstretched to grab me. They were dress forms, and the arms of their dresses hung limp at their sides; I couldn't see how I had made the mistake.

My aunt did most of the chatting at dinner. I kept imagining Fanny Cave in her cottage, her long limbs folded up like a spider's in hiding. The cottage must be larger than it looked, but she certainly lived in a lair in the earth – in the mud, on a day like this.

After dinner we played cards. When I began to nod sleepily my aunt continued playing, though she knew I had a long coach journey in the morning; perhaps she wanted company. By the time I went to bed the rain had stopped; a cheesy moon hung in a rainbow. As I undressed I heard her pegging clothes on the line below my window.

When I'd packed my case I parted the curtains for a last drowsy look at the view. The fells were a moonlit patchwork, black and white. Why was my aunt taking so long to hang out the clothes? I peered down more sharply. There was no sign of her. The clothes were moving by themselves, dancing and swaying in the moonlight, inching along the line towards the house.

When I raised the sash of the window the night seemed perfectly still, no sign of a breeze. Nothing moved on the lawn except the shadows of the clothes, advancing a little and retreating, almost ritualistically. Hovering dresses waved holes where hands should be, nodded the sockets of their necks.

Were they really moving towards the house? Before I could tell, the line gave way, dropping them into the mud of the lawn. When I heard my aunt's vexed cry I slipped the window shut and retreated into bed; somehow I didn't want to admit what I'd seen, whatever it was. Sleep came so quickly that next day I could believe I'd been dreaming.

I didn't tell my parents; I'd learned to suppress details that they might find worrying. They were uneasy with my aunt – she was too careless of propriety, the time she had taken them tramping the fells she'd mocked them for dressing as though they were going out for dinner. I think the only reason they let me stay with her was to get me out of the polluted Birmingham air.

By the time I was due for my next visit I was more than ready. My voice had broken, my body had grown unfamiliar; I felt clumsy, ungainly, neither a man nor myself. My parents didn't help. They'd turned wistful as soon as my voice began to change; my mother treated visitors to photographs of me as a baby. She and my father kept telling me to concentrate on my studies and examining my school books as if pornography might lurk behind the covers. They seemed relieved that I attended a boys' school, until my father started wondering nervously if I was 'particularly fond' of any of the boys. After nine months of this sort of thing I was glad to get away at Easter.

As soon as the coach moved off I felt better. In half an hour it left behind the Midlands hills, reefs built of red brick terraces. Lancashire seemed so flat that the glimpses of distant hills might have been mirages. After a couple of hours the fells began, great deceptively gentle monsters that slept at the edges of lakes blue as ice, two sorts of stillness. At least I would be free for a week.

But I was not, for I'd brought my new feelings with me. I knew that as soon as I saw my aunt walking upstairs. She had always seemed much younger than my mother, though there was only two years between them, and I'd been vaguely aware that she often wore tight jeans; now I saw how round her bottom was. I felt breathless with guilt in case she guessed what I was thinking, yet I couldn't look away.

At dinner, whenever she touched me I felt a shock of excitement, too strange and uncontrollable to be pleasant. Her skirts were considerably shorter than my mother's. My feelings crept up on me like the wine, which seemed to be urging them on. Half my conversation seemed fraught with double meanings. At last I found what I thought was a neutral subject. 'Have you seen Fanny Cave again?' I said.

'Only once.' My aunt seemed reluctant to talk about her. 'She'd given away some more dresses, and Mrs Gibson referred the mother to me. They were nastier than the others – I'm sure she would have thrown them away even if I hadn't said anything. But old Fanny came storming up here, just a few weeks ago. When I wouldn't let her in she stood out there in the pouring rain, threatening all sorts of things.'

'What sorts of things?'

'Oh, just unpleasant things. In the old days they would have burned her at the stake, if that's what they used to do. Anyway,' she said with a frown to close the subject, 'she's gone now.'

'Dead, you mean?' I was impatient with euphemisms.

'Nobody knows for sure. Most people think she's in the pond. To tell you the truth, I don't think anyone's anxious to look.'

Of course I was. I lay in bed and imagined probing the pond that nobody else dared search, a dream that seemed preferable to the thoughts that had been tormenting me recently as I tried to sleep. Next day, as I walked to the path, I peeled myself a fallen branch.

Bypassing the pond, I went first to the cottage. I could hear what sounded like a multitude of flies down in the trough. Was the cottage more overgrown than when I'd last seen it? Was that why it looked shrunken by decay, near to collapse? The single dusty window made me think of a dulling eye, half-engulfed by moss; the façade might have been a dead face that was falling inwards. Surely the flies were attracted by wild flowers – but I didn't want to go down into the crack; I hurried back to the pond.

Flies swarmed there too, bumbling above the scum. As I approached they turned on me. They made the air in front of my face seem dark, oppressive, infected. Nevertheless I poked my stick through the green skin and tried to sound the pond while keeping back from the slippery edge.

The depths felt muddy, soft and clinging. I poked for a while, until I began to imagine what I sought to touch. All at once I was afraid that something might grab the branch, overbalance me, drag me into the opaque depths. Was it a rush of sweat that made my clothes feel heavy and obstructive? As I shoved myself back, a breeze clutched them, hindering my retreat. I fled, skidding on mud, and saw the branch sink lethargically. A moment after it vanished the slime was unbroken.

That night I told Aunt Naomi where I'd been. I didn't think she would mind; after all, Fanny Cave was supposed to be out of the way. But she bent lower over her sewing, as if she didn't want to hear. 'Please don't go there again,' she said. 'Now let's talk about something else.'

'Why?' At that age I had no tact at all.

'Oh, for heaven's sake. Because I think she probably died on her way home from coming here. That's the last time anyone saw her. She must have been in such a rage that she slipped at the edge of the pond – I told you it was pouring with rain. Well, how was I to know what had happened?'

Perhaps her resentment concealed a need for reassurance, but I was unable to help, for I was struggling with the idea that she had been partly responsible for someone's death. Was nothing in my life to be trusted? I was so deep in brooding that I was hardly able to look at her when she cried out.

Presumably her needle had slipped on the thimble; she'd driven the point beneath one of her nails. Yet as she hurried out, furiously sucking her finger, I found that my gaze was drawn to the dress she had been sewing. As she'd cried out – of course it must have been then, not before – the dress had seemed to twist in her hands, jerking the needle.

When I went to bed I couldn't sleep. The room smelled faintly of earth; was that something to do with spring? The wardrobe door kept opening, though it had never behaved like that before, and displaying my clothes suspended bat-like in the dark. Each time I got up to close the door their shapes looked less familiar, more unpleasant. Eventually I managed to sleep, only to dream that dresses were waddling limblessly through the doorway of my room, towards the bed.

The next day, Sunday, my aunt suggested a walk on the fells. I would have settled for Skiddaw, the easiest of them, but it was already swarming with walkers like fleas. 'Let's go somewhere we'll be alone,' Aunt Naomi said, which excited me in ways I'd begun to enjoy but preferred not to define, in case that scared the excitement away.

We climbed Grisedale Pike. Most of it was gentle, until just below the summit we reached an almost vertical scramble up a narrow spiky ridge. I clung there with all my limbs, trapped thousands of feet above the countryside, afraid to go up or down. I was almost hysterical with self-disgust; I'd let my half-admitted fantasies lure me up here, when all my aunt had wanted was to enjoy the walk without being crowded by tourists. Eventually I managed to clamber to the summit, my face blazing.

As we descended, it began to rain. By the time we reached home we were soaked. I felt suffocated by the smell of wet earth, the water flooding down my face, the dangling locks of sodden hair that wouldn't go away. I hurried upstairs to change.

I had just about finished – undressing had felt like peeling wallpaper, except that I was the wall – when my aunt called out. Though she was in the next room, her voice sounded muffled. Before I could go to her she called again, nearer to panic. I hurried across the landing, into her room.

The walls were streaming with shadows. The air was dark as mud, in which she was struggling wildly. A shapeless thing was swallowing her head and arms. When I switched on the light I saw it was nothing; she'd become entangled in the jumper she was trying to remove, that was all.

'Help me,' she cried. She sounded as if she was choking, yet I didn't like to touch her; apart from a bra, her torso was naked. What was wrong with her, for God's sake? Couldn't she take off her jumper by herself? Eventually I helped her as best I could without touching her. It seemed glued to her, by the rain, I assumed. At last she emerged, red faced and panting.

Neither of us said much at dinner. I thought her unease was directed at me, at the way I'd let her struggle. Or was she growing aware of my new feelings? That night, as I drifted into sleep, I thought I heard a jangling of hangers in the wardrobe. Perhaps it was just the start of a dream.

The morning was dull. Clouds swallowed the tops of the fells. My aunt lit fires in the downstairs rooms. I loitered about the house for a while, hoping for a glimpse of customers undressing, until the dimness made me claustrophobic. Firelight set the shadows of dress forms dancing spastically on the walls; when I stood with my back to the forms their shadows seemed to raise their arms.

I caught a bus to Keswick, for want of something to do. The bus had passed Fanny Cave's path before I thought of looking. I glanced back sharply, but a bend in the road intervened. Had I glimpsed a scarecrow by the pond, its sleeves fluttering? But it had seemed to rear up: it must have been a bird.

In Keswick I followed leggy girls up the narrow hilly streets, dawdled nervously outside pubs and wondered if I looked old enough to risk buying a drink. When I found myself in the library, leafing desultorily through broken paperbacks, I went home. There was nothing by the pond that I could see, though closer to Aunt Naomi's house something grey was flapping in the grass – litter, I supposed.

The house seemed more oppressive than ever. Though my aunt tended to use whichever room she was in for sewing, she was generally tidy; now the house was crowded with half-finished clothes, lolling on chairs, their necks yawning. When I tried to chat at dinner my voice sounded muffled by the presence of so much cloth.

My aunt drank more than usual, and seemed not to care if I did too. My drinking made the light seem yellowish, suffocated.

Soon I felt very sleepy. 'Stay down a little longer,' my aunt mumbled, jerking herself awake, when I made to go to bed. I couldn't understand why she didn't go herself. I chatted mechanically, about anything except what might be wrong. Firelight brought clothes nodding forward to listen.

At last she muttered, 'Let's go to bed.' Of course she meant that unambiguously, yet it made me nervous. As I undressed hastily I heard her below me in the kitchen, opening the window a notch for air. A moment later the patch of light from the kitchen went out. I wished it had stayed lit for just another moment, for I'd glimpsed something lying beneath the empty clothesline.

Was it a nightdress? But I'd never seen my aunt hang out a nightdress, nor pyjamas either. It occurred to me that she must sleep naked. That disturbed me so much that I crawled into bed and tried to sleep at once, without thinking.

I dreamed I was buried, unable to breathe, and when I awoke I was. Blankets, which felt heavy as collapsed earth, had settled over my face. I heaved them off me and lay trying to calm myself, so that I would sink back into sleep – but by the time my breathing slowed I realized I was listening.

The room felt padded with silence. Dimness draped the chair and dressing table, blurring their shapes; perhaps the wardrobe door was ajar, for I thought I saw vague forms hanging ominously still. Now I was struggling to fall asleep before I could realize what was keeping me awake. I drew long slow breaths to lull myself, but it was no use. In the silence between them I heard something sodden creeping upstairs.

I lay determined not to hear. Perhaps it was the wind or the creaking of the house, not the sound of a wet thing slopping stealthily upstairs at all. Perhaps if I didn't move, didn't make a noise, I would hear what it really was – but in any case I was incapable of moving, for I'd heard the wet thing flop on the landing outside my door.

For an interminable pause there was silence, thicker than ever, then I heard my aunt's door open next to mine. I braced myself for her scream. If she screamed I would go to her, I would have to. But the scream never came; there was only the sound of her pulling something sodden off the floor. Soon I heard her padding downstairs barefoot, and the click of a lock.

Everything was all right now. Whatever it had been, she'd dealt with it. Perhaps wallpaper had fallen on the stairs, and she'd gone down to throw it out. Now I could sleep – so why couldn't I? Several minutes passed before I was conscious of wondering why she hadn't come back upstairs.

I forced myself to move. There was nothing to fear, nothing now outside my door – but I got dressed to delay going out on the landing. The landing proved to be empty, and so did the house. Beyond the open front door the prints of Aunt Naomi's bare feet led over the moist lawn towards the road.

The moon was doused by clouds. Once I reached the road I couldn't see my aunt's tracks, but I knew instinctively which way she'd gone. I ran wildly towards Fanny Cave's path. Hedges, mounds of congealed night, boxed me in. The only sound I could hear was the ringing of my heels on the asphalt.

I had just reached the gap in the hedge when the moon swam free. A woman was following the path towards the pond, but was it my aunt? Even with the field between us I recognized the grey dress she wore. It was Fanny Cave's.

I was terrified to set foot on the path until the figure turned a bend and I saw my aunt's profile. I plunged across the field, tearing my way through the grass. It might have been quicker to follow the path, for by the time I reached the gap into the second field she was nearly at the pond.

In the moonlight the surface of the pond looked milky, fungoid. The scum was broken only by a rock, plastered with strands of grass, close to the edge towards which my aunt was walking. I threw myself forward, grass slashing my legs.

When I came abreast of her I saw her eyes, empty except for two shrunken reflections of the moon. I knew not to wake a sleepwalker, and so I caught her gently by the shoulders, though my hands wanted to shake, and tried to turn her away from the pond.

She wouldn't turn. She was pulling towards the scummy water, or Fanny Cave's dress was, for the drowned material seemed to writhe beneath my hands. It was pulling towards the rock whose eyes glared just above the scum, through glistening strands which were not grass but hair.

It seemed there was only one thing to do. I grabbed the neck of the dress and tore it down. The material was rotten, and tore easily. I dragged it from my aunt's body and flung it towards the pond. Did it land near the edge then slither into the water? All I knew was that when I dared to look the scum was unbroken.

My aunt stood there naked and unaware until I draped my anorak around her. That seemed to rouse her. She stared about for a moment, then down at herself. 'It's all right, Naomi,' I said awkwardly.

She sobbed only once before she controlled herself, but I could see that the effort was cruel. 'Come on, quickly,' she said in a voice older and harsher than I'd ever heard her use, and strode home without looking at me.

Next day we didn't refer to the events of the night; in fact, we hardly spoke. No doubt she had lain awake all night as I had, as uncomfortably aware of me as I was of her. After breakfast she said that she wanted to be left alone, and asked me to go home early. I never visited her again; she always found a reason why I couldn't stay. I suspect the reasons served only to prevent my parents from questioning me.

Before I went home I found a long branch and went to the pond. It didn't take much probing for me to find something solid but repulsively soft. I drove the branch into it again and again, until I felt things break. My disgust was so violent it was beyond defining. Perhaps I already knew deep in myself that since the night I undressed my aunt I would never be able to touch a woman.